THE GIRL FROM THE WAR ROOM

CATHERINE LAW

Boldwood

First published in Great Britain in 2025 by Boldwood Books Ltd.

Copyright © Catherine Law, 2025

Cover Design by Head Design Ltd

Cover Images: [Mark Owen] / Trevillion and Shutterstock

Interior Image: Tony Fleetwood

A CIP catalogue record for this book is available from the British Library.

Paperback ISBN 978-1-83751-582-0

Large Print ISBN 978-1-83751-581-3

Hardback ISBN 978-1-83751-580-6

Ebook ISBN 978-1-83751-583-7

Kindle ISBN 978-1-83751-584-4

Audio CD ISBN 978-1-83751-575-2

MP3 CD ISBN 978-1-83751-576-9

Digital audio download ISBN 978-1-83751-579-0

This book is printed on certified sustainable paper. Boldwood Books is dedicated to putting sustainability at the heart of our business. For more information please visit https://www.boldwoodbooks.com/about-us/sustainability/

Boldwood Books Ltd, 23 Bowerdean Street, London, SW6 3TN

www.boldwoodbooks.com

For Catriona.

PROLOGUE
LONDON, MAY 1941

When the bus reached Buckingham Gate, Cassie rang the bell and got off before her usual stop. She skirted the pond in St James's Park where a posse of mallards paddled and dipped their beaks, happily oblivious. Vegetables grew in the beds, now, instead of flowers, and barrage balloons drifted eerily above the shattered skyline, catching sunlight, chained to the earth, everything tainted with grime and dust.

Even so, Cassie relished this detour, these few extra moments in the open air, for whichever pathway through the park she took would lead her to the bunker eventually. Within minutes, she would be underground, inhaling unnatural ventilation pumped through a vent in the wall.

Through the thick bank of trees, she spotted the white façades of the Treasury offices, and her stomach contracted, as if her body braced itself and came to attention. But it wasn't nerves. Ho, no. Fortitude, yes, and a kind of hell-bent willingness. An understanding of the importance of her work; to do something, however small, to help. A privilege, as her Uncle Charles had once said.

And yet, as Cassie crossed Horse Guards Road and went through the sandbagged entrance, something deep inside her longed to linger, to feed the ducks, to play as she once had done with her brother and cousins. She yearned for those long summers in the country at Greenaways when fire and death could not possibly rain from the sky. When they had all been together in honeyed sunlight. But that world had vanished now, along with her childhood. And reminiscing about it never did Cassie any good. It made her feel foolish, made her feel old.

* * *

'You know, Miss Marsh,' an RAF officer had said to her on her first day in the War Room bunker beneath the Treasury on Whitehall, 'if they bomb the Thames, we will drown down here.'

And on that same day, as Cassie had descended the wide, spiralling stairs into the basement, she felt as if she were entering the bowels of a ship. She had wondered how she would ever find her way around the underground corridors, the low ceilings latticed with girders and pipes, the lighting murky at the best of times. How would she remember who the important officers were or get to know all the departments and carry out the job she'd come to do?

But this morning, having worked here for over a year, Cassie walked briskly down Staircase Fifteen, a purposeful spring in her step, turning corners by gun racks at the ready if it came to a 'last stand', passing desks squeezed in because they'd needed extra staff, and nodding a good morning to whoever's eye she caught along the way. The weather indicator on the wall stated, correctly, *Clear*, and Cassie gave a little smile. During the worst of the bombing raids during the autumn last year, the sign had been jokingly changed to *Windy*.

Cassie opened the door to the Typing Room, closed it quietly behind her and hurried over to her desk. One or two of the girls finishing their night shift lifted their faces in greeting and went straight back to their work.

She slipped into her chair and pulled her in-tray towards her. Miss Redmond, the supervisor sitting at her corner desk and keeping a beady mother-hen eye on them all, had left a stack of buff files containing hand-written reports and minutes for her to type up, with carbon copies, and *no mistakes*. Cassie leafed through them, checking for the red label stating *Action This Day*. This always struck her as odd, for it meant, in reality, *This Day or Night*.

Cassie had been brought back to the Typing Room from the Mapping Department in the spring when air raids had become less frequent, and focus was turned elsewhere. Reports came in now on Allied soldiers evacuating from Crete, and the situation at Tobruk in Libya. The casualty figures and lists of ships or tanks did not reveal the appalling mess the troops faced every day, but Cassie set to in the most professional manner she could muster. She tried her hardest not to imagine, her hardest not to think about it at all.

As Miss Redmond said, *one has to keep one's head* and she praised Cassie for her efficiency, had hinted at promotion at some point. This seemed neither here nor there. As long as she could simply get through the day's – or night's – work.

'Morning, Cassie,' whispered Esme at the desk beside her, busily compiling a finished report with staples, as Mr Churchill didn't like paperclips. The PM had also given the order for noiseless typewriters to be shipped over from America, as he couldn't bear the clattering. The small typing room and the whole of the underground command centre contained a muffled, industrious hush. Cassie felt everyone was permanently holding their breath.

'How are you?' Esme mouthed.

Cassie nodded her usual smiling response. For how could she explain to her colleague her feelings of detachment, her estrangement from her family? Sinking into the paperwork piled on her desk helped distract her from the drifting sensation that woke with her each morning and lingered with her all day like a strange aftertaste. Her work kept her going, stopped her falling through the cracks. She had been swallowed by her job, swallowed by London, swallowed by the war. And my, how it suited her.

The note on Admiralty-headed paper with its red label appeared to be her first, urgent task, and she wound a new sheet of paper into her machine.

She glanced at the wireless operator's handwriting, and began to type:

Dated this day 4 May 1941... North Atlantic. Shannon, 52 degrees north latitude, 11 degrees west longitude. Castle-class destroyer HMS Westray convoy escort... Lost with all hands.

Cassie's fingers stiffened on the keys. She sucked her breath in through her teeth. An iced fog rose from her toes to her face, engulfing her. She must have cried out, for Esme seemed to be asking her urgent questions, and Miss Redmond appeared, standing over her desk as if to shield her from the other girls. They both spoke to her, but she could not be sure what they were saying. She felt as if she were unravelling, and about to vomit.

Miss Redmond took the sheet of paper from Cassie's typewriter, glanced at it, and passed it to Esme.

'Fetch tea with sugar,' the supervisor said to someone else. 'Now.'

Cassie pressed her hand over her mouth, her stomach buckling. She stared up at Miss Redmond, who looked far from her usual buttoned-up, unruffled self.

'Miss Marsh. Cassandra. This report? Do you... do you know this ship...?'

Cassie nodded, and the girls turned at their desks to stare, their brows pleating in confusion and concern. Time seemed to stretch and expand around her, as if to demonstrate that this unbearable, agonising feeling would stay with her forever.

One of the girls swooped in and planted a teacup on the desk. Liquid splashed over the saucer and onto the paperwork.

Miss Redmond's hand felt heavy on her shoulder.

'Is it...? Who is it, my dear?'

Cassie didn't want to answer, for saying it would make it real. The coldness inside her ballooned, dropping its weight into her bones, sinking to her core.

'My brother,' she managed, her voice distant, as if someone were whispering from the wings.

Miss Redmond pressed the cup into her hands. 'Drink this; it will help with the shock,' she said. 'It will take a while to sink in. And then you can go home, Cassie, if you like. Be with your family.'

Cassie held the cup. She didn't want it to sink in. She did not want it to be true. The tea tasted foul, as if it had been made with bad water.

She shook her head. 'I can't,' she said. 'I can't go home.'

No one in the typing room spoke. Someone gasped.

Miss Redmond persisted. 'Believe me. It's the best place for you...'

Someone else said, 'It's the shock. Go home, Cassie.'

But how could she? How could Cassie appear out of the blue with this news for her mother when she had not seen her, had not spoken to her, for so very long? How could she face her father, when the last time he had visited her, she could hardly bear look at him? How could she tell them – any of them – about Gerard's ship, for it would sound like a lie. A damnable and sinful lie.

She had better leave it for the telegram, she thought. It will reach them soon enough.

Cassie stood up, her legs like liquid, her mind circling in punishing chaos as she shakily gathered her things. She shivered, her fingers fumbling with her coat buttons, the straps of her handbag.

'Do you want me to—?' Esme began.

Cassie crisply shook her head. She said goodbye, and thank you, not daring to catch anyone's eye, and left the room.

She could not remember how she made her way along the corridors and back up the winding staircase to the foyer, but she suddenly found herself in the light of a sublimely beautiful day. Cassie paused on the steps outside the building. St James's Park looked as serene as ever, the mighty trees flickering in a pleasant breeze, the pond shining in sunlight, the ducks circling around each other, all of it goading her with beauty, and normality.

Cassie made her way, a convoluted, jerking route, to a bench by the pond, and sat down. She must think. She must be efficient. She must do the right thing. But how could she do anything, when her whole life, the world she had known, had already been cut loose?

Her lodgings were in Chelsea, and yet there were two other

places that Cassie had once called home. Shock hit her again with a grinding, terrible truth. She sank against the bench and hung her head. It dawned on her.

The thought of going back to her parents' house on Egerton Terrace, South Kensington, where she had been born, repulsed her. And how could she ever return to Greenaways, the house in the country, where she used to go in her dreams?

PART I

1

DEVON, SUMMER 1936

The highways became byways, and byways became lanes, tighter at every turn, worn deep into the earth, twisting, and dipping, leading the way.

Cassie rested her head against the back seat as her father drove through the long tunnel of trees, enclosed by ancient hedges, branches arching overhead. A blushing blur of dog roses, foxglove and wild honeysuckle trailed past the car window, and Cassie tried to capture each flower, every moment. To fix it in her mind. Tickling, dangerous excitement soared, giggling inside her. Almost there.

'Cassie, dear,' her mother in the passenger seat said, seemingly seeing her without even looking around, 'sit up straight; you'll make yourself sick.'

Cassie shuffled her bottom and straightened her shoulders to comply a little, feeling too languid, too downright happy, to manage much more.

She had gone to bed the night before in her clothes – comfy trousers, old blouse and a cardigan – car sickness tablet swallowed with her cocoa. Her mother had woken her in the dark early hours and, in the back of the car, she'd slept again, lulled by the grainy noise of the wheels beneath her as her father turned out of Egerton Terrace, negotiated the deserted South Kensington streets and took them out on to the Great West Road. She'd woken once, alert and knowing that she had travelled deep into the sleeping countryside, and that the night was nearly over.

Now, the car broke from the trees into sunlight, and the view of the Devon landscape unfolded like a cushiony tapestry: fields and hedgerows, and little wooded hills. In the far distance, the purple smudge of the moors. Cassie's mother had once told her about the Celtic name for her beloved county: *Dyfnaint* – 'deep dark valleys', and Cassie, gazing from the car window, understood why her mother looked misty-eyed whenever she talked of *home*.

'In fairness, Miranda,' said her father, yawning as he drove, blinking in the light. 'It always used to be Gerard who was car sick. Isn't that right, son?'

Cassie's big brother, dishevelled, on the edge of being grumpy and far too long-limbed to be comfortable in the cramped back seat, grumbled, 'Only when I read, Dad. And I learnt that lesson.'

Gerard nudged Cassie's arm and showed her his copy of *Sherlock Holmes* concealed inside his balled-up jumper. Cassie giggled behind her hand.

'I think we all learnt that lesson, Gerard.' Her mother sighed.

It fascinated Cassie that her mother, after a such a long journey through the night, could look so immaculate.

The car idled at the crossroads with the wonky, weathered sign on the patch of grass at its centre that pointed in only three directions. The fourth mysteriously unnamed.

'Now, Miranda, I can never remember. Which way is it...?' Cassie's father said, peering through the windscreen.

'Rich, you've been coming here with me for nearly twenty years,' Cassie's mother said, 'and you still don't know...'

They all laughed at his recurring joke, but Cassie caught an odd look on her mother's face, an uncertain smile, as if she always wanted to make sure of something.

'And I get you every time,' her father said, laughing as he turned down the unmarked lane. 'Hey, Cassie,' he prompted as the car rumbled on, the lane now a rutted track, the hedges close enough to catch the paintwork. 'Almost there.'

Cassie leant forward between the two front seats, too elated to speak. Her joy was curious and tentative, as if she didn't want to feel it all at once. Because if she let herself, it would be too tender to bear.

How could she tell them that she often found herself inside Greenaways in her dreams? She'd be moving through the connected rooms, one leading to another. Or she'd be outside, catching glimpses through window after window along the front façade. And upstairs, in the long gallery looking down on to the cobbled courtyard, and in the garden, with the wisteria clinging to sun-drenched bricks and the wide pond brimming with lily pads.

'It always puzzles me,' Cassie's father said, easing the car past the little wooden sign staked into the ground, and through the iron gates rusted permanently open, 'that the house is called Greenaways; the family name is Greenaway. You used to be a Greenaway, Miranda, before I whisked you away from all of this. But surely there should be an apostrophe somewhere on that sign.'

Her mother made an affectionate noise. 'Sometimes, I wish I

could still sign my name Greenaway,' she teased. 'I used to do it with such a lovely flourish.'

'And now you're stuck with Marsh.' He laughed. 'Sorry about that.'

He pulled up on the gravel and Cassie opened her door before he could cut the engine. Inhaling sweet, country air, Cassie shook off the journey, the juddering seat, her aching neck forgotten, and drank in the house where her mother had been born. Greenaways stood as it had done for four hundred summers – 'just an old, smallish manor house' her mother would say – the effortless beauty of its Georgian stone glimmering faintly, concealing its Elizabethan soul.

'Miranda! Richard!' Cassie's uncle, Charles, appeared through the stone porch, pipe in the corner of his mouth as usual. He plucked it out to wave it at them. 'You've made excellent time. Good journey, I trust?'

Cassie's father, opening the boot, said below his voice, 'Here he is. The Colonel-in-brackets-retired.'

'Richard, really,' uttered her mother, evidently cross with him, and went over to embrace her brother.

'Good to see you, Miranda. Rich, old chap,' Charles said, stalking forward to briskly shake his hand. 'Now who do we have here... Gerard, who stretched you? And this young madam. She looks bigger than Marianne now.'

Her uncle Charles talking about her without using her name made Cassie feel both invisible and exposed in one awful, queasy moment.

'I see both you Marsh children are getting your looks from your father.'

'Lucky them,' said Cassie's father, running his hand playfully through his fine fair hair, which, like Gerard's, was annoyingly not as yellow and straw-like as Cassie's.

'Not sure where my own offspring are,' said Uncle Charles, 'but Juno's in the garden.'

'Why don't you go look for them, Cassie dear,' said her mother kindly, knowing that Cassie longed to find her cousins.

'Don't you want some lemonade first?' asked her uncle. 'Your aunt has made it fresh.'

Cassie shook her head, glanced at her mother for brief approval.

'We are hoping for something a little stronger,' her father said, stacking suitcases.

'In the drawing room. Come on.'

Their voices drifted as Cassie headed off along the front of the house, turning the corner under the plumes of wisteria, its stem, ancient and gnarled and as thick as Cassie's thigh, emerging from the foundations. Sweeping away from the side, the field studded with old oaks looked as it should do: serene and unchanged. Closer by, the flower beds enclosed by miniature hedges and linked by gravel pathways sang out, as abundant and as unruly as ever.

Cassie's excitement simmered down to relief. Free of the car at last, she felt the impulse to stretch and sprint and jump, to be a little girl again. To laugh out loud. Shout, even. But she would be fifteen in September, as her mother might remind her, and ought to know better.

The path led her deeper into the garden, alive with hovering bees and fragile butterflies. Behind her, the house settled benignly under the scented midday hour as it tipped into sleepy afternoon. She stopped, feeling suddenly conspicuous, and scanned the windows, upstairs and down, with an impatient wondering about where Oliver and Marianne could possibly be. Gerard had probably found them first, she conceded, and trotted on.

Turning onto a crossways path, Cassie spotted the familiar, lean figure of Aunt Juno in an astonishing, wide straw hat and wafting smock-like thing, earnestly dead-heading roses.

'Cassandra! Is that you? You're here already?' Cassie's aunt appeared surprised, although something in her tone told Cassie that she had known all along. 'I've been beavering away out here, completely forgot the time. Goodness, my dear, what a little lady you're becoming.'

She pecked Cassie on the cheek, her hat chafing on Cassie's ear.

'Have you been sent to fetch me?' she asked, her owl-like eyes widening.

Cassie caught a breath of her musky perfume, more suited to the dark mystery of midwinter solstice than high midsummer. 'No, I am looking for—'

'I think they're indoors, Cassandra. And I better report for duty,' she said, glancing towards the house.

Cassie's father often commented – privately, mind – on her aunt's 'rather hooky' nose, but Cassie only ever thought of her tanned skin, sun-kissed cheekbones and large, all-seeing, pale-green eyes.

'Can't keep guests waiting,' Juno said. 'Come on.'

She dumped her rose trug on the ground and set off, her long, dark hair, streaked with grey, escaping from her hat and straggling over her shoulders. Cassie wanted to giggle. Her mother often said that ladies with 'salt and pepper' hair should wear it short. Not that her mother's hair looked anywhere near grey yet, and she came home from the salon in South Ken once a week, her chestnut hair all glossy and shingled.

Cassie hesitated, knowing she ought to follow – she longed to scoot after her aunt, go back to the house – but she also wanted to linger on her own, to drift around the garden for a little while longer. To relish the prelude to the summer to come.

Spending summer holidays at Greenaways felt like a gift; days and weeks, expanding with possibility, rolling ahead of her. A heady blend of freedom, encouraged by her aunt, tempered by the tapping of a wristwatch from Uncle Charles and a reminder that it was homework time. And Marianne, and Oliver, with Gerard, always, somewhere around.

Cassie went into the house, through the garden door into the vestibule leading to the back area, kitchen, scullery and the pantries, where cooler air lingered and flies peppered the sticky paper hung at the windows. The familiar, piquant aroma greeted her, like fruit falling over into decay, with spice at the bottom. She kept her eye out for mice; last summer, or perhaps it had been the summer before, Oliver had rescued one half in, half out of a trap, and set it free in the garden. Cassie often thought of the mouse. How far had it run? How long had it lived? Did it collapse and die of fright as soon as it reached the shelter of the shrubbery?

From here, she could turn either left or right to eventually get to the main staircase, but she took the shortcut, opening the door onto the courtyard and skipping across the cobbles. At all four corners, statues of King Henry, and his two daughters and his son stared down, but Cassie did not want to catch their opaque, stone eyes. She slipped through the door to the hallway. The staircase lay on her left, wide and oaken, the worn, red carpet turning neat right angles on its way up to the first floor. The front door ahead, and through the door to her right, she peered straight through the dining room down the long line of rooms, one leading onto the other. Light spilled through the windows either side into the dining room, Aunt Juno's small parlour, and then the drawing room, which was so large that it turned the corner. From here, the grown-ups' voices, her mother's gentle laugh and a boom from Uncle Charles, worked their way through the bones of the house.

Cassie wanted to head up the stairs, for she still had no idea where Marianne and Oliver, and Gerard for that matter, could be. But on the dining table stood the pitcher of Aunt Juno's lemonade, as promised by Uncle Charles, cloudy and fruity, the glass perspiring. She poured herself a long tumblerful, watching for drips on the pristine tabletop. As she sipped, she admired the familiar paintings along the wall. A series of little Parisian street scenes, Cassie guessed, with tables and chairs on pavements outside cafés, in the smaller frames. Other larger studies showed different aspects of a sleepy, wide river, overhung with dappled willows, the water sparkling with a hundred brush strokes, and bathers languishing on sunny banks. Each painting signed with the same jagged initials in the bottom right:

AR

Aunt Juno's lemonade tasted as it always did, Cassie thought – good and sweet but with a faint, bitter kick at the finish. Sometimes, it made her hiccup.

For half a breath, Cassie felt aware of someone standing in the doorway, and thought Oliver had come silently down the staircase to find her.

'Aha, caught you.'

She glanced around, wiping the moustache of lemonade off her top lip. But she did not know this boy who leant, arms crossed and rather cocky, against the door jamb. His wire-rimmed glasses gave him a serious, head-boy look. He was dark-haired, short and sturdy, a blazer over his arm, the sleeves of his crisp, white shirt rolled up with precision.

'I was thirsty,' she said.

'You must be the little sister. We were upstairs, and we saw you in the garden from Oliver's window. We're getting ready for tennis. I came down to find you. To stop you being sucked in by the grown-ups.'

'I'm not very good at tennis,' Cassie uttered, disappointed that Oliver had not come to fetch her himself.

'Yes,' the boy said, 'your brother said as much. But you can always be ball boy.' He glanced at the jug. 'Perhaps bring the lemonade, too. Yes, you do that. It's hotting up out there,' he said. 'I'm Woodward, by the way. My name's Luke but they all call me Woodward. Oliver's friend from school. We're in the same House, although we have different Masters, of course, seeing as Oliver's a history and art bod. I'm doing maths, and physics, with extra chemistry. But we both do Latin. And I'm in the Second Rugby Eleven whereas Oliver's captain of the First. But I'm only in the Second because I'm not allowed to play with glasses on, and I'm—'

Half-listening, Cassie realised that she didn't know that Oliver had been made team captain. She blushed with pride.

'Do you play tennis in glasses?' Cassie asked.

'Oh, tennis is easy, so I don't need to wear them,' Luke said. 'It's just that rugby is nigh-on impossible—'

Cassie's attention switched to the voices upstairs on the landing. She went to the doorway to see Oliver and Gerard trotting down the staircase in tennis shoes, their footsteps pummelling a soft rhythm. At least, she *knew* it to be Oliver, even though the sun through the large stairway window had them both in silhouette, and she could not make out Oliver's features properly. But she saw the essence of him, and it had been altered. He looked fuller, his frame smoother, somehow, certainly taller than last summer. *Stretched*, Uncle Charles would say.

Gerard barely gave her a glance as his long strides ate up the hallway parquet, racket perched on his shoulder heading for the garden door, but Oliver slowed his pace when he spotted Cassie. His hair longer at the front, shorter at the back, the wave over his forehead almost covering one eye, gave his face, in that moment, new and fascinating angles. But the way he caught Cassie's attention, that seeking gesture he gave her, had not changed.

Cassie felt Luke brush past her. 'Wait for me, you two,' he said. 'I've got to fetch my own racket from the boot room.'

'Cass, come on,' Oliver said, below his voice, with a wry, subtle jerk of his head, 'time to play tennis.' And he carried on his way.

'I'll wait for Marianne,' Cassie called after him, although he possibly did not hear her, and she sank back into the dining room.

The excitement she'd suppressed in the car as they had drawn near to Greenaways became silly, stunted shyness. Cassie let out a groaning sigh. Her cousin had never made her feel *that* before: confused but elated, and her skin all prickly.

There wasn't enough lemonade for them all, but to top it up would mean going along to the drawing room to ask Aunt Juno if there was any more, interrupting the adults, and having to answer questions. Or she could have a look for herself on the marble shelves in the pantry. But it was the housekeeper, Mrs Poulter's day off; the kitchen had looked pristine, and empty, and Cassie didn't want to be caught snooping in there.

Not knowing quite what to do, Cassie raided the ice bucket on the sideboard, plonking cubes into the jug, filling it back up to the top. She opened each of the cupboard doors, releasing the scent of dust and old wood trapped inside, to find the 'children's' tumblers suitable for outdoors, congratulating herself on knowing where things were kept here at Greenaways. And that's because, she thought, I belong. Never mind her night-time dreams; she came here in daydreams too.

Someone called her name, singing, tunelessly and sweetly, as they came down the stairs.

Marianne! Cassie dashed out to the hallway.

Her cousin drifted down, swinging a string bag of tennis balls, her neat tennis dress white against the summer-glow of her skin. Marianne had grown up; *everyone* had grown up. Everyone, except Cassie.

'Cas-seee...' Marianne sang, and pelted down the last few stairs.

Cassie and Marianne turned circles around each other in the middle of the hallway, greeting each other with laughter. A whole year had passed since they'd last seen each other, but they had no need to speak.

Marianne's hair, caught back in a ponytail, looked as dark as Aunt Juno's had once been. She had the same pale-green eyes, and her face, even with dots of perspiration along her top lip, was as striking as ever. She had something of Aunt Juno about her, but diluted, like the lemonade. Cassie knew she herself must look a fright, her hair a tangled mess from sleeping in the back of the car. She glanced down at her own scruffy travelling trousers and sandals. She should have got changed when she arrived, instead of wandering around the garden on her own. But what did it matter. She was at Greenaways.

Marianne linked her arm through Cassie's and pulled her into the dining room. 'Oliver's been an ass all morning,' she said. 'And I won't tolerate it.'

'Well, Gerard will ignore me now he's got Oliver,' said Cassie, 'and that other boy. What's-his-name.'

'I thought I'd better rescue you from him... Luke. He's a bore, isn't he? Dad said he was a bit of a pipsqueak. You take Ma's lemonade. I expect it's as lethal as ever.' Marianne busied herself stacking the tumblers. 'I'll take these. I suppose we'd better go and find our horrible big brothers. They'll soon complain about being thirsty. And starving. Mrs Poulter has left out plates of sandwiches, Ma said.'

Cassie found the sandwiches in the pantry and fell into step with Marianne, their voices echoing along the back corridor. They crunched over gravel pathways and circled the huge lily-pad pond where fish broke the surface, creating delicate rings, and where dragonflies flickered in mid-air. They walked under the shade of the weeping willows, and Cassie heard the hollow knock-knock of a tennis ball.

'So, why is Oliver being an ass?' Cassie asked.

'Oh, he's been a grumpy so-and-so, bear with a sore head. I think Luke is getting on his nerves and he's only been here two days. Oops, here we are.' Marianne juggled with the tumblers and tennis balls as she opened the gate. 'He'll brighten up now you and Gerard are here.'

The tennis court had certainly seen better days. Bare patches peppered the grass, the net drooped, and the chalk lines disappeared like ghosts into the ground. Gerard and Luke had started already, thwacking competitively at each other, while Oliver fiddled with the net cord.

'Needs to go a tad higher,' he called. 'Someone give me a hand.'

Gerard tipped a volley shot straight past Luke's ankles. 'I thought a lower net would make it easier for the girls,' he called, laughing. 'And the boys.'

'I *nearly* got that ball,' Luke countered, failing to find it funny.

'Really, Gerard?' said Marianne, cheerfully humouring him as she took her own pristine racket out of its press and drummed the taut strings onto the heel of her hand. 'We'll soon see about that.'

Cassie set the sandwiches and lemonade jug on the ground by the old, saggy armchair which had been lined up at the net for whoever might be umpire or, indeed, ball boy. Years ago, it had been in Aunt Juno's parlour but was now delegated to the garden. She added her cardigan to the pile of boys' jumpers and blazer draped over the back.

'Oliver, have you done the measuring thing yet with your tennis racket?' she asked. He didn't seem at all grumpy to her, simply preoccupied and wanting things to be just so. And she knew exactly how he felt.

'Ah, right. You do that while I crank the handle,' Oliver said. 'God, it's rusted into position. Can hardly shift it.'

'Wait a minute!' Cassie called to Luke, who stood poised on the baseline, ready to serve.

He tutted and continued to bounce the ball.

'Not only can girls not play tennis properly,' Luke said. 'They interrupt play.'

Cassie heard Marianne hiss through her teeth.

'Bit uncalled for,' uttered Oliver, under his breath.

He grasped the handle on the post while Cassie took his racket to the centre of the net, stood it vertically against the netting, marked with her finger where the top of the racket came. Then she turned the racket sideways and placed it above her finger.

'Needs to go up at least an inch, Oliver,' she called.

He set to work, grimacing comically, his hair bouncing with his effort.

'Put your back into it, Oliver,' hollered Gerard from the other baseline. 'We're in the middle of a game here.'

Marianne said, 'But are you winning or losing, Gerard?'

'Well, I am about to break Luke's serve, so let's see.'

'That's it, done,' said Oliver. 'And now I'm in no fit state to play. Unfair advantage!'

Cassie handed him back his racket.

'Glad you've brought out provisions, Cass,' he said. 'I will need to be fed and watered. We make a good team, you and I.'

Cassie flicked the compliment away with a shake of her head. 'Is Gerard goading your friend on purpose?' she whispered.

'Probably. Gerard knows how to push buttons... You can have a game, too, you know.'

'I'm happy to be ball boy.'

'Ball *girl*,' he said. 'You are also umpire, then.'

Gerard whizzed through the next game, pounding over the court, his limbs stretching this way and that in an infeasible manner, claiming victory in minutes. Luke looked momentarily thunderstruck, but shook it off, twitching his shoulders in an exaggerated fashion and wiping his palms down his trousers.

'Just warming up, that's all,' he said.

'Where are your specs, Woodward?' Oliver asked.

'In my pocket. But if I was wearing them, I would have beaten Gerard.'

Cassie glanced at Luke. 'But didn't you say tennis was easy...?'

Luke shrugged.

'Right then, let's get on with it,' Marianne announced. 'A sort of mixed doubles, I suppose. Oliver and Woodward against me and Gerard. Cassie, why don't you play in my place with Gerard every other game.'

'No, it's all right. I am half-asleep anyway.' Cassie sat in the armchair. It creaked under her weight and smelt, in a comforting way, of mildew and bonfire smoke. Over the tops of the willows, she spotted the tall chimneys of Greenaways, the weathervane, the stone-tiled roof against a crystalline sky. 'And there is always tomorrow.'

'Cassie, we're waiting,' called Gerard.

'Sorry. Right then. Play!'

Cassie did not have long to relax, for the ball soon hit the net. She dashed to retrieve it, kept the game flowing. Marianne had improved since last year and was nifty when she came to the net; in her new tennis dress, she certainly looked the part. And Oliver sliced the ball low and hard, beating Gerard on some occasions, and sometimes, not. Luke showed off with his serve, bouncing the ball and launching it with menace.

Calling the scores, loud and clear, Cassie felt a peculiar relief in being separate and not quite part of it. Always the youngest, never quite catching up, she had wondered if this summer would feel different. But, watching them play, she still felt like the 'little sister', and really, she did not mind.

'Love-forty!' she cried, as Luke messed up his second serve to Gerard, who cheered in a rather unsporting manner.

'But that was in!' Luke shouted.

'Hard cheese,' Marianne called. 'It was out.'

'Honestly, Woodward,' said Oliver. 'I saw it. I'm closer than you. It was out.'

'I suppose this is set point then?' Luke asked.

'Afraid so,' Marianne called. She caught Cassie's eye and giggled.

Cassie called again: 'Love-forty!'

Luke looked with fury from Marianne to Cassie and back again at Marianne, his glaring silence making Cassie feel curiously unsettled. This wasn't how Greenaways and Marshes played tennis. There had never been such showing off, or complaining, in summers past. The four of them, growing up together, had shared jokes and given each other a gentle ribbing, but none of them had ever been as grumpy as Luke. Perhaps, Cassie thought, it felt different now because they were all older and yet Luke's presence, his mood and his voice disrupted the neat four-square of cousins. He changed the formula and tugged at allegiances.

'You girls have got it in for me,' Luke grumbled.

Oliver lowered his voice to encourage his friend, putting his hand on his shoulder so that they turned their backs on their opponents. 'All right, Woodward... take a breather...' Cassie heard him say. 'Try serving for Marianne's backhand... her weaker side.'

Luke flexed his shoulders again, pounded the ball on the baseline and hit a ferocious serve, the ball skimming over the net. But Marianne moved like a cat, stretching hard to return it, executing a graceful, perfect backhand, her ponytail streaking behind her, and Cassie wished that she could play like her; that she were just like Marianne. That she was a Greenaway.

Cassie clapped, even though the ball was still in play, and Gerard shouted, 'Good shot, Marianne!'

Luke sprinted for his return, lifted his racket behind his ear and volleyed the ball. It slammed straight over the net and hard into Marianne's thigh. She squealed, buckled, and both her knees hit the gritty turf at the same time.

'God, Marianne, sorry!' Luke cried.

Everyone ran to her, but Luke got there first.

'Are you all right...?' he asked. 'I didn't mean...'

Marianne doubled over on the ground, moaned in agony, pressing both palms to her thigh. She looked up at Luke, her mouth gaping, tears rinsing away her prettiness. 'Do I look all right, you beast,' she hissed. 'You did that on purpose, you absolute nasty beast.'

'No really...'

'Come on Marianne,' said Oliver soothingly. 'Let's get you up.'

'He did it on purpose!' she seethed.

'It's okay, Marianne,' Cassie said. She rested her palm on her cousin's back; she could feel the vibrations of her tears and shock racking her body.

Gerard and Oliver took Marianne's elbows and eased her to her feet. She yelped again in pain. Cassie linked Marianne's arm, like they always did to comfort each other. Marianne stared down at her knees, her skin embedded with grains of dirt and bits of grass. A thin trickle of blood eased down to her white socks. Her sobbing rose off the scale.

'Look what you've done!' she screeched.

'Sorry, Marianne...' Luke sounded mortified.

'He didn't mean it, Marianne...' Oliver uttered.

She turned on her brother. 'And you're never on my side!' she yelled.

Wriggling free from Cassie, she stormed over to the armchair and wrenched the pile of jackets to the ground. She kicked them, stamped her heel on them. Her foot caught the sandwich plate, sending it flying. Cassie knew, from the look on her face, that she hadn't meant to. Marianne hobbled out of the court, leaving the gate swinging open.

'Oliver,' Luke said. 'I honestly didn't do that on purpose.'

'I know. Best leave her alone to cool down.'

'Girls, eh?' Luke tried for a laugh.

Gerard tapped Luke on the shoulder. 'Hey, Woodward, game's abandoned,' he said, cheerily, sounding sorry for him. 'Show me where you found those rooks' nests. Down the track by the stream, was it?'

'I better go and find Marianne,' Cassie said.

'I thought we could have a knock about, Cass,' Oliver said.

Cassie gave a hesitant nod, torn between knowing she should comfort Marianne and wanting to spend time with Oliver. Two more summers and he would be going to university. And everything would change once again.

Luke rummaged for his blazer. 'Goddamn it!' he uttered, gingerly fishing in one of his pockets. 'She's gone and broken my glasses.'

'Jeepers, Woodward,' whistled Gerard. 'That's rotten.'

'What's rotten?' Aunt Juno padded through the gate, her long smock trailing around her tanned ankles, red nail varnish flashing on her toes. 'I have just seen Marianne in floods of tears, heading into the house. Oliver, what on earth happened to her?'

Luke presented the smashed spectacles in the palm of his hand. 'She went and stamped on my blazer, Mrs Greenaway,' he said. 'And these were in the pocket.'

'Heavens,' said Juno. 'I hope you have a second pair.'

'As a matter of fact, I do, Mrs Greenaway, but that's not really the—'

'What happened to make her trample your blazer?' Juno's question was framed to perfection.

'All a misunderstanding, Aunt Juno,' Gerard offered. 'I don't think she realised they were in Woodward's pocket.'

'I hit her by mistake with the tennis ball,' Luke mumbled.

'Well then!' Juno said breezily. 'Cassandra, darling, your mother is wondering if you have eaten and whether you need a nap. She was going to come out and find you herself, but she is bushed and has gone upstairs for a lie down. Your father, too, is spark out on the sofa. As for you boys, you are being left to your own devices. Ah, I see Mrs Poulter's sandwiches have hit the deck.'

'Marianne again, Ma,' Oliver said.

'Woodward and I are going off down the track,' Gerard said.

'I'm going to play tennis for a bit,' Cassie added. She felt tired, and past being hungry, but wanted so much to stay out there with Oliver as long as the sun was shining.

'I'll leave you two to it,' said Aunt Juno, her amused gaze whipping between the two of them. She walked out of the court with a flourish of her hand. 'Oliver, don't forget to clear the mess up, will you?'

'Yes, Ma.' Oliver grinned and signalled at Cassie with a flick of his head.

She picked up Marianne's racket and walked to the other side of the net. Without a word, Oliver served a gentle under-arm. The ball bounced near her feet, and she returned it in a perfectly graceful, and quite splendid, arc back to him.

2

Later that same afternoon, Cassie napped in her bedroom, unpacked, and listened to the clocks chime the hours. She explored the Long Gallery for a while, watching the sun lower, leaving the courtyard and its regal statues in shadow. The boys set off on an expedition along the stream, the grown-ups chatted and snoozed with newspapers on their laps in the drawing room, and Marianne stayed in her room.

While Cassie, her mother and aunt ate supper off trays on laps in Juno's parlour, munching cheese on toast, Cassie's uncle and father were playing billiards in the room on the other side of the courtyard. The boys were nowhere to be found. 'Not within earshot of the dinner bell, that's for sure', according to Uncle Charles.

'How do you cope, Juno?' Cassie's mother asked, dabbing her lips with a napkin. 'On Mrs P's day off? I thought her daughter stepped in at such times, or they at least had some sort of rota going on.'

'They're having a family event or other,' said Juno. 'One doesn't like to pry too much. For it means then having to keep on top of things, remembering people's names, etcetera. Mr Poulter will be back, too, tomorrow, which is good news for the garden, bad news for the weeds.'

Cassie's huge yawn brought tears to her eyes.

'Well, someone's tired,' said Aunt Juno.

'I'm not surprised,' said Cassie's mother. 'Did the tennis take it out of you?'

'Everything has,' Cassie said, feeling too content to explain.

The setting sun glimmered softly through her aunt's parlour window voiles onto sea-green wallpaper. Both women's perfumes – her mother's sweet lily of the valley and Aunt Juno's mysterious, dark notes – seemed blended to perfection. Cassie felt reminded of summers long gone, shadows of childhood, of time passing. She yawned again, apologised.

'The first day of the holidays is always disruptive, over-excitable, overwrought, Cassie,' said her mother. 'It will take you a little while to calm down.' She lowered her voice, and mouthed to Juno, 'How's Marianne?'

'Still sulking in her bedroom but I can hardly blame her. I'll take her up some pudding in a minute,' Juno sighed. 'I think it's, you know...'

'Haven't had that yet, with...' Cassie's mother looked over at her. 'Cassie, darling, don't you think you should have an early night? Catch up on your sleep. I'm always good for nothing after that blessed journey through the night and I can see you are. But tomorrow, you'll feel better.'

Cassie conceded, got the feeling her mother and aunt wanted to carry on talking in the way ladies did without her in the room. She helped her mother take the supper trays back out to the kitchen, while Aunt Juno spooned cold rice pudding into a bowl in the pantry and took it upstairs.

'Come back, Mrs Poulter and daughter, all is forgiven,' laughed Cassie's mother. 'I can't remember where the trays go!'

'But Greenaways used to be your home, Mum.'

'Ah, but in those days, I rarely came in here. We had a lot more staff to deal with such things as where the trays go. My mother had a lovely old lady's maid. Such luxury, but when the war started, the butler, the lady's maid, and the likes of Mrs Poulter left for better jobs, better things. The Great War...' She sighed, her mouth crumbled, and Cassie saw a tense sparkle in her eyes, '...put paid to a lot of things.'

Cassie knew not to ask what she meant by *things*. Her uncle, Roland, the boy in the middle of Uncle Charles and her mother, had disappeared into the war and the adults were terribly unforthcoming about it; could never find the words to explain what happened.

'And then...' said her mother, with forced brightness. 'And then, I met Dad and he whisked me away, as he likes to remind us.'

'But you like our house, too, don't you?'

'I love both places,' she said, 'but Greenaways, really, is not my home any more.' She laughed lightly. 'However, I quite like playing kitchen maid. Come on, Cassie, bedtime before you keel over.'

Her mother said goodnight and wandered back along to Juno's parlour with a mug of tea, but Cassie, hearing the boys' voices at the garden door, lingered in the hallway.

Luke appeared around the corner first with Oliver and Gerard following. Spotting Cassie, Luke headed straight for her, making a teasing sound and holding his closed palm out in front of him.

'Look what we found,' he said, gesturing with his hand, close to her face. 'Go on, I dare you.'

'Cass isn't scared of anything,' said Oliver.

'She's boring like that,' said Gerard.

Grinning, Luke said, 'Let's see,' and opened his fist slowly to reveal a tiny bird, eyes closed as if sleeping, brown wings folded, miniature legs curled beneath.

'Oh, it's a wren!' Cassie breathed. 'An adorable little wren.'

'A dead wren, I'm afraid,' said Oliver.

'Lying there in the middle of the path by the stream, just now,' Luke said in triumph, his eyes wide with glee behind his second pair of spectacles.

'We wondered if a rook or an owl had got it,' Gerard said.

'Or a fox. Scared it to death.' This from Luke.

'Let me...' Cassie gestured, and Luke reluctantly tipped the little body into her palm. 'Ah, she is still warm and soft and so light and...' Her voice caught as she gazed at the exquisite creature no bigger than an egg resting in her hand. She ran her little finger over its fragile head. 'Poor thing. Whatever happened to you?'

'Give it back to me, then,' urged Luke. 'I want it for my collection.'

'But,' Cassie said, in all honesty, 'it doesn't belong to you.'

'She's got a point, Woodward,' Oliver said. 'Goods and chattels of Greenaways, I'd say.'

Cradling the bird, Cassie took it outside, hearing Luke complaining and Gerard and Oliver reasoning with him as their voices drifted upstairs.

Dusk had fallen since supper, changing the shape and sound of the garden. Liminal evening shadows blurred the flower beds and the lily pond, where a plopping noise made by a mysterious night-time creature – a toad, perhaps – sounded louder than it ought. Birds sang in a settling down manner, and the silence drew longer between each tentative call.

Cassie carried the wren down beyond the pond and the tennis court to where the brook – which eventually joined the River Dart – curved and bubbled along the boundary. Finding a leaf of a fitting size, she wrapped it around the little body, wondering, hoping for a moment, that it might reawaken. She found the perfect spot and set the parcel down in a mossy crook at the base of a tree, scattering leaves over it.

'You also belong to Greenaways,' Cassie whispered, knowing that the darkening summer night would take care of it.

Even so, with her task done, dusk complete and lamplight glowing like beacons from a handful of windows, Cassie felt a sense of urgency to get herself back to the house.

As she slipped in through the back door, the quietness of the hallway welcomed her – beneath it, a vibration of soft, murmuring voices. Cassie hesitated. Glancing through the dining room towards the partly opened door to Juno's parlour, she decided that she ought to be a polite young lady and say goodnight to her aunt, and reassure her mother that, this time, she really was going to bed. But she jolted to a stop by the dining table, her stomach flipping.

Splash marks tarnished the pristine, polished surface, stark against the rich wood, exactly where, earlier, she had poured her glass of lemonade.

How could she have been so careless? She had spoiled the table.

Cassie hurried out across the hallway and into the kitchen corridor. Mrs Poulter had an enormous cupboard in the scullery filled with cleaning paraphernalia, cloths and dusters, where surely, she would find something to magically remove the stains, put it right and cover up her blunder. She didn't want to be responsible for spoiling the priceless heirloom that must have belonged to her Greenaway grandparents, great-grandparents and all those people in the long-lost past. She didn't want to annoy Aunt Juno, disappoint her mother and, worse, ruin the first day of her holiday.

Cassie opened the cupboard doors, remembering the comforting, chemical scent from the time when she had helped Mrs Poulter clear it out. Pushing aside brushes, matchboxes and bundles of candles, Cassie revealed all manner of tins and bottles containing mysterious household necessities: brown bottles, green bottles and two or three with a black skull on the label to warn of poison. Turpentine, borax, ammonia, and, thank goodness, polish. Cassie grabbed the tin, but the label said:

Grate Polish

Another carton declared itself to be boot polish. Oh goodness, would *that* work? At last: the furniture polish.

Grabbing a duster, Cassie darted back to the dining room, pausing to listen, wondering how long she had before her mother and aunt found her out. But they continued their quiet conversation in the parlour, their voices drifting around the half-open door.

Cassie dibbed a corner of the cloth into the unctuous paste. She had no idea how much or how little she should use. They hadn't got round to teaching her *this* at school. Gingerly dabbing at the marks on the table, she overheard her mother:

'...I know Marianne has a year on Cassie but, my, she is growing up fast... as for Oliver...'

The polish began to seep into the surface, darkening the stains, and Cassie kept rubbing, ignoring her aching arm, her rising panic. Wasn't this how their housekeeper back home at

Egerton Terrace tackled the Chippendale? Or was Cassie simply making it worse?

Her aunt uttered something that Cassie didn't quite catch, and after a moment, her mother said, 'I have to ask, Juno...'

'Go on...'

'Do you see *him* in him?'

Cassie carried on polishing, the stain seemingly no better, glaring accusingly at her. In the parlour next door, Juno gave a shuddering sigh.

'Sometimes... now he has shaken off that adorable, boyish look of his... but I must say, it is hard to tell. Remember, I only knew *him* as a middle-aged man—'

Juno said a few more incomprehensible words.

'As Rich commented to me earlier, "*he's certainly no Greenaway*".' Cassie's mother yawned. 'Lord, I'm tired.'

Cassie glanced at the half-open door, frowning, massaging her elbow. What an odd thing for her father to have said. She felt slighted. *Of course,* Oliver is a Greenaway; he always has been. And weren't they all Greenaways, more or less? Belonging here, like the table, and everything else inside the ancient, rooted house. It didn't seem at all fair that her father should say that about Oliver, and her mother repeat it.

'But in Charles's eyes...?' her mother said.

'Yes... yes... absolutely...' Juno uttered. Another ragged sigh. 'Bedtime, I think.'

'Shall I damp this fire down?'

'No, no, leave it, just put the guard around it.'

Cassie gave the stains one final swipe. She had no idea if the polish had worked or not, so grabbed a napkin from the sideboard and set it on top. Scooting out to the scullery to deposit the cloth and polish, she managed to go up the stairs, two at a time, before her mother and aunt emerged.

Out of breath and her nerves fizzing, Cassie wondered what her mother had meant by whatever lay in Uncle Charles's eyes. However, her mind clouded with tiredness and worry about the stain, on top of the need to tiptoe along the dim upstairs passageway so as not to disturb Marianne, and the puzzle vanished as soon as it had manifested.

But Cassie's cousin must have heard her, for Marianne's door opened and she appeared in nightie and dressing gown to intercept her. She pulled her inside her bedroom.

'I've been waiting for you,' Marianne said, shutting the door. 'What have you been doing?'

'The boys found a dead wren,' Cassie said, which seemed to explain everything.

Marianne uttered, 'Oh!' and her eyes widened in repulsion. 'I bet you that was Woodward,' she said, nodding sagely. 'Look, Cassie, I'm sorry for stamping on your cardigan. I didn't realise yours was there too. Sorry for the sandwiches, and ruining the whole thing. Earlier, I had to go and apologise to Luke for breaking his glasses. Ma said I must, even though I didn't know they were in his pocket, and even though he is a little so-and-so.'

'Is that what she *actually* said?' Cassie asked.

Marianne laughed. 'She didn't have to. I knew she didn't blame me and she brought me some pudding. I can tell what she thinks of him. He has a second pair, and he accepted my apology, but my leg still really hurts. Look. It's stinging.' She showed Cassie the red shadow of a tennis ball, smarting against her skin. 'And I've got the curse.'

'It'll get better,' said Cassie, although she wasn't too sure if the curse, that enigmatic, grown-up, lady thing that her mother kept threatening her with, would ever get better. 'But,' she said, 'Luke will always be a little so-and-so.'

They fell into giggles, but the hilarity soon wore Cassie out.

It had been quite a day, as first days always were, what with tennis, laying the wren to rest and ruining the Greenaways's table. Everything began to merge in her mind, a confusing crowd of voices. She felt exhausted and wanted time alone to think about it all.

Downstairs in the hallway, the clock began to strike for ten.

'It's late,' said Cassie. 'I better go. I'm sure Mum has the ears of a bat. She will know I'm not in bed.'

'My ma seems to know everything I get up to,' said Marianne, 'but never seems to mind. Oh, Cassie, don't go.'

Cassie cast her eyes around Marianne's bedroom. Every detail seemed to be finished with frills of pink and lemon lace: pillows, satin eiderdown, the curtains around the kidney-shaped dressing table.

'You've got all new stuff in here,' she said, wondering why her bedroom at home was never as pretty.

'See, you should stay.'

Cassie shook her head.

'But, I don't know why Ma put you in the guest bedroom this time, when we always used to sleep here together,' Marianne said. 'And look, I have a brand-new, queen-sized bed. We can both fit in with ease. Remember when we had midnight feasts?'

'Yes, but we're nearly grown-up young ladies now,' said Cassie, too tired to enjoy the memory. 'And I'm only next door.'

Yawning, Marianne conceded, took off her dressing gown and hopped under her sheet.

'And remember,' Cassie said, reassuring her cousin. 'There is always tomorrow.'

Marianne smiled. 'And the next day.'

They chimed together: 'And the next day after that.'

3

By the time Cassie came downstairs, the hot plates of eggs, sausages, bacon and tomatoes laid out under silver domes along the sideboard had been all but devoured.

Mrs Poulter would have returned to Greenaways early that morning to prepare breakfast, cycling in from Eastcombe village with her daughter, Maud. The stains on the table, no doubt, had not gone unnoticed, but at least they lay hidden, for now, under a crisp, linen cloth, cluttered with empty plates and steaming cups of tea. Cassie may well have got away with it.

'I know I slept in but...' Cassie said, uncovering an empty dish.

'You know how greedy the boys are,' Marianne said, pouring herself a fresh cup of tea.

Cassie gave Gerard a look.

'But we were starving,' her brother said. 'We hadn't eaten for near enough eighteen hours. Remember what happened to the sandwiches.'

Marianne said, 'Really, Gerard, must you bring that up

again?' And aside to Cassie: 'I'm never going to live it down, am I?'

'It's a poor show when Mrs P has an unexpected day off,' said Aunt Juno, sipping herbal tea at her end of the table. 'Thank God it is now business as usual.'

A faint and comforting clatter of pans emanated across the hallway from the kitchen quarters, along with the sound of running water and the soft tones of music on the wireless. At the sideboard, Cassie secured enough bacon to make herself a sandwich with a dollop of Mrs Poulter's relish on two thick buttered slices of crusty bread. Wondering if she should go and confess to the housekeeper about the stain, she decided against it, and sat down next to Marianne to eat.

Uncle Charles glanced out of the window, folded his newspaper and said, 'Right, it looks like it is set fair for today – perfect for a tramp over Dartmoor. Who's up for it?'

Luke, sitting in shirt and tie, second pair of glasses polished, his clean plate pushed away, raised his hand as if he were at school. Gerard and Oliver nodded a mumbling interest, wiping yolk from their plates with crusts.

'Not you, Oliver, I understand you have not yet finished your agricultural history essay,' said Uncle Charles. 'Ah yes, my boy. I'm keeping tabs. And you know the rule: get it done in the first week of the holiday, then you are free to do as you please.'

Oliver pulled a face. 'Pa, it's taking me all this time because it is a real boring stinker...'

Cassie gave Oliver a sympathetic look, thinking of her own homework – English, French *and* German – which she had yet to plough through.

'And Marianne,' her uncle continued, unperturbed, 'I think after yesterday's debacle, you had better stay put to cool your heels a little more. Plus, there'll be a bit of a crush in the car if you come too.'

'Suits me,' Marianne said, flicking a relieved glance at Cassie.

'Mum, are you going?' Cassie asked.

She blotted her lips with her napkin. 'Where, darling?'

'Dartmoor.'

'Wild horses wouldn't drag me,' she said. 'I have a smashing novel to read, and I know which battles to pick. Walking up to Dartmoor today is not one of them. And, anyway, I didn't bring any sensible shoes.'

'I'm sure Juno has some you can borrow...' Cassie's father said, leaning back in his chair to light a cigarette.

'Miranda has much bigger feet than me,' said Aunt Juno.

Cassie saw her mother glance in surprise down at her own feet, tucked into her comfy 'sloppies'.

'I'd quite like to spend a restful day here at Greenaways,' she said, quietly apologetic, peering at Cassie's father. 'I simply love being... here.'

'I'll stay with you, Mum,' Cassie said.

Her mother gave her a tender look.

Oliver smiled at Cassie across the table. 'You mean, Cass, you don't want to hike all the torturous way to Hound Tor?'

She shook her head.

'I don't know. You women,' said Uncle Charles. 'A good, bracing walk will be just what the doctor ordered. Are you coming, Rich?'

'I most certainly am,' said Cassie's father. 'Need to stretch the old legs. Remember, I have my drive back to London tomorrow to look forward to.'

Cassie's mother began, 'Oh, but, Rich, I thought you might want to...' but stopped herself, concentrating on stirring her tea.

Gerard teased, 'Your old legs, Dad? Do you have new ones hidden away somewhere?'

'Less of your lip, son,' said Cassie's father, laughing, always seeming, and sounding different here at Greenaways.

Aunt Juno gave Cassie's father a sharp look and wafted at his cigarette smoke in an exaggerated fashion, her silvery bangles tinkling at her wrists. Spotting the little sprouting of dark hair under Juno's arms, Cassie suppressed a giggle and caught Marianne's eye.

'And I would like a little fresh air,' Juno said, standing up. 'Don't overdo it, gentlemen. Charles, don't push the boys too far. I know what you're like.' She sighed, with a little stretch of her bare, brown arms. 'And be back in time for cocktails and dinner tonight. Mrs Poulter has the lamb. Now I must go and find Mr Poulter in the garden.'

All the boys and both the men watched, entranced, as Juno drifted out of the doorway, her sandals making gentle slapping sounds that receded across the parquet.

* * *

After those heading for Dartmoor set off, packed boisterously into Uncle Charles's car, Cassie selected a book from the shelf in Aunt Juno's parlour and joined her mother on the west-facing side terrace. Striped deckchairs arranged under the wisteria looked over the undulating sweep of lawn, shadowed here and there by enormous, rugged, old trees.

'What have you there?' her mother asked, lifting her sunglasses to have a look.

'*Great Expectations.*'

'You might regret that. I find him terribly hard work.' Cassie's mother stretched her pale legs out onto the footrest, the light fabric of her tea dress flickering in the breeze. She had eschewed her sloppies for a pair of pretty sandals and wore a wide, soft-brimmed hat that hid first one eye and then the other as she turned her head. 'Aunt Juno has leant me this...' She turned the dog-eared copy of *Cheri* by Colette towards Cassie. 'It's quite an eyebrow raiser, really. I don't think you are ready for it.'

'Why not, Mum?' Cassie asked, mildly aggrieved. One moment, her mother reminded her that she was nearly fifteen and should behave as such; the next, that she was too young for a grown-up book.

'It's decadent, paints quite a picture,' she said. 'But I don't know. Everyone talks about the Twenties as being wild and hedonistic, and they seem to have been for Colette there in Gay Paree. But they certainly weren't if you were stuck at home in South Ken with two young children.'

Cassie glanced at her mother and, for the first time, understood that she had once, long ago, been a girl like her.

'Is Aunt Juno older than you, Mum?'

'Ho, yes!'

'But how old were you when you had Gerard and me?'

'Eighteen with Gerard. Twenty-one with you. I left Greenaways at seventeen to be married. A child bride. Thank goodness for your father.' Her voice deepened. 'But I think no one noticed me go, really.' She glanced up at the house, as if to confirm her memory. 'Because of Uncle Roland...'

Again, the war hinted at, but suppressed, and a tense, drifting silence.

'Is that why Gerard's middle name is Roland?' Cassie asked, suddenly, rashly impelled to fix it.

Her mother nodded. She put her book down, rearranged her skirt, pensively rubbed the fabric between her fingertips.

'Have I not told you this before?'

Cassie shook her head, wondering how she could not know that.

Her mother collected herself, folding her hands on her lap as if this would help her concentrate. 'The year Dad and I got married, 1917,' she said, 'Roland had been reported missing, presumed dead, they said, at Ypres. We could not bury him. And your grandparents never recovered. The beginning of their decline.'

Cassie fixed her eyes on the golden freckles along her mother's arm, avoiding the expression on her face.

'He was their favourite,' she said, as if this explained everything. 'So, the Twenties for me, and our family, and for so many of us, was simply a drab and crushingly awful time. I think some people went a little mad, to be honest.'

'Uncle Charles came home,' Cassie said brightly, wanting to make her mother happy again.

'Yes, he did. He did well out of it. Promotion and medals. Mentioned in dispatches. Married Aunt Juno, the lot...'

Cassie didn't understand what her mother meant by 'the lot' and worried that it would be something else upsetting, so turned back to her book until Maud Poulter came out to ask if they wanted tea and cinnamon buns for elevenses.

Convivial moments drifted by, the light breeze rustling the pages of their books, Cassie daydreaming away from Dickens every other paragraph to the other, rather wonderful, expectation of tea and buns. Her mother's toes, pale and naked and peeping out of her fancy sandals, had perfect half-moons. Even the little ones.

'Mum...' she said.

'Yes, darling?'

'I don't think you have big feet.'

Cassie's mother put her head back and laughed.

* * *

With Mrs Poulter preparing the dinner – and also busy righting Cassie's blunder, for Cassie had spotted her heading into the dining room with the tin of polish and a duster – they ate a lunch of sandwiches out on the terrace, cut by Maud into tiny triangles and presented on a bed of cress. Aunt Juno joined them and, when Marianne appeared and had nibbled her way through one or two, crusts and all, she announced she would go back up to her room.

'But don't you want to go and follow the stream?' Cassie asked.

'Not today...' Marianne said.

'You don't like to play down there any more, do you, darling,' Aunt Juno stated, her words flat and knowing.

It felt like a door closing. Cassie looked at Marianne, amazed. Granted, her cousin was a year older than her, and wonderfully different in many ways, but they had always been the *same*. And following the stream was what they always did. It must be, she decided, because of the curse.

Cassie, rather dumbfounded, licked mayonnaise off her fingers, hoping no one noticed the blob of it on her blouse. Marianne, in her new linen frock, radiated poise and guarded dignity.

'Is your leg still hurting, darling?' Aunt Juno asked. 'That blessed boy! I wanted to give him what-for.'

'A little bit... no.' Marianne's large, clear eyes blinked earnestly. 'It's all right, Ma. It's best all forgotten. Luke is our guest, after all.' She sounded mature, in stark contrast to her outburst yesterday, and her late-night giggling with Cassie. 'Anyway, Pa said I must cool my heels today, and so I will.'

'There's my girl,' Aunt Juno said, stacking plates haphazardly.

'Oh, Cassie, you've not eaten your crusts,' her mother said.

'The birds can have them...'

'The birds will become fat.' Her mother turned to Marianne. 'Remember, dear, to keep your analgesics topped up,' she said, 'Juno, you do have a good supply, don't you?'

'My, yes, of course.'

'And, Marianne,' Cassie's mother went on, 'when people like Luke, are... difficult, and believe me, you will come across many more like him as you grow older, never believe that it is your fault. Always ask yourself, "*Who* would you rather be?".'

Aunt Juno laughed in agreement.

'Thank you, Auntie Miranda,' Marianne said, sounding even less like Marianne. 'I will remember.'

'You do that,' she said. 'Now, I'm going upstairs for a nap. I'll take these leftover sandwiches up to Oliver for you, Juno. And, Cassie darling, don't wear yourself out running wild.'

They all wandered back into the house, leaving Cassie in a rather unsettling silence, the long, empty afternoon stretching ahead. The old, stone walls of Greenaways soaked up the sunlight, and the wisteria hummed with bees. Cassie scattered the crusts across the terrace and set off down through Aunt Juno's rose garden, aware of a sense of loss tugging inside her. Marianne had grown, had moved streaks ahead of her in the past year, clearly leaving grubby rambles along the banks of the stream, and Cassie, behind. And Cassie should have known, should have prepared herself. After all, what better clue had Marianne given her than when she appeared yesterday, gliding down the stairway in her pristine white tennis dress.

Determined not to mind, Cassie went the way she'd gone yesterday at dusk, past the pond and tennis court. She opened the boundary gate that led to the river.

Thickened by elder, brambles and nettles, and in darker corners, vivid, curling ferns, the trees looked different here in broad daylight. Cassie felt for one frightening moment that she'd forgotten where she'd put the wren, that she'd misplaced it, and would never be able to find it again. But she waited, trusted herself and spotted at last the little leaf parcel, still there, untouched, at the foot of the willow. Happily, she carried on down to the riverbank.

* * *

In summers past, she and Marianne would follow the brook, oftentimes with Gerard or Oliver, other times with both. And each year, it had seemed different. Undergrowth would spread to block the path, and they would have to find a way through. Or the track would have been cleared by Mr Poulter or the farmer, and they could trudge on for ages. Whether upstream or down, they kept to the bank, leaping across if the path petered out, or they discovered a new crossing; the rule always to keep on, to see how far they could go.

Cassie stood for a moment with the water running past her toes, coursing over pebbles in the shallows, streaming with green weed, and capturing sunlight in ripples and eddies. On the other side, graceful willow and gnarly hawthorn formed shadowy thickets. She peered along the bank upstream through stooping branches dipping their tips into the flow. But she felt drawn the other way, and set off downstream, wondering if she'd ever be able to reach the Dart, or even the estuary, eventually Dartmouth and the sea. And this she realised, with a light, liberating giggle, despite Marianne's rebuff, was the first time she'd done this on her own.

Tramping over leaf mould and brushing through ferns, she disturbed the scents of the damp river margins, could smell the cool brightness of the water as it bubbled on its way. Birds in the canopy answered each other's calls, a constant chorus to accompany her. And suddenly, above it all, she heard a hollow whistling, a strange, sharp screeching sound. She stopped to listen. The shriek came again. Cassie chuckled to herself and hurried on.

Around the bend, Oliver sat on a fallen log, his heels wedged into a cleft in the trunk, his elbows on his knees. He clasped a thick blade of grass between his thumbs and close to his lips, blowing for all he was worth.

'Careful, you may be doing the mating call of some hungry, ferocious animal,' she said. 'Which will come crashing through the undergrowth to get you.'

Oliver looked around, smiling, 'Such as...?'

'I don't know; I will have to make one up.'

He moved up the log to make space for her.

'Aren't you supposed to be doing your essay?' she asked.

'The blessed Corn Laws have done *me*,' he said. 'I snuck away. I know I have missed lunch, but I am counting on Mrs Poulter's roast lamb tonight to make up for it.'

'Oh, my mum will have found you out. She took your sandwiches up to your room.'

'Foiled again. I hope she won't tell Pa that I've been bunking off.'

'I don't think she will,' Cassie said. 'She does occasionally give me a hard time, but generally, she will take pity and has a nice sense of fairness.'

They sat in easy silence, under the dappled shade. Every so

often, Oliver made his whistling noise with the grass, some attempts better than others. Marianne may have changed, Gerard was too grown-up and not that interested any more, and they had been infiltrated by Luke Woodward, Cassie thought, but she and Oliver were as they'd always been.

'I can never do that... that thing with the grass,' she said.

'Try.'

Oliver bent over to pluck a suitable blade for her, and she gave it a half-hearted go, but it kept slipping from her grasp. She didn't have Oliver's knack, and she worried that the sharp edge may cut her lip. Watching a moorhen paddling among the sedge on the opposite bank, she began to shred the blade of grass.

'At least we can suffer with our homework together,' she said. 'My English Comprehension is nearly finished, but I still have both my French and German to do.'

'Oh, now you've spoilt it, bringing that up again!'

'If I put my mind to it, it won't be too bad. I'll get it done in a couple of days, when Mum and Dad have gone.'

Cassie pictured tomorrow and the day after, and all the days and weeks after that. A whole summer at Greenaways spooling ahead of her.

Oliver picked at a wedge of dead bark on the log, crushing it to dust between his fingers.

'You're good at languages, aren't you, Cass?' he said. 'You're like me. I am a real Latin bore, aren't I, much to my father's dismay? He'd prefer it if I was a mathematician. Or a scientist, like our boffin Woodward. But numbers baffle me.'

Cassie noted a faint break in his voice, a little slice of insecurity.

'And we both like to draw, don't we?' Cassie said, smiling at her own realisation, and the affinity she felt with her cousin.

She had expected to be alone, roaming along the riverbank,

but finding Oliver here had not surprised her in the least. And he almost seemed to have been expecting her.

'But whenever Pa has caught me sketching,' Oliver said, 'it doesn't go down very well... but *German*, Cass!' He laughed. 'Do you like to make a rod for your own back?'

'I could say the same about your Latin, Oliver Greenaway,' she said, teasing him. 'German can be complicated, but that's the fascination, really. I know people think it an ugly language, but I find it descriptive, rhythmic, almost poetic. And the words make sense to me, especially with their English connection. *Die Vogel singen*; *der schone Fluss*; *die Blaue Blumen*. Even *Eine Kleine Nachtmusik*. As long as you know the root of the word, you're away!'

Oliver puzzled for a moment. 'Singing birds, a beautiful river, blue flowers... a little night music? Ah, lovely old Mozart. But all those capital letters, Cass!' he said. 'At least what you are studying will be useful. Latin is dead.'

'But it means you are very good at crosswords, Oliver.'

Their chuckling faded in with the sounds of the riverbank: the bubbling water and the gentle breeze whispering in the treetops.

'Anyway, how is Marianne?' Oliver asked. 'Smashed or stamped on anything else this morning?'

'Oh no, she's—' Cassie faltered, wanting to say *different*, but felt stumped. 'One minute, she is all giggles, wanting a midnight feast; the next, she is all prim and proper.' Cassie did not want to elaborate; she felt disloyal. 'But she's all right. I am wondering why Luke is... sorry, he's your friend, but he seems to be—'

'A pain in the backside?'

Cassie nodded and laughed.

'Pa called him a pipsqueak again this morning, out of his

hearing, of course,' said Oliver. 'I laughed but now I think it was rather unkind.'

'Yes, I suppose it was.'

'Did Woodward upset you last night, Cass? With the wren?' The softness in his voice felt so familiar, trusted and comforting that she didn't dare look at him.

'No,' she said, even though he had. 'I found a safe place for it.'

'I guessed as much,' Oliver said. 'Right, swear to secrecy.'

He turned on the log towards her, his face closer than she expected. His features had altered since last summer most certainly, but before now, Cassie could not say how. Close up, his jawline looked stronger. His brow a little heavier, his eyes deeper in their sockets, their colour intense. She stared at his mouth.

'I swear.'

'His parents are divorcing.'

Cassie gasped. She barely understood what that word meant, for it had never been uttered at home. But she knew it sounded like something scandalous, ruinous and disastrous, all rolled into one.

'Why?'

'His mother had her head turned. Ran off with some other fellow. A Scotsman, apparently. It is an absolute scandal. My parents know, of course. And it is going to be in the newspapers, apparently. A court case. The school had to intervene with Luke, for he was not coping. That's why he's here for the summer: to keep him out of the way of it all. His parents are filthy rich, Pa told me, but I already knew that. Very wealthy indeed.'

'No wonder he is at sixes and sevens. His mother running off like that.' Cassie felt sorry for Luke, began to understand why he behaved like he did. 'But... but Woodward isn't a particularly posh, rich person's surname, is it?'

'No, that's his nickname,' Oliver said. 'Luke's surname is Dubois, from the French. He told me they were Huguenots. Made pots of money in silk weaving in the old days. *Du bois* – "of the wood", see? So we took it further, us boys at school. He is Lucien Dubois. We went with Woodward.'

Cassie smiled. 'He even calls himself that.'

'He's not all bad, you know. Quite a good chap, really, deep down. Just understandably troubled at the moment. Oh, Cass, did you see...?' Oliver leant forward, pointed to a patch of fern.

'No, what?'

'A wren, just there, beneath the tree.' He held her arm, pulled her over, to guide her, to see what he had seen. 'See, they like to be near water.'

Cassie peered at the undergrowth, thought she saw movement in its dark spaces, but couldn't be sure. She heard the slightest of rustling sounds.

'They're so well camouflaged,' she whispered, not wanting it to hear her or she may scare it. Perhaps, she thought, it was searching for the other wren, which lay wrapped in its leafy tomb.

The crop of curling ferns shuddered, and she saw the tiny bird, with its short, cocked tail, flit free and fly up and away, vanishing into the trees, to safety.

'I wonder if she was looking for her mate,' she said. 'But the one Luke found was brown, so she can't be...'

'Why not...?'

'But aren't male birds always the opposite to the female, always bright and showy?' she asked. 'Like drakes and black-birds and cockerels...' she trailed off.

'No, wrens all look the same,' said Oliver, catching her eye with an amused twinkle.

'I get that now,' Cassie said. 'I'm thinking of swans.'

And, after a moment, he said, 'But you're different, Cass.'

'Different?' Cassie uttered. Water birds piped intermittently. She swore she heard the whistling trill of the wren far up in the branches. 'Why?' She didn't want to be *different*.

'When Woodward tried to scare you last night,' Oliver said, 'with the dead bird, you were so... lovely. Marianne would have screamed for certain. And other girls would have cried, been disgusted, and not dare touch it, or care for it like you did. You're not like other girls.'

Admiration expanded his voice and she felt herself fold in, adding protective layers, for she wouldn't dare let herself think that Oliver might feel as she did right at that moment: so deeply free and happy. She remained still, drumming her heels gently on the side of the fallen log, trying to keep the smile off her face.

* * *

Uncle Charles's car pulled up in the late afternoon, and its passengers emerged; Gerard looked sunburnt and sulky, and Luke uncharacteristically unkempt, while Uncle Charles appeared invigorated as he gave a good stretch and expounded on the joys of hiking.

Cassie's father, looking rather dishevelled himself, made a beeline for the drawing room where Aunt Juno was opening the gin and clinking ice cubes into glasses. As he passed Cassie in the hallway, he ruffled her hair in greeting, uttering, 'Dubois is a bit of a pain, isn't he?'

Cassie giggled in automatic response, enjoying his brief attention, but soon felt an itch of shame, after what Oliver had told her.

She followed her father through to the drawing room and joined Marianne on the sofa. Her cousin had been curled into the corner, cradling *Jane Eyre* and drinking her mother's lemonade, but she unfolded herself and gave Cassie a bright-eyed greeting.

'We're going to play hide-and-seek after dinner,' she said with relish, the young girl re-emerging. 'And Luke will be *it*, as he doesn't know Greenaways.'

'Oh really? Isn't that mean?'

'No, he volunteered.' Marianne lowered her voice, laughing, but sounding kind. 'He must be a bit barmy.'

'Or eager to please,' said Cassie, joining in.

'Ah, so the gigglers are back on form,' said her father, putting his feet on the footstool and accepting a hefty, cut-glass tumbler from Aunt Juno, complete with expertly pared lemon rind.

'Had a good day, Rich?' Juno asked, settling herself in the armchair opposite him. Her tanned arms emerged from the folds of her loose, gold-thread tabard, which clung and shifted mysteriously around her frame. She had applied mascara, enhancing her large eyes, and her hair was arranged on top of her head so that it sat in cloudy puffs, reminding Cassie of a stormy sky.

'A good day, Juno?' he smirked. 'Yes. No. Not really.'

'Oh, come on, man,' said Uncle Charles, blustering in, still full of the joys. 'Isn't that what you wanted? All that fresh air is good for the soul. You should have come with us, Juno.'

'Yes, you should have,' said Cassie's father, lighting a cigarette in an unreasonably aggressive way, blowing a grey plume to the ceiling.

There was something odd in his voice, and Aunt Juno bristled, squaring her shoulders.

'Oh no, Richard, dear,' she said, with a caustic spark. 'We had a nice quiet lady's afternoon, didn't we, Marianne and Cassie?' She glanced at the doorway. 'Didn't we, Miranda?'

Cassie's mother walked in, dressed for dinner and looking delicate and lovely in soft white, her waist tiny, and the skirt of her dress fluttering above her ankles. She wore a dab of pink lipstick on her mouth.

'Didn't we just,' she said. Her eyes looked wide, expectant and happy. 'Bring your drink upstairs, Rich; I have run you a bath.'

Cassie's father let out an exaggerated sigh and got rather laboriously to his feet.

'That's me told,' he said.

* * *

Dinner over, the dessert plates cleared away, Uncle Charles brought the port from the sideboard and began to set out glasses. 'I can see from you youngsters' faces that you are dying to get down from the table,' he said. 'What is it tonight?'

'Hide-and-seek, Pa,' said Oliver.

'Ah yes,' Cassie's mother said. 'The Long Gallery is perfect for it. I remember we used to play there when we were children. Can find all manner of hidey-holes.'

'Don't go giving Luke any clues, Mum,' Gerard said. 'He is *it*.'

'Didn't we used to call it sardines, Charles, when we were first married? That's the adult version,' Aunt Juno said, 'Always a bit rakish back when we played it in our day. Honestly, we were born so-called staid Victorians, but what happened?'

'The war happened, Juno,' said Cassie's father evenly.

Juno retorted, 'Well, yes, I know *that*, Rich...'

Cassie watched her mother look first at Aunt Juno and then at her father, two bright points of red appearing on her pale cheeks. The little spat lingered in the air and it felt odd to

Cassie. If anyone would argue with Aunt Juno, surely it would be Uncle Charles.

'Can we get down, please, Mum?' Cassie asked, and her mother nodded distractedly.

The cousins and Luke began to scrape back their chairs.

'Ah, you, young lady,' Uncle Charles said, and Cassie's heart sank. She hated her uncle singling her out, was worried he'd make her stay behind and talk to him about her schoolwork. Her uncle always seemed to want to find out how clever she was. 'You enjoyed your lamb tonight, didn't you?' he said. 'I remember a time when you cried over Sunday lunch here because you realised you'd been tucking in to slices of the sweet creatures that had been gambling in the fields all spring.'

'Pa, come on,' said Oliver quietly. 'Don't remind her.'

'It's okay, Uncle Charles, I am over that now,' Cassie said brightly, not ready to admit to the tremor of guilt she'd felt enjoying Mrs Poulter's delicious roast.

'Go on then. The lot of you.' Uncle Charles dismissed them. 'We grown-ups have the port to tackle.'

The cousins hurried up the stairs, laughing, shushing one another, while Luke stayed behind in a corner of the hallway, facing the wall, eyes shut and counting loudly to one hundred. At the top of the stairs, Gerard and Oliver split, heading in different directions, and Marianne tugged Cassie along the landing towards her parents' bedroom.

Like the drawing room below it, the huge room turned the corner of the house. Cassie followed Marianne in but stopped halfway across the carpet, shocked by the size of the wooden bed. Both the glossy headboard and footboard curved around the top and bottom of the mattress as if they might trap the sleepers. The stained-glass shades on the lamps sent a rosy glow over the rumbled, unmade sheets and blankets. Aunt Juno's earthy perfume seemed to have sunk into the very walls. Her unstoppered scent and make-up bottles crowded the dusty dressing tabletop, her brushes and combs lying haphazardly, tufted with her hair. One of Uncle Charles's shirts lay crumpled by the bed, his ties draped over a chair. A pair of underpants had been kicked towards the skirting board.

'Come on,' hissed Marianne, nudging her. 'Luke'll never find us. He wouldn't dare come in here.'

She trotted over, opened a second door on the other side and gestured that Cassie should follow her. In this smaller room, two huge, full-length mirrors propped against one wall faced two polished-wood wardrobes, almost reaching the ceiling and quite nightmarish in size.

'Ma's dressing room,' Marianne said. 'We can choose a wardrobe each. Even if he finds one of us, he might not find the other. Come on, hurry. He must be up to seventy or eighty now.'

But Cassie could not move. She stared at the painting hanging between two mirrors. 'Who's that?' she asked, her eyes smarting.

Marianne giggled. 'Ma. When she was an artist's model. Awful, isn't it?'

Cassie didn't know what to say. She didn't know what might be awful or not awful about it, but she could not stop gaping. In the painting, Aunt Juno – definitely her, for Cassie recognised her huge eyes and her 'hooky' nose – lay stretched on a couch in a gloomy, lamp-lit room, gazing straight out of the canvas at whoever had painted her, the angles of her knees, hips and shoulders yielding into the cushions, her hands behind her head, her long hair almost to her waist, a faint smile on her lips. Aunt Juno, naked.

'Crumbs, Marianne,' Cassie said, 'do you think we will look like that when we grow up?'

'Hope not. Come *on*.' Marianne pinched her arm, opened the door to one of the wardrobes, her eyes gleamed with excitement. She pulled Cassie towards it. 'God, hurry up. He's coming!'

Cassie gave her a look. 'Are you feeling better, Marianne?'

'Much better, Ma's tablets worked a treat. Now hurry up!'

Cassie pushed aside the coats and dresses hanging inside the wardrobe and climbed in between them, her face brushing up against draped cashmere, and heavy worsted wool, the pungent scent of moth balls and Aunt Juno thickening the air. Marianne shut the door on her and Cassie felt around in the cramped gloom to find something soft to perch on. An old gaberdine car coat had been left folded up on the bottom of the wardrobe, and, with some difficulty, she eased herself down.

'I'm going to lock you in, Cassie!' Marianne hissed. 'Or the door might swing open!'

The key turned and Cassie shifted to find a more comfortable position, her fingertips brushing against something nestled in the folds of the coat, dislodging it. She picked it up, squinting at it in the thin shafts of light piercing the gaps around the hinges. An old sepia photograph: an image captured in shades of taupe and brown.

A gentleman with a grey, clipped beard sat in a café staring straight into the camera; either side of him, young ladies in hats leaning towards him to crowd into the photograph and, equally, to attract his attention. They all looked towards the camera except one. The young lady right next to the gentleman gazed at him instead. She seemed distinct from the other women, hatless and with unruly, dark hair, her profile as striking and as strong as Aunt Juno's.

Marianne snapped off the dressing room light, and the sudden, plunging darkness startled Cassie. On reflex, she slipped the photograph in her pocket for safekeeping.

Cassie heard Marianne climb into the wardrobe beside her, the low thump of the door and a hat box or something falling over inside it. She strained to listen for Luke's footsteps, for him opening the main bedroom door, and walking across to the dressing room. But would he dare come into her aunt and uncle's bedroom? *Surely*, he wouldn't dare.

In the close, stifling, blacked-out silence, Marianne's chortling began, reaching Cassie in irresistible, low, muffled waves through the sides of the wardrobes. Cassie felt the fur from Juno's sable prickling her nose and she was in danger of sneezing. Her legs started to go to sleep, her tummy began to quiver, her own giggles surfacing in irresistible waves.

'Shush, Marianne, shush,' Cassie whispered to herself. She heard the door to the dressing room open, and froze. The light flicked on, slivers of yellow appeared through the hinges and around the wardrobe door, and a quiet footstep approached. The back of Cassie's neck prickled with an almost pleasurable fear. She held her breath, squeezed her eyes shut, thinking this might save her, and make her invisible. The key turned in the lock, the wardrobe door swung open, and she blinked in the light.

'Thought I'd find you here,' said Oliver. 'This is by far the best place to hide.'

'Oliver, get lost!' came Marianne's disembodied command from the next wardrobe. 'We were here first. You will give us away!'

'There's no chance he'll hear us. He is prowling the Long

Gallery, although I think Gerard might be the first victim – he went for the broom cupboard behind the stairs. Far too obvious.'

'Oliver, bugger off!' hissed Marianne. 'There's no room for you.'

Cassie pressed her hand over her mouth, trying her hardest not to laugh.

'She's right,' he said, gazing down at Cassie with his wide, playful smile. 'I better go. Stay put, Cass, and keep quiet.'

He began to push the door closed but Cassie, without thinking, reached up to touch his hand, plucked at it, wanting him to stay, wanting him to continue the game.

Oliver chuckled affectionately, leant down into the wardrobe, wrapped his arm around the back of her head, pulled her towards him, and kissed the top of her hair. He shut the door, locked her back in, switched off the light in the dressing room, and crept away.

Cassie squatted back down, clutching her knees to her chest, with happiness, almost like a pain, coursing through her body. Aunt Juno's musty old coats might be suffocating her, and her back ached from doubling up on the old, folded gaberdine, but Oliver had found her. Oliver had made her feel looked after, and held securely, in the newest, most intense and exciting way possible.

And while Marianne giggled in the wardrobe beside her, Cassie smiled serenely in the pitch-black darkness.

* * *

Luke found everyone eventually and, the game over and high spirits depleted, they all sauntered down to the drawing room. The grown-ups were playing rummy with the French windows open, the last glow of the sunset streaming over the sky. Cassie perched on the arm of her mother's chair and sleepily looked over her shoulder at her cards.

'Who was found first?' her mother asked.

'Gerard, wasn't it...?'

'Only because I made the fatal error of choosing Mrs Poulter's broom cupboard.'

'I knew where you all were in minutes,' Luke said. 'I just played it out for a bit.'

'I wish you had been quicker,' Marianne said, 'because I've got a crick in my neck.'

Uncle Charles set down his tumbler of whisky.

'Cocoa time for the youngsters, I think,' he said. 'I'll go and put a pan of milk on.'

'Very domesticated, Charles,' said Cassie's father.

He gave him a look. 'Well, I know what my troops want.'

'Pa, we're hardly children,' Oliver said. 'Can I have a brandy in mine?'

Juno bristled. 'Certainly not, Oliver. Some things have to wait until you are older,' she said.

'Gone are the days when you were all upstairs by seven,' said Cassie's father, 'tucked in and content with a bedtime story.'

Juno laid down her cards. 'There. That's the winning hand.'

'Thank goodness for that,' Cassie's mother sighed, putting her own cards on the table. 'I am ready for bed. As are you, young lady.' She patted Cassie's knee. 'You can take your cocoa upstairs. Are you coming, Rich?'

'No... I fancy another game.'

'Early start tomorrow, remember.'

'Don't I know it,' Cassie's father said, gathering the cards and shuffling them.

Charles quaffed the last of his drink. 'Come on, youngsters, if you want cocoa, follow me.'

With playful, unenthusiastic groans, the cousins and Luke followed Charles out to the kitchen, where he put them all to work, collecting mugs and spoons, and fetching the quart of milk from the cold shelf in the pantry. And, within half an hour or so, with bedtime drinks made, the house grew quiet, everyone settling down for the night.

In her room, Cassie got ready for bed, relishing the simple pleasure of a day done, a comfy bed to snuggle into and the prospect of another lovely day tomorrow. She opened the window to let in the night air, got under the covers and switched off her lamp. But as soon as she lay her head on her pillow, the cocoa made her want to use the lavatory. Thank goodness the bathroom was just along the landing.

A sort of listening silence seeped around corners and up the darkened stairs as Cassie made her way along the passageway. Across the courtyard, a light still shone in the upper-floor windows, the boys no doubt still awake and larking about. From a distant room somewhere on Cassie's floor came the sound of gentle snoring.

Back in her bedroom, Cassie felt thrilled by the lateness of the hour and how it made her feel a less like a girl and more like a young lady. No one else around to tell her she must go to sleep. She leant on her windowsill and gazed out into the darkness, at the night-time world of Greenaways. As her eyes adjusted, the shapes of flower beds and the silvery pathways emerged, lit serenely by the waxing half-moon. But she could only see so far; beyond the garden, everything else sank into deep country blackness.

'Goodnight, Greenaways,' Cassie whispered, listening for the owl or the nightjar, or indeed the elusive toad in the lily pond.

A crunch of gravel, one step and then another, crackled in the silence, with a gentle rustling and a low voice murmuring from the centre of Aunt Juno's roses. In the darkness, two shapes, one taller than the other. A faint movement.

'...and this one's a damask, Richard.'

'Smells delicious. As an old rose should... but I can hardly see it in the gloom...'

'It's deep burgundy. The colour of wine.'

'Ah yes, I can just about make it out... the scent is intense...'

'...often things are in darkness...'

At the window, Cassie chuckled gently at Aunt Juno proving to be the perfect hostess by showing her father around her garden when she probably wanted to turn in for the night.

'...this one's easy to look after... and very beautiful...'

'Beautiful, you say? Easy to look after?' Her father's voice changed. It deepened, became urgent, sending out a warning that crept, prickling over Cassie's scalp. 'Like you, my dear... but not so easy to look after... are you, June?'

Cassie's aunt uttered a reply, but her words escaped into the night as the two figures moved away, as one shape, disappearing into shadows.

Baffled, Cassie drew back behind her curtains and crawled into bed. She didn't know her father had such an interest in flowers and wanted to giggle at the absurdity of the grown-ups walking around the garden at night, admiring roses. But she felt too tired even for that, to think any more about it, except a small, fleeting wondering as she drifted to sleep, as to why she'd never heard her father call Aunt Juno 'June' before.

4

LONDON, SUMMER 1939

Cassie promised her mother that she would tidy her bedroom that morning. But, after half-making her bed, folding a handful of clothes and flicking the duster over her shelves, without moving any ornaments, she curled up on the window seat with her book. At last, she was allowed to read *Cheri*. But, despite the unnervingly risqué story, all beautifully sensuous and Parisian, Cassie felt too languid, too troubled to continue.

Raising the window sash which overlooked the gardens along the rear of Egerton Terrace and those of the mansions in the Crescent behind, she hoped some fresh air would help. Long ago, she had decided that the backs of people's houses, less-than symmetrical and sometimes rather unkempt, and with their motley layout of London-brick garden walls, proved far more interesting than the fronts. She had sketched the view she had grown up with many times, capturing bare, brown, wintry trees and sumptuous, summer green.

But today, the view did nothing to ease her troubles. For beyond this enclave of white mansions, with their fine frontages, their railings and polished-brass letter boxes, the outside world shifted and groaned in turmoil. Even now, soldiers dug trenches and erected an artillery battery a stone's throw away in Hyde Park.

Cassie gave up on her book and collected her diaries from her bedside table – something to distract her from her simmering anxiety. The Christmas after her last true summer at Greenaways – the one with the dead wren, the combative tennis match and hide-and-seek in the dark – Cassie had found a Lett's lady's diary at the bottom of her stocking. She had been delighted, had thanked her parents passionately, for it meant they thought her grown-up enough for a proper diary, along with the usual chocolates, new fountain pen, satsuma and bag of Brazil nuts. Three years on, she had a trio of the little books, with identical leather covers and pencils tucked into their spines.

With the sound of children on their school holidays playing outside, Cassie sat by her open window and turned to the first page of her first diary.

There hadn't been much for her to write about in January 1937, but she had scrawled right across the page for the first week of July:

To Greenaways!

It hadn't been until a few months later that she found out that Luke had invited Oliver to his family estate in Buckinghamshire for the summer. Gerard had declared himself too grown-up to go to Greenaways, anyway, and so Cassie and Marianne had spent that holiday mooching about reading, daydreaming, and declaring they were bored – frankly, wasting their days – the path along the riverbank forgotten about, and the tennis court sprouting weeds.

Cassie gave up on 1937 and picked up her diary for 1938. In June, the month she had left her girls' day school in the red-brick mansion behind the Royal Albert Hall, she'd written:

Last day ever at boring Kensington Gore!

She had filled the page with her School Certificate results, drawing a ring around her '*Very Good*' results, with a double ring around German. She had written:

Wunderbar!!!

Sitting there on her window seat, she gave a shudder. She had always thought the language evocative but realised now why such a beautiful-sounding word like *Kristallnacht* had, since last autumn, held such sinister meaning.

Cassie turned a few more pages into August 1938:

Dad drove Mum and me to Nice to celebrate exam results. Car sick three times. But Mum said it didn't beat Gerard's record.

Cassie gave a little laugh, warming to the memory despite the uncomfortable journey down to the South of France. Here, she had viewed art, tasted wine and eaten fine food. She had written out the names of each new dish she'd tried; when it contained garlic, and cream, and noted the particular names of the shellfish. She had felt very grown-up on the Cote d'Azur. She finally got the curse, had had her hair restyled, swum in the Med, worn lipstick for the first time, and had sent Oliver a post-card from Saint-Tropez. She did not receive one back.

Perhaps he does not know our address. Perhaps it was lost in the post, she thought, feeling suddenly as if she herself was lost. A sort of slipping away of the girl she had been. As if the glorious Greenaways summers had never happened. It had been three years since she'd seen Oliver, and she felt as if he, too, had vanished.

Cassie shut the diary, tossed it aside and the grainy old photograph flew out. So that's where it had been. All this time, she had meant to give it back. She'd taken it with her to Greenaways the summer after the game of hide-and-seek, but did not find the chance to slip it back into her aunt's wardrobe. For if her aunt or uncle had caught her, how could she explain that she had unwittingly filched it in the first place? She would sound absurd.

Cassie had not looked at the photograph in a long while; how young the women appeared now, whereas it still proved difficult to judge the gentleman's age. In any case, he seemed very distinguished. She guessed, from the women's wide-brimmed hats and high-neck blouses, that the picture had been taken before the Great War. And, for one strange moment, she decided that the girl looking away from the camera and straight at the man could easily be Marianne.

But, of course, Cassie thought, slotting the photograph into the back of the diary and putting it away, it must be Aunt Juno.

* * *

Marianne *always* wrote back by return of post. In her latest letter, serving as Cassie's bookmark in *Cheri*, she gushed on about her long-standing school friend Victoria – or Vee as she, apparently, now wanted to be known – and how if they finally got round to declaring war, it would be a relief. Vee couldn't wait, Marianne wrote, because she'd heard that they wanted girls for the WRAF and Marianne and Vee, seeing as they were both eighteen, were going to sign up together.

The uniforms are the nicest, too!

'Coo-eee!' Cassie's mother knocked on the door and came in, casting a humorously judging look around her bedroom. 'I see you've been busy, Cassie, dear. Second post's arrived. There's a letter for you.'

'Is it from the College?'

'Open it and see. You don't receive many official, brown envelopes with our address typed out on them, do you?'

Cassie began to open the envelope but fumbled and started to tear it.

Her mother, peering over her shoulder, sighed in frustration, whispering, 'Come on, come on'.

'I've been accepted,' Cassie said, handing her the letter. 'I can start in two weeks.'

'Well, well. This is wonderful news. More feathers in your cap. Dad will be pleased.'

He would, Cassie conceded, but going on a secretarial course sounded so trifling and unimportant when the whole world around them seemed about to crumble. She fitted the letter back into the envelope, unable to shake off the feeling of something bad approaching. The news bulletins on the radio did not help: relentless and urgent. Only yesterday evening, before she settled down to sleep, she had written in her diary:

At dinner, Dad said there was going to be a war.

No exclamation marks this time.

Cassie's mother wandered over to her bed and began to straighten her wonky eiderdown.

'Mum,' Cassie said, 'what's the WRAF?'

'The women's branch of the RAF. Why?'

'Marianne and her friend Vee are going to join up.'

'Are they now?' Cassie's mother glanced at her, suddenly looking sad and frightened all at once. 'You're not thinking...?'

'I don't know,' Cassie said. 'I feel that I want to do something *consequential*.'

'Oh, Cassie, remember you are a year behind Marianne, not yet eighteen.'

'I will be next month, Mum.'

'Yes, yes. Well, go on the secretarial course – then see how you get on. It will be useful; *you* will be useful. There are so many things you could do, although... Dad is suggesting that we – you and I – evacuate.'

'But *children* evacuate,' Cassie said, aghast.

'He's getting very worried and wants us to be safe. He will stay here, of course, so that he can keep going into the office.'

'But Mum, I want Dad to be safe.'

'I do, too, darling,' said her mother, her eyes brightening with worry. She seemed pensive for a moment but shook herself and laughed. 'I wonder when it was that you stopped calling me "Mummy".' She gazed in admiration at Cassie. 'You seem to have become a young lady without me noticing.'

This surprised Cassie and pleased her. For a good while now, she had been taking more care of her clothes and her hair, gone with her mother to the salon; they'd shopped together, picking out dresses and shoes that suited her, gave her confidence a boost. Instilled in her a little, she hoped, elegance to match Marianne's.

'Where would we evacuate?' she asked as her mother ran a finger over one of her shelves, checking for dust.

'Greenaways of course.'

Cassie cried out, 'Oh!', wondering immediately how nice it would be if Oliver was there.

Her mother gave her a puzzled look.

Cassie countered quickly, 'But what about my secretarial course?'

'After that, then,' her mother said. 'It's only four weeks long, isn't it? Intensive, they said. We can talk it over with Dad tonight. Now, come on, let's think of something nice to bake him this afternoon.'

Cassie followed her mother down their elegantly pristine stairs with the curving bannisters as she reeled off some of her father's favourite puddings.

'Do you think, Mum, that we should see what Mrs Blake has left us in the pantry?' Cassie ventured, remembering that her mother's attempts in the kitchen were not always a success. 'She made a whole batch of apple pies the other day. And there's a huge jug of custard on the cold shelf.'

'Ho, no, *I* want to make the pudding. He will be pleased. I want to surprise your father and it's about time I did.'

* * *

Later, as they ate supper, Cassie's father talked at length about the contingencies the company he worked for – a shipping firm on the Strand – had in mind in case of war and she watched her mother grow more pale as the dinner candles burnt lower. The rumours her mother had heard and relayed to Cassie now spun around her head: of the Germans using gas, of them parachuting into England in their thousands, that they'd had plenty of practice bombing people during the war in Spain. Her mother reeled them off now.

'All the more reason, Miranda dear,' her father said, 'for you and Cassie to go to Greenaways.'

'I wonder if we can persuade Gerard...'

'Unlikely. He's a grown man, Miranda.' Her father put his hand over her mother's on the tablecloth, and Cassie saw her mother's apprehension melt away, at least in that moment. 'There will probably be conscription. You've heard him talking about the navy. He might as well choose where he wants to go now. And anyway, you know we can't stop him.'

'At least we managed to convince him not to go off to Spain to fight against Franco,' Cassie's mother said. 'Although one of his university friends went, you know?'

Cassie, listening, didn't know. She batted away her shock, kept perfectly still, didn't dare ask if Gerard's friend ever came home again.

'Spain was just a trial run,' her father uttered, tipping wine into his glass. 'I think we are really in for it now.'

'Rich! Really.'

Normally, her father would have added a witticism, lightened the mood. But this evening, it seemed, he was out of jokes.

'We shouldn't be speaking like this,' said her mother. 'Let's get on to better things. Hey, Cassie, darling, where's your letter? Show Dad the letter.'

He read it through in silence, seemed rather unenthusiastic, but raised his glass of merlot to her.

'Well done, Cassie,' he said lightly. 'Get that under your belt and who knows where you will end up?'

But Cassie didn't have the confidence or the energy to think too far ahead, for her parents' conversation had stilted her appetite. She longed for a time when, instead of picking over her mother's dried-out pear pudding, they were tucking into one of Mrs Blake's delights, that Gerard was at home more often, and that she herself – even though she was loath to admit – was still at school. It hadn't been *completely* perfect when she'd been younger – she'd had little worries and contradictions to contend with – but nothing like this.

When had she, Cassie wondered, stopped calling her mother 'Mummy'? When had she stopped dreaming of Greenaways?

5

After lunch a week or so later, Cassie settled down in the pleasant little nook that her mother had created at the end of the first-floor landing. The tall window, with its shutters folded back, overlooked the street; there was space for a small desk, perfect for writing letters, and an armchair for a pleasant afternoon of reading. She drew out a sheet of Egerton Terrace headed paper to begin a letter to Marianne.

It's been a quiet summer so far here in South Ken, but guess what? I am halfway through Cheri!

Cassie paused. Aunt Juno's oils of little cobbled Paris quarters rose inexplicably through her mind.

'Oh good, there you are,' her mother said, hurrying out of her parents' bedroom, buttoning her jacket. 'I'm off to the King's Road – I must see if Peter Jones have that lipstick I like. They say there are shortages already and I want to stock up. But you will be in this afternoon, won't you?'

Cassie said she would, even though the sunshine was

already tempting her out for a walk around Hyde Park, and she would like to post her letter to Marianne later.

'Good, well you can do that before supper,' said her mother, rummaging in her handbag. 'Someone needs to be here in the meantime when Oliver arrives.'

'*Oliver?*'

'Yes, I clean forget about it.' She had not noticed the excitedly horrified tone in Cassie's voice. 'But Dad reminded me this morning, thank goodness. Where are my *keys*? Oliver is travelling en route to Sandhurst for his interview. The trains don't work for him otherwise, from wherever he is coming from. So, he is going to stay the night. It'll please Uncle Charles no end, no doubt, if he gets his commission. Not sure what Aunt Juno thinks of it, mind.'

'Oliver?' Cassie repeated, quietly to herself as her mother trilled, 'Found them. See you later on!', before going downstairs and out of the front door.

Cassie stared for some moments at the few lines she had written to Marianne, placed the lid on her pen and set it down. She honestly thought this feeling would have stopped, that she had consigned it to her girlhood, and had forgotten about it, along with so many of those hazy, long-ago, summer days. But at the mention of his name, this strange yearning, this instinctive drive to see her cousin, talk with him, rushed straight back to her, and settled inside her. How unnerving it felt, she thought, for her past to come right here into her present.

She abandoned her letter and went into the bathroom to run a bath, her ears straining above the noise of the cistern for the front doorbell as she quickly washed her hair. She hadn't thought to ask her mother when, exactly, Oliver would arrive. It could be in three minutes; it could be in three hours. Still, she felt an urgent need to prepare herself.

Back in her bedroom, Cassie picked out her new, olive-green dress with the cap sleeves and navy stitching, and carefully dried her hair, smoothing it and curling the ends like her mother had shown her. The straw colour of old, she noted, had evolved recently into a pleasing golden shade but gazing at herself in the mirror, she became irritated. She had never felt the need to make a good impression for Oliver before, so why all the fuss? But perhaps now, she reasoned, now she was a grown-up young lady, she would change her clothes when expecting any visitor. A friend from school. Her aunt or uncle. Anyone.

* * *

The doorbell rang all too soon, jolting Cassie, sending a shrill echo through her mind. Hovering on the landing, she heard Mrs Blake pad along downstairs to answer it, a pleasant exchange, the shutting of the front door.

'I'll just fetch her, sir.'

'No need, Mrs Blake,' Cassie called. 'Here I am.'

She walked down the stairs, just like Marianne might, as unhurriedly, as elegantly, as she could bear, but feeling as if she were rushing forward, unable to feel the treads under her feet. Oliver was taking off his hat, setting his suitcase down, shaking Mrs Blake's hand. The housekeeper seemed delighted with their overnight guest, saying that she was sure she remembered him as a little boy.

He glanced up at Cassie. His face cleared as if he did not know her, and then a slow and astonished look of wonder and recognition deepened across his features as she approached, and his mouth widened into a luxurious grin.

'Cass? I can't believe it!'

Wearing a suit and a raincoat, he appeared taller, broader,

his hair shorter, showing more of his face, and he had shaved himself closely that morning so that he looked fresh, young and vulnerable. Not in the least like a man, Cassie thought, ready to sign up for the army.

'You look like a gentleman!' she blurted out.

'I should hope so.' His laugh sounded richer, deeper.

She walked towards him, laughing, too, and she knew there was no need to be nervous or feel frightened, for her cousin simply gave her the feeling, as always, of tumultuous joy.

Mrs Blake offered to go and make them tea and to bring it out into the garden.

Cassie thanked her and took Oliver's trilby for him. She had never seen him wear such a hat before; the inside of it still felt warm as she hung it on the coat stand.

'I think your housekeeper may be mistaken,' Oliver said, below his voice. 'I am sure I have never been here before. But perhaps I visited when we were very small?'

'Perhaps,' Cassie said, enjoying his playful, querying tone.

She led the way along the hallway to the garden door, feeling proud suddenly of the graceful home her mother had created, and out onto the terrace.

'I think our garden would fit inside the tennis court at Greenaways,' she said, as they sat on the garden chairs among her mother's sunny geranium pots. 'Seems such a long while ago now,' she said tentatively, even though she didn't believe so, for all those Greenaways summers were now sitting here, right beside her.

Oliver chuckled. 'Sometimes it does, sometimes it doesn't,' he said. 'Do you remember the wren?'

'Of *course* I do! Poor little thing.' Despite the poignancy, the possible sadness, Cassie laughed, and her happiness seemed to come from nowhere with breathless speed, expanding around her like a new, second skin. She felt herself grow into it, moving into the next stage of her life, a new maturity, where she could handle such baffling, intense emotions.

Oliver looked around at her father's neat borders and clipped topiary. 'No, I think I would have remembered being here...' He shot a look at Cassie. 'If I may say so, Cass, you look very well.'

Mrs Blake set down the tray on the table between them and gave Cassie an inscrutable smile. Cassie felt so bright in that moment that she wanted to ask the housekeeper to sit with them and have tea. But it would not be appropriate and anyway, Mrs Blake had to make their fish pie for supper before she went home.

Cassie and Oliver sipped tea and nibbled Mrs Blake's short-bread biscuits. The children who lived in the house behind began a game and their voices rose and fell like cheerful sparrows.

'They will all be gone soon, I bet. Evacuated to the country,' Oliver said.

'Dad wants Mum and me to evacuate. The plan is to go to Greenaways, for a short while, at least.'

Oliver glanced at her in delight. 'Really? Well, that is a splendid idea.' His face fell. 'The news isn't looking good, is it?'

'Dad must stay here for his job, and I've got to do a secretarial course first. But I feel that I want to do so much more. I don't know how much use I will be at Greenaways.' With the outside world encroaching into their private one, Cassie sank with disappointment. However, rallying herself, she said, 'And so, you will be joining the army?'

'That's the plan. Pa is cock-a-hoop, seeing as he has always been an army man himself. It means leaving university a year early, but nobody seems to mind that.'

'Gerard is determined to join the navy,' said Cassie. 'Last time he was home, he mentioned being a wireless operator on a ship. Ha, I remember him building his own cat's whisker radio receiver in his bedroom, even though Mum and Dad had a perfectly good wireless in the sitting room. He would let me listen to broadcasts on the earphone. I couldn't walk past his bedroom door without him ambushing me to come and admire a new gadget to help him send a Morse code message to his friend who lived out in Surrey, or somewhere.'

Oliver chuckled. 'Good old Gerard. He loves his radio stuff.'

'Mum did get annoyed with him,' said Cassie. 'All that equipment in his bedroom, gathering dust... but I think she is not so much annoyed now, but frightened... thinking of Uncle Roland?'

Oliver agreed. His gaze deepened in thought, a frown drawn between his brows.

'My parents never really talk about that time,' Cassie said.

'Pa will if you press him,' Oliver said. 'But only about the triumphs. Not the outright disasters.'

'And now, we are...' Cassie stopped, conscious of them all, the young Marshes and Greenaways, all moving towards something unknown. To a place where they could no longer be children.

'We're all scattering, aren't we?' Oliver said, catching her eye.

'Even Marianne,' she said. 'She wants to be in the WRAF.'

'Ah, that's that friend of hers,' said Oliver. 'Victoria, isn't it?'

'Vee, now,' said Cassie.

'And Luke, Woodward, the utterly brilliant Lucien Dubois,' said Oliver. 'He's been head-hunted by the War Office, assisting a top bod there in one of those grand buildings along Whitehall. Snatched away from university. They couldn't wait, apparently.'

'How is he?'

'Oh, he is happy as Larry living in the family townhouse in Chelsea. Has the place to himself, lucky fellow. His father is at the house in Buckinghamshire. His mother, as you may remember, high-tailed it to Scotland a while ago. His job suits him. Last time we spoke, he seemed much more cheery. And, in a way, much more reasonable.'

It could only be a good thing, they both agreed, and settled back into one of their convivial quiet times, sipping and nibbling. Cassie peered up at the friendly, fair weather clouds against the blue sky, marred a tad with coal smoke puffing from a chimney along the way. The sounds of a normal South Kensington summer's day reached her in little currents of air: the polite honk of a car horn on Egerton Crescent, the rumble of a bus along the Brompton Road, and voices carrying from open windows and across the gardens like snatches of a tune.

'You wouldn't think, on a day like today, would you...?' Cassie said.

She did not have to go any further. Oliver knew.

The breeze caught at a lock of her hair, and it flickered in front of her eyes, gilded by sunlight. Oliver appeared captivated by it.

'It will be good for you and Auntie Miranda to go down to Greenaways and stay out of harm's way,' he said. 'Pa is talking about taking in evacuees, school children from Plymouth, although Ma is still determined to come up to London quite regularly for exhibitions and gallery openings, and says Hitler is not going to stop her viewing her beloved art. But now that the galleries and museums are clearing out of London, something tells me she will have to.'

'I had forgotten that your mother comes up to London for the galleries,' Cassie said. 'But, of course, she has lots of lovely paintings.'

'Quite a collection – Ma's a real art lover,' said Oliver. 'She spent more than a year in Paris when she was younger, and met the artist who painted the landscapes, those lovely views of the Seine and the Marne, and the little street scenes in the Marais.'

Cassie's mind filled with the image of the portrait hanging in Aunt Juno's dressing room.

'Oh,' she said, feeling her cheeks burn. 'When she does come to London, we never see her here.'

Oliver gave a little humorous shrug. 'That's Ma for you. She isn't particularly sociable.'

'We've all been a bit distant these last few years, haven't we?'

'Things, life, changes,' Oliver said lightly, stretching his legs out into the sun. 'We have moved on and grown up but not necessarily apart.'

Cassie, still struck by the man Oliver had become, took a moment to admire the shine of his good leather shoes, the fine tailoring of his shirt. Her mother once said that while girls often went through a brief 'rabbity', somewhat ugly, stage where their adult teeth were too large for their young mouths, boys took far longer to 'grow into their looks'. But Oliver had matured in the space of a few years; his features had widened and deepened, and yet he remained, unmistakably, Oliver.

'Thank you for my postcard, by the way.'

'Oh, that.' Cassie gave a wave of her hand. 'That was ages ago. I was probably just showing off. Look at me, I am in Saint-Tropez!'

'No, it was lovely and thoughtful.' Oliver smiled on a memory. 'I think I was at Luke's again that summer, or at home, can't remember... but not half as exciting as the South of France.' He held her gaze for a moment longer than necessary. 'Thank you, Cass.'

'Do you know, you are the only one who calls me Cass,' she said. 'I like it.'

Instinctively, a mirror of her younger self came to her mind, crouched in Aunt Juno's wardrobe, reaching for Oliver's hand. But she resisted this time, holding her palms firmly together on her lap and waiting for the moment to pass before looking his way again.

Cassie offered him more tea, pressed on him another short-bread biscuit, chattered about her secretarial course. They both wondered whether, if things worked out, they might all be together at Greenaways at Christmas. But Cassie knew she shouldn't count on it. He asked about her holiday on the Cote d'Azur, and she regaled him with stories, but mixed up Cannes with Caen, muddling her words and giggling at herself, making Oliver laugh. The sound of it felt so deliciously familiar, and yet an unsavoury detail jarred her memory: overhearing her mother and aunt at Greenaways, while frantically polishing the table, and what her father had said about Oliver.

Sitting beside him here, talking about summers past, Cassie felt the same outrage, the same need to defend him. And yet, stealing a sideways glance, a strange doubt surfaced. She saw a new element in his matured face: a morsel of the gentleman in the old sepia photograph.

But, despite a strange, unsettling confusion, the kiss Oliver had planted on the top of her head in the half-darkness of Aunt Juno's wardrobe remained in her mind like a rare radiant jewel.

* * *

Oliver had said goodnight, thank you and goodbye the night before to Cassie and her parents, and said that he hoped he wouldn't disturb them in the morning. But Cassie woke at dawn to the sounds of someone who didn't know the house moving around and trying not to make a noise. She heard the spare bedroom door across the landing open with its usual creak. The floorboard outside the bathroom groaned and she, eventually, heard Oliver stealing down the stairs and leaving the house to catch a bus to Waterloo for his early train.

As the front door shut, Cassie got out of bed, fumbled into her dressing gown and scooted barefoot along to the landing window. Peering around the shutters, she watched Oliver stride away through the glimmering early light, a fine-looking silhouette in his suit and trilby, swinging his suitcase with purpose.

Cassie smiled sleepily to herself, offering him luck, and herself hope that she would see him again soon.

At the bottom of Egerton Terrace, he was almost out of sight and Cassie craned her neck to capture a little more of him before he disappeared. But he stopped and hesitated, turning to look back the way he'd come. Cassie thought that perhaps he had left something behind. He stood for some moments, gazing back along the street towards the house, and Cassie, on impulse, waved.

Oliver did not see her – he *couldn't* have seen her – and he turned again, crossed the road and set off in the direction of the Underground, vanishing into the morning.

6

DEVON, DECEMBER 1939

'Ah, here he is, at last,' said Cassie's mother as they stood shivering in the rainy gloom outside Exeter Station. It was a cold late afternoon in the middle of December.

Charles pulled up in his car and leapt out, waving.

'If it's not my favourite sister,' he called.

'Your *only*, Charles,' she said, her 'Ugh, what a journey—' smothered by Charles's huge, woollen-coated embrace.

He turned to Cassie. 'And here's my clever niece.'

Cassie braved his over-long hug, sincerely pleased to see her uncle after such a torturously long time travelling.

'No cardboard labels on your coats like parcels, I see,' he said, as he quickly stowed their suitcases in the boot, 'but our newest evacuees. Come on, away to Greenaways.'

Charles drove along empty streets, the blackout hanging heavily over the town and the evening falling fast, and out into the bleak, darkening, winter countryside. Deep valleys and wooded hills retreated into nightfall, and hedgerows were barely illuminated by the car's shrouded headlights as the lanes wound endlessly up and down, and the windscreen wiper creaked and whooshed.

'As you know, we've had our little posse of evacuees since September,' Cassie's uncle said.

Her mother, in the front seat, made a disgruntled sound.

'Schoolboys from Plymouth,' he went on, cheerily. 'The Long Gallery is their dormitory. The back kitchen their refectory, the courtyard their playground. They have had history lessons there, of course, courtesy of good old Henry the Eighth. And off they troop to the village school each morning.'

'So, the days will be peaceful, then...' Cassie's mother uttered.

'Mrs Poulter is in her element, it has to be said. She used to be Matron at a boys' school so looks after them very well.'

'Thank goodness for Mrs P.'

'She's becoming quite creative with portion control and scrutinising their ration books. There are places that are out of bounds, of course. Juno has put No Entry notices up everywhere.'

'Gosh, I wonder how Juno can bear it.'

'Oh no, Miranda,' said Charles. 'The boys may be rowdy at times, but they are quite entertaining. There's only a dozen of them and they are thoroughly enjoying themselves. Although, Mr Brough, their teacher is suggesting they will go home for Christmas, and some of them might not even come back.'

'I'm not surprised,' said Cassie's mother. 'It seems like a pointless exercise, all of this. It's all gone very quiet out there. As if there is no war.' Her voice sounded small and hopeful in the darkness inside the car.

But Cassie, listening from the back seat, hadn't been given the impression of 'no war' during her recent interviews in one of the white-stucco government buildings along Whitehall, a building which she would have walked straight past without a backward glance a few months before. Her uncle 'knew people' at the War Office, and once she had graduated from her secretarial course with a Distinction, he had put her name forward for the job. Now, she understood all too well the immense bureaucratic machinery churning behind the façade's blank windows.

'Mum, you know it's safer to be out of London,' she said. 'And Dad will be down here for Christmas.'

'Cassie is right,' her uncle said, rallying her mother cheerily. 'Back home in the county of Sea Kings, Miranda. You will be in your element.'

'I know, I know I should be grateful.' Her sigh lingered, filling the car as the rain continued to fall.

The journey stretched on through pitch-black countryside. Cassie thought she knew it well, but felt completely lost, wondering at each slowing down of the car and at each turning at a junction that *surely*, they'd be nearly there. At last, her uncle eased the car through the gates and Greenaways appeared before her, a blacked-out, huge, oblong block, looking empty and forlorn in the darkness, and with not a chink of light showing.

* * *

Cassie woke the next morning to the sound of clumpy footsteps and a suppressed clamour of youthful voices seeping along the landing outside her bedroom door. She pulled on her dressing gown and opened the blackout to let in the thin, morning light, gasping in surprise at the transformation.

Winter had shifted Greenaways out of Cassie's sleepy summer daydream. Naked branches drew sketchy lines across the colourless sky; flower beds lay broken-down, soggy and brown. Her aunt's rose garden appeared as a spiky, pruned forest, dripping with raindrops. A robin, invisible somewhere in the trees, piped away. Cassie wondered about the wren, laid to rest in the undergrowth, and felt sure her fragile bones must be part of the earth by now.

She dressed quickly – and warmly – and waited for the chattering along the landing to fade, before slipping out and down the stairs to the hallway. The boys in school caps and with satchels over their shoulders had formed into an orderly single file on the gravel outside. They looked to be all under eleven, their breath puffing in small clouds, and some of them only half the height of the lanky teacher, Mr Brough, who stood at the head of the line, hatless but in a smart overcoat, surveying his charges. He gave them a proud, encouraging smile before leading them off across the gravel and out through the gates.

'Good morning, Cassandra,' said Juno, emerging from the dining room and drifting towards her in a woollen poncho reaching almost to her ankles. 'I hardly recognised you standing there. Charles said how much you'd changed. Sorry I wasn't around when you arrived yesterday; I was in bed with a sniffle.'

She rested her hands on Cassie's shoulders and leant in briefly to give her one of her usual restrained hugs.

'It's lovely to be back,' Cassie said, not quite sure how much she meant it.

'Come through to the parlour. Your mother is there toasting bread like a Girl Guide. You will find Greenaways a totally different prospect, you know, in winter, and at war.'

'I can tell,' Cassie said. 'Yesterday, Mrs Poulter didn't as much say hello to me as say: *can I have your ration book?*.'

'She has, dare I say, become rather formidable. Quite

admirable, really. She will commandeer you for kitchen duties, I don't doubt.'

Cassie followed her aunt through the door into the dining room, with a sign tacked to it saying:

Do Not Enter

The notice on the door to Juno's parlour read:

Entrée interdite

'Ha, that's my little joke,' said her aunt. 'Harry Brough told me the boys are starting French next term.'

Juno's parlour felt like a comforting, warm cave compared to the icy stairs and hallway. She shut the door behind them and kicked the draught excluder back into place.

'Here you are, Cassie, dear,' said her mother, wearing her fur stole and brandishing the toasting fork. 'The last piece before we must damp the fire down to preserve the fuel. I had forgotten how cold this place gets. It must have been like this when I was a child, but when you're younger, you don't seem to feel it like you do as a grown-up.'

'You must be spoilt at Egerton Terrace, Miranda,' said Juno. 'Never feels cold—' She stopped herself, before adding, '— must be because it's a terraced house.'

Cassie saw her mother give her aunt a brief, puzzled look before turning back to poke the fire.

Biting into her buttered toast, Cassie could not recall her aunt ever visiting them in London. But memory, she decided, often proved fickle, for Mrs Blake seemed to have remembered Oliver from some time or other.

Juno busied herself with the stack of post, sorting out

government information pamphlets, and sifting through bills and Christmas cards. 'These leaflets will make good kindling, Miranda, for this evening's fire,' she said. 'Ah, Cassie, here's a card for you.' Her aunt glanced again at the writing on the envelope. 'My, how thoughtful of him.'

She handed it to Cassie, who peered at the postmark stamped somewhere in Berkshire.

'Who has caught up with you here, Cassie?' her mother asked.

'I really don't... know.' She hesitated, slitting the envelope open, feeling her mother's and aunt's eyes piercing her as she pulled out a dear little Christmas card with a picture of a robin sitting on a postbox on the front. A rush of joy tingled over her scalp, and she gave in to a full and delighted smile.

'It's Oliver.'

'How lovely, dear,' said her mother.

'How thoughtful,' Juno said again.

Cassie quickly read the card and, in sudden embarrassment, slipped it safely back inside the envelope.

'You can put it with the rest of them on the mantelpiece, Cassandra,' her aunt said.

'Yes, yes, I will...' Cassie gave a quick glance at the cards arranged on the shelf over the fireplace but instead, put it into her cardigan pocket, instinctively wanting to keep it private.

'Well!' said her mother, breaking the unexpected silence. 'As well as peeling a mountain of potatoes today, Cassie, your task is to help me get this place looking Christmassy.'

'And Marianne is back, later, on two days' leave,' said Juno. 'She will certainly want to get involved. She always loves Christmas.'

'Oh, I didn't realise. That's wonderful,' said Cassie. It had been over two years since she'd last seen her cousin.

'Her friend Vee is coming too,' her aunt added. 'So, we are beginning to have a house full. I must say, Miranda, I have never taken to her.'

'Like you didn't take to Luke, Juno?' said Cassie's mother.

'I suppose I didn't, although Oliver has said that he's a lot less hard work now. I suppose that's what's called maturing. Works as an assistant to some head honcho at the War Office. But, of course, can't tell him any more than that. As for Vee,' said Juno, 'you've not met her, have you, Cassandra?'

Cassie shook her head. But as Vee trickled through every line of Marianne's letters, she felt as if she knew her intimately.

'I think that I am going to slip up and call her Victoria by mistake,' said Juno. 'Or worse, Vicky.'

* * *

Later that morning, the mountain of potatoes peeled, Cassie and her mother wrapped up warm and headed out the back door into the garden, with her aunt's garden trugs, gloves, and her trusty secateurs.

'I wonder if I can remember where the best holly is,' said Cassie's mother. 'And let's see if we can find some fir boughs. Let's try along the edge of the park.'

They walked down the wide stretch of grass at the side of the house under the huge, bare, wintry trees, their boots squelching on the sodden ground. Cassie glanced back at the house, and seeing it now in daylight, it appeared as if it had aged in the two and a half years since she'd last visited. It looked fragile, the stonework brittle and half-naked without the creeping roses and wisteria that clothed it all summer. She realised in that moment that she would never have known during their final true summer here, when they had all been together, that it had, in fact, been the last one.

'You seem distracted, Cassie,' her mother said. 'You look worried.'

'I suppose I am,' Cassie said, with sudden lucidity, admiring her mother's perception.

They had reached the boundary hedgerow thick with holly and her mother set to work on cutting her prize specimens.

'Go on...' she said.

'I'm thinking about the job at the War Office, and the interviews,' said Cassie. 'I go over and over them again in my mind. What I said. What I didn't say. And I have absolutely no idea if I did well, or awfully badly. And I'm not even sure I want the job if I am offered it...'

'Cassie, whatever happens will be right for you. Ouch, these gloves of Juno's must be ancient. That went right through.' She stripped off a glove and put her finger in her mouth. 'It vexes me to say it, as I really don't want you in London, I want you here with me, but I think you will thrive there. And you will be back at home with Dad in South Ken. Although of course, I wish he was here, too, but you can't have everything. That's me doing my bit, I suppose. Letting my children go. Gerard training on his ship in Southampton, off to sea soon. And you, dear Cassie, at the War Office.'

Cassie began to clip at some holly. 'Not yet,' she said. 'And I feel so nervous.'

'Of course you do. You wouldn't be *you* if you didn't. And Uncle Charles would not have recommended you if he didn't think you were right for it.'

'But I wonder why he didn't put Marianne forward?'

'Oh, I asked him that and he said she is not clever enough. She is happily training for the WRAF, apparently learning to drive. She will be ferrying pilots to and from their planes, loading munitions. I can't see her doing that, to be honest. She has never struck me as someone who wanted to get her hands dirty, but she may surprise me.'

Cassie knew Marianne to be tougher than people thought but simply didn't necessarily like to show it. Her cousin certainly had a gritty interior.

She chuckled. 'If the uniform looks good,' she said, 'Marianne will love it.'

They turned their attention to the little copse of fir trees over in the corner of the field.

'These are all our old Christmas trees, planted out all that time ago, in the years before the war.' Cassie's mother looked at her. 'The *other* war.'

Cassie began to fill her basket with cuttings from the lower branches, catching tantalising wafts of their clean, evergreen scent, as a robin accompanied them, perched on top of the hedge. Seeing it, Cassie immediately thought of the one on Oliver's card.

'It was nice of Oliver to send you a card...' her mother said, as if she had, again, read her mind. 'I'm guessing it's because he won't be here for Christmas.'

'Yes, it was nice,' Cassie said, trying not to show how happy, how surprised, it made her. 'But it's only because I sent him a postcard from Saint-Tropez that time, and he must feel he owes me some correspondence.'

Her mother gave her a quizzical glance. 'Well, whatever the reason, it seems to have taken the worried look off your face, darling.'

* * *

After lunch, a small car trundled in and parked on the gravel outside the parlour window. Marianne hopped out in her Air Force blue and from the driver's seat sprang a small, neat girl with glossy, conker-brown hair, also in uniform, her bright laughter cutting through the still, cold air.

Juno went out to greet them. Marianne held onto her mother in a huge, squeezing embrace, and Juno broke free eventually to give Vee one of her swift, lukewarm hugs.

'My, they do look good, don't they?' said Cassie's mother, peering through the parlour window. 'I feel we ought to go out, too, and be part of the VIP welcoming committee.'

'Come on then,' Cassie said brightly, although feeling suddenly, inexplicably shy.

The young woman laughing in the hallway with her best friend seemed an entirely different person to the cousin Cassie had known all her life and had been writing to almost every week for the past few years. Marianne looked even more poised and polished than before, with her dark hair neatly coiled at the nape of her neck and her pale-green eyes flashing with good humour. She wore a supremely confident shade of red lipstick.

'Ah, here is lovely Cassie,' Marianne said, hugging her, and pulling back as if to measure her up. 'Cassie, this is Vee.'

Marianne's friend leapt forward. 'It's lovely to meet you at last,' she said. 'I've heard so much about you.'

Close up, Vee's eyes were a sparkling brown, her skin luminous.

'I do like your uniforms,' Cassie said.

'Oh, we can't wait to get out of them,' said Marianne, hauling off her cap. 'I said, didn't I, Vee, as soon as I get home, I want to put on a pretty dress.'

'Trouble is,' said Vee, 'they only issue one size. I had to cut my trousers off at the knee.'

Her laughter filled the hallway to its rafters.

'Ma,' said Marianne, 'we are starving. I hope Mrs Poulter has something for us in the larder.'

Juno began, 'I expect she has. You must go and say hello—'

'Come on, Vee,' Marianne broke in, 'let's go up and change. You're in with me.'

'Would you like Pa to take your suitcases?' Juno asked.

'Oh no, Ma, we are WRAF girls now; we can manage our own suitcases.'

They made their way up the stairs, bumping their luggage over each step, their laughter and conversation waning as they turned the corner.

'Where are all these schoolboys then?'

'...at *school*, silly...'

'Marianne, your home is *posh*... My, look at your bedroom... all this frilly lace...!'

Cassie thought of how she used to giggle with Marianne like that; how it proved to be their perfect form of communication. But as she retreated to the parlour, she felt mild irritation with both Marianne and Vee, for she didn't feel there was a great deal these days to laugh about.

Marianne came down soon enough dressed in a warm, elegant dress carrying a box of Christmas baubles. Vee, in ruby-coloured wool and with her delicately radiant, elfin face, reminded Cassie of the Hawthorn Flower Fairy from one of her childhood books. She made a beeline for the footstool to perch on, but Cassie stood up, gave her a generous smile, and offered her the armchair. After all, she told herself, she was a guest of Greenaways.

Her uncle blustered in, ruddy-cheeked from his constitutional walk, and distributed his usual huge greetings, and leaving the last special one for Marianne.

'It's nice and cosy in here, Ma,' said Marianne, as the parlour filled up and more chairs had to be brought in. 'But aren't we going to be a bit cramped?'

'The drawing room is too large and draughty to use in winter,' said Juno. 'We are trying to save on firewood and coal. But now you are here, let's get the fire going.'

'But where are we going to put the Christmas tree?'

'Out in the hall, Marianne, if I can be bothered to dig one up this year,' said Charles. 'Although Harry Brough – the teacher, Marianne – has said he will give me a hand, get the boys involved. They'd enjoy that.'

'Oh yes, you must, Charles,' said Cassie's mother. 'You must do a tree. I want it like old times.'

'But Miranda,' he said, stoking his pipe and sucking on it. The air grew rich with dark, tobacco scent. 'It can never be like old times.'

'Be that as it may,' Juno said, giving her husband a hard look. 'We will have a tree. For Miranda.'

Cassie's mother placed her hand on her aunt's arm and mouthed, 'Thank you, Juno.'

As Cassie began to decorate the mantelpiece with fir boughs and holly sprigs above the picture frames, she realised that she hadn't noticed any usual coolness between her mother and aunt. Perhaps, she thought, now that they were always to be in each other's company, they had become closer.

And now, with the fire popping in the grate, and Marianne and Vee making paper chains, draping them around their necks like feather boas as they grew longer, Cassie felt the Christmas spirit enter the house, and herself.

'We better get that blackout down. It's getting dark,' said her uncle, going to the window. 'Ah, the urchins are returned.'

Cassie spotted the boys trooping back in through the gates,

headed up by Mr Brough, on their way around to the garden door. And presently, as they tucked into Mrs Poulter's high tea, the chattering hubbub emanating from the kitchen quarters amplified the festive mood.

'I see that the boys are not allowed in here,' said Vee playfully, 'But will their teacher be gracing us with his presence this evening, I wonder? What do *you* think, Marianne?'

* * *

Harry Brough, indeed, joined them later after supper, and offered to play the piano next door in the drawing room, the door slightly ajar, while they sat and had a game of cards. Cassie's mother came in from telephoning her father in Charles's study, her eyes glowing with tearful joy as she accepted a glass of sherry from her brother.

'How *is* Rich?' Juno asked.

'Working himself to the bone, it seems,' Cassie's mother answered.

'That's Rich for you...' Juno trailed off.

'Try not to fret, Miranda,' Charles said. 'He's a sensible one. He won't take risks. And here's to Poland.' He raised his glass as the fire crackled and the mesmerising notes of one of Chopin's 'Nocturnes' drifted through.

Cassie, realising her uncle's measures of sherry were rather on the large side, felt as if she might drift off to sleep, but Vee's sporadic bursts of laughter wouldn't allow it. She even began to not mind them so much.

And then, came a sharp knock on the front door.

'Goodness me, who is it at this hour?' Cassie's uncle said, launching himself out of his armchair and marching out of the parlour.

They waited, exchanging looks and straining to listen, while Cassie imagined her uncle in the hallway grappling with the blackout curtain over the front door, while listening for the bolts to be released.

'Good God, boy!' came her uncle's booming voice, through the dining room and into the parlour. 'We weren't expecting— What in the name of—!'

Marianne squealed and leapt to her feet.

The piano music from the drawing room stopped dead.

'Oh my!' Juno cried, her eyes widening in startled joy. 'Is Oliver here?'

Vee flicked her gaze in confusion from one person to the next. And Cassie, her mind whirring madly and her stomach flipping, wished, suddenly, that she had put Oliver's card on the mantelpiece, for then he would see it when he walked in the room.

'My *dear* boy!' cried Cassie's mother, getting to her feet and hurrying to the parlour door.

Cassie's brief, but sharp, sense of disappointment evaporated in a joyful rush as Gerard came into the room, his dark, naval coat, a smart contrast with his fair hair, tall and impressive, his cap under his arm, grinning, his eyes sparking with mischief.

'I got a lift from my CO,' he said. 'He was coming this way. Had to walk the last mile and a half, mind. No joke when your torch is on the blink.'

'But why? How?' uttered Cassie's mother, extracting herself from her son's arms. 'Oh, you're cold and damp; come in, come closer to the fire.' She tugged him to her armchair.

Everyone exclaimed in joy, and Cassie struggled to hear her brother's explanation – 'unexpected leave... one day only' – as to why he was here. Harry Brough came through, wondering at the uproar. Gerard shook hands with him, and with Vee, hugged

Cassie and her mother again, who wiped at her eyes when she thought he hadn't noticed.

'Oh, Gerard,' said Cassie, beaming at him as she passed him a brimming glass of sherry, 'you have made Mum's Christmas. A bit early, but what a wonderful surprise.'

'Such a surprise. And only two people missing now,' said Juno, curling herself up in her armchair and Cassie caught a strange, wretched edge to her voice. 'Oliver. And Richard.'

* * *

Later, Cassie went up to her bedroom clutching a hot-water bottle, a little light-headed from the shock of Gerard's arrival, the sherry and the laughter. She lit a night light and placed Oliver's Christmas card alongside snippets of holly and fir on the bedside table. There was not a peep from the boys in the Long Gallery, but along the landing came Marianne and Vee's suppressed mirth from her bedroom. Cassie decided to read Oliver's card one more time before she blew out the light. He had written:

Sorry I will miss you at Christmas. Have a warm and happy time.

Oliver may not be at Greenaways, Cassie thought, but Gerard was here, although briefly. And soon enough, Dad would join them for Christmas. They would make the best of it, and they would be warm and happy.

Everything felt good and right in that moment as Cassie drifted to sleep. Everything as it used to be.

7

LONDON, FEBRUARY 1940

Cassie sat on the edge of the chair in front of a huge desk in the wood-panelled office, listening while the man opposite issued her instructions. She had to memorise them, for she was not allowed to write anything down.

'You are to report to the unmarked entrance of New Public Offices, on Horse Guards Road, at oh-eight-hundred hours on the date specified. Show all your necessary identification, naturally, and sign in. You will be issued a pass presently. Find your way to Staircase Fifteen. Go down the stairs, and you will be met at the bottom.'

'Yes, sir.'

'Never tell anyone where you work, or what you are doing.'

'Of course, sir.'

'That includes your family, your friends. Your boyfriend...?'

Cassie shook her head.

'You tell no one.'

'Yes, sir.'

He kept very still, looking at her for some moments, appraising her, then reached in his desk drawer for a buff file.

Through the window, Cassie saw the leafless branches of a London plane tree; she heard the muffled sound of a bus chugging past along Whitehall. The clock on the desk had a slow, ominous tick.

The man passed some paperwork across the desk towards her.

'Read and sign this,' he said. 'And this. And this. Take your time.'

Cassie did as he asked, reading, absorbing the rules and regulations, and handed the signed documents back to him.

He collated the forms, checked them, cross-referenced the information with a ledger at his right hand, and then stuffed them into the file, shutting it back in his drawer.

'What you are about to do, Miss Marsh, is of the gravest importance to the security of our country.' He gave her another grim, searching look. 'You understand.'

It had not been a question, Cassie realised, but a command.

He stood up and extended his hand across the table to shake hers. In that instance, his steely mask dropped, and Cassie noticed a trace of a smile.

'Welcome to the War Room, Miss Marsh. I wish you the best of luck.'

* * *

Stepping outside at the end of that afternoon, Cassie felt buoyed by a little wave of euphoria. The setting sun, although not at all warm, brightened the air, and the mighty Cenotaph cast a long shadow down the wide avenue. Light-headed with excitement, and a touch of disbelief at how quickly her life could change, and the enormity of what she had been entrusted with, she hurried along to Parliament Square to catch a bus to South Kensington.

That morning, her uncle had driven her through darkness to Exeter, where she caught a fiendishly early train. She had arrived at Paddington an hour and a half ago and headed straight to Whitehall for her final interview. She didn't have time to realise how tired or anxious she'd been but felt better now that she sat in her favourite spot, the front seat at the top of the bus, with the prospect of soon being home. As the vehicle swayed and lurched around corners, as she gazed down on familiar streets in the darkening early evening, she wanted to laugh with joy at her achievement.

Cassie alighted on the King's Road and headed north through the graceful Brompton streets, dinking this way and that to tackle the maze of mews and shortcuts that she knew so well. She'd be home before her father got in from the office: a wonderful surprise for him as she hadn't seen him since Christmas. He did not know she'd been invited for the final interview; the telegram had only arrived at Greenaways yesterday.

Dusk had fallen by the time she reached Egerton Terrace. The streetlamps were not on, of course, and the elegant, white, Georgian houses glowed like beacons. Cassie, her heels clipping along the deserted pavement, shivered at the thought of air raids. Before Christmas, their housekeeper, Mrs Blake, had left London for her sister's in the country – *time for a fresh start* she had written to Cassie's mother. But Cassie had guessed the real reason. She could hardly blame her.

Climbing the steps to the front door, Cassie felt sure her father would be thrilled with her news. She could, of course, never tell him any precise detail but perhaps, she thought, glimmering with expectation, he'd take her out to dinner to celebrate. Beauville's in Knightsbridge had always been her favourite and was still open, apparently.

As she let herself in the front door and stepped into the darkened house, the quietness of the street switched to extraordinarily loud music, a robust concerto playing on the wireless upstairs.

'Dad?' she called, her ears filled with soaring violins, but remembered he'd still be at work. And, in any case, if he was upstairs, he'd never hear her above the music.

Mindful of switching on any lights in case he hadn't put the blackout down, she took her jacket off in the dark hallway and felt her way to the coat stand. Her fingertips brushed against fur, reminding her of hide-and-seek, and crouching inside her aunt's wardrobe. Cassie wondered if her mother realised that she'd left her coat behind. Surely, the one thing she should have taken with her to spend winter at Greenaways would have been her fox fur.

Cassie hung up her own jacket and turned to the stairs.

The music grew louder as she walked up. Her father must have tuned into the Third Programme that morning in the bedroom, forgetting to switch it off before he left. He didn't need to have it so monstrously loud, Cassie thought. What would the neighbours say?

Her father had also forgotten to switch off his lamp. Its glow filtered through her parents' open bedroom door and across the upstairs landing, casting shadows of the bannisters over the dark stairwell. But at least one thing seemed right: he had left the blackout down at the landing window.

Cassie needed to go to her bedroom to change her clothes, but didn't want to do anything – she could not think straight – until she had switched off the wireless. It was far too loud to be enjoyable, although she felt sure she recognised the piece.

Perhaps she had heard it on the gramophone at Greenaways, she thought as she walked along to her parents' bedroom. Or perhaps Harry Brough had played part of it on the piano over Christmas?

Cassie stopped in her parents' bedroom doorway. Shock, like a hard, violent screeching inside her head, drowned out the concerto blasting from the radio. She recoiled, pressing her hand over her mouth to stop herself screaming.

On the bed lay two figures, naked and curled together, clutching at each other's bodies, deep in sleep among crumpled sheets, illuminated by lamplight, seemingly deaf to the music, oblivious to Cassie. The tableau of bare skin, pale arms around a long, tanned, swan-like back thumped her in the chest. An aggressive and vulnerable image bound in one queasy vision, like a forbidden, erotic painting.

Cassie turned and ran along the landing, stumbling a little on the dim stairway, missing her footing, taking two stairs at a time. She sprang down onto the hallway tiles, imagining her footsteps crashing up through the house and yet the concerto played on and on, seemingly endless. Breathing hard against the cold soup of repulsion churning in her guts, she fumbled for her jacket by the front door and knocked the fur coat to the floor. A musky fragrance came to her, a memory, a tickling of her nose. Juno's coat, hanging in the pitch-black inside her wardrobe.

Cassie left the house, pulling on her jacket as she ran along the dark street. She stopped at the corner, threw down her handbag, bent double and vomited into a drain. She found a tissue, and a mint at the bottom of her handbag and, panting, she hurried on.

At the next corner, she thought it would happen again, and she clutched at the railings, gulping on the cold night air, wondering, for a fleeting, illogical moment, why she should be so shocked. Hadn't she seen already Aunt Juno naked in the painting hanging in her dressing room? But, she corrected herself, she had never seen her father in bed like that, with no clothes on and his fingers entangled in Juno's dishevelled, long hair.

* * *

On the King's Road, shops were closing, shutters coming down, but Peter Jones looked to be still open for business, and the doorman didn't say otherwise as Cassie walked straight past him and headed for the ladies' cloakroom.

Inside the cloistered, scented sanctuary, she ran the tap at the basin, filling her palm and rinsing out her mouth, wanting the tepid water to warm her fingers. But her hands continued to tremble, cold, as if they belonged to someone else. And her body shuddered, turning in on itself, queasiness returning in threatening waves.

She took long, ragged breaths, trying to grasp hold of a sense of reality, to keep her head up above the suffocating shock. Sitting down at one of the mirrors, Cassie dabbed a little complimentary cologne behind her ears and stared at the blanched face looking back at her. She had to do something about that. Finding the lipstick that Marianne had given her for Christmas in her bag, she shakily put it on. No better.

Cassie grimaced at her reflection. It didn't matter what she looked like; she simply did not know what to do.

She could go to Paddington, she thought, after some moments. That could be a possibility. Catch a night train to Exeter, go back to Greenaways. But what would happen then? Her mother would be excited to hear about her new job but wondering why she had travelled to Devon through the night.

And she would ask her questions. So many questions. But at least, Cassie thought, Juno wouldn't be there.

And Egerton Terrace was impossible. Cassie could never go home again. Even though a small instinct told her that her father and aunt had not been aware of her, how could she look her father in the eye, speak to him, be in the same room as him, and be normal with him, when she had seen... that?

Cassie felt her middle give way in despair. She hung her head, wondering where her tears were. She had forgotten how to cry. The shock, the betrayal, the misery, had wiped out the softest, most vulnerable part of her. The part that would have wept at witnessing her father and aunt... Such an unspeakable shattering of her family.

And what would Gerard have to say about it? And Oliver and Marianne? Oh, her poor mother! She could never tell anyone what she had seen. She wondered what it would do to them; would they, indeed, believe her?

Cassie stared at herself in the mirror, seeking comfort from her own reflection. The image of her father with Aunt Juno lay like a sheet of lead over her mind: another terrible secret to bear, on top of overhearing her mother and what her father had said about Oliver.

... certainly no Greenaway...

Confusion seeped through Cassie, like a virus might, chilling her bones and prickling her skin. Aunt Juno going to bed with her father may well mean her also being with other men. A strange truth crept up on Cassie. Her scalp tightened, the sweat on the back of her neck soaking her collar, an idea scratching at her mind; the bond between her and Oliver had always felt special, different to the one she had with Marianne. And, in many ways, *Oliver* was different.

A tinny voice came through the Tannoy to announce the

store would be closing in fifteen minutes, making Cassie jump. She gathered her things and, her knees about to give way, wandered out into the corridor, unsure which way to turn.

At counters, tills gave a final ring, customers collected packages, and store assistants said their cheery farewells, signalling the end of another working day. But as Cassie made her way slowly towards the exit, the air, such ordinary, everyday air, around her seemed to expand and then swallow her. Her distress resurfaced, hitting her again, keen, like a wound.

Spotting the public telephone booth by the escalator, Cassie slipped inside, pulling the folding glass door shut behind her. The small space smelt of tobacco, expensive perfume and something sweet and unidentifiable. It felt like a refuge. Perhaps, she thought, if she curled up on the floor, and they switched off all the lights, no one would notice her, and she could close her eyes and forget what had happened. But the doorman walked past and gave her a look that told her she must leave.

Cassie lifted her finger, to signal 'one moment', pulled out the A-E telephone book and began to leaf through it. She couldn't, she realised with clear, iced precision, turn to Gerard, or Oliver, or anyone in her family. And her school friends had scattered long ago. But there was one person in London she could call, perhaps could rely on, who might take pity, even though she had not seen him in years. She ran her finger down the long columns of Ds.

'Come on, come on,' she uttered. 'There can't be *that* many Duboises in London.'

Cassie found a likely address in Chelsea, dialled the number, let it ring, wondering if she got it right. He might not be in; he might not remember her. He might not care. The doorman tapped on the window.

She gave him an appealing look, shook her head, fed the

tuppence into the slot when someone, finally, answered the telephone.

'Hello? Hello?' The voice sounded as if he was standing beside her in the booth.

'Is that Luke, Lucien Dubois? Hello, it's Cassie, Cassandra Marsh, I... sorry to disturb you, I...'

What could she say? What words could she use to describe, to explain, the utter bleak misery, the panic pounding through her blood?

'Are you free this evening?' she managed, trying to make herself, her situation sound normal. She tried to picture him, could only think of the troubled boy, the sore loser with the broken spectacles, who had teased her with a dead bird.

'I am, yes. Why?'

'Can I...?' she stumbled. 'Would it be all right if I... visited you?'

'Cassie, of course you can.'

Her 'thank you' came out as a sodden whisper. Tears, at last, coursed down her face. She replaced the receiver, sat down on the stool, put her face in her hands and wept.

8

LONDON, MAY 1940

'Thank goodness,' Luke said. 'We now have the right man for the job. I never rated Chamberlain, personally. In fact, I feel sorry for him. Would you like more toast, Cassie?'

'He did his best, we can see that now,' Cassie said, pouring tea at the kitchen table. 'He was duped by the Germans. We all were. And yes, please.'

Luke handed her a fresh piece of toast and she began to scrape it with a smidgen of butter and jam. Kipling, Luke's tabby cat, sat on the table at her elbow, watching proceedings in his usual poised and rather judging manner.

They often started their days here in the basement at Cheyne Row, with its large kitchen and separate scullery, and passageways painted sensible brown: appropriate décor, it seemed, for servants long passed. 'Our own air raid shelter if it comes to it,' Luke had said, even though South Ken Station – with its deep Piccadilly Line platforms – was their nearest Underground, but Cassie had baulked at the idea of going there. It was rather too close to Egerton Terrace for her liking and, so far, she had avoided explaining why.

All outdoor Anderson shelters, according to the latest government directive, must be built by the 11 June. But, as Cheyne Row did not have a large enough garden for one, Luke had conceded that the kitchen table seemed sturdy enough.

'Do you ever see Mr Churchill down there in the bunker?' he asked, bringing slices of toast over to the table. 'Ah, this looks like the last of Mrs P's marmalade from Greenaways.' He picked up the jar and peered into it. 'Goodness knows when we shall ever taste that delight again. So, do you and the PM ever cross paths?'

'From time to time, I see him, walking around, hands behind his back, deep in thought. He has this certain, unmistakable bearing,' Cassie said. 'How can I say it...? He's *larger* than any other minister, any other person, in every way. He has quite the presence, even more so now as PM.' She smiled. 'But he will always acknowledge you if you walk past him. A nod, and a sort of grumbling murmur as he goes on his way.'

'This is dire,' Luke said, indicating the wireless.

The bulletin came to end, and swing music began to trill through the airwaves. The Low Countries had fallen, the British forces were retreating to Dunkirk, and the German army had left no one in doubt of its ambitions. Gazing out of the kitchen windows – criss-crossed now with protective tape – up at the little slice of clear, Chelsea sky beyond the basement steps, Cassie thought about what the BBC left out of its bulletins: the detail she dealt with at her desk each day deemed too sensitive, too damn frightening, for public consumption.

'Luke, I've been here nearly three months,' she said, to lighten the mood. 'I owe you more than the kitty for tea, bread and jam. I must pay you rent.'

'Come on, Cassie, we have talked about this,' Luke said, getting up to peer into the mirror on the back of the kitchen door to adjust his tie. 'You buy the groceries. You do a good job at pooling our rations. You cook occasional meals...'

She caught his glance in the reflection and laughed. 'Badly! Always trying to think what Mrs Poulter would do.'

'Save your money. You might need it – a contingency fund. And if I can't help you out, then who can?'

Who indeed, thought Cassie. The Dubois property on the elegant enclave of Cheyne Row, Chelsea, had been her sanctuary since the evening in February when she'd telephoned Luke from the booth in Peter Jones. Fifteen minutes later, after a juddering walk through the blackout down the King's Road, Luke had opened the front door to her and had taken her through into the sparsely elegant drawing room – 'Christ, Cassie, what has happened to you?' – and sat her down with a brandy. She couldn't answer him, of course. In all honesty, she didn't know how to.

Cassie had concentrated hard on a spot on the wall behind Luke's head, wondering if the colour of the panels was a Wedgwood or a Dresden blue, sipping, trying her best not to cry. She had never felt more confused, inarticulate, and alone.

'I did wonder if you would know who I was,' Cassie had uttered, as Luke stoked the coals in the hearth and Kipling, curled on the rug, had blinked at her with disinterest.

Luke had looked around at her. 'I'd know you anywhere, Cassie.'

Although she hadn't been sure if she would have known him.

He was, of course, no longer a youth, but a slightly taller, slightly more robust version of that youth, with dark, cropped hair and grown-up, horn-rimmed glasses. Now in the kitchen, as he pulled on the jacket of his Jermyn Street suit – tailored to perfection – put on his hat, and rearranged the handkerchief in his top pocket, he appeared quite the important civil servant.

'Right, see you later,' he said, picking up his briefcase. 'Enjoy your day off, Cassie. You won't know what to do with yourself.'

Kipling the cat, sitting at her elbow, bumped his head against her hand, and she let him lick the buttery crumbs from her fingers.

'I'll find something,' she said. 'Even if it's just acting as maid-servant for this fellow.'

Luke laughed briefly and then his face fell like it did when he seemed deep in thought. He contemplated her, looked like he wanted to say something more.

'Cheerio, then,' Cassie said brightly, as if to help him out.

She took a cup of tea with her up the dim basement stairs, and then the three flights of house stairs that curved their way airily to the top of the house. Her bedroom-cum-sitting room under the eaves spanned the width of the property. 'It was once the servants' quarters, remodelled,' Luke had said, when he showed her up that first evening. 'You don't mind, do you?', which had given Cassie nervous, out-of-control giggles. How could she possibly mind being let in to such a miraculous haven? The room had enough space for a queen-sized bed, wardrobe, and a comfy armchair by the little hearth, while next door, her own little bathroom. Two huge dormer windows faced south, one of which had a stepladder propped permanently under it.

This morning, Cassie climbed up the ladder, dexterously balancing her cup, opened the window and stepped out onto the sloping roof. Sitting down on the tiles, which always gave her a mild wobbly feeling, she propped her feet against the robust, stone balustrade and sipped her tea in the spring sunshine.

Luke's house sat only a few streets from the river and, Cassie realised soon after taking up his offer to become his lodger, stood an entirely walkable distance away from her family home in South Kensington. When she had first got her bearings, she felt gratified that her windows faced south. Somehow, she thought, it may help to keep what she had seen at Egerton Terrace that cold, February evening behind her and out of her mind.

Today, the trees in Battersea Park across the river looked fluffy with blossom, the great chimneys of the power station beyond churned out their usual plumes of smoke, joined by smoke from the hearths of endless rows of terraced houses in Clapham, Wandsworth and beyond. Below, the curve of the river sparkled as it made its way towards Westminster.

Cassie felt warm pressure against her ankles as Kipling, having silently followed her upstairs and out of the window, settled himself at her feet. She smiled and lifted her face to the sun, relishing the contrast to a usual working day, below ground in the War Room.

* * *

The morning after she had arrived at Cheyne Row, Luke had insisted that she use his telephone to call her mother.

'She'll want to know about your job, Cassie. Surely, she will be expecting a telephone call?' he had said. 'Everything else can wait.'

Luke did not ask about *everything else* for she had already asked him not to. But she knew, from the way she caught him looking at her, that he could see pain on her face and could hear it in her voice.

Cassie had lifted the receiver and asked the operator to be

put through to the Greenaways number, feeling a strange pinch of assurance that there would be no danger of her aunt being at home to answer the telephone. And still, her stomach had flipped in relief when she heard Mrs Poulter say hello.

The housekeeper's voice had pealed across the hallway: 'Hurry, Mrs Marsh. It's Miss Cassie in London.'

Her mother, breathless and joyful, picked up the receiver. 'Darling Cassie! What news do you have?'

'I have been offered the job, Mum. I start... very soon indeed.'

'Marvellous, marvellous, oh, Cassie, well done. I expect Dad is over the moon!'

'I... I don't know. I haven't told him. I'm at a friend's. I haven't been home.'

Cassie's lie had felt like a bee sting piercing her tongue.

'Oh really? Well, he will be so very proud, and so very pleased. I will call him.'

Cassie, trying not to imagine the telephone ringing through the house on Egerton Terrace and waking the occupants in the bedroom on the first floor, had fired off what practical details she could in answer to her mother's questions. She fought to divert the conversation away from any more mention of her father, and to counter the surge of repulsion rising in her gut. In any case, she could not tell her mother, or anyone, where she would be working, or in what capacity. Of course, her uncle would have had a fair idea, but he knew the important secrecy of such matters.

'You're at a friend's, you say?' Cassie's mother had asked. 'I didn't quite catch that, Cassie? The line is very bad. What did you say?'

And Cassie had never felt so thankful for the wartime regulation three minutes allowed for a telephone call.

'Mum, I have to go...'

'Bye, Cassie darling...'

She had wandered back into the blue-panelled drawing room, her stomach pulsing with a stew of the half-truths she'd told her mother, the horror of the night before, the scene at Egerton Terrace, lingering. She already knew she must get used to it: the utter sorrow, the two-headed shame that she must carry with her.

Luke had glanced up at her, his features stretched with concern, but he sensed not to ask any more questions.

'Cassie, you can stay here as long as you like,' he had said. 'You are always welcome.'

She had uttered her thanks, left the room and shut herself in the scullery downstairs to cry.

* * *

This morning, up on the roof, with the skyline of chimney pots laid out before her under the balmy sky, and Kipling keeping pleasant company, Cassie's tears had long dried and yet she continued to exist in limbo, floundering with uncertainty. But she couldn't, she had realised, stay silent at Cheyne Row forever.

'Do you need to go back to Egerton Terrace to pick up your things?' Luke had asked at the end of her first week. He had possibly noted her hand-washed stockings drying out every evening on the kitchen stove. 'I can come with you and give you a hand if you like.'

'No,' Cassie had said, for most of her clothes were at Greenaways anyway, and in the meantime, she had gone out to the King's Road and bought herself one new outfit and some underwear. It would do for now. Her drawings, her diaries, her ornaments and books in her bedroom belonged to another time, another world, which had been shattered and trampled on, pulverised to dust. 'There is nothing I want or need there.'

Luke looked shocked at her curt answer, had appeared on the verge of asking more, but had held his tongue instead, and that afternoon, Cassie had thought there was nothing else for it but to sit down and write to her mother in Devon. She filled her in as much as she could about her new job, which, she wrote, she was sure she would understand, amounted to very little. And because of time constraints and travelling restrictions, she asked her mother to package up the clothes on the list enclosed, plus a couple of pairs of shoes.

Do send me the postage bill. And please, send to me here:

She wrote down Luke's address.

PS: Don't worry about me, I am lodging with a friend.

Which was all – Cassie decided as she basked in the sun on the roof, the tiles warming deliciously beneath her – her mother, or anyone, needed to know.

Kipling stretched and rested his chin flat on her foot. She gently rubbed the space between his sleepy, blinking eyes, realising how easy it would be to simply do nothing, to stay here, remain quiet, work hard, and keep her own counsel on the secrets she knew. To exile herself from her family.

9

LONDON, AUGUST 1940

Cassie woke and for one blissful moment thought she must be back at Greenaways. She knew that she wasn't at Egerton Terrace and, while sleeping, had forgotten about Cheyne Row. Sunlight warmed her closed eyelids, birds whistled and sang nearby, and a summer from long ago glimmered in her mind. But her dream, whatever it had been, evaporated when a barge over on the Thames honked. Cassie opened her eyes.

Kipling lay curled on the bed, a compact weight by her feet. One of the shutters at the dormer windows stood open; she had left it like that after switching off the light to go to bed, mindful of the blackout but longing to see the sky. She wanted to wake to natural light because she must, now, get up and dressed, have tea and toast in the kitchen, and head off to spend the best part of the day in the stifling gloom of the bunker.

Walking into the building, Cassie gave a wry chuckle, remembering that she had thought, after Dunkirk, that it couldn't get much worse. How wrong, she reminded herself, could she have been?

Inside the foyer, she showed her pass, signed in and headed

to Staircase Fifteen, passing the usual unsmiling Royal Marine in red-banded cap poised with his rifle. Downstairs in the bunker, extra staff were being crammed into every nook and cranny. Miss Redmond, Cassie's supervisor in the Typing Room had asked, or rather had told, her to move to a cubby hole outside on the corridor, as she wanted to keep an eye on a less-experienced recruit in the office.

Cassie enjoyed working in her little booth, feeling the raw, vital energy radiating from the people bustling past. She got to know the faces – the RAF, the army and the navy chiefs – swooping along for debriefs with Intelligence, jaws clenched with responsibility, paperwork clutched in their hands. Everyone seemed to be improvising, constantly finding opportunities for resistance, all focused on stopping the enemy breaking through the country's last line of defence: the battle in the sky.

And Cassie spent each shift in a frenzy. She typed up piles of reports about the outcome of every dog fight, every attack on airfields, on shipping in the Channel and radar stations; every raid on towns and ports from Aberdeen to Dover, from Land's End to Liverpool, to be circulated to Mr Churchill, the Chiefs of Staff and the King. She detailed the planes involved and the outcome: Junkers or Messerschmidt, Hurricane or Spitfire; German losses, British losses; the pilots bailed out, injured, lost, killed. The casualties on the ground: crew and civilians, individual souls condensed into figures. As each day unfolded during that long, sleep-deprived summer and fortunes improved one moment, and deteriorated the next, everyone hoped for the best, feared the worst. The words Cassie typed sounded concise, callous but necessary.

She barely had a moment to herself, and did not expect one. She worked either from eight in the morning until four; or two in the afternoon to nine at night. Once every fortnight, she would start at 3 p.m. and work all through the night. That morning, as Cassie had settled into her booth, Miss Redmond had said she'd be back in a moment with her next task but had been gone a while.

Idle times, however, proved equally unsettling. Cassie's thoughts drifted to her mother ensconced at Greenaways and Gerard on his ship, docked at Southampton. Oliver, as far as she knew, was still at Sandhurst and Marianne, dear Marianne, must be in the most danger working at the airfield in Kent. But Cassie would not allow her imaginings to go any further. She turned her notebook over and began to doodle with her ink pen, her drawing evolving into a wren. And then she remembered. The image of her father with Juno rose like a menacing spectre, and she stopped drawing, put the lid back on her pen. Even the precious, peaceful memories of sitting with Oliver on the log by the river had been sullied.

'Ah, young lady, I see that you like to draw.'

Cassie glanced up at the man in a civilian suit standing by her cubby hole, his shadow momentarily blocking the light.

'Sorry, sir.' Embarrassed, Cassie closed the book. 'Only until Miss Redmond gives me the next assignment,' she said. 'She will be along in a moment.'

'But you like to draw?' The man seemed to be head-to-toe in brown, from his slick-backed hair and spectacle frames to his suit and his tobacco-stained fingertips.

'Yes, sir.'

'Right, you can start working for us tomorrow in Room 64 with the Maps Ops. I will clear it with Miss Redmond. And brief you tomorrow, oh-eight-hundred hours, Miss er...'

'Miss Marsh, sir.'

'Carry on, Miss Marsh.' He gave her another glance, and half a smile. 'That looked rather good, by the way.'

* * *

Cassie thought she knew her way around the bunker. Certainly, there were many sections out of bounds and each guarded by a Marine – the Cabinet Room and the Map Room – and lots of other doors with *Do Not Enter* signs. But she had never heard of Room 64.

Early the next morning, Cassie dropped in to the Typing Room to see Miss Redmond, to check with her that the man, Mr Frederick, had spoken with her, and that she approved her move.

'Lucky thing,' Esme said, sitting at her desk behind a stack of paperwork in her in-tray. 'You'll be in the thick of it. And the map boys are always so glamorous.'

'Is that what they are, Esme?' said Miss Redmond flatly. 'Now, Cassie, I understand from Mr Frederick that it may well be a temporary post, because frankly, they are scrambling around for people to help. I told him I was loath to let you go, and so, in due course, you may well find yourself back with us. Are you happy with that?'

'Do I have a choice, Miss Redmond?'

'Not really.' Her supervisor gave her a faint, admiring smile. 'But top marks if you can actually find where it is you are supposed to be.'

Cassie eventually asked the sentry by the main door, and after turning the corner at the PM's kitchen, and doubling back by the Switchboard Room, and passing the sign that read, *No whistling or unnecessary noise in this corridor*, she at last found Room 64. She knocked on the usual blank, non-descript door and entered a larger than expected space – the Typing Room had always felt claustrophobic – with Mr Frederick sitting behind his desk at one end under a haze of cigarette smoke, huge plan chests lined up all around the walls and three draughtsmen beavering away at their easels.

'Ah, here's our artist,' Mr Frederick said, and the other men turned their pale, weary and rather relieved faces towards her.

'I wouldn't put it quite like that, Mr Frederick,' she said. 'More of a doodler, sir. You saw the drawing.'

He looked at her for a second, sucking on his cigarette, and Cassie thought she'd overstepped the mark. Perhaps her desire to please and to show him she had the nerve to do the job must have sounded cheeky.

But he said, 'That's what we need. Along with speed and accuracy, yes, a sense of humour. Thomas, show Miss Marsh the ropes, will you? I have a meeting.'

'Right you are, sir.'

Thomas, the younger-looking chap, but seemingly the most experienced, gestured to Cassie to join him at a plan chest. He hauled open each enormous flat draw to show her the maps of various parts of the British Isles and Northern Europe.

'We work on these, labelling them as events progress,' he said. 'When you've completed the task, they are taken along to the Cabinet Room each day for the briefings. We work at a terrific pace, and you will be given the grotty jobs here, I'm afraid. And you must expect to work night shifts.'

Cassie expected nothing less.

Thomas led her back to his desk. The map pinned to his drawing board showed the south of England and the northern coast of the Netherlands, Belgium and part of France. Dotted along the continental coast were dozens of labels with black squares on them.

'These labels are the German air bases within striking distance of the south-east of England, and London,' he said. 'And these...' He pointed out the red circles dotted over the

English countryside. 'Here, the bombers have broken through and dropped their payload.'

There were hundreds of raid sights scattered through Kent, Sussex and Hampshire, while the pale-blue Channel appeared, to Cassie far too narrow and vulnerable.

'We need you to draw the labels, and amend the maps as the intelligence comes in,' Thomas said. 'Sometimes, we have hand-written notes, sometimes proper typed-up reports. Like this.'

He handed her a sheaf of paper, stapled at the corner.

'Ah, yes,' said Cassie. 'I usually type these up.'

'Then you will know exactly what we are dealing with,' Thomas said. 'This morning, I need you to update the map for the raids over the south-east late yesterday. As you will see from this report, they struck bases in Sussex, Portland Harbour and the Isle of Wight, along with radar stations on the High Weald. But the RAF pushed them back, made them drop most of their bombs into the sea. There's only so much flying time the Junkers have, you see, or they run out of fuel. Our boys are doing the same job every day: turn the bombers or get them down. Stop them getting to London.'

Cassie peered at the map. 'My cousin is in the WRAF at Manston, in Kent; I can see they have been targeted.'

One of the other men lifted his head from his work. 'The bastards always seem to hit at teatime, for some reason,' he said. 'It's getting pretty hot nearer home, too. They got up the estuary as far as Gravesend Docks the other day. It's only a matter of time.' He ran his hand over his slicked-back hair, his eyes glinting behind his spectacles, it seemed to Cassie, with admiration. 'How long the RAF can keep this up is anyone's guess. The airfields must feel like they are sitting ducks.'

'That sort of comment, Eddie, doesn't get us anywhere,' Thomas said. 'The Big Man said, didn't he: "we go on to the end"? And, didn't you hear what Miss Marsh said? Her cousin is at Manston, so perhaps that sort of attitude can be kept for the pub.'

'But it's the reality,' Eddie replied, catching Cassie's eye and giving a mocking shake of his head. 'If we stopped to think each time something bad happened, we'd never get anywhere. Something to remember Miss... er, Marsh.'

Cassie lifted her chin. 'I know how vital it is to remain impartial,' she said, steadily returning Eddie's gaze. 'The importance of my work keeps me going.'

Eddie gave a cocky shrug and lowered his head to his drawing board, and Cassie followed Thomas over to her desk in the corner.

'Wait here while I fetch the map that I need you to update,' he said. 'There are dozens stored in the plan chests so I won't expect you to find your first one for now. All in good time.'

Cassie sat down at her desk behind the sloping drawing board. Beside it were wooden trays of pens, bottles of coloured inks, boxes of labels, and a huge anglepoise lamp, its dome focusing its light on the board. Someone had left a map of the North Atlantic pinned there, the blue, empty tract of ocean peppered with pin holes and markers indicating shipping routes, the convoys, a graceful, sweeping shape across the water. Her predecessor had drawn English flags on some of the labels, and Swastikas on others; some labels indicated U-boats and submarines. Some labels showed neat little ships lying on their sides.

Cassie shuddered, staring at the map and the positions of the Royal Navy, the Merchant Navy and their enemies, frozen in time. One of these could be Gerard's ship, but she *must* not think of it. *The end*, Cassie thought. Mr Churchill had said they would go on to the end. But how would any of them know when the end had come?

'Ah, this is obsolete, we don't need this.' Thomas unpinned the map, rolled it up and set it aside. 'It's at least a month old. Things move fast around here, as you will soon discover. Now, Miss Marsh,' he said, unrolling the new map and tapping it with his pen. 'Back to the English Channel, the Thames Estuary and the Stuka dive bombers we are contending with.'

Eddie piped up, 'Hey, Tom, did you hear? Goering named yesterday *Adlertag* – Eagle Day. He thinks he will destroy us.'

'Yes, he thinks does,' said Thomas. 'But we, Miss Marsh,' he looked at her, 'have other plans.'

10

LONDON, SEPTEMBER 1940

Now that Cassie worked nights in Map Ops, and Luke a more normal routine of days in his Whitehall office, they would pass each other either in the morning or evening on the stairs, along the hallway or walking up from the basement kitchen and offer each other sleepy greetings.

'You look as tired as I feel, Cassie,' Luke would joke.

And Cassie would say, 'I will see you on the other side.'

They were both exhausted but, as Luke reminded her, his job was above ground and at least he didn't have to do night shifts or breathe in stale, piped-in air.

But Cassie would say, 'Oh, it's not too bad.'

Working in Room 64 with its different purpose and focus, gave Cassie a strange sense of gratitude; she felt invigorated, as long as she could keep batting Eddie's pointed comments away. While the Battle of Britain raged on and Mr Churchill paid tribute to The Few, life at Cheyne Row continued the best way it could. And Cassie could leave her deplorable family secrets in a dark space at the back of her mind.

She pinned up a rota on the kitchen cupboard for shopping,

cooking, and making sure the tea ration stayed intact. Cassie and Luke fell into their routines, 'like an old married couple,' Luke joked. Twice a week, Luke's charlady, Mrs Ennis, came by to sort out the laundry and other chores. And whoever was at home would make sure the cat had his dinner.

In the late afternoon of that early September day, Cassie got up and dressed for work and began to heat up leftover soup on the stove for her 4 p.m. 'breakfast'. But, as she sat down at the kitchen table, exhaling a sigh, preparing herself for another night in the War Room, the air raid siren started, mournful and sickening, shuddering through the air. She put her spoon down and went to look for Kipling.

Cassie walked up the basement stairs and along the hall, calling out, making her voice as sweet and encouraging as she could above the grinding wail of the siren that trailed along with her wherever she went.

Most of the rooms at Cheyne Row had been shut up: the dining room and the salon on the ground floor, the library, and several bedrooms, leaving the smaller, blue-panelled drawing room as a haven for Cassie and Luke to spend quiet evenings with the wireless. The Dubois family valuables and breakables had been packed away or shipped out to Mr Dubois's country seat. And Mrs Ennis once or twice had run a feather duster around the closed-up rooms, but after a fashion, Luke had told her not to bother.

No sign of Kipling, but Cassie noticed the door ajar to the salon and poked her head into the darkened room. Furniture and mirrors shrouded in dust sheets loomed like pale ghosts: an accumulation of wealth locked in a time capsule. She often wondered about this empty house, the long-gone people and the lives past. And what had turned Mrs Dubois's head? What had made her bolt? Luke never mentioned his mother, even though post still arrived for her, and it lay unopened on the hallway console. And Cassie did not press him. In the same way, she did not mention her own father, even though he lived just streets away. Luke seemed to understand their mutual reticence.

'Oh, Kipling!' Cassie cried, spotting a curled-up shape on an armchair. The dustsheet had fallen to the floor and the fine silk seat was grubby and matted with fur, tiny, claw-sized holes speckling the surface. 'Naughty cat, how long have you been coming in here?'

She scooped him up, wrapped her arms around him as if to shield him from the bawling siren, and took him downstairs. Shutting the kitchen door behind her, she took her bowl of soup and crawled under the table, which Luke had set against the wall in the corner furthest from the window. A mattress cushioned the floor, and bolster cushions made an almost-comfortable nest. Kipling found a spot on her lap and tucked his nose under his paw.

'I know, it's horrible, isn't it, but we must sit this one out,' she whispered to him.

He purred as the awful sound continued, shifting the air as it rose and fell.

'Heavens, I will be late for work.'

Cassie thought briefly about her father, whether he was at home, hearing the siren, too, or over in the Strand in his office, or sheltering in one of the Underground stations. Her mother, inevitably, followed him through her mind. But Cassie could only picture her with guilt, shame and the unsettling realisation that Cassie's childhood and family had been splintered, with her the only witness.

The siren stopped. Cassie held her breath, waiting for the all-clear, clinging onto the cat so hard, he began to wriggle. Silence. And no all-clear. She kept still, listening, suffering the unbearable suspense of cowering, waiting for the enemy's next move.

She felt, then, rather than heard, a crumping deep within the ground beneath her. Again, and again. A constant thumping, punishing the earth. Sound began to reach her in waves, like eerie, approaching thunder. Bombs exploding, somewhere. No longer red squares that she might place on a map, but real and vivid, tearing into London, invading the city, and yet still strangely distant, like someone angrily kicking a barrel in another room.

Hadn't Eddie said only a few days ago, 'The bombers always get through...'? Hearing him, Cassie had thought him entirely unpatriotic. But crouched under the table, her scalp tight and her mouth dry, the planes evidently scoring their way across the London skyline, Eddie, also, seemed to be right.

She must think, she must get her bearings, work out which direction the explosions were coming from. Leaning tentatively forward, she peered up at the taped-up window to catch a glimpse of the outside, in case this would help her. But the late-afternoon sky over Chelsea only teased her with its clear, September blue. The kettle stood on the draining board. In her panic, she had forgotten to fill it when the siren went off; one of their rules, in case the water main was cut so at least they could have a cup of tea.

And she had no idea where she'd left her gas mask.

The distant bombing continued, the noise like the playing of a terrible, out-of-tune symphony, and far away, the sound of aircraft banking and droning, cutting through the sky.

'Christ, Kipling,' Cassie whispered, planting a kiss on his little, striped head, fear gouging a gulley through her stomach. 'I don't know what to do. Oh!'

She heard the clunk of the front door opening above, and

footsteps – two pairs, it sounded like – walking along the hall. The cat jumped off her lap and sat by the kitchen door, scratching it with his paw, his ears twitching back and forth.

'Ah, so Luke Dubois comes home from work, bravely making his way through the air raid,' she whispered to Kipling, her voice trembling, 'and you don't want Cassie Marsh any more.'

The footsteps descended the basement stairs, and Cassie began to crawl out from under the table. She could hear Luke's voice. He was talking to someone. Perhaps he had come across a person in need of shelter? Had they enough soup left, she wondered. She felt sure the tea leaves were running low.

The kitchen door opened and Cassie, still on her hands and knees, saw two pairs of smart, polished shoes walk into the room. The cat scooted straight past and out the door. She looked up and cried out, 'Oh,' again, knocking her head on the underside of the table.

'Cassie, it's Oliver,' Luke said.

'She can see it's me,' Oliver laughed. Reaching down, he gripped Cassie's hand and helped her to stand. 'God, you're shaking, Cass. Did you hurt your head?'

'No, no,' she replied, although she had done and, embarrassed, gave it a rub. She found she could barely say another word. Fear, switching so abruptly to relief, made her want to be sick.

Cassie had not recognised him in that brief first moment. But, as always, although so much time passed between the occasions they saw each other, the essence of Oliver beamed in his smile and shone out through his eyes as it had done at Greenaways and again at Egerton Terrace last year. This time, from under the peak of his army captain's cap. He looked pristine, his khaki pressed, new and splendid, buttons shining. And shyness and confusion slammed into her. She remembered, suddenly, what she knew, and did not trust herself to speak.

'Oliver's on embarkation leave, Cassie,' Luke said, opening a cupboard door. He pulled out a bottle of red wine. 'Ah, this will do.'

'Luke, that's not from the famed Dubois cellar, is it?' Oliver asked, removing his cap and setting it on the table. He pulled out a chair to sit down, and Cassie stared at him. Didn't he want to get under the table? 'One your father wanted to lay down for at least a decade?'

'No, no, all the good stuff has gone to Buckinghamshire, with my father.' Luke rummaged for three glasses.

Cassie looked from Luke to Oliver and back again, wondering how they could be so relaxed, so breezy. The siren's wail might have stopped, and, for now, she could no longer feel or hear any bombs, but the noise and terror continued to blast through her bones.

'But... but, the bombers...' she said, waving her hand skywards. 'What's going on?'

Luke cocked his head to listen. 'Sounds like they've moved on. For now.'

Cassie dipped to retrieve her soup dish from under the table, clattered it into the sink and busily started to wash up. Her mind juddered once more with the indelible image of Oliver's mother with *her* father, and she did not want to look at him.

'The news isn't good, Cass, I'm afraid,' Oliver said gently. 'What was that you said, Luke, on our way over here, the report of today's RAF losses being the heaviest so far?'

'My boss *thinks* that Goering *thinks* that the RAF is finished,' Luke said, plonking the wine glasses onto the table.

Cassie, fearful of the answer, remembering what Eddie had said, asked, 'Are we finished?'

'Can't say,' Luke said. He uncorked the bottle and glugged wine into glasses. 'But the Luftwaffe broke through this afternoon, found a weak spot. Came straight up the Thames, right into London. Not surprised, really. Our boys must be spent. They've hit the docks and the East End.' He sounded all-knowing, reminding Cassie of how annoying he'd been that summer at Greenaways.

'I heard it,' Cassie whispered, staring out the window behind the kitchen sink, her hands in the washing-up water, shaking. 'I heard them.'

'Yes, the poor blighters,' Luke said. 'They have issued code name Cromwell in certain quarters. Invasion imminent.'

Cassie gasped, turned to glare at him. Tears seared her eyes.

'*Luke*, really,' Oliver said under his breath.

'But leave the washing-up now, Cassie,' Luke said. 'Come on, chin up. We need to toast Captain Greenaway, who will be tomorrow, *a-way* to North Africa.'

'I need to get to work,' Cassie said, briskly drying her hands.

'You're not going anywhere,' said Luke.

Cassie, defiant, shook her head at him.

'Too dangerous,' he said. 'They haven't sounded the all-clear.'

'I need to get to Whitehall, to track the raids. Produce the maps for The Cabinet Room. I need to *help*. My colleague said this would happen. My colleague was right.'

Oliver pulled out a chair. 'Come and sit down, Cass,' he said, his voice low and insistent, as comforting as always. 'You can't do anything to help those people at the moment.'

Cassie gazed at her cousin, gave in and sat down. She accepted a glass of wine from Luke and, as she sipped, she stopped fighting, and got used to the shrieking crisis inside her. She relaxed, felt a little safer, and it seemed such a novelty, for things hadn't been that way in a long while. Was it simply the company, the conversation, sitting with Oliver and Luke at the kitchen table like they might on any other day? And yet it had been such a long time since she'd seen Oliver; they had never been together like this, as adults, drinking wine. But with bombers prowling overhead, and the secret about her father and Oliver's mother smouldering inside her, how could this be like any other day?

'Cass, you will be able to help others tomorrow,' Oliver assured her. 'Tomorrow, you will be stronger, in a better frame of mind.'

The siren sounded again, this time in a different pitch, and Cassie jolted with relief.

'There. All-clear,' said Luke, draining his glass and topping up the others. 'Come on, let's do this *Chateauneuf-du-Pape* some justice. And, come on, Captain Greenaway, tell all.'

Oliver sat back in the chair and stretched his legs out in his habitual relaxed way, reminding Cassie of the last time they met, sitting in the garden at Egerton Terrace over a year before. How harmless everything had seemed then, despite the war breaking out: how exciting, almost carefree.

He took a sip of wine. 'I'm shipping out to Tobruk. That's as much, of course, that I can tell you both.' He gave Cassie a wry smile. 'You, Cass, will probably know more than I do, once you start getting the reports through. But we all know the Italians bombed Malta a couple of months ago, and now their army is moving through Libya into Egypt.'

'I don't think the Eyeties will give you much trouble,' Luke said, slurring a little. He had drunk far more wine than Cassie or Oliver. He took his spectacles off to polish them.

Oliver glanced at him. 'Woodward, we don't know that.'

Luke beamed, seemed to enjoy being challenged, raised his

glass at Oliver. But for Cassie, her cousin's ominous words sliced through her pleasant, wine-induced haze. She squared her shoulders, kept her face still, as if to brace herself, to try to disguise the panic rising again inside her.

Seeing through her veneer, Oliver said, 'I will write to you this time, Cass. I promise.'

'You two... honestly...' Luke uttered, looking at them both and laughingly shaking his head. 'I'm starving. Anyone for toast?' He got up, stumbling a little as he went over to the counter and began to slice the loaf, rummaging in the drawer for the butter knife.

'Oliver, how's Marianne?' Cassie asked.

Oliver's face broke into a grin. 'Ah, don't you know? She is *stepping out* with Harry Brough, the teacher, when she can – when she can get home to Greenaways. They write to each other *every* day.'

'Oh goodness, how wonderful. I didn't know!' cried Cassie. 'Marianne is such a good letter writer, but, I admit, I haven't heard from her recently.'

'Well, he seems a fine chap,' Oliver said. 'Quite a lot older than her, but I think that suits her.'

Luke sat down with a plate of burnt toast and Cassie watched as he scraped butter over it, contaminating the butter dish with crumbs. She felt herself grimace with distaste, but reminded herself that this was his house, and he could do as he liked.

'No wonder you don't know what's going on in your family, Cassie,' Luke said. 'No wonder you haven't had a letter from Marianne. Because no one really knows where you are.'

Oliver sputtered in surprise.

'But we are all scattered now,' Cassie said, bristling with guilt at the distance she had put between herself and everyone. 'And anyway, my mother knows...'

'I wonder what your mother thinks about it,' Luke said, munching toast, his eyes bright behind his glasses, his cheeks glowing from the wine, coaxing the troublesome youth out of hiding. 'And your father? Does he mind you lodging here with me? Perhaps they all think there's something going on. A *frisson* between us.'

Embarrassed, Cassie caught Oliver's eye, but the look on his face – crooked astonishment – made her want to giggle.

'We both know that is not the case, Luke. And, Oliver, any news about Vee?' Cassie asked, desperate to change the subject. 'You know, Victoria?'

'Ah yes, I believe she is still around,' Oliver said. 'She and Marianne are still at Manston together.'

Luke wiped his buttery fingers down his shirt and leant over the table towards Cassie.

'But why, Cassie, why have you distanced yourself from your family?' he slurred, pointing at her. 'What are you hiding from?'

'N-nothing,' she uttered.

'But you came here...'

Luke stared at Cassie and somehow, the promise he'd made her that terrible evening in February found its way to the surface, and he stopped his train of thought.

'Come on, you two,' he said. 'Let's go up while it's quiet and have a look.'

* * *

They went upstairs to Cassie's attic room, the house in twilight now that evening was falling and the blackout down. Oliver led the way up the ladder out of the window and onto the roof.

Cassie followed, and last up was Luke; Oliver had to help him, as he now seemed entirely intoxicated.

As Cassie looked eastwards, her mouth dropped open. Beyond the City, the air raged and burnt, a fierce red seeping upwards, tainting the clouds and the darker sky above it. Searchlights crossed and needled their way through black, billowing smoke; the horizon glowed, inflamed, like a sunset. Cassie shook her head and leant against the sloping roof, disorientated momentarily, her shift work playing havoc with her senses. For it was the end of the day, she told herself, and the sunset would be behind her in the west.

'God in heaven,' Oliver breathed. 'It's on fire.'

'The docks,' Luke said, wiping the back of his hand over his mouth. 'Must be Wapping, Bermondsey, Poplar...'

Cassie wanted to look away but found herself staring instead at the distant East End obliterated by an inferno with the Palace of Westminster closer on the curve of the river, its towers in silhouette against the glowering sky.

'What can we do?' she uttered. 'Those poor... poor souls.'

'The artillery will have got as many down as they could, picked out by the searchlights. Our RAF fighters won't be able to do so much in darkness,' Oliver said. 'But we do have the barrage...'

Cassie looked at him. She knew they both realised his attempt at comfort was futile.

In that moment, the sirens began another round of ominous wailing.

'Mother of God,' Cassie said. 'They're flying in again.'

'Come on, back inside,' Oliver said.

Luke gave him a mock salute. 'Yes, sir.'

Cassie went first, easing herself down the ladder, while Oliver gripped her hand, supporting her. She didn't need his help, for she had climbed up and down the ladder many times, but she welcomed it, her palm against his cold with fear.

Downstairs in the kitchen, with blackout drawn and the lamp on, the noise and the taste of fear stayed with Cassie. Oliver put the kettle on the stove, and Luke rested his head on the table, about to drop off to sleep.

'Hey, Woodward,' Oliver said, shaking his shoulder. 'I think you better call it a night.'

Luke lifted his head, his eyes blurred in the soft, yellow light, a wide, silly smile over his face. 'Ah, Oliver. Captain Greenaway. My very best friend. All through school, and beyond. My very best friend.'

'Shall I get you a blanket, Luke?' Cassie asked.

'Ah, Cassie,' he mumbled, grabbing her hand. 'Thank you. I love you. And Oliver loves you too. Why do you think he is here?'

Oliver laughed. 'I'm here to see both of you. Come on, Luke. You've never been able to handle your drink, have you?' Oliver turned to Cassie. 'We used to smuggle scrumpy at school to drink in the dorm after lights out but had to hide it from Woodward, here, because after two sips, with all his blabbering and stumbling, he would give us away to Matron.'

'Is that so...!?' Luke shook his head, chuckling.

Cassie went to fetch a blanket from the under-stairs cupboard, deciding that Luke, with all this chattering, must be very drunk indeed. When she came back in, he had crawled onto the mattress under the table and was already snoring.

'We should go to a shelter,' Oliver said.

Cassie shivered. 'I don't want to go outside,' she said. 'Luke says this is safe enough. Let's stay down here. Anyway, we need to keep an eye on him.'

Oliver agreed. 'Switch on the wireless, then,' he said. 'And we will listen for the news.'

Cassie glanced at the ceiling. Aircraft engines ebbed and flowed, goading and menacing; the distant explosions continued, booming steadily, relentlessly. Pouring their tea, Oliver seemed pensive but not, Cassie deduced, from fear of the raid.

Finally, he said, 'What did Luke mean, Cass, that no one seems to know where you are, that you're living here?'

'Oh, there's certainly no *frisson*.' Cassie's giggle sounded forced as she accepted her cup from him.

'That's not what I meant.' Oliver ignored her laughter. 'Are you not in touch with your family?'

'It has been hard,' she said, in truth, but found she could not look at Oliver.

Cassie had barely spoken to her mother after the first stilted telephone conversation when she had moved into Cheyne Row. And since then, in their rare, brief, three-minute calls, Cassie had steered the conversation to the day-to-day life at Greenaways with the schoolboy evacuees, and to Gerard.

'His latest letter arrived yesterday, posted from Southampton,' her mother had told her a few weeks before. 'Oh, Cassie, it was brief, but you know your brother. He doesn't give much away, does he? But I can tell he is happy there with his mates on his ship. He has all but finished his training... But, darling, Dad spoke to me the other day. He has been wondering, can he—?' And the line had cut out.

'It's my job, Oliver.' Cassie sighed. 'It has all but taken over my life like it has for all of us. For you, Marianne, Gerard. And, of course, I can't *tell* them anything about it.'

'I am simply surprised that you are living here with Luke, when your family home is only a fifteen-minute walk away. I mean, Woodward is great company...' he glanced under the table with a wry smile, 'but...?'

'I wanted...' Cassie felt tears swelling behind her eyes. 'I wanted a change,' she said weakly, her fib trailing off. She hated to be untruthful with Oliver; it opened a yawning, lonely gulf between them, even though he – miraculously it seemed – was sitting opposite her at Luke's kitchen table. But how could she possibly explain what happened? How could she confide her terrible secret to him? 'And I can understand...' Cassie faltered. '...why me not living at Egerton Terrace might be on everyone's mind. But it's nothing to do with Luke... in *that* way.' She looked Oliver in the eye, wanting him to understand. 'Luke has been wonderful. He has a lovely cat. And I... I prefer it here.'

'You don't have to explain,' he said. 'Please don't cry, Cass.'

'I'm not!' she cried, rousing herself, wiping her eyes and laughing a little, relishing Oliver's ability to cut through any crisis she may have. 'I simply realise that it is so hard to please everyone.'

'Then it's simple. Don't even try.'

The raid continued and Cassie tried to blank out her thoughts; she did not want to imagine what was happening to the people, to London. How on earth could she? How could anyone truly visualise hell? As a distraction, she thought of a map she'd worked on recently, and did a quick calculation: the East End lay seven or so miles away.

Oliver watched her. 'You know that if they do fly overhead, chances are they won't have any payload left,' he said.

'I was thinking that,' Cassie said, 'but it sounded so selfish inside my head.'

'You are never selfish, Cass. You always have this utter, innate kindness.' Oliver held her gaze, his pupils dark, enlarged in the lamplight. 'And that kindness... you. You never seek attention.

The way you quietly gathered up the dead wren and cared for it. And you worrying about the fate of the lambs. I could have socked my father in the jaw for teasing you about that. Remember, that time at Greenaways...?'

'Yes, yes, I do.'

Cassie remembered all too well. At Greenaways, she and Marianne would say, *There is always tomorrow*, but she had come to learn that this might not always be the case.

'I know you are frightened and are putting on a brave face,' Oliver said. 'So am I.'

Cassie smiled at him, suddenly not afraid to do so, and wondered whether this clarity, this feeling of knowing him, and knowing herself, was like falling in love. Something odd seemed to be happening: a settling of the chaos, the grating uncertainty that had started one summer night, long ago. Her yearning for Oliver, and his friendship, seemed wholly justified.

But Juno's garden, her roses, and a muffled conversation in darkness about the scent of flowers crashed through her mind. Cassie jolted, snuffed it out.

'Are you all right?' Oliver asked.

'I am. For now.' Cassie gave him her best smile.

He got up to put the kettle on again, and found, thank goodness, Luke's new loaf and Cassie's egg ration so they could have some supper. Luke's snores, from beneath the table, grew louder.

'Nudge him with your toe,' Oliver said, glancing over his shoulder, his smile a delight amid the sludge of fear and confusion inside Cassie's head.

She did so, and their friend turned over, and slept peacefully.

Cassie cocked her ear. 'Dare I say, it seems a lot quieter out there now?'

'Amen to that.'

They ate, Cassie mesmerised by the blurry shadows cast on the wall by the warm lamplight. Their shadows looked so ordinary, so reassuring, as if she were watching a simple, domestic play.

Oliver followed her gaze.

'Ah. *Pulvis et umbra sumus,*' he said. 'We are but dust and shadows.'

He made perfect sense to Cassie, seemed to speak to something deep inside her. Deeper than she knew existed. His words sounded like confirmation.

'That's from the *Odes of Horace,*' he said. 'Comforting, in a way, isn't it?'

'Yes... of course...' she said. 'You did Latin.'

They continued with their supper, their shadows against the wall mirroring them. Cassie felt herself relax, her limbs, her muscles, all of her melting into a more tolerable condition. And, astonishingly, whatever love or regard she felt towards Oliver did not seem like happiness to her: more of a calling.

She wanted him to keep speaking. It would see them both through the night, knowing that they – and their fear – were fleeting and insignificant when compared with the imploding world outside.

11

The next morning did its best to right itself. When Cassie woke up, soon after dawn, she climbed the ladder in her bedroom and poked her head out of the skylight window. On the eastern horizon sat a low, hazy smog; she smelt lingering traces of burning in the air. The houses nearby, from what she could see, looked as pristine and as polished as they ever did here in Chelsea. The river's great curve around Battersea appeared its usual fluid grey.

Downstairs in the kitchen, Oliver was busy making a pot of tea, and Luke had already left for work.

'I don't know how he does it,' Oliver said. 'He was pie-eyed last night.'

'Neither do I,' she said. 'How was Mrs Dubois's chaise longue?'

'Sublimely comfortable,' Oliver said. 'As to be expected. I take it you are going in?'

'Of course. I have missed a shift. They'll need as many of us as possible, there's no doubt. I will drink this, eat some toast and set off.'

'I will go along with you,' Oliver said. 'The buses might be disrupted. We can take our chances on the Circle Line to Westminster. It's not a deep line but fingers crossed, it should be running.'

'Oliver, you don't have to...'

'I know I don't. Just to keep you company. It was quite a night.'

'And then you're off?'

'And then I'm off.'

Cassie mechanically buttered her toast, sipped her tea, preparing her mind and body for the day ahead. She felt her insides harden as she tried not to think about Oliver leaving to face the Italians in the deserts of Western Egypt; his departure would be over in moments, she fooled herself, and she would have to get on with her day.

* * *

They caught the Underground at Sloane Square along with other grey-faced, subdued, wary passengers, and trundled along to Parliament Square surprisingly quickly. Here, it appeared business as usual: civil servants intent on getting to work in suits, carrying briefcases; secretaries hurrying along in their second-best coats and hats; younger girls, their fashionable, rolled hairstyles covered by snoods, well turned out, and with either guarded fear or brave determination in their eyes. A bus or two chugged around from Westminster Bridge, followed by cruising taxicabs. But the air itself did not feel the same, as if London had entered a new and frightening era. They could all smell the burning, too, thought Cassie. The news vendors' billboard outside the station entrance read:

London's Biggest Raid. Wave After Wave of Bombers.

'No one quite knows what to do, do they?' Cassie said as they waited to cross over to Whitehall. She peered up at the strangely unremarkable sky as if she'd expected it to look different, ripped apart. 'Everyone is stunned.'

'Life is changing at an almighty speed, hurtling into the unknown...' Oliver's words drifted as they hurried across the street. Ahead of them, the Cenotaph stood defiantly in the centre of Whitehall. Beyond it, the sandbagged entrance to Downing Street. 'But this, last night, feels like the beginning of something entirely sobering. Honestly, my mother has only just given up with her excursions to London. At last, she has seen sense,' he said. 'Or rather, perhaps my father has put his foot down. He probably said, "June, enough is enough", or something.'

A memory juddered through Cassie's mind, raking cold, prickling sensations up the back of her neck.

Cassie swallowed. *'June...?'* The feeling lingered, creeping into her scalp.

'Yes, that's my mother's real name, but she does not let anyone call her it,' Oliver said, with a chuckle to himself. 'She changed it when she was an artist's model, way back in the old days. I can only guess she wanted to be thought as something of a goddess. Pa only calls her June when he particularly wants to make a point. You are someone very special if she lets you use that name. She doesn't even let her own sister call her June.'

Cassie slowed her pace as the overhead conversation between her father and aunt in the darkness of the rose garden at Greenaways years before emerged into clear daylight: her father's voice saying, *'June'*. And her secret returned like a horror show, confusing and frustrating, and downright abhorrent. Her parents' bed. The entwined limbs, their sleeping, oblivious faces. The wireless at full volume. The tangle of Juno's hair. She felt her knees about to give way, the confusion of her younger years falling into place.

It must have been going on for ages, this lascivious affair. Since they had all been children, for who knew how long. At Egerton Terrace, at Greenaways, and probably – and possibly – other seedy, desperate places.

Cassie stopped in her tracks, sucking in her breath, willing it to give her strength. A chasm had opened between her and Oliver, as if the pavement caved in between them.

'All right, Oliver, thank you,' she said politely, on the edge of anger. 'We're nearly there, so you can leave me here.'

Oliver, realising she had come to a halt, turned back and peered up the street. 'Oh yes, of course. If you like. I just wanted to make sure you were safe, that's all.'

'You mentioned that earlier.' Cassie heard fury snapping in her voice. Better anger, she thought, than despair. 'And in all honesty, I think that it is rather an unfair thing to say.'

'What...?' Oliver's smile froze. His brow creased in confusion. 'Cass? What do you mean?'

She gazed at her cousin, his lovely, familiar face, his eyes searching hers for answers. Treacherous tears pricked her eyelids. She blinked them away, praying he had not noticed. She felt herself stiffen and close down, as if she stood in front of a stranger. For the first time in her life, she couldn't be herself with him; she could not be *Cass*.

'It is unfair,' Cassie said, 'because I can't say that to you. *Oh, Oliver, please don't go off and be a soldier, it's unsafe.* But you think you can happily say it to me. And I don't like it.'

'Cass, I was only...'

She offered her hand, to shake his in farewell, gritting her teeth against the rage simmering inside her, against *her* father and *his* mother, their utter contempt for the family. Marshes and Greenaways alike. She forced herself to keep calm, to save face.

'Good luck, Oliver,' she said, and her voice cracked, threatened to break wide open into a scream of frustration. But she must not let on that her blood raced with pain, that turmoil collided in her bones, that she loved him.

Cassie could never tell Oliver this, or what she had seen in the bedroom at Egerton Terrace; her simmering doubts about him being *no Greenaway*, and Uncle Charles not being his father, especially when he was leaving that day for war.

'Goodbye, Oliver.'

He gripped her hand, his expression flinching in confusion.

'Well, yes, goodbye, Cass...'

Cassie turned and walked quickly, to stop herself saying anything else. She might blurt out what she knew about their parents; she might tell him she needed him. And neither of those things would do.

When she reached the corner of King Charles Street, which led down to the War Room entrance, she could see St James's Park like a hazy, green Eden at its end. She dared to glance back. Oliver remained where she'd left him, fine and pristine in his captain's uniform, as if standing to attention, in expectation, waiting for her to look round. She lifted her hand, a silent gesture, an apology. And he saluted her in return, his arm firing out to the side, bending at the elbow, his hand stiff and pressed firm against his cap.

Cassie felt something break inside her, a sob mixed with the beginnings of a giggle. How they had laughed when he had shown her how to salute that time at Egerton Terrace when he'd been on his way to Sandhurst.

Long way up, short way down. Long way up, short way down.

Now, his eyes, shielded by his cap, gave nothing away; his face looked blank and concentrated. His mouth a firm line. Utterly serious: an exemplary army officer. But the simplicity of his gesture, the unreserved respect in it, for Cassie, made the complications within their family, and her rage, feel so much worse.

She turned again and walked down towards the park. She must hurry; she must not be late. There was so much to do.

Veering left onto Horse Guards Road, she slipped into the War Room entrance, to take herself once more underground.

12

LONDON, OCTOBER 1940

Every evening, since the first huge raid on the East End, when she had said goodbye to Oliver, the bombers had come. They had breached further into the city each time to drop their high explosives, screamers and incendiaries on houses, hospitals, schools. Relentless, terrifying and yet almost, now, tediously predictable.

Sitting at her desk in Room 64, Cassie worked on the maps, marking out Germany's airborne *Blitzkrieg*, the information filtering through to the hallowed Map and Cabinet Rooms. The heavy bombing soon spread over the whole of the country: Birmingham, Southampton, Bristol, Liverpool, Glasgow, Plymouth. And, of course, much closer to home. A fortnight ago, a bomb had sliced through the west window of the Holy Redeemer church around the corner from Cheyne Row, and scores of people, sheltering in the crypt, had died. Luke had gone out to help, and returned home hours later, his clothes filthy, his face ashen, his eyes guarded and a shade darker. He said that he'd heard someone cry out, *God take me!* And refused to tell Cassie anything more about it.

But for weeks now, Cassie had barely been back to Cheyne Row; it felt much safer to sleep in the 'Dock', the dank dormitory in the War Room's sub-basement. She would emerge whenever she had the chance, blinking in daylight, for a brief walk around St James's Park, sometimes meeting Luke, whose office was in Whitehall, or having a chat with Esme, depending on what shifts they were on, before going back underground again.

'My bus wasn't running this morning,' Esme said that lunchtime as they sat together on a bench overlooking the pond, tilting their faces to the weak, autumnal sun. 'I had to walk from Holborn as far as Piccadilly, stepping over hosepipes, skirting around piles of rubble, still smoking. Oh, Cassie, there was a ruined row of houses, doors blown out. I saw a birdcage swinging in a shattered window, with a dead canary inside it. And my shoes are ruined. But I prefer to risk that, than spend a night in the "Dock", Cassie. I don't know how you bear it.'

Cassie didn't feel she needed to explain that she preferred the distinctly uncomfortable sleeping quarters deep beneath the War Room to the dangers of trying to get home during an air raid.

'I am past worrying about how scruffy my shoes are,' she said. 'But I suppose we must keep up appearances. It wouldn't do to let ourselves go.'

'Not now you are working with the Map boys,' Esme laughed.

'Oh, Esme,' Cassie said, 'it is the last thing on my mind. They really are rather—'

'Disappointingly dull?'

'No, I was going to say, "oddballs" is a better way to describe them.' Cassie shuddered, reminded of the way Eddie often caught her eye. 'Mr Frederick is the boss, Thomas is kind and patient, Frank is a lot older, rather grandfather-like. But let's not think about them or my work while we have a chance to sit and enjoy the fresh air. Although today, not so fresh... What's that smell?'

'Smells like burning sugar and fat...' Esme said, her nose twitching.

'The wind is coming from the east,' Cassie said. 'The East End docks must have been hit again. Those poor souls.'

Esme nodded in silent, exhausted agreement, and Cassie gazed at the areas of grass now turned over to muddy rows of potatoes, at the ripples over the pond, resembling cold silver over the surface. The trees in the park shed their dusty leaves, drifting into dirty mounds along the path. Even the beauty of autumn had been altered by the war.

Esme glanced at her watch. 'I need to go. Only three-quarters of an hour for lunch, or Miss Redmond wants to know why. Oh, we miss you in the Typing Pool, Cassie.'

'We have to do as we are told,' Cassie said. 'And I had better get back too. Or, likewise, Mr Frederick will give me one of his old-fashioned looks.'

* * *

On Cassie's desk in the Maps Op Room, Thomas had left a report on the previous night's raids over the counties south of London, with a listing of more than one hundred co-ordinates of where the bombers had let loose their payloads. Cassie went to the plan chest to find a corresponding map and began to annotate where the bombs had fallen with small circles in red ink.

'They want this one urgently, Miss Marsh,' Eddie said, sidling up to her desk and leaning over her shoulder. 'Because RAF Croydon and the nearby aircraft factories have been targeted – again. I'll give you a hand.'

Cassie drew back. 'I don't see how you can help me do it any quicker,' she said. 'Unless you read out the co-ordinates to me.'

'Good idea,' he said.

Cassie felt a sinking disappointment as he pulled his own chair over and sat next to her, close enough for her to be able to smell his hair oil, shuffling the pages of the report through his long, slender hands.

'Right, come on, Miss Marsh. Let's start from the beginning, in case you have missed any. Here's the first: Bexley, 51.441 degrees north, 0.149 degrees east.'

Cassie fixed her eyes on the map to hide her annoyance, refilled her pen with red ink and set to work, wondering if Eddie would be better occupied getting on with his own tasks. But he was her senior, and she felt she ought to humour him. Or at least do as he asked. After all, she had only been brought in because they were short-staffed. Thomas wouldn't be in until the night shift, and wasn't there to clarify procedures as he usually did. Mr Frederick was in a meeting and Frank, the other draughtsman, was pouring over his map of raids along the Sussex coast. Perhaps this was how they worked when information was needed by the Map Room immediately. But then, Cassie thought, each piece of the work they did was urgent.

Eddie fired off the list of co-ordinates, and Cassie worked swiftly, using her rule to find the correct spot on the map and quickly marking it on.

'51.434 degrees north, 0.464 degrees west. Ashford,' Eddie said. 'They must have been going for Lydd airbase on the Kent coast and overshot their target.'

Cassie hesitated, asked him to repeat the details.

'Come on, Miss Marsh. You know how to read maps, don't you? You go in the door before you go up the stairs. Longitude before latitude. And there you find your target.' He dictated the map reference to her again, slowly, and with sharp sarcasm.

'This isn't right, sir,' she said. 'The co-ordinate you have just given me is too far west. It's not in Kent. Can I see the details for myself?'

The tone of her voice caught Frank's attention, and he looked over at them.

'Miss Marsh is right. Did you say Ashford, mistaken for Lydd on the Kent coast? The co-ordinates don't sound like anywhere south-east of London to me, Eddie,' he said.

Cassie set her ruler over the map. 'It's here. I have found it. Ashford in Surrey. Look, south-west of London.' She looked at Eddie. 'Not Ashford in Kent, sir...'

Eddie stared at her, his face blank, almost slack with indifference, but his eyes glinted with fury.

The strip lighting on the ceiling began to flicker, the bulbs making a buzzing sound, and the room instantly plunged into pitch-black darkness.

'Electrical blackout,' Frank said, his calm voice an otherworldly echo from the far corner. 'They must have hit a substation somewhere. Common occurrence, I'm afraid. Hold on...'

Cassie heard a rustling, the shake of a box of matches and she felt a pressure on her thigh, a brief stroking of her leg through her skirt. A spark flashed, cutting through the sheer blackness, and the short stub of candle on Frank's desk began to glow, small at first, expanding like a halo.

The yellow light reflected on the lenses of Eddie's glasses, his face looming uncomfortably close to hers.

'You weren't afraid, were you, Miss Marsh?' he said, his voice cold and flat.

'Not at all,' she said evenly, her flesh shrinking. She held her nerve. 'But I can certainly get on with this myself, thank you.'

Gritting her teeth, she took the report, turned away from him and refilled her pen.

Even an hour later, when she had finished, she could still feel the sensation of Eddie's hand touching her leg, as if it had burnt her.

* * *

There was no question of Cassie going home at the end of her shift. The fireworks, as Frank called them, were 'really going off'. Even if Cassie made it back to Cheyne Row, the journey back in tomorrow would be equally perilous.

After eating a sandwich at her desk, Cassie said 'goodnight' to Frank and Mr Frederick, and 'hello' to Thomas, who had just arrived for his night shift. She collected a fresh set of bed sheets from the store and climbed down the wrought-iron ladder to the sub-basement, backwards, wondering if this must be how Gerard felt, going down into the hold of his ship. Immediately, the confines of the 'Dock', with its bare, brick walls, heat and fuggy atmosphere, closed in on her, the feeling of claustrophobia like an acute, intense illness.

As Cassie walked along to the women's sleeping quarters, she stooped to go under doorways with signs reading:

Mind Your Head.

The air supply system rattled like someone with a hoarse throat, and mice darted quite blatantly along the concrete floor. But at least, even in this revolting place, where she could settle down on one of the hard, wooden bunk beds, Cassie would snatch a reasonably good night's sleep. So deep was the 'Dock',

Cassie had come to realise, that she wouldn't hear the bombs raining down.

She smiled hello to familiar faces as they walked past: staff, having slept in pyjamas and dressing gowns, emerging bleary-eyed and in desperate need of a cuppa, for their next shift. The 'Dock', if anything, proved to be a great leveller.

'Ah, Miss Marsh. Cassie... Glad I caught you.'

She turned, and in the gloom of the low-watt bulbs, Eddie appeared behind her, as if he had followed her, his tie loosened, ready, Cassie assumed, to turn in, too. He had never called her by her first name before and it felt worse than the touch of his hand on her knee in the darkness of the power cut.

'I don't want to get you into any trouble, but...' he said, lowering his voice and glancing beyond her shoulder in dramatic fashion in case anyone should overhear.

'*Trouble*, sir?' Cassie said, instantly on her guard.

'I noticed a blunder with one of your co-ordinates on the London South report that you completed this afternoon. I can see that you're new to the job, Cassie...' Eddie sighed like a patronising schoolteacher might when finding a spelling mistake. He gazed into her face, gestured, his hand brushing her sleeve. 'And I am happy to say nothing to Mr Frederick if...'

Cassie peered straight at him in disbelief, holding her ground, the bundle of bedding in her arms a buffer between them.

'If...?'

'We're all tired and lonely these days, aren't we?' He gave a confident jerk of his head towards one of the sleeping quarters, as if he thought she'd grasped his meaning.

Cassie stood perfectly still, fighting the impulse to run, to seek the sanctuary of the female dormitory.

'You obviously didn't realise, sir... Eddie,' she said, her voice clear amid the rumbling racket of the ventilator. 'Mr Frederick and I went through the final map and corrected the minor error together. He was happy with my work and sent it straight on to the Cabinet Room.'

Eddie drew his chin back in surprise, looking doubtful for a second, before grinning and nodding as if he already knew.

'I see... I see...' he uttered. 'Good to check these things.'

But Cassie saw bleak anger beneath his smile.

Eddie began to mumble about doing a thorough job and not letting the side down. Stooping somewhat as he must under the low ceiling of the sub-basement, he seemed diminished; his slicked-back hair had lost its sheen under the weak lighting. Dull, indeed, Cassie would be able to tell Esme. And deceitful. Eddie most probably had inserted the error himself on purpose to catch her out.

'If that's all,' Cassie said, 'I don't want to sound rude, but it has been a long day and I want to go to sleep.'

She walked away, and yet felt him move with her, as if he would escort her to the bunks.

Cassie stopped dead, and he almost bumped into her.

'Eddie, are you forgetting,' she said, her own brittle anger surfacing, 'the men's quarters are down that way?'

13

LONDON, NOVEMBER 1940

Cassie finished her 8 a.m. 'til 4 p.m. shift promptly that afternoon and, as she had two days off, caught the bus home through the foggy murk of the damp, autumnal blackout. Leaning her head against the window frame from her favourite top-deck seat, she sleepily spied a fragment of the street below around the edge of the blind. Hooded car headlights captured tiny darts of moisture in soupy-yellow beams and people, dark shapes muffled by hats and scarfs, shuffled head down, making their way home before 'the fireworks' started again.

It was strange, Cassie decided, what a person could get used to.

She shivered, and peered through the bus window, expecting to see the row of shops before her stop but she did not recognise the street. Ringing the bell, she made her way down the precarious spiral stair.

'Where are we?' she asked the bus conductor.

'Pimlico. We're all being diverted along Chelsea Embankment,' he said. 'Sloane Square Station took a direct hit this morning. Straight through that brand-spanking-new glass roof as the train was leaving the station – so our depot gaffer told us.'

Cassie could only thank him and utter futile sympathies. Finding a seat downstairs, among fellow resigned passengers, she fixed her jaw, determined not to think about what had happened to the people on the train at Sloane Square, simply making their way to work.

A newspaper headline back in September had irritated her:

Cockneys in the Fight – Homes Shattered, But Not Their Hearts.

But Cassie had thought, the reporter could not *genuinely* know how those ragged, sleepless people felt as they trekked away in their hundreds from their smashed houses and their wrecked lives. She looked at the faces around her on the bus, and knew she could never comprehend someone else's miseries, unless the very same had happened to her.

The bus pulled up near the Albert Bridge and Cassie alighted, wondering how much more of the map of London would change each day while she worked below in the bunker. She heard the Thames making an angry, rushing sound in the chilled darkness as it flowed around Cadogan Pier; she'd forgotten how cold it always felt by the river. Even so, she was grateful for it sharpening her senses as she made her way past the sublime patrician houses of Cheyne Row.

Letting herself in with her latch key, she noticed lamplight glowing around the half-closed, drawing-room door. Cassie pushed it open.

'Hello, Luke, how are—'

She stopped in the doorway, jolted, exclaiming in surprise. Her father was sitting in the armchair by the fire, his fair hair brightened by the flames, looking very much at home, smoking and reading yesterday's newspaper.

'Cassie, there you are, thank God.' He got up, stubbed out his cigarette and strode over towards her. 'You look astonished. Are you all right? I heard about the bomb at Sloane Square, and guessed it was your nearest station. That's why I came over. I needed to check. The cut-and-cover lines are really not safe. You weren't anywhere near there, were you...?'

'But how?' Cassie stuttered in confusion, her mind whirring as her father gripped the tops of her arms and hugged her. 'How?'

'Mrs Ennis let me in, and very kindly lit the fire,' he said. 'Dubois is still at work, I believe. But never mind that. It is very good to see you, at long last. You have become quite the stranger, haven't you?'

Cassie found she could not look at him; his presence, unexpected and invasive, set off sparks of memory: half-happy, half-appalling.

'I have telephoned this house several times these last few months, you know, worried sick with all this madness going on,' he went on, sounding puzzled. 'The housekeeper said she would leave you a message...?'

Cassie went over to the other armchair to hide the look of shame on her face. Mrs Ennis had certainly left her messages on the telephone pad to say that her father had called, and Cassie had torn each sheet off and secreted it in her pocket, hoping Luke hadn't seen it first. For, without doubt, he would gently berate her for ignoring her father.

'Sorry, Dad, I have been extremely tied up with my job, and my...' Cassie trailed off, too drained and bewildered to explain.

'I know, that is what your mother has said. She has told me not to make a nuisance of myself and distract you. I understand.

I didn't want to bother you, but the bomb this morning at Sloane Square was too much. I had to see you. To make sure you are all right.' Her father sat down opposite her. 'I haven't seen you in so long.'

His gaze lingered in an unnervingly accusing manner and Cassie garnered her strength to meet it. He looked a tad thinner, his hair sparser than she remembered. His hands as pale as they'd been when intertwined with Aunt Juno's hair. Cassie swallowed; she wanted to cry.

'And I am not at all sure why you choose to live here,' he went on, like he did when telling her off as a little girl. 'Why wouldn't you want to live at home? All your things are still there, Cassie. Your bedroom is exactly the same. And I have a perfectly good Anderson shelter in the garden. I had the gardener help me dig up my lawn. Can you believe that? I understand from Mrs Ennis that here, you make use of the kitchen table.'

'It's perfectly safe, Dad. A good, old, solid heirloom, in the basement.'

'Is Dubois charging rent? Can you afford it?'

'Luke and I have an arrangement,' she said, and her father lifted an eyebrow. 'I am earning two pounds, ten shillings a week now,' she continued quickly, feeling an unwelcome blush spread over her cheeks, hating having to explain. 'And I *like* living here. I am a grown-up now, Dad.' She tried to soften her voice, laugh a little.

'Be that as it may,' he said, his concern tempered a little. 'A father can ask after his daughter's welfare, can't he?' He glanced at his watch. 'Look, it's still early. Let me take you out to dinner. You love Beauville's, don't you, although they only have a set menu these days.'

'How can we go to dinner,' Cassie asked, aghast, 'when people are dying on their way to work?'

'Fair point,' he said with a look of admiration.

Against her instinct for respect and courtesy, Cassie wished her father would say goodbye and leave.

'I say, Cassie,' he declared, 'Mrs Ennis poured me a drink, and it needs refreshing. Looks like you need one? A gin and tonic?'

Cassie mumbled that she did. Perhaps a snifter would calm her down, help her sleep later.

'No lemons or ice, but there we are,' he said brightly.

Cassie looked up at him through her lowered lids, almost daring herself to watch as he busied himself at Luke's drinks trolley. While the coal in the grate crackled gently and her father clattered the tumblers, she remembered the oddly tender way that Aunt Juno had made his gin and tonics at Greenaways, slowly paring the lemon rind and rubbing it around the rim of the glass. She pictured the times her aunt had glanced at her father as if on the verge of fury; her aunt gliding around in her sensual, floating gowns, as if to entice him, enrage him. Admiring the roses in the dark. Herself, stumbling into Egerton Terrace in the blackout.

Swallowing the rotten lump clogging in her throat, Cassie took the tumbler from her father, thanking him.

'Cheers,' he said, settling himself back in the armchair and glancing around the softly lit room, the panels a rich corn-flower-blue in the shadows. 'Dubois certainly has a very nice place here, I must say. And the Buckinghamshire property...' He let out an admiring whistle. 'The family is richer than God, Uncle Charles tells me. No wonder the divorce was a bloody bitter battle. With Madam Dubois flitting off like that. I suppose you were too young to remember...'

But Cassie knew and understood all too well Luke's misdi-rected pain that summer at Greenaways.

'Luke does not talk about it,' she said.

'Well, well, it's all water under the bridge anyway,' said her father, appearing barely interested. 'We can certainly stay here 'til Goering sends the bombers in again, and then we must find a shelter. A *proper* shelter. South Ken Underground is a brisk walk away, but there is always *home*, Cassie.'

'Dad, I always feel perfectly safe here,' she said, although this was not entirely true.

He sipped his drink, appraising her. 'How is your job going, my dear?'

'I can't really—' she began.

'I'm sorry. Silly me,' he said. 'I shouldn't ask. I realise how sensitive the information you are dealing with is. And how harrowing it must be, Cassie. I simply want to know that you are doing okay. You do look tired and pale. Mum is worried about you. We all are.'

'It is the shift work,' she offered, trying to rally herself and keep her mind in the present, the conversation at an acceptable level. 'I have been working mostly nights and, when the raids are particularly bad, I haven't been able to get home. We sleep there in the dormitory in the sub-basement. It is horrible, but at least I feel relatively protected down there.' As long as Eddie wasn't around, she thought.

Cassie paused, thinking about the peculiar, secure feeling the dank little basement gave her, despite it being so grotty. How she felt especially safe if, on her way, she caught the distinctive whiff of the PM's cigar smoke along the corridor or heard his comforting, rumbling voice from inside his quarters. She glanced at her father, instantly aware that it would nearly be a year since she had last felt reassured by his presence. And how she could never do so again.

'I feel I am living like a mole,' Cassie said. 'At least now for the next few days, I can snatch a little sunlight.'

'No wonder you look tired.' Her father glanced at her, as if noticing for the first time the extent of her exhaustion. 'We are certainly in the thick of it, aren't we?' he went on, sipping his drink. 'Every aspect of life, impacted. With the docks devastated, my firm are under the cosh, normal procedures turned on their head. As for the submarines stalking the Atlantic...'

He drifted, glanced past her, and Cassie knew that he was thinking about the convoys. Thinking about Gerard.

'I'm proud of you,' he said brightly, but Cassie heard a break in his voice, noticed unexpected emotion surge over his face. And yet, she felt too confused, too angry with him to feel sorry for him worrying about Gerard, or to accept his praise.

Steering the conversation to routine detail, she told her father that she had been working on maps these past few months but was due to go back to the Typing Room soon. Possibly before Christmas.

'My friend Esme misses me. Miss Redmond misses me,' she said.

'I don't doubt they do.' Her father's eyes flickered. He looked pensive, his features clouding with contrition. Perhaps, Cassie supposed, he was thinking of her mother, or more likely Juno.

'And they fit their bombing raids around the river tides,' she said. 'When they know the Thames is low, they hit the docks, making it more difficult for the firemen to get the water.'

'My goodness, I had no idea...'

'And Mr Churchill has put out a directive: St Paul's must be saved. At any cost.'

'Christ almighty, of course he has.' Her father flicked his lighter and sucked greedily on another cigarette. 'As for what happened at Coventry. A fire storm, I heard. No wonder we drink.'

In the past, his comment would have made Cassie laugh, eased her mind. But now, it seemed that nothing he could say would help.

They both fell quiet, the street outside, silent. It felt far too peaceful. Cassie listened, fearing the siren.

The door to the drawing room moved an inch and Kipling nudged his way in, seeking the warmth of the fire. He rubbed his body around Cassie's calves once or twice in his usual obligatory fashion, leaving a drift of fur on her stockings, before settling on the rug.

'As we aren't going for dinner, shall I rustle us up some omelettes, Dad?'

'My goodness,' he exclaimed, over-jovial, 'what a wonderful idea. I'm famished. Come on, I will give you a hand.'

* * *

Downstairs in the kitchen, Luke had left a note by the kettle to say that he would not be home until late. Cassie's father, offering to make the tea, spotted it. And, filling the kettle and setting it on the hob, he said, 'We *are* curious, Cassie, *surprised*, as to why are you living here with Dubois.'

'Who is *we*?' Cassie asked, her scalp stinging in irritation, clattering the bowl as she whisked eggs with a spoonful of milk to make them go further.

'Your mother, Charles and Juno. And Marianne, I expect.'

Cassie tensed with anger at the way he said her aunt's name, seeming to relish it. Outrage blinded her for a moment. She kept her back to him, swirling melting lard in the frying pan.

'Luke is my friend. I am his lodger,' she offered, conscious that she was repeating herself, hating having to explain. The omelette spat and bubbled in the pan, speckles of fat landing on her hand.

She put the plates down in silence. Her father poured out the tea, cut into his omelette, and Cassie hoped he would drop the subject.

'But, Cassie, what will people think? It does seem rather improper.'

'Are you saying people are gossiping about me?' Cassie retorted.

'The simple question is, I suppose, why you won't live at home? It's but a short hop and a skip away.' He gave her an encouraging smile across the table. 'I won't charge you rent, you know.'

Cassie forced her own smile. 'I want my independence, Dad. Lots of girls my age live away. Especially now. Look at Marianne; she is billeted in Margate. There's no gossip about her, I take it.'

'Apart from her and Harry Brough being sweet on each other.'

'Luke Dubois and I are not sweet on each other, I assure you.' She laughed lightly, trying to pacify him. 'And, as you know, my job... I have been caught up with so many things. I speak to Mum whenever I can.' And yet it had become a very rare occurrence indeed.

'But she hasn't seen you, *I* haven't seen you – not since last Christmas, Cassie.' He sounded plaintive, hurt. 'And here we are. It's already November.'

She swallowed a bite of omelette, not daring herself to speak, feeling her eyes smart as the unsettling image of the last time *she* had seen her father returned.

'No argument, I will take you to Greenaways for Christmas,' he continued, now half-angry, half-exasperated, like he had been when she or Gerard had misbehaved as children. 'I assume you will have some days off? Let me know, and I will pick you up early on Christmas Eve, so you have no need to worry about train fares. Your mother will love to see you.'

Cassie did not doubt it. She nodded, to appease him, but she had no idea about taking any leave over Christmas; it seemed such a trivial thing to be even considering.

Supper finished, although Cassie had barely tasted the omelette, they washed up, their conversation veering on to Marianne and Harry, and how their romance had blossomed over the year. The schoolboys had soon caught on to it, apparently, making up little chants and singing them up the stairs and around the breakfast table about Miss Greenaway and Mr Brough 'sitting in a tree'.

As they both laughed softly, Cassie remembered how she used to enjoy her father's company, and yet as soon as she relaxed into it, the pain of what he had done returned to bite her, exhausting her.

They sat back upstairs until the clock in the Dubois drawing room chimed for nine o'clock. No sirens had sounded, and Cassie longed for her bed in the attic room, to sink into sleep with Kipling curled at her feet.

'I better take my leave,' her father said, gathering his coat and scarf. 'But I will telephone soon about arrangements for Christmas Eve. Be prepared for the journey, Cassie, for I can guess it will be lengthy. Every Tom, Dick and Harry will want to be out of London.'

Cassie followed him to the front door, and he pecked her cheek goodbye as if all was well and normal in the world. But Cassie's world had shattered long ago.

'Dad, I don't want to go to Greenaways,' she said. 'I won't be coming.'

He stopped halfway down the steps, turning in surprise.

'But Cassie, *why*?' he said aghast, peering up at her in the gloom. 'Look, I know everything is difficult these days but think of your mother. She won't have seen you or Gerard in a year. It's unlikely he will make it home for Christmas again, so the least you could do is spend some time with her.'

But Cassie *did* think of her mother, and the tender, bewildered look on her face when she thought no one was looking. Cassie thought of the ways her mother tried her best for her father, whether putting on a nice new dress, or baking his favourite pudding. She remembered the vulnerability and the shame in her mother's eyes when she had glanced down at her own feet, that summer long ago, after Aunt Juno had insinuated that they were big and, Cassie was sure, ugly in her mother's mind.

Cassie hated Juno. And she hated her father for his betrayal, his stupidity and his arrogance. But, standing on the doorstep at Cheyne Row, even hating him felt confusing and wrong. As if somehow, it had become Cassie's fault.

'I'm not coming to Greenaways, Dad, because I know.'

'Know what?' His face looked crooked, his mouth working, his eyes piercing up at her from beneath the rim of his hat.

'I know about you and Aunt Juno,' she said, her legs weakening but her voice as clear as a bell. 'And I don't want to come home, or go to Greenaways. Or go anywhere with you.'

'*What*?'

'I saw you in bed together. And I don't want to see either of you ever again.'

He began to walk back up the steps. 'Oh, Cassie, really, I—'

She slammed the door shut and turned for the stairs, the sound of it reverberating through her bones. As she reached the landing, he began to bang the knocker, and she heard a thin, disembodied version of his voice, pleading, 'Cassie, Cassie. Can I talk to you? Cassie?'

But she carried on up to her attic room, where in the darkness, Kipling lay as a soft mound on her bed. High up here, at the top of the house, at least she could no longer hear her father calling her name. Here, even if the sirens sounded, she would feel detached and alone, yes, but safe from any more harm.

PART II

14

LONDON, MAY 1941

Cassie had no idea how long she had been sitting on the bench in St James's Park.

From time to time, she looked up to watch the ducks dabbling in the pond while the sun came lazily out from behind the clouds over Mayfair and went back in again. But mostly, she stared down at her hands clutched on her lap, at the fingertips that had typed out the report, and the truth, in stark, precise, horrifying black and white:

HMS Westray... 52 degrees north latitude, 11 degrees west longitude... Lost with all hands.

And Miss Redmond asking her, 'Miss Marsh? Cassandra? This report. Do you... do you know this ship...?'

Cassie shivered despite the spring sunshine, the chill coming from inside her. She felt a desperate instinct that she was wasting time, that she ought to get going, be somewhere else. But she had no idea where to go, or how to get there. She glanced around the park, as if to seek support. A handful of people, some in uniform, some in ordinary clothes, were on their way to appointments or taking mid-morning strolls around the pond. But how could anyone possibly help her? There was nothing any of them could do.

Cassie stood up, as dazed and as vulnerable as a baby learning to walk. She realised that, among strangers' faces, she had been looking for Oliver. He would understand; his presence would be enough. But how ridiculous, she chided herself; her cousin was fighting with the army in the Western Desert. And, besides, she must remember, when she cut herself off from her father and her family, this had to mean Oliver too. When Oliver had visited Cheyne Row last September, her secret had sat like poison on the tip of her tongue. She had been in danger of hurting him with what she knew about their parents, and she could not put herself in that position again.

Cassie took a huge, ragged breath, and tentatively headed off along the path. She felt small and transparent. Such an insignificant wisp of a girl that any gust of wind would blow her clean over.

* * *

As Cassie let herself in the front door of Cheyne Row, it felt odd to be arriving there in the middle of the day, and she wondered how on earth she had managed the short journey on the bus. Miss Redmond and the girls in the Typing Room had urged her to go home, but even the Dubois house could not be her sanctuary for long.

An incendiary had hit the chimney pots above her bed during 'The Wednesday' raid a month ago, damaging the roof. Thank goodness, Luke had said, it had been while they were both out and he had begun to look for somewhere else for them to live until repairs could be done. The point of fixing the roof when bombs could fall again any day, at any time, was lost on

Cassie, but she had felt too resigned to reason with him and had moved her things down to a bedroom on the second floor.

Lying on top of the covers now, Cassie curled herself up. She had made it here, the first step 'home', but had no idea what to do now. The telegram would arrive at Egerton Terrace in due course, courtesy of naval bureaucracy, she thought, staring dry-eyed at the wall, but what about the meantime?

She thought for one blissful moment that she might fall asleep. At least, then the agony and the aching numbness might momentarily disappear. But she could not sleep, and the pain stayed with her, a chilling, suffocating shroud, with the words, *Lost with all hands* rolling through her mind.

Half an hour, an hour later, Cassie could not be sure, she heard a vehicle pull up outside, car doors slam, and a woman's cheerful voice saying, 'Thank you,' followed by footfalls up the steps to the front door. Cassie sat up, straining to listen as a key turned in the lock downstairs. Someone had arrived in a taxicab and let themselves in.

She went out of the bedroom, stood at the top of the stairs and peered down into the hallway. A petite woman in a spring coat, heels, and elaborately perched hat stood leafing through the post on the telephone table. What Cassie could see of her dark hair was punctuated with confident streaks of grey over her temples; her skirt beneath the coat was certainly not 'Utility' but light wool, draped and silky.

By the front door stood a suitcase and a cat basket.

'Hello?' Cassie said, her voice rasping with fatigue. The effort of her greeting wearing her out, she sat down on the top step.

The woman jumped, turned, stared up at her and broke into a wide, red-lipsticked smile.

'Oh, are you Cassie? You look as pretty as I imagined. Anthea

McKinnon. Dubois as was.' She held her hand out as if Cassie would be able to reach it and shake it in greeting. 'Lucien's mother,' she said, introducing herself. 'He speaks so highly of you.' She peered quizzically. 'Why are you sitting up there?'

'I have just heard about my brother, and I don't know what to do.'

'Oh, my dear.'

Anthea came quickly up the stairs and sat beside Cassie, holding both of her hands in hers. It seemed she didn't need to ask *what* had happened to her brother.

'My goodness how cold you are,' she said, her voice calm and reassuring and, for such a slight woman, rich and mellow. 'First thing you do is get into bed, and I will make a hot water bottle.'

Cassie thought it a silly idea. She simply wanted to remain there at the top of the stairs, feeling the comforting texture of Anthea Dubois's fine cotton lace gloves rubbing her hands, and breathing in her powdery-scented perfume. If she stayed like that, frozen and immobile, then she wouldn't have to tell anyone else about Gerard and perhaps it would cease to be true.

'Come on.' Anthea stood up and, surprisingly strong, hauled Cassie to her feet. 'Which bedroom? You're no longer in the attic, I take it? I hear you've been bombed out up there.'

Glancing at her, Cassie noticed in her surprisingly young-looking face a little, pointed nose and large, brown eyes – even darker than Luke's – and she had the clearest skin Cassie had ever seen. Anthea must have been a child bride, she decided, and then remembered how young her mother had been when she had married her father. She clenched Anthea's hands.

'The bedroom on the second floor, at the front,' she uttered.

'Ah, Lucien's old nursery whenever we were in town. Come on.'

Anthea made Cassie put her dressing gown on over her clothes and get into bed, tucking the covers around her.

'Back in a sec.'

She left the room, and Cassie could hear her calling for Kipling as she went down the stairs. Presently, she came back in with a hot water bottle and a hot toddy.

'I've raided my former husband's whisky,' she said with a naughty giggle. 'If I am to be labelled the scarlet woman for leaving Lucien's father, then I may as well make the most of it.' She plumped pillows behind Cassie's back, handing her the tumbler. 'Sip that. Let it sink in.'

Anthea sat in the chair in the corner, pulled the pins from her hat, removed it and began to sift through the post, opening the odd letter here and there – Cassie assumed the ones addressed to her – and uttering little exclamations. Cassie rested back against the pillows, sipping the warm liquid. It offered her faltering darts of comfort, but this did not feel right, and she fought the sensation.

Luke's mother, she decided, was a woman whose hair, with its dark and grey streaks, always looked wonderful, even though she had just taken her hat off.

'May I ask—' she started.

'Of course.'

'Why are you here, Mrs... um...?'

'Call me Anthea, dear. It is much easier,' she said. 'I'm here to collect the rest of my things. When Lucien wrote to me about the damage, I thought that it was high time I came for the last of my belongings. I needed to be in London to sign off something boring with the solicitor, anyway, which is where I was this morning. Plus, I want to take Kipling back with me. London is no place for a cat these days. He will be fine on the Sleeper, I'm sure. I've got about two hours while my driver has his afternoon break. He'll take my luggage to King's Cross. I am due to have dinner with friends, then... Oh my dear, you don't want to hear about all my nonsense, do you?'

'Oh, I don't mind.' Listening to Anthea chatter helped Cassie feel like she might manage to peer through a black cloud, although something horrendous still hovered at the corner of her eye. 'So, it wasn't a cab that I heard?'

Anthea blushed, dipped her head. 'No, I have a driver whenever I am in London. I know, I know, a terrible extravagance in wartime, but he is an honest, loyal chap, Wickham, has been with me for a long while. He can fit ferrying me from place to place around his ARP duties.'

Cassie sipped at her toddy, relishing an insight into Luke's infamous mother's life.

'Where do you live now, Anthea?'

'Edinburgh. In New Town, it's a delightful spot. A nice view of the Castle,' she said, and gave Cassie a searching look. 'I take it you know what happened five years ago?'

Unsure whether to say how much she knew, Cassie gave half a nod, half a shake of her head.

'I'm now married to Max McKinnon, or "the Scottish man" as people say, talking about him as if he is some sort of unmentionable Macbeth.' Anthea gave a light laugh. 'I fell in love, Cassie, and that was the problem. It was horrendous. I felt awful about it, and what it did to Lucien, and to his father. Lucien went to Greenaways that summer, I'm sure you remember? Your aunt and uncle, your whole family were very good to him.'

Cassie winced; at times, none of them had been entirely patient with Luke.

'As he has been to me, here,' Cassie said. 'He gave me a place to stay when I started my job...' She did not wish to elaborate.

Anthea gave her a puzzled smile, as if sensing something

more. 'He enjoys your company. He has said as much to me when he writes. Poor boy. He is settled now, but he has been through it, and I think he was made to suffer unduly. As soon as it became clear to his father what had happened between Max and me, I was out,' she said. 'And I mean *out*. I had to leave... Of course, I *wanted* to leave but I wasn't given the opportunity to help Lucien through it. I was not allowed to speak to him for at least a year.'

Cassie set her cup down, considering the entirely new take on the Dubois divorce.

'But you have managed to renew your relationship with Luke... Lucien?' she asked shakily. It had been months since she'd told her father she never wanted to see him again, and she had not stopped wondering how the situation would ever be resolved.

'We have. We talked, Lucien and I. We have indeed... an understanding... But of course, my name is mud with the rest of the family. There's not a lot I can do about that but give it time.' Anthea stirred herself. 'Do you need anything else at the moment, Cassie, for I want to start having a rummage? I won't be taking much, just some evening gowns, and shoes, and books that belonged to my mother in the library here. And also, believe it or not, a little painting that Lucien's father gave me on our wedding day. I want it because at the time, it meant so much. He would not let me take a bean from the country house.'

'I might try to sleep,' Cassie said, although knowing she could not. 'And decide what to do.'

Anthea flashed her a concerned look. 'Your family home is only in South Ken, isn't it? Is your father still there?'

Cassie nodded, squeezing her eyes shut for a moment. She gave in, and lay down.

'I'll leave you to rest and come back up shortly. If there is anything else I can do...' Anthea's gaze acknowledged Cassie's pain. 'Now, where is the damn cat...' She walked out of the door, making a kissing noise with her mouth, calling lightly for Kipling.

Cassie sat up. 'Oh, Anthea, did Luke not tell you?' she called. 'Kipling went missing the day the house was damaged. During the awful raids in April. We haven't seen him since.'

Anthea gasped, came back into the room, her face pale.

'Oh no, not my little one...'

The ache in Anthea's voice, the way she struggled to contain her sorrow, stung Cassie. She remembered, then, that Luke had wanted to tell his mother face to face about poor Kipling.

Guilt, an overwhelming grief, scorched a deep, searing channel through her.

Cassie erupted into tears, pressing her hands over face, doubling over on the bed. Her crying, a terrifying melding of pain and fear, seemed to break off parts of her. The scale and pitch of her cries frightened her, immobilised her until there seemed to be no point in trying to do anything else.

She felt Anthea sit beside her on the bed, her hand on her shoulder.

'This isn't necessarily for the cat is it, Cassie?' she asked gently, her voice honeyed. 'It's for your brother...'

'Of course it is!' cried Cassie, her face still pressed into the covers. 'But I cannot see my father. I cannot see my parents.' Her voice came out as a hollow wail. 'How can I go to them with the news about Gerard, when I haven't spoken to them in so long?'

'Oh, my dear...'

'My mother will hate me. My father will hate me even more than he does now. I can't go home. I can't face them.'

Cassie sensed Anthea wanting to ask, but how could Cassie begin to explain the reason why she had cut herself off, had untethered herself from everyone in an act of such anger, embarrassment, self-preservation?

Anthea said, instead, 'I understand that Lucien is looking for somewhere else for you both to live. And, until then, you know you can stay here as long as you like, as long as it is comfortable.' She stopped to peer at Cassie, as if to make sure she was listening. 'He thinks the world of you, you know. But I also feel sure that now you need to be with your family.'

'My mother is at Greenaways, and the telegram will reach my father soon enough,' came Cassie's muffled response.

'Possibly not. Max's son, William, was killed at Dunkirk, but we thought he had made it home, during that utterly confusing time, because we didn't hear. It was only weeks afterward... Some sort of muck up. And there we were, living our lives, carrying on, not knowing. Max was tormented with guilt when he found out.' Anthea paused. 'I think you know, Cassie, you can't leave it to the telegram.'

Cassie lifted her sodden face, blinked fresh tears out of her eyes, and whispered, 'I am sorry about Max's son. I am so sorry about Kipling.'

Anthea's eyes glistened.

'Now, Cassie,' she said firmly, jutting her chin, 'do you think your father will be at home? Remember, it is a Saturday. Yes? Pack a small bag, my dear. All my stuff can wait. I can catch the Sleeper back any time. I will ask Wickham to drive you home, and if necessary, he can drive you and your father to Devon, to your mother.'

'I can't tell him,' Cassie uttered. 'I can't see him.'

'Then I will,' said Anthea. 'I will come with you, and I will break it to him. It might be better coming from a stranger, don't you think?'

'I... I really don't know.'

'Neither do I, really,' said Anthea.

Cassie stared at Luke's mother, seeking her friendship, her confidence. 'Could it... could it possibly be a mistake?'

'Only you know that,' she said gently. 'You deal with these reports every day, don't you?'

Cassie nodded and began to cry again, weakly, at her own futility.

'Come on,' said Anthea. 'Let's do this one thing at a time. Get out of bed, Cassie, and wash your face. Then let's see if you can pack a bag.'

* * *

As Anthea's driver made his way past the Brompton Hospital and up the Fulham Road towards South Kensington, Cassie noticed intermittent damage where bombs had fallen with deadly precision on every other street. Whole terraces remained intact and pristine as if there was no such thing as war, until the one gaping hole in the centre of a façade, and a family's life torn open, exposed it for the world to see. Egerton Terrace appeared unscathed, as serene as it had ever been, but what did that matter when Gerard could never, would never, come home again?

The car slowed down outside her house, drawing up behind her father's car. Cassie glanced up at the clear sky, the afternoon sun flickering at her through the trees and, for a moment, felt consoled by its warmth. The driver cranked the handbrake and Anthea, next to her on the back seat, patted her hand, pulling her back to the brutality of here and now.

'I'll go and knock on the door,' she whispered. 'Follow when you feel ready.'

Cassie, watching through the car window as Anthea went up

the steps to her childhood home, remembered gangly, loose-limbed Gerard – in shorts and school cap – sliding down the handrail, whooping loudly, to execute a perfect dismount onto the pavement, his cap still in place. And her mother, scolding him from the front door but laughing too much for her reproach to have any effect, while gripping hold of little Cassie as she tried to hook her leg over the rail to copy him.

Cassie looked back up at the sky, wondering if Gerard, on board *HMS Westray*, had known he had been about to die; whether he thought of his home here, of their long summer holidays, their last Christmas together at Greenaways. Had he remembered, had he *known*, how much they all loved him?

Her father opened the front door, unshaven, pale and looking undernourished, and in need of a haircut. Cassie's stomach jolted in agony, in pity, as she watched his expression change from curiosity as he greeted Anthea with a cocking of his head, to disbelief and distress. His mouth dropped open as he listened and recoiled. He looked puzzled, shaking his head, peering past Anthea's shoulder when she indicated the car. Spotting Cassie sitting in the back seat, he shuffled down the steps in his slippers, calling her name.

The driver leapt out of the car to perform his duty, but her father uttered, 'I can open a car door myself, man.' He leant inside the vehicle, his eyes sharp, his pain manifesting as anger, his face as crumpled as old parchment. 'Come inside, Cassie, for the love of God.'

She followed him in a stupor up to the front door, the past whirring beside her, offering memories, laughter and a repeat of the terrible, twisting devastation the last time she'd been home. The hallway smelt of stale cigarette smoke, her father's shoes lay kicked into a corner and unread post peppered the floor beneath the console. She glanced at the coat stand, in fear of seeing something of Juno's: a fur, a shawl, one of her horrible floppy hats. Through the open dining-room door, Cassie spotted a clutter of dirty plates and an empty whisky bottle on the table.

Her father showed Anthea through to the sitting room, and held the door for Cassie as if she would not know the way.

'Excuse the mess in here,' he said, heading for the drink's table. 'I can't get a daily woman to stay. Sit down please, Mrs Dubois— Sorry, um Mrs... a gin and tonic?'

'It's McKinnon now,' Anthea said, taking a seat. 'And it's Anthea, please.'

Cassie, conforming on reflex, also sat, and her father, seeming to forget what he was doing, plonked himself on the sofa opposite, leaning forward, his long arms resting on his knees. It struck Cassie how alike Gerard and her father were. Why had she never noticed before?

'Cassie,' he said, peering at her, his voice grainy. 'Can you tell me precisely what you know?'

She nodded, her mouth dry; she had not said a word since she and Anthea had left Cheyne Row.

'A report came through,' she said, her tongue stiff, as if she had forgotten how to talk. 'And I began to type it up, but within moments, I realised what... who. I hoped straight away that it was wrong. A mistake. A lie.' She held her father's gaze longer than she wanted to. 'I couldn't believe it. But I knew. I knew.' She uttered the name of the ship. 'Lost with all hands.'

Her father flinched, groaned, pressing his palms together between his knees, chafing them over and over.

'I assume there will be a telegram, Cassie?' Anthea prompted.

'Yes, yes,' she said, feeling nausea rising in a cold, anxious spasm through her stomach, 'from the Admiralty.'

'Gerard changed Greenaways to be the contact address,' her

father said. 'When he realised that more of us were likely to be there in the circumstances...'

Cassie stared into his eyes and saw in them a double layer of anguish.

'We need to get down to Greenaways,' he said. 'I must get to your mother. My goodness, we must get there before the telegram.'

Anthea said, 'My driver Wickham will gladly drive you.'

'No, no.' Cassie's father stood up and paced to the window and back again. 'I will drive. I will do what I am supposed to do as a father. As a husband.'

Cassie could not bear to watch him, and stared instead at the rug, at the photographs on the mantel, at her mother's favourite armchair, the wireless in the corner, as if she no longer recognised them. Along the bookshelf, neatly arranged, was Gerard's collection of *Sherlock Holmes* stories.

Anthea, seeing the look on Cassie's face, came to sit beside her, her soft voice asking if there was there anything else she needed, anything at all?

Cassie gazed at Anthea, shaking her head.

'No,' she said, trying to smile, her numbness returning to protect her. 'Nothing at all...' She caught Anthea's eye, wondering how she could ask for the impossible.

'I will let Lucien know, of course,' Anthea said. 'I'm sure he will be in touch at once.'

Cassie had no doubt. Luke would easily step in to the practicalities, mastering the logistics, making plans for her welfare. But how could Cassie say that she also wanted Oliver? He would support her simply by being by her side. If only she could tell him why she needed him: his understanding and his trust. Layers of confusion and panic built up inside her like rock strata smothering her core, while tears seeped silently from her eyes. My, how she needed Oliver now.

But she wiped her eyes and pressed Anthea's hand. 'We looked for Kipling, you know,' she said. 'We searched for days, up and down the street. Knocking on doors. But it was no use. And I am so desperately sorry.'

'Please, Cassie,' Anthea said. 'Please don't worry.'

'It's just that... we miss him terribly.'

* * *

They drove through the night, the highways becoming byways, the early-summer dawn rising stealthily and clear, a half-light which seemed to linger as they went mile upon mile into deep countryside. Until in an instant, the day arrived, and the car nosed its way down familiar, rich-green lanes.

As she watched through the car window, Cassie's childhood journeys to Greenaways clustered together as one. The drowsiness, mild hunger, the vague, uncomfortable sensation of travelling, the excitement, the marvel at arriving somewhere sublime, her very own heaven, having left all her day-to-day troubles and grumbles behind. But that feeling had now been eradicated, and she had never sat in the passenger seat before. If Gerard had been with them, she thought, he'd have plenty of room to stretch out on the back seat. Her father, by now, would have said, *Not long to go.*

They approached the crossroads, where four lanes met at the little grassy rise, the signpost on top. But Cassie's father did not slow the car, hardly took his foot off the pedal. He steered down the unmarked track and drove on in silence.

Bumping through the gates at Greenaways, tyres crunching gravel, he cleared his throat, breaking hours of silence.

'It is... Cassie...' He sounded broken, his words dropping like shards of glass. '...with your aunt and I... it has been extremely... complicated.'

Her anger surged, reviving her, snapping like elastic.

'Define *complicated*,' she said through her teeth.

'I can't really explain now. We don't have time. Look, we're here. Maybe later, I will sit down with you, and we can talk it through...' His voice trailed off. 'First things first, we need to see your mother.'

'You've had the whole journey to explain yourself to me,' Cassie said evenly.

'I understand why you are angry,' he said and exhaled a shattered groan. 'I am an undoubted coward.'

He parked the car, cranking on the handbrake. Cassie remained still, her stomach churning, her limbs frozen in protest, staring through the windscreen. Her mother's quizzical face popped up at Aunt Juno's parlour window where she must have been taking breakfast. A moment later, Juno appeared beside her, immediately ducking away.

'There she is,' Cassie whispered. 'There they both are.'

The front door opened, and her mother emerged in her slippers and dressing gown, her hair under her scarf in curlers. She hurried forward, her face fixed in a wide but hesitant smile, staring at them while they remained sitting in the car, confusion flickering around her eyes.

'I think we must have beaten the telegram,' Cassie's father uttered.

Juno appeared at the front door, waiting. Cassie glared at her, trying to deduce whether she knew that Cassie knew. And yet her aunt remained inscrutable. Puzzled and furious, she seemed, at their unexpected arrival, and yet giving nothing else away.

Cassie glanced at her father beside her in the car and then at her mother's face as she dipped her head down to peer through the window, rapping it playfully with her knuckle.

'Rich, Cassie, why are you here?' Her mother's voice became thin, frightened and childlike through the glass. 'What's going on?'

An elongating sensation enveloped Cassie, grasping her, pulling her in two opposite directions. Love for her mother, love for her family. Grief solidified into rage, and it could not be sustained – none of it. Clammy sweat prickled over her scalp as if she were about to vomit.

'If you haven't given up Juno already, Dad,' she whispered, staring straight ahead, dry-eyed, furious and guttural, 'and told her that it is over between you, that it is utterly wrong and is never going to happen again, then you must do so. You must tell her, Dad. Put a stop to it. Today.'

15

DEVON, AUGUST 1941

The church at Eastcombe sat on a hill a short distance from the village, its squat, stone tower shimmering in sunlight against the rippling, purple carpet of moorland beyond. Cassie hadn't been here for a long while; she hadn't been brought up in a particularly 'churchy' way, and her aunt and uncle hadn't insisted she went with them when they came to worship on Sundays. But she remembered the August Lammas Fairs on the village green, when the folks of Eastcombe celebrated the first harvest, and summer fetes: sunny afternoons playing tombola or throwing rings over sticks, with Gerard, Oliver and Marianne.

'Here we are,' Luke said unnecessarily, parking his car in the layby.

He tucked it close to the hedge, as Charles had instructed; the lane up to the church simply wasn't wide enough for two vehicles to pass each other with ease. Killing the engine, he glanced around at Cassie sitting in the back seat and gave her a questioning smile.

She offered him her usual nod to indicate that all was well, even when it wasn't.

'Thank you for driving us, Luke,' said Cassie's mother, sitting beside her.

Juno in the passenger seat also offered her thanks but, despite it being Marianne's wedding day, a positive boost for everyone in the months after Gerard's death, she seemed unable to raise much of a smile. Cassie, noticing her aunt's usual fiery edge extinguished, put it down to her father having done as she'd insisted. And yet that possibility did not do much to make her feel any better.

Luke got out of the car and, dapper in his immaculate suit, hurried around the front to open the passenger door for Juno. He returned swiftly, ever chivalrous, to give Cassie's mother a hand. Cassie opened her own door, not wanting to linger a moment more inside the car breathing in the smell of her aunt's perfume.

'Can you manage, Cassie?' Luke asked. 'I haven't left you much room.'

'I'm fine,' she said, even though she had to squeeze out and caught her sleeve on the hedge.

Luke lifted his elbow for her to take, and they strolled up the lane – like 'the old married couple' Luke often teased that they'd become – while Cassie's mother and Juno trotted off ahead, clamping their hats to their heads as the steady breeze came off the moors.

Juno had piled her long hair into a knot and seemed to have chosen an especially out-of-fashion cloche to wear. Cassie's mother, on the other hand, had bought herself a smart new outfit and hat. Any unsuspecting guest from Harry Brough's side would think that *she,* and not Juno, was mother-of-the-bride.

Earlier, as they had readied themselves to leave for East-combe, Juno had suggested: 'Miranda, you must sit in the front passenger seat.'

'No, you should, Juno. You're the bride's mother,' she had argued, and they had danced around each other in an odd contest of courtesy.

Juno, it felt to Cassie, had stopped short of saying, *But, Miranda, you should... you have lost your son...*

With Cassie adding in her mind, *And you, Juno, have been sleeping with my father.*

Her mother had slipped into the back seat to settle the matter.

Watching her now, walking up to the church beside her sister-in-law, Cassie hoped, with all her might, that she was none the wiser about Juno. For how could her mother possibly bear that too?

Since the dreadful news about Gerard, Cassie's mother had been an unstable shadow of herself, holding onto a fragile casing of hope. She had whispered to Cassie from time to time that she hoped there had been a mistake. That Gerard would turn up, like he had done the Christmas before last, out of the blue, safe and well, all gangly in his uniform and laughing his hellos.

But the Admiralty telegram had been delivered to Greenaways soon after Cassie and her father had arrived there that terrible May morning. Once again, the rarified Greenaway world had been ripped open. First Uncle Roland and now Gerard.

For Marianne's wedding, however, her mother had steadied herself and made a supreme effort to smile and look forward to it. And the pride and compassion that Cassie felt for her mother made her loathe her father even more.

Cassie shook off this awful sensation as she crossed over to the lychgate with Luke. To counter it, she drank in the beauty of the little tract of Dartmoor beyond, the heather its most vivid purple, the gorse yolky-yellow, the air sweet with the scent of loam. She relished this brief freshening of her senses, to shake off the traces of London with its perpetual dust, gloom and grime, and her consuming, damaging misery.

'Do you know, Cassie, why churches often are set apart, a short distance from their village?' Luke asked.

Cassie did know but thought she'd let him tell her anyway. Luke's presence continued its firm and steady course; he was her comforting, if somewhat clinging, shadow. He would often chat away to her in the kitchen at Cheyne Row, not realising that Cassie only half-listened, her mind drifting but, thankfully, not dwelling, in those moments at least, on Gerard's death.

'...because of the plague,' Luke was saying. 'You see, Cassie, the houses would have originally been much closer to the church...'

They walked through the churchyard, along the path sheltered by ancient yews, and Cassie heard the organist playing 'Ave Maria'. Its simplicity, its beauty, lifted her from her relentless cycle of sorrow, surprised her with a brief and almost unrecognisable glimmer of, dare she say, joy?

'...but they burnt down the plague-ridden dwellings around the church and rebuilt the village further away...' Luke said, '...those that were left behind, that is.'

'I see,' Cassie said, as reality clamped its binds around her once again. *Here we are*, she thought, *those that are left behind.*

They went under the porch and through the ancient door into a chatter of hushed voices rising and falling around the organ music. Pews on the groom's side were filling with Harry's family and friends from Plymouth and a handful of evacuee schoolboys, and their parents. The bride's side looked a little depleted. So many were scattered and unable to come, Oliver being one of them. Among the villagers, Cassie spotted Mr and

Mrs Poulter with their daughter, Maud, and there, at the end of the third row from the front, on her own, sat Vee.

Since Cassie had last seen her, Marianne's friend looked like she had shaken off her girlish, dimply looks; her face had lost its plumpness and now bore even prettier angles. The eighteen or more months working at Manston airfield must have matured her, Cassie thought, like a fine wine. Vee spotted Cassie and gave her a perky wave.

'Is that Marianne's friend from school?' Luke, who had caught up with Cassie along the aisle, half-whispered.

'Yes, indeed, and from the WRAFs. The famous Vee,' she said. 'I will make introductions.' Cassie slotted herself into the pew. 'Vee, hello, it's lovely to see you.'

Vee stood up to greet Cassie, gripping her hands. Up close, she seemed to have evolved into a sophisticated little half-pint bristling with energy in a perfectly tailored jacket and skirt. Her green hat with a long feather reminded Cassie of a female Robin Hood.

'I'm so dreadfully sorry to hear about Gerard,' Vee said, her burnished-brown eyes glimmering and troubled. 'It must be appalling for you.'

'Thank you, yes, absolutely...' Cassie wavered, still not able to accept condolences. 'This is Luke... Lucien Dubois. Oliver's old school friend. And also...' Cassie gave a little laugh. 'My landlord.'

'Really, Cassie, not quite,' Luke chuckled, 'and less of the *old*.' Grinning, he shook Vee's hand.

'I've heard all about you, Luke,' Vee said, twinkling at him. 'Let's sit here together.' She beckoned him forward so that he would sit between her and Cassie. 'Like the three wise monkeys,' Vee added.

Perching on the hard, wooden seat in her best clothes, with

the musty scent of books prickling her nostrils, Cassie felt she were back at school and ought to be sitting to attention.

While Luke and Vee made small talk, she took in the majesty-in-miniature of the little church: the arching beams against the stone ceiling, the rood screen in front of the altar carved with rustic Green Man's faces, and the flower arrangement on the altar steps: white roses spilling out of a pillow of baby's breath to match Marianne's bouquet.

Cassie's father had arrived early to bring the flowers and act as usher, and there he was, talking with Harry Brough, who loitered, his chin red from shaving too closely, on the groom's side. When Marianne had suggested that, with Gerard gone, she and Harry should have a quiet ceremony at the registry office in Exeter, Cassie's father had become exceedingly magnanimous. Had all the benevolent uncle performance, wondered Cassie, stemmed from his guilt?

'If you want a church wedding, have a church wedding,' he'd said. 'We'll be here to celebrate as a family with you.'

'Of course, Marianne, you must be married at Eastcombe, as Uncle Richard and I were,' Cassie's mother had added. 'And Gerard would have loved it.'

But all Cassie had noticed was her father trying far too hard on every score, from his attentiveness to her mother, to offering to pay for the wedding car. A sign, she hoped, of outright discomfort and remorse.

Cassie jolted. Juno and her mother had finished their conversation with Harry's parents and both drifted over to join her father. As she watched them gathering like old friends might do, she felt a fresh pang of turmoil. Life, she realised, would forever more be as awkward and unsavoury as it felt now.

The organist stopped playing and everyone returned to the pews, settling into silence. The vicar gave a signal, the 'Bridal

March' began, the congregation stood, and heads turned in simmering excitement to watch Marianne walk in on Uncle Charles's arm.

Cassie's eyes prickled as she gazed at her cousin in her white dress, her red-lipped smile flickering through her veil. How elated she looked, how thrilled and not one bit nervous, as she made her way towards Harry waiting for her at the altar. Cassie's uncle escorted his beloved daughter with his usual confidence, resplendent in his fine suit, his top pocket lined with Great War medals. And in that moment, seeing Charles's pride and his pleasure, Cassie grasped suddenly that he didn't know about Juno and her father. He *couldn't* know.

As Cassie caught Marianne's eye, and her cousin responded with a glittering look of affection, she remembered how she had always wanted to be just like Marianne. And today, nothing had changed.

I want to be *happy*, Cassie thought.

The vicar welcomed everyone, started the ceremony with the declaration and swiftly moved on to Marianne and Harry exchanging their vows. The sudden solemnity of the moment caught Cassie by surprise, and she felt tears swimming in her eyes as the vicar continued with a short reading: 'Love is patient, love is kind. It does not envy, it does not boast... It keeps no record of wrongs...' he said. 'Love never fails...'

The door at the rear of the church clunked open, and some guests glanced around with curiosity, but Cassie was too busy scrabbling for her handkerchief to take much notice.

'Shuffle along, Cass,' someone whispered.

She glanced up at Oliver standing beside her in the aisle in his captain's uniform, his face older, tanned and weathered by the desert sun, his cap clamped under his arm, his eyes as intense and expressive as they'd ever been. Dazed, she moved along the seat, her mind whirring backwards to the last time they had seen each other, their difficult and bewildering farewell on Whitehall.

The organ wheezed into life again and everyone stood up to sing the first hymn. Charles rested over the back of his pew to pat Oliver on the shoulder and Juno swivelled in her seat, reaching to clutch silently at his hand. Luke leant around Cassie to greet Oliver, uttering his delight at seeing his friend, and Vee peered past Luke to mouth '*hello*' too. The bride and groom, facing the altar, seemed oblivious to the latecomer and Cassie kept her face forward, her eyes down, the hymn book juddering in her hands.

Feeling Oliver sitting close to her, the cloth of his jacket brushing her arm, she hadn't realised how much she had missed him and how sorry she felt for how she had left things. With Gerard's death, she had woken up to how much she needed Oliver in a way that seemed imperative, and in such a contrast to how she felt about Luke and his practical, level-headed support.

The ceremony continued around her: another reading, this time by Harry's best man; Marianne drawing back her veil; Marianne and Harry signing the register.

During the last hymn, while the congregation sang, 'I vow to thee, my country, all earthly things above...', the bride and groom walked over to the plaque on the side wall inscribed:

Our Glorious Dead of the Great War, 1914-1918

Five names were listed, men and boys from the village, and etched at the bottom:

Roland Greenaway, aged 20

As Marianne placed her bouquet in the niche beneath the plaque, grief flashed a warning beacon through Cassie's mind, threatening to engulf her. She began to weep silently in confusion, her stomach trembling, tears running in channels down her cheeks, splashing onto the open hymn book.

Everyone continued to sing, '...and her ways are ways of gentleness, and all her paths are peace...' but Cassie could only mouth the words.

Turning to go back to the altar, Marianne spotted Oliver among the faces and, with a cry of happiness, she scooted over, silk and lace rustling.

'My Oliver, my Oliver!' Marianne said, laughing with delight. 'My horrid big brother Oliver!'

Cassie watched, wiping her eyes, as Oliver enfolded Marianne in a huge hug and Marianne buried her face in his shoulder. The wedding guests carried on singing, their voices rising in strength and joy, and Oliver lifted his face to smile at Cassie around his sister's veil. And in that instant, Cassie felt lighter, her fears and grief tempered, at least for a while.

* * *

They all trooped back to Greenaways to celebrate, sitting down to afternoon tea made by Mrs Poulter and Maud, rations and shortages permitting. A long line of tables had been set up in the courtyard that morning, covered in pristine linen and decorated with vases of sunflowers, dahlias and roses gathered from Juno's garden. Marianne and Harry sat together as a couple at the head, while everyone else took a seat where they could, a happy mix of family and friends.

The schoolboys – who had formed a motley guard of honour as the bride and groom left the church – were ferrying out the plates of sandwiches, the tea and lemonade from the kitchen. And Cassie, sitting halfway down, kept being asked to pass plates, the salt and pots of chutney up and down the table as everyone started to tuck in.

'You've chosen the wrong place there, Cassie, my dear,' her uncle called down the table, chuckling. 'Having to hand everything back and forth.'

But Cassie didn't mind. She felt comforted by the old, stone walls surrounding her, with Oliver close by, and Marianne so radiantly happy, realising that they were all but one small part of the long and chequered history of Greenaways. Cassie saw Vee regaling her mother with a funny scrape she had got into with some RAF lads, while Luke appeared to be telling Harry's father a particularly earnest story.

Beneath the murmur of conversation, she heard Juno say, 'Your hair looks lovely, Cassandra. I like the way you've styled it.'

Cassie looked up to see her aunt sitting diagonally opposite, her all-seeing eyes peering at her across a jug of celery stalks.

'It's gone a lovely shade of blonde hasn't it, as you've got older,' Juno persisted.

Cassie touched the wave of hair over her ear and felt herself blush, as if Juno knew that Cassie knew, and the rotten shock and disgust of her discovery rose once more to overwhelm her.

'Your hair, Cassie,' Juno went on, her expression sincere, thinking perhaps that Cassie had not heard her. 'Days like this, I wish I could do something better with mine.'

Cassie stared at Juno, wondering if she ought to return the compliment. She remembered the torturous journey she took with her father from London that night a few months ago, bearing the terrible news about Gerard. They had barely spoken but, in the darkness of the car, somewhere between Salisbury and Tiverton, she had uttered, 'Dad, you must never tell Juno that I saw you both, that I know.'

And she hoped to God that he had heard her and had paid heed.

'Thank you,' Cassie replied. 'Hasn't it been a wonderful day?'

'Absolutely. We all need some brightness in our life.'

But beneath her aunt's pleasantries, Cassie sensed a hidden layer, another meaning, that her aunt had picked up on something, had listened in on Cassie's thoughts. That she was now overplaying her kindness, in the way that Cassie's father seemed to be doing these days.

The colour of Juno's eyes intensified with unreadable, locked-in emotion.

'The wedding, Marianne told me this morning,' she said, 'is for everyone.'

Juno turned away, distracted by one of the schoolboys filling her glass with lemonade, and Cassie, hearing Harry's mother ask her to pass the salt, did so. And, shaken by Juno's tender admission, she began to chat with the elder Mrs Brough, complimenting her on her choice of hat.

* * *

After the speeches and before the sun had set, Marianne and Harry left for their hotel in Dartmouth, waved off by everyone with whoops and cheers from the front steps. Then the guests gathered on the west-facing terrace where Charles popped champagne corks, Cassie helped Maud bring out trays of glasses, and Oliver set up the wireless, tuning it to a music programme.

'I think my dancing days are over,' Cassie's father said, settling back into the garden chair next to her mother, who sipped delicately at her drink and gave him an indulgent smile, squeezing his hand.

'Did they ever begin, Rich?' Juno asked with a hard laugh, breezing past them holding a brimming champagne flute in each hand for Harry's parents.

The sound of conversation tinkled around Cassie's ears and a cheery ragtime tune came from the radio. She paused to take in the beauty of the moment: the golden, evening light slanting across the park, making long shadows of the trees and glimmering over faces and crystal glasses. On reflex, and with an insistent, tantalising yearning, she looked around for Oliver.

Instead, she saw her uncle lead Juno into the centre of the terrace to dance. And other couples, including Harry's parents, went to join in. Cassie's mother, her cheeks flushed from only a few sips of champagne, got up and hauled her father to his feet.

'Come on, Rich, let's show them,' she said.

As her father took her mother into hold, poised for a moment to find the beat, he glanced over at Cassie as if looking for her approval. But how could she give it when her trust still lay in tatters? How could she forgive and forget when the scenario and the players paraded in front of her? She turned and made her way through the guests.

'Here she is,' said Luke. 'Wondering where you'd got to. Is that Duke Ellington on the radio?' he asked, gesturing with his glass to chink it against hers, then Vee's and Oliver's.

'Ah yes,' said Cassie. 'I love these old Cotton Club tunes.'

'You like to dance, don't you?' Luke said.

'I do but I barely seem to have the time these days.'

'You mean, you don't go down to the Café de Paris or over to the Coalhole?' asked Vee. 'Honestly, if I was in London, I'd be out every night. Air raids allowing.'

'It's easing up now, don't you think, Cassie?' Oliver said.

'Now Hitler's turned his sights on Russia. It must feel a little safer in London?'

'Even so, it's my shifts, you see; I can't fit in a lot of social life,' Cassie said.

The idea of being back in the city felt exhausting. She wanted to stay here, on the terrace at Greenaways for this warm, summer evening with the joyful music swinging into her limbs. She began to tap her toes, the old-time tunes on the wireless like honey in her ears. Oh, to forget about London, about the bunker, the grinding reality of her work. It felt such a relief to be able to put on a pretty dress for a change. And if Oliver asked her, she thought, she would most certainly dance tonight.

'What is that saying... There's a time to weep, a time to laugh, and a time to dance,' said Oliver. 'I can't remember the rest... but now is our time to dance. Well, well!' He let out a playful whistle. 'Look at my ma and pa. Don't they look good together?'

Charles was certainly an excellent lead, Cassie thought, and Juno as graceful and loose-limbed as ever, their bodies moving with serious concentration to the rhythmic melody. But seeing her aunt and uncle together felt unsettling. Poor dear Uncle Charles, she thought. He continued to work tirelessly to hold his grieving sister and the family together in the wake of Gerard's loss, oblivious to the deceit on his doorstep.

Cassie took a mouthful of champagne to bolster her nerves and dared herself to pick out her parents among the dancers again. They moved slowly among the other pairs, tenderly, oblivious to the speed of the music. Together, in their own world, supporting each other inside their mutual mourning. But whatever effort her father had been making with her mother behind the scenes, she decided, could never seem enough.

Sensing someone standing close beside her, she uttered, 'Imagine Gerard here, with all of us. He would have loved this.'

'He would indeed.'

She turned, expecting to see Oliver, but found it was Luke who had spoken. He gestured towards her, cocking his head to the side, his eyes glittering and serious behind his specs.

'Come on, Cassie, let's have a dance.'

Cassie opened her mouth to say, *No, thank you,* but felt powerless and heady from champagne. The terrace had filled up, everyone giggling and jostling, bumping elbows. With the blackout down, no lights showing inside the house, and faces and figures blurred in the fading light, she decided to surrender to the evening. She allowed Luke to lead her into the throng.

He steered her gently around, a strong, solid presence, his stocky figure surprisingly supple, the side of his face close to hers. She shut her eyes, absorbing the rich tones of the singer's voice, the tune's gorgeous, earthy tempo. She could hear Luke speaking close to her ear, but did not catch the words. He gripped her hand a little tighter. Swaying gently with him, she felt liberated and something inside her began to melt.

Perhaps this, she thought, *this is how I will be happy. Like Marianne.*

After all, she remembered, Luke had been the one she had turned to that terrible evening in London when she had stumbled in on her father and Juno. She had thought of Oliver at first, but how could she go to him with that information? Even though she had easily found Luke's name in the phonebook, she still felt it had been a miracle that he'd been at home, had answered her call, taken her in. Truth be told, she had depended on him ever since. And he had taken care of her.

The song finished and everyone paused, straining to listen for the next tune to break through the crackling airwaves. She drew back from Luke, thinking she'd like to sit down, perhaps have something more to eat, but he held onto her.

'Let's wait for them to play the next record,' he said, his expression palpable, despite the falling dusk. Deep and brown, his eyes seemed sharp with questions, and longing. He started to say something and Cassie turned her head, ready to listen. But he cleared his throat instead. 'Honestly, the suspense!' he joked. 'You can imagine the man in the booth at the BBC, dusting off the long player, checking for scratches... lifting the needle... or perhaps Charles's wireless has gone out of tune. The signal out here must be very poor... you see... Cassie...' He reached up and smoothed her hair behind her ear.

The next tune started with a lively flourish of jazz horns, and Cassie felt a strange dropping sensation, a sharp realisation. Luke's mother's voice echoed in her mind. *He thinks the world of you, you know.*

It became achingly clear, as they began to shuffle around the terrace again, that Luke liked her, more than liked her. She thought of him at other moments: becoming drunk that evening when he arrived at Cheyne Row with Oliver; teasing her with the dead bird when he'd been a disturbed boy. How much he had taken care of her.

But how much he bored her. A dull fist of shame, wrapped up with disappointment, hit Cassie in the stomach.

Perhaps she should tell him she wanted to sit down, find a quiet spot, talk with him properly, let him know that she didn't feel the same. And yet she carried on dancing. At the corner of her eye, she noticed Oliver and Vee get up to do a turn, but they seemed unable to dance for laughing.

'He's got two left feet,' Vee called as Luke and Cassie brushed passed them, and they fell back again into their laughter.

A sudden, blinding thought shook Cassie's core, and she

realised then that Vee found Oliver attractive. And why wouldn't she? It seemed so obvious now, that other people, other girls would like Oliver, and would make him happy, give him everything that he wanted, and deserved. And yet it felt to Cassie that Vee had just raked her face with her fingernails.

Oliver and Vee gave up dancing and stood together, engaged in close and fascinated conversation, Vee talking with her little fairy hands, plucking ideas out of the air, while other couples moved around them.

The music drifted out across the terrace into the shadowed garden, with the night horizon a deep, sapphire-blue above the darker hills. The wedding party chatter, the tinkling of glasses and the laughter, rose into the warm, night air scented with the jasmine climbing up the old stones of Greenaways, with Vee's voice the loudest of all.

16

Cassie woke the next morning and opened her blind to let in the gentle sunlight. Moving slowly, hampered by a mild fogginess in her head, she washed and dressed, and went downstairs, not at all surprised that most of the family were still in bed, apart from her uncle who, true to form, had gone out early on one of his constitutional walks. She ate her breakfast at the kitchen table with Mrs Poulter, chatting about the wedding, before giving her a hand to clear up the remains of the party.

One by one, people emerged, either still worse for wear or perfectly fine once they had a strong cup of tea, toast and Mrs Poulter's bramble jam. And as Cassie stacked the last of the heirloom serving platters in the china cupboard, the remaining few guests left in cars and taxis, and the house settled back to its familiar rhythms and sounds.

'We're missing at least two dozen glasses, Miss Cassie,' said Mrs Poulter, coming back into the kitchen. 'I must say I was too tired last night to go looking for them.'

'I'll go on the hunt,' Cassie said, taking a tray with her out to the terrace.

She began to find them, tumblers, champagne flutes and wine glasses, in the bird bath, on window ledges and tucked into the corners of the steps leading down to the garden. Gathering up the relics of the fun and laughter of the night before, she heard footsteps, and Oliver call her name.

'We are going for a trip up to the moor, Cass. Do you fancy that? Luke's driving. Mrs Poulter is going to pack us a hamper of leftover sandwiches.'

'Don't tell me,' Cassie said. 'A trek up to Hound Tor?'

'Oh no, it's not going to be one of Pa's infamous hikes. We'll go as far as we can up the drover's road in the car and stop there. It's short walk to the Tor. We can have a picnic.'

'In that case...' Cassie said. 'Yes, I could do with some fresh air.'

She hadn't had a chance to spend much time with Oliver since his arrival yesterday, and a trip to Dartmoor sounded a perfect opportunity.

'That's good. So, it's the four of us. We're just waiting for Vee... Hey, let me give you a hand with those.'

Hearing him mention Marianne's friend so casually jolted Cassie; she remembered suddenly how well he and Vee had clicked during the evening. Falling quiet, she put the tray on the garden table and began to arrange the dirty glasses as Oliver brought them to her, cloudy with dregs or with lipstick marks on the rim.

'These are going to take some cleaning,' she said.

'And this one is cracked. Sign of a good party. At least it's not Ma's best crystal.' Oliver perched on the low terrace wall, looking over his shoulder at the sweep of grass, glittering under the lingering dew. 'I'm glad I made it back for the wedding. Only just in time, mind.'

Cassie gave a light laugh. 'When I heard you come into the

church, I thought, oh God, is it that moment when someone bursts in to protest at the union or forever hold their peace?' She caught his eye. 'I'm glad you made it, too.'

Oliver sighed, gazed up at the house, as if seeing it for the first time or admiring it in a new light. 'I haven't chatted with you properly since I got here, have I?'

'Oh, we've all been too busy enjoying ourselves.' Cassie paused, noticing the guarded look on his face. She placed the last of the glasses on the tray, the last time they had seen each other, their parting on Whitehall, on her mind. 'How are you, Oliver?'

He exhaled a wry laugh. 'Now there's a tale. But being here, seeing this...' He stared along to the edge of the garden, brimming with mellow, end-of-summer colour. 'I've missed home.'

'I can see that,' she said tenderly. 'But Greenaways always works its magic. As magnificent as it is, it has had a humbling effect on me. Quite comforting.'

'Yes... I wondered how you felt, Cass, coming back here, after Gerard... I think... that...'

Hearing him struggling to find the words, she waited, didn't want to press him.

'Greenaways soothes wounds...' Oliver said eventually. 'Wounds that cannot be seen.'

Frightened by the shake in his voice, Cassie noticed the rash of freckles over his tanned forehead, the mark of the desert sun. But how much more of him had changed, on the inside?

'Despite that, and all this English country garden glory,' Oliver said, rousing himself, 'I can still feel sand between my toes.'

He was making light of it, but she saw a scarring in his eyes, a creeping memory of incidents, of scenes, once seen, he may not be able to forget. It felt quite possible to Cassie that Oliver would never be able to erase these things, and they would suck away a little piece of his soul.

'How long are you going to be here? In England?' she asked, immediately hating herself, for it sounded selfish and inappropriate.

'Not sure yet. Certainly, for a while. I'm helping with the training of new recruits, back at Sandhurst. That's where I came from yesterday. I had told Ma and Pa that it may not be possible for me to make it to the wedding, so they didn't tell Marianne.'

'The look on her face...' Cassie smiled, picturing it.

'No one else knew,' he said. 'I would have told you, Cass, but I didn't want to jinx it. And also...' His gaze trailed over her face. 'I am sorry I haven't written, as I promised to. And no, I didn't forget your address. I know you are still at Cheyne Row. I simply thought that you wouldn't want to hear from me.'

'Oh, Oliver, not true.' Cassie gasped. 'I am sorry how I left things that morning. I was frightened, overwhelmed. So very frightened, and it didn't come across well.'

'I should have admitted that I was pretty much scared to death myself. And then we would have understood each other. And I wasn't here when you lost Gerard. I'm sorry.'

Cassie sat beside him on the terrace wall. 'There's no need for that,' she said. 'And you are here now.'

Oliver turned to smile at her, hooked his arm around her head, as he had done during hide-and-seek in the wardrobe, and planted a kiss on her forehead.

'You see, Cass, you always say the right thing to me. You know me better than anyone.'

Cassie felt an impulse to lean her head on his shoulder, for him to hold her for the rest of the day, but Oliver shuffled away a little, leant forward to rearrange some of the glasses on the tray.

'So, in answer to your question...'

'My question?'

'About how long I'm going to be here,' he said. 'Me being stationed at Sandhurst is open-ended for now. But I could get my orders at any time to return. Our dealings with the Afrika Korps in the Western Desert are sadly not over yet. Not by a long chalk. Compared to the Italians, the German troops are an entirely different calibre.'

'I've seen the reports,' Cassie said gently. 'Not that I can pretend for one minute to know what it is like to be there.'

'I will be sent back to that dust-choking hell eventually, that's for sure. No amount of champagne will make that sound any better.'

He picked up a glass that had been tucked in a niche in the wall and put it with the others.

'Talk to me about it, Oliver,' Cassie urged. 'If you want to. I have, unfortunately, become hardened to a lot of different kinds of hell – going by the information that crosses my desk every day. I will listen, even if I cannot totally understand.'

'No,' said Oliver. 'I wouldn't want to do that to you. I know you are strong, Cass, stronger than even you think you are, but I wouldn't want to distress you any further. I remember how upset you were when we said goodbye before.' He threw her an anxious glance. 'And now, with Gerard...'

Cassie flinched at the mention of her brother's name and braced against the onslaught of pain. But Oliver was the one person she could forgive, apart from her mother, for throwing Gerard's name at her.

'What about Luke?' she asked. 'He is good to talk to. He seems to have a constant ability to see the bright side of every-thing.' Cassie chose her words carefully. 'Maintains a positive outlook at all costs.'

'That's the problem. He doesn't seem to want to delve

beneath the surface. And anyway, we're men.' Oliver gave a dry chuckle. 'We don't talk about such things with each other. Especially the fear.'

Cassie did not know this to be entirely true. But she wanted to help Oliver, in any way she could, even if he would not accept help from her.

'Then, perhaps Vee?'

Oliver shook his head. 'I hardly know her.'

'But that might be a good thing?'

'No,' he said, 'not her.'

Cassie felt Oliver gazing at her for some moments, and then past her, taking in the trees in the distance, the far-off smudge of Dartmoor on the horizon, his eyes shining, their colour deepening.

'It's the green,' he said, sounding like he needed to explain. 'It's like I have never seen it before.' He sighed. 'England's green and pleasant land. Like a heaven.'

'Compared to...?' Cassie coaxed.

'Oh God, Cass, compared to endless, scorching, bleak terrain, the sand and rock and dirt, all the same monotonous... the blind uncertainty of running forward into a smoke screen caused by the latest shell explosion.' He waited, his thoughts aligning. 'It's the intense heat that slays you. There's no shelter, or hardly any to speak of. It's like a weight on top of my head. And by the middle of the morning, the heat is rising in waves, shimmering, moving. It's an odd thing. We feel that we can walk around without hesitation. You see, they can see you, but only in a distorted way because of the strange, dizzying haze. And I'd watch them do the same. But I'd see a man walking upside down, fourteen feet in the air. You couldn't aim at him, because you didn't know where he was. The desert fools you. It traps you. A mysterious, strange trick of the light. And then, it reverts back in a second and we would have a complete view of the front for, say, fifteen minutes. Then it would distort again. Like the air has thickened, baked in the heat.' Oliver shook his head, not understanding his own explanation. 'Now I know why you hear tales of mirages. How a man can be deceived, to think he may be in a sanctuary, that he may be, possibly, safe.'

Cassie wanted to tell him, *You are safe here* but knew it to be trite and meaningless.

'The heat haze would clear once more, and everyone would dive for cover,' he said. 'Because the war started again.' He stopped.

Cassie waited, gathering her strength to listen to whatever Oliver needed to tell her. For it would be the reality, the moment when the reports and briefs, the figures and the lists of casualties, all the cold, military terminology dissolved. What the men go through seemed to be ignored or lost along the way, and in Gerard's case reduced to four words: *Lost with all hands*.

'I look for omens in the sky,' Oliver said, with a half-laugh. 'Ridiculous, really, when I think about it now. The shapes of clouds might suggest good things, might remind me of home. That it might be a good day. And there is a lot of sky out there, Cass. But I never think about being killed. It is always the other man who is going to die. One moment there, the next gone. But I am kidding myself. I have seen it too often.'

'Oliver, I...' Cassie began, but unable to match something so desperately profound and important, words failed her.

She locked eyes with him, noticing the myriad new crinkles around them. He flicked his gaze away and back, away and back, as if he could not bear to look at her but urgently needed to. She wanted to do, to say something reassuring or sympathetic about the war, about his experiences in the desert wasteland, but how could she possibly comfort him, or give him hope, when she had none herself?

'You see, you're the one person...' he whispered, his voice heavy with unexpressed feeling. 'But it's all right, Cass, you don't have to...'

They sat for some moments, while the air sang with birds, and the Devon soil gently heated, forcing out the scent of cut grass and, on its tail, the rich fragrance of Juno's roses. And in that silence, their bond mended. Cassie held it like a nugget of gold in the palm of her hand, as pure and as precious as childhood.

'Come on, you two!' Luke called, appearing around the corner, beaming with boyish excitement. 'We're ready to go!'

But, seeing them sitting on the wall together, Luke's face fell, puzzled and serious, as if he had witnessed something that neither of them was aware of.

Oliver gave him a cursory wave, and Cassie furtively dashed away her tears.

'Our marching orders,' Oliver uttered, giving Cassie half a smile.

'Come on, then,' she said, 'We can't keep Dartmoor waiting.'

* * *

They all met by the car, Vee looking fresher, Cassie thought, than she ought to, her story-book features enriched somehow by lack of sleep. Cassie got into the passenger seat, Oliver and Vee in the back, and Luke drove down the lanes towards Eastcombe, passing the church and turning onto the unclassified road that became the track that trailed up to the moor.

'You're not looking so green around the gills any more, Vee, if I may say so,' Oliver said.

'Oh, I soon recover from overindulging.' Vee laughed. 'Cast-iron constitution. And fresh air will soon put the colour back into my cheeks. Although this juddering road isn't helping. How are you feeling, Cassie?'

'Surprising well, thank you,' she said cautiously, not quite knowing how to answer. 'But I am glad Mrs Poulter gave us a huge flask of strong tea to bring with us.'

'You were restrained last night, Cassie,' said Luke, negotiating the tight, stone walls on either side of the lane. 'A lesson for all of us.'

'At least Pa wasn't serving red wine last night, hey Woodward?' Oliver laughed. 'Red wine is often not your friend.'

'Well, I am certainly looking forward to indulging in wedding cake,' Luke said. 'Mrs Poulter put in a huge slice of that too.'

'That should work wonders,' Cassie said, winding down her window to bathe her face in the cool air coming down from the moor.

As they went higher and higher, she watched the moorland unroll like a bolt of fabric woven in purple and brown. Its undulations hid and then revealed its Neolithic secrets, its stones, and boulders standing as temples to earth and sky. Birds flitted up from the heath and dived down, and a group of ponies watched them nonchalantly as they drove by slowly, chewing their cud, their long manes trailing across their long, wise faces.

'How about here?' Luke asked as he pulled up by a monumental stack of flat boulders, the peak of Hound Tor beyond.

The stones looked to Cassie as if they had been placed just so by prehistoric deities. She got out of the car and walked a little way on her own to take in the horizon, her face warmed by the sun as it peeped in and out of friendly, white clouds. The spongy, primeval earth yielded beneath her footfalls, and the heather flowed on and on, punctuated by feathery grasses and stunted gorse, and the odd tumbled-down wall. At her feet, fragile harebells shuddered, weathering the breeze, and Cassie felt a surge of new confidence. It matched the joyful hope sparked by hearing 'Ave Maria' playing at the church, but this time came from somewhere more mysterious and shadowy: a place, like the moor, the rocks and the sky, that had been here long before them all.

'It is sublime, isn't it?' Oliver said, his voice low in admiration.

Cassie had no idea how long he'd been standing beside her.

'That's *it*,' she whispered, matching his tone. 'I have been struggling to explain it to myself. But yes, pure and sublime.'

They stood together without speaking for a spell or two. Cassie could sense Oliver's hand naturally close to hers by her side, and part of her wanted to catch hold of it; the other part resisted, telling her not to be so silly. She had been a child when she had fallen in love with Oliver, in *filial* love, she reminded herself. It wasn't the love in films or the stories in the magazines, or even in the novels she'd read. But something else, in disguise? Trust, yes. And a recognition. And yet that trust, that confidence, had worked itself so deep that it felt part of her.

'Cass,' Oliver said, 'I want to say again, I'm sorry I wasn't here for you when we lost Gerard.'

So many people had offered their sorrow to her, but only Oliver's found its way in.

'I know.'

Below, on the lower reaches of the moors, where they merged with farmland, walls meandered and criss-crossed, and sheep grazed in little flocks and families within the crooked fields.

'If I'm right, I think those sheep over there are Whiteface,' Oliver said.

Cassie giggled. 'You can tell from this distance? I am impressed.'

'Don't forget, Cass,' he said, 'I grew up around here. Pa used to test us when he took us on his hikes.'

'Ah yes. We used to have family picnics up here, didn't we, somewhere...?' Cassie pictured the gatherings, her parents, Oliver's parents, Marianne, and Gerard. The joy crippled now, ever since she stumbled in on her father and Juno's secret. And Gerard, gone. 'I remember your pa telling me that sheep must never hear the same church bells twice in one week. They must always be driven to new pastures.'

Oliver sighed. 'If there wasn't a war, and the bells all muffled, we might be able to hear the Eastcombe church bell up here, depending on the way the wind blows.'

'I miss that,' Cassie said. 'Growing up in London, I'd hear all manner of bells.'

'Like "Oranges and Lemons"?' Oliver smiled.

'And the chiming city clocks,' said Cassie. 'But now we have a sort of tense, panicked silence, now that the raids have eased off.'

'I can't wait...' Oliver's voice cracked, and he looked at Cassie, his expression an appeal, 'to hear the bells again.'

Cassie wanted to hold his hand, so they could comfort each other, and look after each other. Like people who love each other do. But now they were grown-ups, it must remain in the past.

'Oliver! Cassie!' Luke, unloading the car, called out. 'Guess what! Vee has brought champagne!'

Laughing, with relief it seemed to Cassie, they went back

over to help Vee and Luke spread out the blanket on the leeside of the boulders.

'Goodness me, Vee,' Cassie said, 'You are one brave girl.'

'Hair of the dog always helps.' Vee laughed. 'Your father gave it to me, Oliver, for our picnic.'

'That sounds rather encouraging of him,' Oliver said, picking up the bottle. 'Thank goodness, it's still icy cold.'

Luke lugged the hamper from the boot, setting it in the middle of the blanket. Vee spread out cushions, and Cassie began to unpack the plates and sandwiches.

Oliver popped the champagne cork.

'Not sure this is a good idea,' he said, pouring glasses, 'but at least we can have the flask of tea later.'

They each found a spot around the blanket, fell quiet, munching and sipping, with Vee giggling a little more, it seemed to Cassie, with each mouthful.

'Luke, have you told Cassie yet about the house you found in Richmond?' Oliver asked.

'Oh yes,' said Vee, intrigued. 'Luke the Landlord.'

'Ah no, it slipped my mind.'

'I know you're looking for another place to live, Luke,' Cassie said between bites. 'So, you've had some luck? Luke's house was damaged, Vee, in a raid back in April and it is unsafe to stay there. And we lost the cat. Kipling hasn't been seen since.'

Luke rested his hand on Cassie's arm to comfort her; she could see Oliver's gaze looking down at it, while Vee made sympathetic noises.

'But I have been wondering, Luke,' Cassie went on, subtly flinching her arm, and he took his hand away, 'if now is the time for me to find my own place? My friend Esme at work shares a flat, and she mentioned the other day that the girl was going to go off to get married.'

'But *Richmond*, Cassie!' Vee said.

'It's a lovely place, detached, Edwardian I think, only one street away from the river,' Luke said. 'I've just signed the lease.'

'Sounds delightful,' said Vee. 'When you're billeted in a room in a draughty old cottage like I am.'

'The ideal place to settle down, when all this is over,' Oliver said, looking from Cassie to Luke and back again. 'And how wonderful to be near a river. Like Greenaways.'

'Although, of course, the Thames at Richmond is much the mightier,' Luke said, sounding delighted at the prospect.

'And that area is still like a village, isn't it?' Oliver said. 'But not too far into town? It all sounds wonderful, Cass.'

'And the trains go into Waterloo,' Luke said.

Cassie realised that everyone assumed she would happily continue living with Luke, as his lodger, or did they all think it was, or would be, something more? The old married couple joke had worn rather thin in her mind.

She felt their eyes on her, Oliver's the most intense, and a sensation of expectation closed in on her, as if doors were shutting, blotting out her horizon.

'What about your job, Cassie?' Vee asked.

'What do you mean?' she countered.

'I'm just curious. Is it something you wish to continue?'

'I can't say I enjoy my job. I mean, is anything *enjoyable* these days?' Cassie admitted. 'But I know how important it is. Like all of us, a small cog inside something far bigger than ourselves.'

'I'm not sure you will be able to travel in from Richmond to Westminster every day, with your shifts,' Luke said.

'But, if I do live in Richmond for a short while, I will stay in the Dock during the awkward shifts,' Cassie said resolutely. 'Which is the rather unpleasant sleeping quarters, Vee, in the sub-basement. Not something anyone wants to get used to, but—'

'We can't have that, Cassie,' Luke said.

Vee asked, 'Where is your friend's flat?'

'In a mews in Bloomsbury, but...'

'You will be safer out in Richmond, Cass,' Oliver said.

Cassie glanced at him, puzzled. Usually, he would take her side, understand how she felt, back her up. He must see, she thought, that she looked uncomfortable with everyone talking around her, about her.

Beside him, Vee vehemently nodded.

'Are any of us safe?' Cassie said, feeling prickly, not really wanting to explain herself, even to Oliver, and certainly not in front of everyone else.

The conversation waned, but Cassie heard a warning sound in her mind, as if the wind had got up and was beating across the moor: a storm approaching. Although the sky remained clear and constant, she felt put upon by Luke and Vee, and even a little bit by Oliver. She knew he would want the best for her, but carrying on living with Luke was not it, especially now that she had begun to notice the depth of his affection for her. Cassie had never wanted to conform to what other people expected her to do. She felt on the brink of losing the independence that she had carved out for herself, away from her parents, while keeping the secret that she alone had to bear.

Luke topped up their glasses, and Vee began to chat with Oliver, her shoulder turned as if to block Cassie and Luke out, her voice as low and as intimate as it had been last night. Cassie placed her hand over her glass when Luke leant over to her with the bottle and cocked her head to listen. As their conversation simmered out of earshot, Cassie knew that her admiration for

Oliver had become Vee's; that Vee shared Cassie's vision of her cousin: a simply wonderful human.

And yet, again, Cassie felt a chasm widen between them, the intimacy of her exchange with Oliver not a quarter of an hour before as they had taken in the view now negated and irrelevant.

The chaos battering Cassie's mind exhausted her, and the champagne certainly hadn't been a good idea.

'I'm going to have forty winks,' she said.

'Good idea,' Luke said, although the others didn't appear to hear her.

She curled up on the blanket, rested her head on a cushion, closed her eyes and began to doze, feeling the tender sunrays on her cheek and hearing quietened voices and occasional laughter: Luke enthusiastic about the house in Richmond, Oliver chatting about Sandhurst, and Vee promising to visit him there.

* * *

Cassie must have fallen asleep for, with a sudden, plunging sensation, she woke, her mouth parched and her head aching. She sat up, blinking. The day had progressed into a luminous, golden afternoon and Luke sat alone on the other side of the blanket, reading. He glanced at her over the top of his book.

'Ah, so you're awake...' he said, his smile indulgent and almost paternal.

She rubbed her eyes. 'Where are the others...?'

'Don't ask...'

Cassie gave Luke a puzzled look and turned her head at the sound of distant laughter. After some moments, two figures emerged where the moor fell away beyond the nearby huddle of boulders: Oliver and Vee stumbling back up the slope, their arms around each other.

Squinting, and disorientated after waking from her nap, Cassie didn't pay much attention, noticing instead how much shorter Vee looked than Oliver. As they drew nearer, she saw that Vee's wedge-heeled sandals dangled from her hand, her naked, dainty feet tiptoeing over the heath. And in that moment, Cassie felt her world changing; the way Oliver appeared, the way he held himself, he looked like a stranger. And Cassie no longer knew him.

'Time to get the tea out,' Luke said brightly, putting his book away and giving Cassie a concerned look. 'Do you feel better for your nap?'

She shook her head, mutely smoothed her hair, gathered herself together. As Oliver detached himself from Vee's arm, and Vee coiled down onto the rug, all giggly and warm, her cheeks flushed, her face ridiculously pretty, Cassie understood all too clearly, and with a strange, ludicrous kind of fury what had happened between them behind the boulders. Earlier, on the terrace at Greenaways, when Cassie had urged Oliver to confide in Vee and he had said, '*No, not her,*' she had thought, as she had done throughout her life, that he had spoken the truth.

Oliver remained standing, detached and silent. With his back against the sun, Cassie could not read his expression and found she no longer wanted to, for she may see another lie.

'There had better be some cake left, Luke,' Vee said, touching her hair behind her ear to pull out a sprig of heather. 'Although I feel I have had a little slice of heaven today already.'

Luke's chuckle sounded forced and embarrassed, and he gave Cassie a look, as if he desperately needed her to join in.

But she busied herself with the teacups, while Luke rummaged for the cake in the hamper. Oliver finally sat down, cross-legged, on the other side of the rug to Vee, who chattered away, oblivious to the tension, intent on drawing Oliver in. But he sat quietly, his jaw set, shielding his eyes from the sun. Cassie dared herself to steal a glance at him. He had missed a button when doing up his shirt, and he hadn't tucked it in to his trousers.

Luke filled the silence with observations: the types of clouds overhead, his own amateur weather forecast; even the species of bee that foraged along the edge of the rug. And Cassie nibbled her cake, barely tasting it, the crumbs like grit in her mouth while she felt a seismic shift in friendship and kinship, now fractured and destroyed. Breathing in air thickened by Vee and Oliver's carnal exchange, she braced against the onslaught of jealousy, the loss of trust gouging out her insides.

'What's the matter, Cass?' Oliver asked, evidently noticing her discomfort and sounding defensive, irritated and so unlike himself.

But Cassie gave him her broadest smile.

'Nothing is the matter, Oliver,' she said.

Vee yawned and said something bright and silly to Oliver, who gave a barely audible response. Luke, glancing at his watch, began to pack up the plates and glasses. Everyone, swamped by unspoken unease, the day finished, followed his lead, emptying dregs of tea onto the grass in silence.

As they bumped back down the track in the car, leaving the quiet, blessed beauty of Dartmoor behind, Cassie felt that her universe that afternoon had once again altered its course. But, she rallied. She told herself, why shouldn't Oliver want to be with Vee? Even marry Vee? Oliver did not have to answer to anyone, including her. He was his own man; he could do exactly as he pleased. They were no longer children, and she really shouldn't be so prissy about it.

And yet, Cassie thought, as her sickening confusion

returned, it wasn't that Oliver had been with Vee, but that he had broken her trust.

Luke, negotiating his way along the lanes, began to whistle a tune.

'Anyone recognise that?' he asked. 'It was on the wireless last night when we were all dancing and it's driving me crazy.'

He looked at Cassie and she shook her head. No one else spoke.

Cassie glanced behind to the back seat. Oliver and Vee sat apart, each against their side of the car. Vee appeared to be asleep, her head lolling against the headrest, and Oliver had turned to stare out of his window, his arms folded, his jaw stiff, shutting himself away.

Luke shrugged and carried on whistling, turning in through the gates at Greenaways.

As soon as the car had stopped, without a word, Oliver got out and walked off alone into the house. And Cassie, watching him go, made a vow to herself: from that moment on, whatever Oliver did or did not do would not devastate her.

17

LONDON, AUGUST 1941

Two days later, Luke set their suitcases down on the doorstep at Cheyne Row and fumbled in his pocket for the latch key.

'I've got mine,' Cassie said, 'if you can't—'

But before she'd opened her handbag, or Luke could answer, the front door swung open and Mrs Ennis leapt out, crying, 'He's here, he's here,' tugging at Luke's sleeve.

'Mrs Ennis, what on earth!' Luke said. 'Who's here?'

'I've been watching out for you all afternoon,' the house-keeper stage-whispered, her eyes bright in her ruddy face, gesturing for them to come in. 'He's in the salon. Quietly, though. Shut the door quickly, in case he...'

Cassie exchanged a puzzled look with Luke as they walked in, and he meticulously closed the front door behind him. They followed Mrs Ennis, breathless, as she tiptoed down the hallway, surprisingly light-footed for a such a rotund woman.

'Here, he's here...' the housekeeper hissed again, placing her finger over her lips. 'Don't scare him off...'

'Scare who...?' Luke uttered.

But Cassie, as she slipped past Mrs Ennis into the gloom of

the shuttered salon, with its white-shrouded furniture and still, stale air, grasped what – and who – the housekeeper meant. There he was, the little telltale form tucked in the corner of one of Anthea Dubois's best silk chairs. Cassie sucked her breath in with joy.

'Kipling...'

She carefully stepped forward and sat on the floor by the chair to peer at the cat. He looked leaner, a little unkempt; there appeared to be a nick in his ear where an adversary had taken a bite.

'Oh, thank God, you're home,' Cassie whispered. 'You naughty cat.'

Kipling woke, lifted his head and gave a little bleat.

'The little monkey was sitting at the kitchen window when I went down, looking all forlorn, and, in a way, quite outraged,' Mrs Ennis said. 'I gave him some fish scraps and a dash of milk. Lord knows where he has been all this time.'

'Poor creature,' Cassie uttered. 'It's been four months! What tales you could tell.'

She gently touched his paw, her fingertip trembling, her face suddenly wet with tears.

Mrs Ennis said, 'I'll leave you both to it then... put the kettle on.'

Luke sat down on the floor beside Cassie, his arm around her waist, something he had never done before, apart from when they'd danced at Marianne's wedding. His touch felt heavy, and grounding. He pressed a handkerchief into her trembling hand. In the half-light, Kipling rearranged himself and settled down with a sigh.

'Ah, thank goodness, little man,' Luke said. 'We have been worried. Now you are home, you can ruin my mother's chair all you like.'

Cassie's laugh, brief and cleansing, burst out of her, but she continued to weep, silently, and seemed unable to stop. Luke pulled her closer and she sensed the comfort he offered, and yet it felt tentative, and rather awkward.

'You can't go and live with Esme now,' he said playfully, persuasively. 'For what would Kipling think?'

Mopping her tears with the handkerchief, Cassie rallied and politely eased herself out of his embrace.

'We must telegram your mother to tell her that he is home,' she said brightly. 'She will want to send for him.'

'I expect she will make the trip herself to fetch him back to Edinburgh. Then she will see you,' Luke said. 'She thinks you are wonderful, Cassie...'

Cassie gestured, wanting him to stop there, fresh tears stinging her eyes.

'Honestly,' she said, forcing a laugh to break through the compliment, 'why am I crying? I should be happy, over the moon. Kipling is home.'

'I know why you are crying, Cassie.'

His low, serious voice cut through the dim light and forced her to look at him. The daylight glancing in through the door from the hallway settled on the rim of his spectacles. Behind the lenses, intelligence glittered in his eyes, ponderous and searching.

Panic began to smoulder in Cassie's belly. 'You do...?'

'You have been through so much. Kipling coming home is the one happy thing that has happened in a long time.'

'We've all been through—'

'I'm not talking about other people. Especially not myself. I am talking about you.'

Luke sat back a little, and in doing so, seemed even closer, for he could see the whole of Cassie, from top to toe. He reached over to take hold of both of her hands and cradled them, resting on her lap. Kipling shifted on the chair and gave a healthy, teeth-baring yawn. Cassie wanted to release herself from Luke's grasp, from his concern, but it would seem so entirely rude, when he had been so caring for all this time.

'Cassie. Cassandra Marsh,' Luke uttered, with a shake of his head. 'As if I would ever have forgotten you.'

His proximity, and his flattery, confused her. And then she remembered.

'You mean, that evening? Is that what I said on the telephone? When I called from Peter Jones?' she asked. 'I was in a frightful state.'

'I heard the pain in your voice, down the line,' he said. 'And I saw it when you got here. You were shattered.'

'You were so kind, Luke, I...' Cassie thought that she had got away with it. That Luke knew nothing of how devastated she had been. But at least the reason, her terrible secret, would forever stay locked away.

'And all I could do, from that moment on, was take care of you, Cassie,' Luke said. 'To do all I could for you. I ask nothing of you. Except to know that I love you. And have done since the first summer at Oliver's.'

She shook her head as understanding seeped through her bones. That from the moment the little rotter of a boy had found her in the dining room at Greenaways, sipping Juno's lemonade, that his teasing her and challenging her, and often, let's be honest, ignoring her, came down to him loving her.

'No, Luke...' she breathed with shattering clarity.

He hadn't heard. Surely, if he had, he would not have continued off in his own world of reasoning and words, his desire to constantly impart information. Surely if he had listened to her, he'd know that she didn't feel the same way. She felt desperate to release her fingers from his grasp.

'It seems entirely the right moment to ask you,' Luke's face broke into the happiest of grins, beaming, obviously not reading the expression on her face, 'because people are talking already... you living here with me. It isn't, really, the done thing. Vee joked about me being your landlord... it might sound seedy, so perhaps you *should* go to live with Esme for a while... while we sort everything... because if they already think...'

'I don't care what people think,' Cassie said.

'But I do,' he said. He rearranged himself so that he faced her, gathering her hands even tighter in his. His fingers, immaculately manicured from his latest trip to the barbers, were damp with sweat. And yet, overriding that uncomfortable sensation, and the excruciating closeness of him, thundered her realisation of what was about to happen.

'Cassie, will you marry me?'

'Oh, Luke...'

He beamed at her in the gloom, as if she had said, *Yes*.

And Cassie knew that if she were a weaker person, that would have been her answer. She would have consented and be done with it. What girl, these days, wouldn't want to be taken away from it all? To leave the city, live in a beautiful, big house in the suburbs by the river, with a kind, wealthy and generous man. But she knew that wherever he took her off to, whatever life he would make for her, her troubles would follow her and set up home there too. *Yes* would not fix the turmoil and grief raging in the background.

'I'm sorry, Luke,' she said. 'I am saying no.'

His face fell. Finally, he had heard her, and his mouth gave a little twist as if to clip down his disappointment. Cassie's guilt slammed into her; she felt she had sunk him, like a ship *lost with all hands*.

'But thank you, Luke, so much. You are such a great friend.' She sincerely wanted to comfort him. He didn't deserve to have that look on his face, after everything he had done for her. She couldn't tell him that she didn't love him, not in the way she wanted to. 'You see, I don't want to marry anyone.'

Cassie pulled her hands away and Luke's head drooped. She gazed at him, and an icy shell began to form around her, protecting her, isolating her. It shielded her from daring to think about the pain she'd caused Luke; it eased the burden of her family secret; and diluted her confusion, her feelings for Oliver. Behind frozen walls, she could detach herself even further from the unkindness in the outside world, and even her own.

'If I marry you, Luke,' she said, 'then I will have to give up my job, as you know. Married women don't do what I do. And I want to keep working, I want to keep fighting. I must. I want to do that for all of us.' She took a ragged breath. 'You can see that, can't you, Luke? I need to work.'

He nodded. 'I'm sorry I have embarrassed you, Cassie. I have messed everything up.'

'No, no,' she said cheerfully. 'I'm not embarrassed. We are still friends, aren't we? If that is what you want.'

Luke shrugged and turned to Kipling on the chair to gently stroke his head. And Cassie felt her icy wall thicken. She could see through the shield, certainly, she mused as she watched Luke fuss with the cat, and yet she felt so dreadfully cold. And alone. Luke mattered to her, his friendship mattered, but he had changed it forever.

'Perhaps,' she said, her voice weakened by the darkness in the room, 'it is best that when I see Esme at work tomorrow, I ask if I can sleep on her sofa until her friend moves out. I don't want to be in your way here.'

Luke turned to her, aghast, his eyes bright and earnest.

'In my way? No. That will never be the case, Cassie. And I can't have you sleeping on someone's sofa. That won't do at all. Stay here until everything is arranged. Please.' Luke's mouth found its way into a smile. 'Kipling insists.'

Cassie laughed lightly but tears scalded her eyes.

'In that case,' she said, getting up to leave the room; she needed to busy herself, felt in danger of changing her mind. 'I had better go and fetch you that cup of tea that Mrs Ennis promised us.'

At the door, Cassie paused and turned in confusion, wanting to thank Luke for his understanding, to echo her vow of friendship; to ask him if he would forgive her, and if they could put it all right.

But he spoke before she could muster the words.

'Cassie, whatever happens, wherever you go, nothing will change,' Luke said. 'My offer will stand. Always.'

* * *

Esme's flat, a pretty place tucked away in a cobbled mews behind a row of Bloomsbury mansions, proved the perfect bolt-hole for Cassie. A month or so after Marianne's wedding, and the return of Kipling, and as soon as Esme's friend had vacated, Cassie moved in.

Luke came with her on the Underground to Holborn, to carry her suitcase. Cassie, having fitted the rest of her belongings into a small carpet bag, felt buoyant and light of foot at making a fresh start. And yet the feeling of being exposed and vulnerable crept over her as she carted her life with her on and off Tube trains, packed into two pieces of luggage.

'Well, he's a fine figure of a man,' Esme whispered to Cassie by the front door, as Luke disappeared up the stairs and around the corner with the suitcase. 'Is he a bachelor?'

'He most certainly is,' Cassie said, giving her an encouraging smile.

Cassie knew her friend of old, having watched her enjoying the company of male colleagues in the staff canteen at Whitehall, or at the Lyon's tearoom around the corner, giving all manner of gentlemen the glad-eye.

And she smiled as Esme hurried up the stairs, calling, 'Will you stay for a cup of tea Mr Dubois? Luke, is it?'

Cassie, following her friend, heard him say, 'I won't actually, thank you; I have much to do.' And when she reached the sunny little first-floor living room, Luke continued with, 'Except to say cheerio to Cassie.'

She thanked him, feeling shy and aching with guilt, unable to completely meet his eye, even when he rested his hand on her shoulder, his gaze wide and earnest.

'Remember what I told you, Miss Cassandra Marsh,' he said.

Cassie nodded her assurance and saw him out, sensing an ending that had happened all too quickly. It felt as if another person had passed out of her life, even before she had shut the door behind him.

* * *

A few weeks after she had moved into Esme's, Miss Redmond and Mr Frederick realised that Cassie had a flair for languages. It was certainly listed on her CV but, her supervisors admitted, her aptitude must have been overlooked in the early days of recruitment mayhem.

And when the important man behind his polished-oak desk in his Whitehall office told Cassie, without giving much away, naturally, that they needed linguists with Signals Intelligence, in a headquarters somewhere in the Home Counties, she felt a brightening sense of anticipation. Distance, space, and a new challenge felt like the answer to a puzzle that she had been struggling with for years. A chance, perhaps, to put her thorny family issues to one side, to stop thinking about Oliver, and for her to be kind, do the right thing, and keep out of Luke's way.

And not long afterwards, Cassie again packed her suitcase, not forgetting her German school dictionary, and caught a train out of London, on her way to the Kentish coast.

PART III

18

KENT, APRIL 1943

Spring came to this south-eastern corner of England later than it ever had done at Greenaways, far away in the West Country. But, after working in London, in the smothering underground bunker, and making her way home past bombsites and along dusty streets, Cassie didn't mind that at all. At least she could breathe fresh sea air and work half of her shifts in daylight.

Local people called Capel-le-Ferne, along the coast from Dover, 'the village in the clouds', and it seemed to inhabit its own world, with its own peculiar climate. Moist sea air rose up the chalky cliff faces, bowling in as mysterious, low-lying cloud, scattering droplets on whatever it touched – windowpanes, eyelashes, and the lush-green, unfurling ferns that thrived on banks and in hollows, spilling over garden walls. And, as Cassie left her billet that morning in this, her second spring here, and walked past flint-walled houses, and the medieval church – the 'chapel in the ferns' indeed – on her way to the headquarters, she felt cleansed and nourished, gulping on the sweet, salty air as if it were feeding her.

As she walked along, the sky cleared for a moment and over

the sea, the coast of France emerged on the horizon. Cassie felt as if she could touch Calais, the distance entirely swimmable. And, a stone's throw along her clifftop, sat the Capel battery, its three mighty guns trained across the Channel, where the bombardiers were at their stations morning, noon and night. Further up the rise, like a beacon perched on the sea cliff, stood Ferne House, the Victorian mansion requisitioned by Signals Intelligence and Cassie's place of work. Or, more officially, Station Y. And a mere twenty-one miles to the south, over the water, the enemy waited, watching.

'Good morning,' Cassie said, showing her identity card to the sentry at the entrance, and he let her through with a jovial salute.

Two of the newly recruited WRAF girls in their tidy uniforms were walking ahead of her up the long, sweeping path to the house. They caught sight of Cassie and waved. Cassie slowed her pace, but they waited for her.

'We're going into the village at lunchtime, to have a look around, if you'd like to come,' said one. 'You can show us the sights.'

'We thought we'd stop in at the café. Have a sandwich,' said the other.

Cassie patted her shoulder bag. 'Ah, thank you, but no. I have my own sandwiches. And a letter from my cousin to read.'

'Ah well, another time.'

Cassie smiled and nodded, feeling awful that she could not remember their names, but also relieved that she had a genuine excuse for not joining them. She had been at Ferne House for eighteen months now but, as one of the few civilians, still felt like an outsider – and preferred it that way. Not long after she had first arrived, she had overhead someone say, 'Who's that?' as she walked by, and another had answered, 'Oh, that's the girl from the War Room...' And Cassie had decided how well it summed her up; there felt no need for them to know anything more about her.

She went through the front door and walked across the large hallway, with its graceful, arched ceilings, to her office, once an elegant parlour. Compared to the energetic, intense atmosphere of the Westminster bunker, the airy rooms at Ferne House had an altogether more restrained, hushed, peaceful air. Cassie put this down to everyone simply *listening*, and the silence suited her well.

Margaret, the Signals Officer, at her desk in front of the grand fireplace, lifted her head to greet her.

'Morning, ma'am,' Cassie said, keeping her voice low so as not to disturb her colleagues already at work.

Sitting down at her desk, she switched on her receiver, fitted her headphones and ran her usual, early-morning frequency tests. The aerials on the roof picked up short-range radio streaming across from the Continent, and over the airwaves, down the wires and into Cassie's ears surged staccato voices, clipped and truncated by signals and static. Merely noise and interference to the untrained. But Cassie, her notepad at the ready, gently teased the dial with her fingertips to tune in past expectant, yawning silence, to pick up words, sentences, information. Gerard, she thought, his boyhood wireless obsession often on her mind, would have been proud.

And she listened.

Messages filtered through the channels: communications between German Majors and their subordinates stationed in Haute-Normandie or Picardie, and between marine *Kapitans* and sailors on patrol between Calais and Dieppe. Cassie detected, isolated, and wrote down what she heard. She added her translation underneath, tore the sheet from her pad and handed it to the clerk, who took it immediately to the signallers in the next room. They forwarded it in scrambled code straight to Station X at Bletchley, somewhere in Bedfordshire.

And Cassie would close her eyes, concentrate, turn the dial and listen.

Whether any of her intercepted messages, when followed up or acted on, had a positive outcome, she had no idea. But she prayed that each piece of information she collected would build a picture, would help someone, somewhere, be they a downed bomber crew, resistance fighters in hiding in the Bocage, or sailors in trouble at sea.

* * *

At lunchtime, Cassie took her flask and sandwiches outside to sit on a bench by the small lawn overlooking the sea. The sky had cleared again and beyond the balustrade, she could see a wide sweep of water, and the curving pier at Folkestone. Relishing having this moment to herself, Cassie sighed with pleasure and drew out Marianne's letter. By the looks of the postmark, it had reached her at her billet in the village via the War Office PO Box after some delay.

My dear Cassie,

I hope this finds you well. All is continuing here at Green-aways as it always does. A little chaotic, as usual, with Harry's boys – although so many of them want to go home now, that Harry hints that this will be the case after the summer term. Ma is keeping her fingers crossed! Pa doesn't mind, though. He organises hikes for them at weekends, now the weather is better, up to his favourite spots on Dartmoor. There isn't

*much moaning from the boys. I think they love it. And they
love Pa too!*

The sun warmed Cassie's face and she smiled, remembering
her uncle's enthusiasm for the wild, open moorland, imagining
all too well how infectious it would be for the schoolboys.

*Little Lilibet is, as you may guess, the light of our lives. Nearly
a year old now, can you believe it, Cassie? Our dear honey-
moon child. Although, I am sure Ma was counting months on
her fingers when I told her I was pregnant. Lilibet is losing her
baby fat, now that she is trotting around, which I feel is rather
something to be mourned in my scatty mother's mind. But,
lo! I have other news. I am expecting again!*

Cassie, thrown for a moment, gasped and looked back at the
view. Her cousin, streaking ahead of her again on her life's
mission, married and with a second child on the way – it made
Cassie feel left behind again. She folded the letter, experienced
a bewildering prickle of envy, similar, she was able to admit to
herself now, to how she felt watching Marianne play tennis,
arrive at Greenaways resplendent in her WRAF uniform, and
walk down the aisle in her dazzling wedding dress.

But she only had herself to blame.

Glancing across the lawn, Cassie spotted Margaret with a
pair of male officers chatting, sharing cigarettes on their break;
another young man, the office clerk, was with one of the new
WRAF girls, making her laugh. She had probably invited him to
go with her to the village instead. The men appeared confident
and attractive, certainly, and yet Cassie barely engaged with any
of them. She would not allow the idea of making friends, or

meeting a boyfriend, never mind progressing to marriage and motherhood, to cross her mind.

As she had told Luke, when he proposed to her, there seemed to be far too much else to do.

Even during the short while Cassie had been living at Esme's, Luke had popped in regularly for the cup of tea that her friend had promised him the day Cassie moved in. And while Esme flirted with him, he had remained oblivious, his attention firmly on Cassie.

Sitting on the bench, Cassie's eyes stung with remorse and her old, tired guilt blazed once again. She blinked, and a seagull caught her eye, drifting over the clifftop, riding the warm air, wings pure white against the sky, and she felt engulfed by regret; the chance of an ordinary, happy life – just like Marianne's – missed.

Cassie unfolded the letter, found her place again.

There's room aplenty here for us at lovely old Greenaways, but I feel Harry may be itching to get back to Plymouth. Perhaps we will when all this madness is over. Your mother is contemplating going back to town, as you probably know. We will miss her, but she said that she so desperately wants to be with your father.

Cassie swallowed mild nausea, the sense of pity that goaded her whenever she thought of her mother. But it always seemed to be displaced, quite swiftly, by pure anger towards her father.

Vee, as you know now is married to her handsome RAF chap and lives near Canterbury.

Cassie had no idea about Vee, had half-expected, over the past year or so, to hear of her and Oliver's engagement.

As you are stationed 'somewhere in Kent', Vee wondered if you would like to meet up – we're both not sure of distances but I will include her address, anyway, at the bottom of this letter. Perhaps you will write to her? It might be nice for you both to see a friendly face.

We haven't heard from Oliver in a long while, have you? I never know if it is a good thing or bad. And I always think too much. Ma constantly worries, and so do we all. Do let us know if you hear from him.

Cassie flinched at the mention of Oliver's name. She ought to be used to it by now, should have expected it.

After Marianne's wedding, he had drifted away from her, the family, from everyone. Cassie had heard nothing from him since then. She could blame the war, of course, for letters not getting through. Sitting on the bench at Ferne House, taking in the noon-day sun, she allowed her sorrow to flow; she did not fight it. She must let it run its course and be done with.

Cassie turned back to the letter, now somewhat creased in her hands:

Write soon and let us know how you are, Cassie. We all miss you dearly.

19

KENT, JUNE 1943

Cassie's bus followed the Roman road out of Dover on its straight-as-an-arrow way to Canterbury, chugging alongside fields, pastures and woodland all maturing steadily in the warmth of early summer. The last of the blossoms had been scattered in the orchards, and vines burgeoned on the hop frames, turning their tendrils and their leaves towards the sun. The air inland had a more rounded, honeyed scent, Cassie decided as she walked up through the village that lay halfway thereabouts between Capel and Canterbury, where Vee had suggested they meet.

As she approached The Gardeners Arms, a long, low, red-brick public house with undulating roof and foundations that seemed to have settled deep into the earth, Cassie hoped Vee would do as she asked in her letter and wait for her outside the pub. She had never been inside one on her own before, and didn't relish doing so now.

Truth be told, Cassie also didn't relish coming to meet Vee in the first place and had only agreed to because her cousin had suggested it. She feared uncomfortable memories surfacing,

Vee's prying questions. But life at Ferne House, Cassie had to admit, proved rather lonely all the while she kept herself to herself.

Quickening her pace, she skirted the village green where a huge, ancient oak tree grew, wondering if she'd recognise Marianne's friend after all this time. But as she crossed the road, shielding her eyes from the sun, an unmistakable, cheery voice called out from one of the tables in the pub front garden.

'Cassie, over here! Here I am!' Vee stood up, waving both her hands. 'I've got you half a pale ale,' she said. 'We could have had Bishop's Finger, but the barman said it is rather strong, and we can't have it going to our heads, can we? They can cut us some sandwiches, if you like.'

Vee's cheeks looked as rosy as ever, her rich-brown hair longer and rolled to perfection, her energy barely contained inside her neat jacket and skirt as she hauled out a chair for Cassie to sit, planting a friendly kiss on her cheek.

'My, my, it's been a while!' Vee breezed, sitting back down and taking neat sips from her drink.

Cassie saw the gold band on Vee's left hand and tapped it with her fingertip.

'Congratulations,' she said. 'Tell me when, how, who?'

'Ah, my lovely Reggie. I am Mrs Reginald Carey now. He's Flight Lieutenant at Biggin Hill, although, as you probably have guessed, we met at Manston. We live in Stourmarsh, on the other side of Canterbury. It's quiet, a little dull if you ask me, proper country. But when Reggie comes home. Well!'

Cassie smiled, drank her ale, tasting its mellow, light and somewhat addictive sweetness. The flavour, she concluded, of a Kentish summer. 'A Flight Lieutenant, no less, Vee…' she mused. She had been expecting a young navigator or bomb loader.

Picking up on Cassie's train of thought, Vee said, 'Reggie is a few years older than me, granted, but not *that* old. The airmen get younger and younger these days.' She laughed. 'But I think it's what I needed, really. A nice, sensible, experienced man. An officer, no less! Marianne will tell you. I have calmed down a bit these days. And it is all thanks to Reggie.'

'You must worry about him...?'

'We all worry, though, don't we?' Vee gave her a serious, experienced look.

Cassie glanced around at the other tables, at the villagers and farm workers, and a few people in military uniform basking in the sunshine, taking their leave from the war for a simple lunchtime, and felt among equals. She noticed the blackboard on the pub wall listing sandwiches: sardine, spam or cucumber. Dessert: Gypsy tart (mock).

'And when, Vee?' Cassie asked. 'Last time I saw you, it was Marianne's wedding. Did you know Reggie then?' As soon as she spoke, she realised the pertinence of her question.

Vee's face clouded, thinking about it. 'Hmmm, no, it was after that. Not long after. I really thought I had had enough of men. The way some of them treat you... ah, I don't want to speak out of turn... but your cousin...'

Cassie wanted to pretend that she didn't know what she meant, but didn't have it in her.

She swallowed the dryness in her throat. 'You mean Oliver?'

Sipping her drink, Vee nodded. She turned to read the menu.

'Hmm, slim pickings, as always. I'll go in and order. What do you fancy?'

'Cucumber.' Cassie gave her a five-shilling note, her hand trembling. It had been nearly two years ago, but the picnic on Dartmoor, and whatever had happened between Oliver and Vee, had changed them all. 'Please, I'll buy these.'

When Vee came back, she sprinkled change into Cassie's hand.

'So, your cousin,' she said, with a humorous grimace of disdain.

'I thought that you had hit if off at the wedding?' Cassie said cautiously. 'You were dancing, laughing. You...'

Cassie gazed at Vee, mesmerised by her hands: small, plump, manicured. And Vee's mouth, her sweet, Flower Fairy lips, and her bubbling laughter always beneath the surface. No wonder Oliver had found Vee attractive, wanted Vee, instinctively, even for one moment. Cassie imagined, she understood how Oliver would have been entranced, for she *knew* Oliver.

'Why, yes, we did all those things, dancing, having a good time, and I thought we were getting on. That he liked me,' Vee said. 'But really, I think it was all down to Dutch courage. You know.' Vee tapped the side of her glass with her fingernail. 'I admit, Cassie, I was making a downright play for him. I think he is quite the chap. And he seemed to welcome it, at first. But he certainly puts up his defences.'

Cassie shook her head in surprise. This did not sound like Oliver, apart from at the end of the picnic and in Luke's car on the way back to Greenaways from Dartmoor, when he seemed to have crawled inside himself.

Vee dipped her head, looking rather shamefaced, and said, 'You must have noticed that we stole away to have a roll in the hay on Dartmoor that time... As nice as it was, I never felt that I got anywhere close to him. Always a barrier, his mind somewhere else.'

The barman set their sandwiches down in front of them, but Cassie had lost her appetite, her belly full with a stew of churning, muddled memories.

Annoyed at herself for being weak, for going back down that

path when she had fought so hard to resolve it, she took a bite of her sandwich, hoping it would help settle her stomach.

'You both looked like you were having a good time...?' she pressed on, hating herself for asking.

'But even when we were dancing at the wedding, I didn't feel he was *with* me. All very confusing, frankly. Obviously, he was not for me. He cut himself off.' Vee sighed. 'I wrote to him soon after, and wish I hadn't. I must...' Vee blushed. 'I must have sounded *pathetic*. I know there's a war on, and I expect he has used that as an excuse. A blessing, really.'

'You haven't seen him since—?'

'Absolutely not! Soon after that, I met Reggie and realised what type of man I wanted.' Vee drained her glass. 'Let's have another. This ale's delicious.'

They finished their sandwiches, shared a slice of mock Gypsy tart, and the pub garden began to empty as people drifted off. Sunbeams scattered by the oak tree on the green caught in their glasses of ale, turning the honey colour to gold.

'What luxury this is,' Vee beamed at Cassie. 'Supping ale in the afternoon. So, Miss Cassie Marsh,' she said, teasingly. 'How are you? How is the wonderful Lucien Dubois, your ex-land-lord? I bet he misses you, now you are out here in Kent.'

Cassie squared her shoulders. 'I think he is well,' she said, cautiously. 'He writes to me but doesn't tell me much about himself. I think he just likes to share his news about his cat.'

'His cat?' Vee said. 'My, my, a man who likes cats. Something tells me that he certainly *is* Mr Wonderful.'

Cassie found herself smiling in agreement.

In Luke's recent letter, he told her that his mother was planning to take Kipling away to Edinburgh the next time she came down to London, but that he had persuaded her that it was not a good idea.

After all,

Luke had written,

it didn't seem fair to subject the creature to such a long journey, and I know how fond you are of him, Cassie.

'He has moved out of London to Richmond, and Kipling, the cat, loves it out there, apparently,' she said. 'There is a huge garden and lots of trees... I expect Luke is excelling at his job, as usual, but that's all, really...'

Vee winked. 'Oliver told me that Luke liked you a great deal.'

'When did he, when did Oliver...?'

Cassie faltered, her mind switching back to the picnic.

'Ah, I think it is obvious to everyone,' Vee said. 'Written all over Luke's face. You must notice how he looks at you, Cassie.'

Cassie thought of Luke in the salon at Cheyne Row, proposing to her, and her cheeks burnt with contrition.

'Ah, I see a little blush there, Cassie,' Vee chortled. 'I must say, you never give much away. You have poise, a certain reticence, and I think people, men in particular, find it intriguing.'

Cassie shook her head. 'No, I don't think so...'

'Have you looked in the mirror recently?' Vee said. 'You have the quality of a lady – unlike me.' She laughed. 'And as for your hair. Where does that refined, pure blonde come from?'

'My father, actually...'

But Cassie could not absorb Vee's compliments, she could not grasp Luke's feelings for her or how she felt about him, for an immense, breathtaking relief shuddered through her, astounding her and leaving her mute. It had taken time that afternoon, while sitting here with Vee, for realisation to hit her. Whatever had gone on between Vee and Oliver had not mattered. Had meant nothing. And yet her relief made her feel rotten. There must be something terribly wrong with her, she decided, for it to matter so much.

Cassie picked up her glass, her hand trembling as she sipped.

'Ah, it's fine, Cassie. Don't look so alarmed. You should relish it, enjoy the utter admiration of a completely eligible bachelor,' Vee said.

It took Cassie some moments to remember that Vee had been talking about Luke. She nodded, tried to smile.

'But look out,' Vee laughed, 'someone will snatch him up. I must tell you, this happened to a friend of mine... She didn't make her feelings clear... needed to communicate... I said to her, write a letter, make a telephone call...'

As Vee chattered on, Cassie tried once again to reconcile the turmoil pounding through her mind. She had thought that, by coming out here to Kent, and throwing herself deeper into her work, closing herself off, that she may leave it all behind. But her life followed her wherever she went, her own trail of dust: her own shadow.

20

LONDON, OCTOBER 1943

As soon as she walked into the sitting room at Egerton Terrace, Cassie could see that it had benefitted from her mother's touch. Apart from it looking brighter and smelling fresher, the coffee table no longer sported rings from glasses and cups, and newspapers and periodicals lay in neat stacks. Golden chrysanthemums sat in a vase at the window and the layer of dust along the bookshelves had been wiped away, making it look like the home that Cassie had once known. Beside Gerard's *Sherlock Holmes* series, her mother had slotted Cassie's Jane Austen collection.

'It took quite a while to get this place ship-shape,' Cassie's mother said, watching her as she looked around. 'And I gave your room a tidy; thought it would be nice to bring some of your old books down. I think the house, and Dad, went to pieces when Mrs Blake left for the country. He couldn't seem to get a char for love nor money.'

The sitting room felt rather chilly, so Cassie leant over the fire to give it a poke, remembering the certain knack this fireplace needed to help it draw.

'That's better,' she said, aware of the elusive sensation of belonging, suddenly. Since she had last lived here, she had lingered alone in a halfway house between childhood and adulthood. Her life had stalled, and, she felt ready to admit, she had put herself there. Perhaps now, she could do something about it and build her first tentative bridge.

Her mother cut slices of cake, and poured tea. Autumn rain sparkled on the windowpanes, pattering with a soothing rhythm. The room began to warm up.

'I see you are growing flowers again, Mum?' Cassie said, nodding towards the window.

'Ah, I have a confession to make. I treated myself to them while browsing at Peter Jones yesterday. They had just had a delivery from Covent Garden. I was there at exactly the right time. Within half an hour, they'd all but gone. God, I have missed that shop. I have, in a way, missed London.' Her eyes glistened as she handed Cassie a plate. 'And you, Cassie dear.'

'Glad to know where I am in the pecking order.' Cassie laughed, but thought that surely her father should be buying her mother flowers.

'Oh, *you*. You get that from Dad, the little jokes. Are you sure you can't stay for dinner, at least? It has been so long since we were all together – Marianne's wedding was over two years ago!'

'My work, Mum... it has been hard,' Cassie said, hearing the twang of guilt in her voice.

'What time is your train? Dad will be home by six. Can you get a later one?'

'I really can't, Mum. It is important that I report there for seven this evening. Half past at the latest.'

'Sounds like a curfew.'

'It is for security, Mum.'

'I know I shouldn't ask where or why,' her mother said, 'so I won't.'

Travelling up from Kent that morning, Cassie had decided to drop in en route before catching the train to the facility on the outskirts of London, where she was to be taught how to use a new type of radio receiver. Her mother had been back at Egerton Terrace since the summer and had written to Cassie that the threat of air raids had dwindled enough for her to feel safe to leave Greenaways. And that she wanted to spend more time at home, with Cassie's father.

I want to get back to a semblance of normality, to our old life, if that will ever be possible.

And Cassie guessed, between the lines, that she had meant life at Egerton Terrace without Gerard.

'Sorry, Mum, I do seem to have sprung this visit on you,' she said.

'Cassie, dear, never apologise for that. This is your home!'

Except Cassie did not always feel it to be the case.

'But you know how things are, with my work,' she said instead. 'It is impossible to make firm plans.'

'I'm just thinking how disappointed Dad will be to miss you. If only you'd told us beforehand, perhaps he could have taken the afternoon off?'

Cassie set her cup down. 'So, what news from Greenaways? How is your lovely grandniece?'

'Ah, Lilibet is adorable. I have a new photograph of her with Marianne and Harry. They went to a studio in Dartmouth, all in their Sunday best. Remind me to fetch it before you go. But goodness me, poor Marianne, a child under two and another one on the way. It is exactly what happened to Juno, when she had Oliver and then Marianne, although...'

Cassie waited, wondering what her mother had wanted to

say. She had been vague before, that summer of 1936 at Green-aways, when she had said that Uncle Charles had *come home from the Great War, married Juno, the lot...* Perhaps she had meant what Cassie had overheard about Oliver. That he was *no Greenaway.*

'Although, Mum...?' Cassie prompted her. 'Times were different then, is that what you mean?'

Her mother shook her head, gave her an inscrutable look.

'And did you hear, Cassie?' she went on. 'Oliver is back in England – a huge relief for Juno. But who knows where he will go next. He didn't manage to visit Greenaways, however. Uncle Charles mentioned something about possibly the Scottish Highlands...'

'Yes, I know. I got a letter from Marianne yesterday.' Cassie arranged her expression into one of natural curiosity, folding her emotions into a tight parcel inside her heart. 'A relief for all of us,' she said.

'For now.'

Cassie nodded, understanding. Allied troops had invaded Sicily in the summer and started their hard slog up into Italy, and yet Oliver wasn't with them. Being sent to the Highlands could only mean more training. She smiled inwardly, tingling with pride; she imagined how good Oliver would be at leading his soldiers, winning their respect, their admiration. He'd been like that at school, Luke had once told her. As captain of the rugby team, he commanded discipline; they held the line, worked together, obeyed the rules. All those hours on the playing field would have paid off for Captain Greenaway.

But she did not want to, she must not, think about, worry about Oliver.

Cassie gazed at a painting in the alcove by the window: a wide, peaceful river with overhanging trees, sunlight glowing on water, dappled shade along the banks. The Seine on its way to the sea. And, in its corner, the jagged initials:

AR

'That's new,' she said, and then instantly realised that she had seen it before at Greenaways.

'Aunt Juno gave it to me, as a parting gift,' said her mother. 'Painted at the turn of the century. She knew how much I admired it while I was there. She is good like that. Very observant, and sensitive to people's needs.'

'Hmm.' Cassie preferred to blot Juno, and her cool, knowing eyes, from her mind.

'And she knows a great deal about art. She has such enthralling stories to tell from her heyday. She was an artist's model, did you know that? She went to Paris when she was eighteen: around 1911, I think. Before we knew her.' Her eyes glittered with intrigue. 'What a life! Juno is fascinating. She was muse to Alberte Rene; he painted that,' Cassie's mother indicated the painting, 'and many of the other pieces she has.'

Hearing her mother say the enigmatic artist's name, Cassie felt a long-standing puzzle settle in her mind. Among the other paintings that graced the walls of Greenaways, Alberte Rene must have painted Juno in all her nude splendour. Could it be that he was Oliver's father? No wonder, she thought, the photograph of the artist with his group of admirers, and Juno, had been secreted in an old coat at the bottom of the wardrobe.

'I saw the painting of Aunt Juno once, in her dressing room,' Cassie said, immediately wishing she hadn't. 'We were playing hide-and-seek,' she added. A spark of nostalgia lit up her mind: dreamy, halcyon days caught in amber.

'It's quite something, isn't it? That nude. Of course, Rene is long dead. He was quite an old man. Well, I should say, a lot older than Juno. Died in England soon after the end of the Great War.'

Her mother gave a troubled sigh, fell quiet, and gazed past Cassie at the rain on the window. With her sad, wistful expression, Cassie wondered if she thought of Gerard and, indeed, Uncle Roland.

'Is it good to be back, Mum?' she asked, to rally her. 'Home at last?'

'Ah, yes and no,' she said. 'You see, Greenaways is my childhood home. So many memories, layers and layers of them. But these days, the old house gives me a strange feeling of... how can I put it? Looking and being the same as it ever was, and yet it speaks a different language... and this is down to Juno being chatelaine, of course, taking over from your grandmother all those years ago. She has certainly put her stamp on it.'

'Was it difficult, being there...?'

Cassie's mother gave her a sharp glance. 'It is difficult everywhere.'

'I can imagine.'

'Can you, Cassie dear?' She looked sad and guarded.

'Mum, I know it is terribly hard, with us losing Gerard.' Tears pooled briefly in Cassie's eyes. She knew too well there could be many other reasons for her mother's distress.

'So many things,' her mother uttered to herself. 'It is such a muddle.'

Cassie waited, watched as her mother ruminated, seemed to do battle with her own thoughts, giving little shakes of her head, as if to crush them before they rose to the surface.

'I said, just now, that I find Juno fascinating,' she said cautiously, peering at Cassie as if to check how to proceed. 'And... your father does too. Has done so for many years.'

'We all find Juno fascin—' Cassie stopped. Seeing the knowing look on her mother's face, horror drenched her body.

'Darling...' Her mother leant forward, her face creasing with sorrow, her eyes sharp with pain. 'Dad told me that you know about your aunt and him. I am so sorry, what an awful thing for you to have to deal with. On top of everything else—'

Cassie exhaled a rush of scorching air. 'You *know* about them? I had hoped to God that you didn't. That they had stopped, and that you were none the wiser.'

Her mother shuffled in her armchair, curled her knees up and hugged them to her body, her mouth working into an ugly shape. Her voice trickled out, small and childlike: 'I have always known.'

Cassie's horror switched to nausea, bubbling through her stomach; her scalp tightened in a chilled sweat. She barely remembered how to breathe.

'Dear God, Mum...'

'It started, apparently, during a game of Sardines at Greenaways, way back,' she said. 'Your father always has been a flirt. And your aunt... well! She has a certain appeal, doesn't she? Not in the classic way, I grant you. More a mysterious allure. Remember, she had been Rene's muse, and...' She took a deep breath, moved her head slowly as if her neck caused her pain. 'Juno and Charles used to host big Friday to Monday house parties. You children were all small; Gerard was eight and you were only about four. You wouldn't have remembered this, but we used to put you all to bed on the nursery floor, you know, where Oliver and Gerard would sleep during the summer holidays. We had a children's nurse in those days. She kept an eye on you. Dad and Juno must have chosen the same hiding place. You know the game. People pack into the tiniest spaces, all sorts of merriment ensues, while they wait to be found...'

Cassie shut her eyes, willing herself not to picture it. She had seen far too much already.

'How?' Cassie's thoughts floundered. 'How did you find out?' she asked, praying that it hadn't been in the same way she had.

'Juno told me.'

'*When?*' Cassie cried, aghast. Her question felt irrelevant, but she struggled to find the right things to say.

'She wanted to apologise, almost to ask my permission. My blessing. Ha, yes. As I have said before, Cassie, the 1920s were rather chaotic times. You see, I didn't particularly want to join in, with two young children...' She paused. Pain flickered over her face and yet her poise remained firm, her lipstick immaculate, her hair dressed as neatly as ever. 'And still mourning my brother, I must not have been entirely *there*.'

'But *Juno* had two young children.'

'Juno is Juno,' she said, inhaling as if air would work as an analgesic. 'Remember how I used to bake puddings for Dad, although they never seemed to look like they did in the recipe book, and I put so much effort into creating our lovely home.' She gave a wistful glance around the room. 'Because I couldn't or didn't want to do other things... Too damn tired all the time. Your father needed something extra that I could not give him. And Juno obviously had something about her that he needed.'

Cassie hated how defeated her mother sounded. Her mind reeled and doubled back, remembering how her father used to mention Juno's 'hooky nose', and, at times, go out of his way to avoid her. Their simmering anger towards each other, their little spats: a smoke screen.

'Cassie, please don't look so wounded,' her mother said, her voice verging on the positive. 'I gave them my blessing. For the sake of the family. Why make people unhappy, if you are yourself happy with the status quo? But it was all unmentionable. No one talked about it. All terribly English. That was, still is, the way of the world.'

'Oh, Mum, you knew from the start?' Cassie breathed, incredulous.

'Pretty much. But I loved your father. *Love* your father,' she said stoutly, sitting up straight and smoothing her skirt. 'Always will. As for Juno, she is my friend, above all else. She was there for me when Uncle Roland died. Also, with Gerard...'

'But it must have affected you. Damaged you?' Cassie cried with indignation. 'When I was younger, I remember you sometimes looking so unhappy but at the same time trying your hardest with Dad. It is all so... objectionable.'

'Oh, my beautiful daughter, always so polite.'

Cassie felt a snap of irritation. She wondered how her mother could be so blasé, shaking pain off like raindrops from an umbrella. But she had had far more time than Cassie to get used to it. Even so, no one should have to get used to *that*.

Her anger surged, directed once again at her father. How he could have been so arrogant, self-absorbed, so careless with her mother?

She hesitated. 'Does Uncle Charles know?'

'Ho, no. I don't think Charles could take it.'

'Then why should you and *I* take it?' Tears of rage, of frustration, burst from Cassie's eyes. 'And I can barely look Dad in the face at the best of times. Let alone Juno.'

Her mother leapt to her feet and sat on the arm of Cassie's chair, pulling her head towards her shoulder, stroking her hair like she might have done when Cassie was a child. The room grew quiet; a piece of coal fell in the grate, sending up a spike of orange flame.

'Cassie, Cassie. Me coming home here, to be with your father, where I belong, is all part of the healing. We are working on it,' her mother whispered, soothing her. 'He told me that you had guessed about him and Juno. And that it was time to stop. I have no idea what Juno thought, but perhaps she saw the sense in it. Time to move on... Maybe we will talk about it one day.'

Cassie's tears scorched her cheeks, as raw as her anger.

'How can we be sure it is really over?' She scrabbled for her handkerchief in her cuff.

'He finished it, he said, around the time that the news came though about Gerard. Perhaps they both felt sorry for me. Even more sorry than usual.'

'But this is what is so utterly horrible...' muttered Cassie, blotting her face. 'They have no respect for you, or dear Uncle Charles.'

'Ah, but strangely...' Her mother sat forward so she could look at Cassie properly. Her smile was crooked as she gently wiped Cassie's cheeks with her fingertips. 'I feel powerful, in a way. Isn't that odd?'

Cassie wanted to burst out laughing at the absurdity but felt too exhausted. 'But,' she said, 'it seems to me, whatever happens, someone will get hurt.'

'Everyone is hurt,' said her mother. 'What's that pain, when you have lost both a brother and a son?'

Cassie faltered, her anger spent, unable to counter the argument.

Her mother went back to her own armchair and began to stoke the fire.

'Anyway, at times, it certainly worked for me. As I said: a sense of power.' She paused. 'Also, I like Juno.'

'I don't,' Cassie blurted out, surprising herself.

Her mother stared at her in humorous surprise, then nodded, acknowledging her honesty. 'Are you all right, Cassie?'

She shook her head, swallowed a mouthful of cold tea to ease her parched mouth and her aching throat. She grimaced.

'Come on, we can do better than that,' said her mother. 'I will put the kettle on again.'

Cassie slumped back in her armchair, her mind spinning. She felt twitchy, on edge, her whole body unsettled as she tried to adjust to her mother's revelation, her renewed confusion, and the shock which, she felt sure, was yet to hit her.

Her mind switched to Oliver, as it inevitably did in distress. He always had the ability to take on her misery, whatever it may be, talk it out, absorb it and set it straight. But, as usual, he was somewhere far away. And even if he were beside her right now, ready to listen, she could not possibly tell him about *this*. And yet if Oliver was here, she thought, trying not to smile at the idea, he would fill the room with light.

Cassie wiped her eyes again, took a deep breath, reminded herself that she did not and could never have a claim over him. She must release herself from her own muddle, her own pain. And finally, she may grow up.

'Is it *definitely* over between Dad and Juno?' Cassie asked, making her mother stop on her way out the room. 'Because, to be honest with you, the thought of it makes me feel sick.'

Her mother pondered and inhaled, bolstering herself with a little more strength.

'It is, Cassie,' she said. 'But I often ask myself, when are things *really* over?'

* * *

An hour or so later, they hugged on the doorstep. The rain had passed, and the late-afternoon sky, as it gradually darkened, held a deep, pure indigo tinge over the South Ken chimney pots.

'Don't leave it so long next time,' her mother said.

'I'll try not to.'

'You're catching the Tube?'

'Yes, it's not quite rush hour yet, so it shouldn't be too busy.'

'Ugh, but the trains are so dusty and dirty, and you are looking so pressed and fine in your coat and good shoes.' Her mother turned back for her handbag, hanging from the coat stand near the front door. 'Here, take this.' She pressed a ten-shilling note into her hand. 'I will treat you to a taxi, with lots to spare. You should have no trouble finding one on the Brompton Road. You can ride in style.'

Cassie laughed lightly. 'Thank you, Mum.'

But she did not return her smile. 'Write to me, when you've had a chance to take all of this... this news in,' she said, peering at her in earnest. 'Or we can talk on the telephone if you like.'

They both turned at the sound of a vehicle coming up Egerton Terrace. It stopped next to the pavement on the opposite side and an elderly, well-groomed lady got out. She began to count out coins into the driver's hand.

'As luck would have it!' Cassie's mother said. 'Here is my neighbour, Miss Willmott, home from one of her excursions to Fortnum's. You can take her taxi.'

Cassie gave her another quick embrace and hurried across the street, lifting her hand in case the cab should escape her.

As she settled into the back seat and the vehicle set off, a strange lightness, somewhere near relief, teased her. But Cassie's stubborn determination, as usual, won her over. She simply wanted to get on, catch her train in good time, throw herself into the new skills she would be learning, and be as far away as possible from everything else.

The taxi slowed at the junction with the Brompton Road,

and a pedestrian, careworn and haggard-looking, caught her eye as he turned the corner to make his way along Egerton Terrace.

'Oh, my goodness, Dad...' Cassie cried.

'Do you want to stop, miss?' the driver asked.

'No, no...' she uttered, staring as her father walked along the pavement, his hat low over his eyes, his shoulders stooping under his mackintosh. He held his briefcase as if it carried half a dozen bricks.

Something – his sadness, his conscience, perhaps, Cassie had thought later – made him glance at the cab and he caught sight of her peering through its rear window. He looked puzzled, recoiling for a second, frozen with surprise. But his face broke into a smile, the wide, joyful grin that she remembered from years ago, when they had all been together, when they had all been happy.

Cassie waved. Her father put his briefcase down, lifted his hat to her, and stood watching as her cab made a right turn and headed off to Paddington.

* * *

The traffic had been tediously slow along Park Lane, and, having paid the driver and bought her ticket, Cassie found she had only seven minutes before her train left.

'I have enough time,' she uttered to herself as she headed for the public telephone booths under one of the arches.

She put down her suitcase and thrust her hand into her bag for her *Lett's Ladies Diary 1943*, quickly turning to the telephone numbers scribbled on the back page. Even as she gave the operator the number, she realised that it was a weekday, before half past five in the afternoon, and therefore unlikely that anyone would be at home to pick up the call. Yet, she let it ring, watching the minute hand on the huge station clock as it hovered between two and three, promising herself that she would hang up when it moved to the three.

A couple strode past her, arm in arm on their way to the platforms, looking ordinary, steady and happy, their footsteps perfectly in tune. Cassie felt an intense pang of yearning as she listened to the telephone peeling cheerfully away at the other end of the line. And, in her mind's eye, a new and glorious sunrise slowly grew brighter. Seeing the couple, she decided, had confirmed everything.

Cassie had always wanted to be Luke's friend; she knew that he would do anything for her. But she had never wanted to ask, not until now. She swapped the receiver to her other ear; she had been pressing so hard that it began to hurt.

Oh, to be normal, she thought, thinking of the couple. Oh, to live a quiet, ordinary, respectful life. Of course, she wanted to be loved, she reminded herself, coiling the telephone cord around her finger. She did not want to be like Juno and her father, loving everyone, respecting no one, and making a miserable mess of their families in the most unsavoury of manners.

'Dubois speaking.'

'Luke? Is that you?' She shoved her pennies into the slot, and they rattled loudly against metal.

'Of course it is me, Cassie. How are you?'

'There's a question,' she said. 'I haven't long enough.'

She closed her eyes to shut off the station. An announcement bellowed right above her, almost drowning out Luke's voice, but it didn't matter to her one jot that he had begun to explain at length why he happened to be home at that time of day. She liked Luke; nothing horrible would ever happen to her with Luke.

'Luke,' she said. 'Can you hear me?'

'Loud and clear.'

'Luke, will you marry me?'

21

KENT, MAY 1944

Cassie tuned her dial and listened. From across the Channel, German messages filtered through – reports of the destruction of bridges, railways and roads in the area around Pas de Calais across the Straits of Dover, courtesy of Bomber Command.

She translated and wrote the messages down, understanding that deception tactics were in play. The enemy, predicting an imminent Allied offensive, had been building up reinforcements and defences just across the water, expecting the troops to land on the French coast via the shortest way across the Channel. And the RAF, Cassie understood, were in the act of destroying those regiments' means of moving to the right position when the real invasion took place.

With an intense surge of urgency, Cassie turned in her chair to look for the clerk, gesturing for him to take her paperwork; the messages were coming in thick and fast, and she did not want to miss any. He noticed and walked across the room towards her and, for a second, Cassie thought she knew him. She blinked. She must be mistaken, but as he drew closer, her stomach turned on itself and plummeted.

'Ah, I know you... Miss Marsh, isn't it?' Eddie said, his grin expectant, but his eyes vacant behind his spectacles.

She lifted one earpiece and cocked her head.

'I didn't hear you,' she said evenly.

He drew closer, and his proximity sent a rash of irritation and unease over her skin.

'Miss Marsh,' he said. 'It's Eddie.'

'And these are highly urgent.' She gestured with the pages containing the messages, holding them towards him at arm's length.

Eddie's eyes flicked up and down as if to question her, scrutinising her face and her body. But she held fast, refusing to react to his grubby, ungentlemanly manners; she had been through far too much since their last encounter to allow this pipsqueak of a man – as her uncle Charles would call him – bother her any more.

Cassie jerked the papers and Eddie took them.

'I know they're *urgent*,' he said, looking deliberately bemused, as if she had spoken nonsense. 'That's why I've been brought in from London to help out down here. Things are hotting up, as I understand. But Miss Marsh, Cassandra, isn't it? You must remember me? From Maps Ops, in the Westminster bunker?'

'I'm sorry,' Cassie said, smiling faintly, amusing herself. 'We are not allowed to talk about it. And no. I don't remember you. Now, I must press on.'

She replaced her earpiece, turned in her chair and tuned in again to the voices whispering through the airwaves.

* * *

Cassie kept her head down for the rest of the afternoon, wondering if Eddie would approach her again, to try to initiate another awkward conversation. How much longer she could pretend not to remember him, she didn't know, but she planned to snub him and not engage with him for as long as possible. After all, she only had three more weeks to go before she left Ferne House, and the War Office services for good.

At six o'clock, Margaret, her boss suggested Cassie take a break.

'Make us some tea, and I'll come out with you,' she said. 'Could do with some fresh air.'

Cassie brought the mugs out to the clifftop by the balustrade where Margaret stood, her idea of fresh air seemingly to be to fill it with her cigarette smoke.

'I hear that you will soon be leaving us, Cassandra?'

Cassie jolted. 'Ah yes, ma'am. I didn't know that you had been told yet.' She paused, adding shyly, 'I'm getting married.'

'Lucky you. I'm married to the job and have been forever, it seems, certainly before all of this.' Margaret caught Cassie's eye. 'You *have* been a dark horse. None of the girls knew that you were even courting. Who's the lucky chap?'

'It's Luke. Lucien Dubois. A dear old friend. I have known him forever.'

'Very sensible, Cassandra. As long as he hasn't simply swooped in and swept you off your feet.' Margaret chuckled.

'That certainly hasn't been the case,' Cassie said, realising straight away it was a sad thing to admit. 'Although...'

Margaret lifted an eyebrow. 'Although?'

Despite being her superior who she would always call *ma'am*, Margaret had become someone who Cassie felt she could confide in, if she needed to. Margaret had at least a decade on her, had been in the forces before the war, wore her WRAF uniform like a second skin, and was clearly a woman of the world. But, unlike with Miss Redmond at Westminster, Cassie didn't feel quite so intimidated; it felt natural to fall into conversation with her. Perhaps, Cassie decided, because she herself had grown up since her days in the bunker.

'Oh, nothing, ma'am...' Cassie forced a laugh. 'Certainly, in my case. No swooping or sweeping.'

'Because, believe me,' Margaret said, 'that sort of thing fizzles out soon enough. I've seen it happen far too often.'

Luke had, of course, after the hasty telephone call from Paddington Station the previous autumn, wanted them to be married straight away. But Cassie had insisted that she carry on working for at least a year. She wanted to do her duty; she wanted to see it through. But soon after New Year, her mother and Anthea had begun to correspond excitedly, and finally, Cassie had given in and set a date for this August. Like so much else in her life, out of her hands.

'I must say, the name Dubois rings a bell...' Margaret said, grinding out her cigarette under her toe. 'Wasn't there a big divorce case, in the newspapers, some years ago now?'

'I know nothing about that; I would have been far too young,' Cassie said, rather lamely, but not wishing to encourage *that* sort of conversation. 'Must be another Dubois you're thinking of, ma'am.' Although, she knew all too well, there weren't that many listed in the phonebook.

It felt strange to talk out loud about Luke, to Margaret or anyone, for their courtship, if she could call it that, had been perfunctory, almost peripheral to her. Cassie had seen Luke at Christmas at Egerton Terrace, and once since then when he showed her the Richmond house. Certainly, no great romance. But when she thought about how her mother had reminisced quite fondly about her father whisking her away, she felt marginally better. At least this meant that marriage to Luke would be a better, more settled prospect.

What a gentleman Luke had always been: kind and understanding. And yet after each of his chaste kisses on her cheek, or squeeze of her shoulder, Cassie had struggled to return affection, feeling confusion and a trace of pity.

'If I may, Cassandra...' Margaret began, peering at her as the Capel mist drifted around them, blotting out the early-evening sun. 'You don't look so happy about it. Sorry, I'm being flippant; it must be the effect of the work we're doing here. I know there is so much to deal with, so much that becomes vital matters of life and death, that a wedding must feel... unimportant?'

'Yes, it does sometimes feel like that...' Cassie said.

But despite their relationship feeling far too convenient for its own good, Cassie decided that Luke must be the right man for her. Hadn't she turned to him when she had needed him? Firstly, in the booth at Peter Jones, and again, at Paddington Station. Luke had been a solid friend, a comfort, had offered her a home, while her family tore itself open like an overripe, rotten fruit.

Fighting the dropping sensation of helplessness, Cassie nodded vague agreement with Margaret.

'None of us here have really got to know you, Cassandra, and now you're leaving us, it seems such a shame. You've been here, what, two and a half years...? I know we've had our chats, but you don't open up much, do you?' she said, with kindness.

'If I open up, ma'am, I may never stop,' she uttered, gesturing towards the Channel, the sound of the waves muffled by the fog, as if this might explain everything.

'I know exactly what you mean. And that would never do. Not when we have so much work to be getting on with,' Margaret said firmly, reverting to her officer role. She noticed

Cassie gazing at the sea. 'Is there someone you know, someone close, out there...?'

Cassie nodded, misunderstanding. She said, 'My brother...'

'Ah, yes, all very difficult,' Margaret said, distracted by something over Cassie's shoulder. 'We do need to keep going the best we can.'

Margaret's response irritated Cassie. People had been saying much the same thing to each other for a long while, and its banality had begun to grate. Cassie knew full well that she had to carry on, for there proved to be no other option. But not one part of her training had ever covered how she might feel, drowning under the responsibility, walking the fine lines between saving lives and destroying them. No one had shown her how on earth she must endure it.

Margaret drained her mug and indicated behind Cassie's shoulder.

'There he goes... shift over, back to his digs,' she said. 'We have unfortunately inherited some trouble from Westminster, Cassandra.'

Cassie peered around Margaret and spotted Eddie striking a scrawny, inconsequential figure as he headed away from Ferne House up the long, sweeping path.

'There were complaints about that man, and he has been foisted on us,' Margaret said. 'But we will sort him out. He won't last five minutes if he carries on with that sort of behaviour here.'

'Absolutely. Yes, ma'am.' There seemed to be nothing more Cassie wanted to say about it.

'Ah, but this is better news,' Margaret said. 'I see the dignitaries are already here. I had better go. Finish your tea, Cassandra. See you back inside.'

* * *

While they had been talking, the mist had all but evaporated, and the sun beamed through from the west, highlighting clouds with liquid gold. Silhouetted in the sudden brightness, Cassie saw a small group of men approaching along the grassy clifftop, light winking off uniform buttons and epaulettes. Squinting, Cassie could make out the deep blue of the two naval officers, and the red flashes of the military policeman. As they drew closer, there at the centre, despite wearing army fatigues and cap, walked the unmistakable, rotund figure of the Prime Minister, his bulk and energy, his gait, the cigar in hand, giving him away, even from this distance. Beside him, taller, more upright and in his distinguished uniform, strode General Eisenhower.

'Good God,' Cassie uttered to herself, watching them strolling along, deep in conversation, as if taking the evening air together. 'So, *these* are our dignitaries...'

And she understood.

The sea fog had cleared, and German lookouts peering through binoculars on the other side of the Channel, training their sights along these cliffs, would see Mr Churchill, and the American General. Would feasibly, hopefully, believe the invasion was about to be launched from this corner of Kent: from Ramsgate, Deal, Dover and Folkestone. The shortest, most obvious route to Calais.

Watching Mr Churchill, Cassie felt her heart expand. She brimmed with admiration, and wanted to laugh at his audacity. The simplest of ruses, to be the decoy and to do the exact opposite of what would be expected, to do the trick. Confuse the enemy, fool the enemy, at least for a moment, a day, maybe two.

22

JUNE 1944

A fraction after dawn, Cassie left Ferne House and walked in twilight around to the little area of lawn overlooking the sea, her legs brushing against ferns unfurling along the pathway. Fog streamed upwards over the edge of the cliff, drifting like ghosts might, wherever it will. It enveloped Cassie, deadening sound and blocking the view.

She stood at the balustrade, facing an uncanny wall of white, the rising sun, somewhere to her left on the far eastern horizon, not strong enough yet to burn away the haze. Five minutes ago, Margaret had tapped her on the shoulder to give her leave to take a break, and yet voices continued to ring in her ears. Garbled intelligence, vague suspicions and sightings, uttered in German, had streamed through her earphones all night. Five times in the space of an hour, she had heard mention of Pas de Calais and the Straits of Dover, promptly reporting it to her supervisor. Had the tricks and subterfuge, the double-crossing that had been put in place over the past few years, begun to pay off?

Cassie shuddered, not daring to hope, to believe. For she did not know enough, and yet sometimes, felt she knew too much. Inside Ferne House, senior naval men had gathered in the drawing room, now conference room, filling the space with low voices, cigarette smoke, and excruciating anticipation. They drank tea and waited for news, while the signallers remained hunched over their desks, sending false messages out into the airwaves.

She leant her arms on the ledge, lifted her face into the damp, salty air to refresh her skin. Her neck and shoulders ached from working through the night, and she felt numb, strangely, almost pleasantly, light-headed with fatigue. No one had told her specifically, but she guessed that vast ranks of Allied soldiers had been amassing these past weeks along the south coast further to the west: from Portsmouth to Poole, Southampton and Dartmouth, and beyond, waiting and poised to go. And in the early hours of this short summer night, they would have embarked in darkness, a huge armada crossing the Channel for Normandy. And Oliver would be among them: one tiny part of the enormous seaborne invasion.

Cassie flinched, as if stung, and forced herself to picture happier things: Marianne's little children, the prospect of Luke's lovely house in Richmond, the beauty of Greenaways on a summer's afternoon. She concentrated on the muffled splash of the waves against chalky scree below, and heard the odd cry of a seagull, lost somewhere in the fog, seeming to come through from another world. Behind her, Ferne House glimmered inside the haze, white against white, while the ferns, like a blended smudge of green, drank in the cool, suspended droplets.

But it was no use. Her mind, as always, spun with familiar, nostalgic yearning, wavered into homesickness and switched back to Oliver.

She didn't even dare imagine what he might be doing at that

very moment. Already halfway across the Channel? The pale sand of the Normandy beaches rising into view through the breaking dawn. She buckled up her feelings, as if tightening a belt. Not thinking about Oliver, or loving Oliver, had always been the right thing to do.

'Hello, Cassandra.' Margaret appeared by her side, carrying two steaming mugs of tea. 'They have just made a fresh urn. And I thought you might appreciate this.' She pressed a mug into Cassie's hands.

Thanking her, Cassie accepted it. The heat through the ceramic warming her fingers felt gloriously comforting, catching her unawares. She took a long, grateful sip, tears of relief prickling her eyes.

'Goodness, you are right, ma'am,' she said. 'I didn't know how much I needed this.'

'It's been quite a night, I can tell you.' Margaret exhaled, turning to lean the small of her back against the balustrade. Despite having put in a gruelling shift, she looked immaculate in her uniform, her hair neat under her cap. 'And yet we all know this is only the beginning. But perhaps... the beginning of the end.'

'I can't even think beyond the next minute,' Cassie said, fighting niggling fear, her throat aching with tiredness.

'That's the way to get through it.'

Holding her mug in one hand, Margaret expertly removed a cigarette from the packet with the other and planted it between her rouged lips. She sparked her lighter, glancing at Cassie. 'No need to worry. You're doing an excellent job, Cassandra. And the geologists have certainly done theirs.' Margaret puffed her cigarette. 'They have studied the terrain, the elevation, the gradient, down to the type of sand on the beaches. They have looked into the rhythm, the ebb and flow of the tides. The meteorologists have been reading and predicting the weather for weeks. It must, it will, happen today.'

'I feel as if we are teetering on the verge of something monumental,' Cassie said with a groan of hope. 'That the whole world is suspended, watching and waiting.'

Margaret glanced at her in admiration.

'You're not wrong,' she said. 'Whatever the outcome, the sixth of June will be carved deeply into everyone's memories.'

They stood silently, contemplatively, for some moments. Cassie, listening to the faint rush of the surf below, understood in that tiny, private part of herself, that the geologists, the meteorologists, must have got it right.

In that moment, the air felt a little warmer, the sun a little higher, the mist dispersing to reveal the long, wide sweep of rough grass along the clifftop where Mr Churchill had been walking not a fortnight ago.

'I better get back inside,' Margaret said. 'See you back in there.' She glanced at her watch. 'Five minutes. And don't forget to bring the mug in with you. Must keep things ship-shape.'

Margaret gave a light, departing laugh, and Cassie leant on the balustrade, giving herself another moment to prepare herself for the rest of the day. Simply being near the water reassured her. She could almost feel the push and pull of the waves and Gerard – the memory, or an impression of him – drew close, as if he stood by her side, listening and waiting, too.

'I do it for you, Gerard,' she whispered, peering down at the rocky, screeded shore, emerging through the mist. After all, her brother was now part of the sea, that one great body of water. 'I do this work in the best way I can. I do it for you.'

Time pressed on. Cassie ought to be getting back to her desk, although the weight of it felt far too momentous to bear. She'd heard that the PM was back at the War Room, back at the heart of it all, and she could well imagine the monumental activity, the sense of purpose, the strained, hushed conversations, channelling through that labyrinth of underground rooms. But this, she thought, was what everyone had been working towards.

Taking a deep breath, she walked around to the entrance, feeling boosted and stronger than ever. Only a month or so ago, during a dry spell, the ferns along the path had been brittle and brown in places, as if burnt, worn out and fading. But, Cassie noticed, they had revived themselves, started anew, and no longer looked so beaten.

Remembering how she'd heard, a fortnight before, Mr Churchill's deep, rumbling voice carrying across the clifftop, she felt ready to go back to work.

For Cassie, after the exhausting, taut hours of darkness, the longest day had begun.

23

JULY 1944

'Always nice to be here,' Luke said, turning the car through the rusted, old gates at Greenaways, the tyres crunching over the gravel drive. 'Almost like coming home... our second home, Cassie, don't you think?'

'I feel I have had lots of "second homes" over the years,' Cassie said, stifling a yawn. The journey down on the train had been tiring, but she had felt somewhat revived as soon as it broke through into the rich-green Devon hills. Luke had picked her up at Exeter Station and now, catching sight of the exquisite, familiar façade and the purple, draping wisteria as resplendent as ever, she sighed with pleasure. 'But this, I may say, is one of the loveliest.'

'What about Cheyne Row?' Luke asked, cranking on the handbrake, chuckling. 'Joking of course... We went through it there, didn't we? Air raids, missing cats...' He stripped off his driving gloves and reached for her hand. 'Well, soon-to-be Mrs Dubois, I certainly have cherished memories of *this* place.' He scraped his thumb over the engagement ring on her finger. 'After all, it's where we first met.' He leant over and kissed her cheek, moving his lips around to her mouth. 'It feels like an age since *your* rather romantic proposal. I was a blethering idiot when I asked you. The poor cat did not know where to look. Thank God you're the sensible one. And how I have missed you, my darling. But, not long to go now...'

'Come on then,' Cassie said lightly, eager to get out of the car and stretch her legs. She gave him a gentle shove and glanced back at the house. Charles had come out through the porch to bellow his greetings, and Anthea appeared beside him on the step. 'Oh, how lovely, your mother's here already.'

Anthea trotted across the gravel towards them.

'The happy couple!' she trilled, squeezing both Cassie's hands in hers and turning to Luke for a bear hug. 'I knew it would happen eventually. I always knew it,' she laughed.

In her finely cut, linen dress and with her calm, melodious voice, Luke's mother appeared as elegant and energetic as Cassie remembered. The day she first met her – the day she had found out about Gerard – had been a terribly bleak time but Cassie didn't attach horrible memories to Anthea. Much had moved on since that awful day, and yet so little. But Anthea, buoyant with positivity, seemed to clear the air wherever she went.

Charles breezed over. 'What's this, what's this... My favourite niece has arrived. And don't say it, Cassie. I know, I know. My *only* niece.'

Cassie hugged her uncle, looking around for her father's car.

'Where—?' she began. 'Where are my...?'

'Ah, so news is your mother and father have had to delay by a day,' Charles said. 'Something going on at Rich's office.'

Cassie felt a smidgeon of relief, for she had not been with her parents in the company of Juno since Marianne's wedding. The awkward, anticipated situation had been boiling at the back of her mind all the way to Greenaways. But then a strangely childlike disappointment took over, for she had been expecting them and hadn't seen them since Christmas. She wanted to see them, to feel settled, and have everything back to normal. She just hadn't realised how much.

'But never mind that, Cassie,' continued her uncle. 'You are here now. And they will be here tomorrow. And of course, we have our lovely guest of honour, Madame Dubois-McKinnon...'

'I like the sound of that.' Anthea gave a humorous curtsey. 'An honour indeed.'

'Come on, Dubois,' Charles said to Luke. 'I will give you a hand with the luggage.'

Anthea linked Cassie's arm, and they walked together over to the house, while her uncle and Luke dealt with the suitcases.

'This is so exciting, only a month to go,' Anthea said, patting her hand. 'And Luke is the happiest I have ever seen him. Kipling coming home when he did was a sign, I am sure of it.'

Marianne appeared at the front door, holding her chubby baby boy in one arm, and the hand of her daughter with the other. The little two-year-old sucked her fingers, her eyes widening with curiosity.

'Cassie... Cass... eee!' Marianne called. 'Look who's here, Lilibet and Georgie! It's Auntie Cassie.'

'Am I *Auntie* to them?' Cassie asked as she embraced Marianne and Georgie in one go, and bent down to say hello to Lilibet, who gazed at her, nonplussed, with the same wide, pale-green eyes as her mother, and Juno.

'I think you'll find it's first cousin once removed,' Luke said, following them into the hallway with the suitcases. 'Or is it second cousin? Hmmm. I feel I need to check that.'

'Isn't Georgie a bit of a pudding?' Marianne said, plonking him into Cassie's arms.

'Oh my...' Cassie uttered in awe and delight, feeling the

child's compact weight settle comfortably into her arms. He blinked up at her, his face close to hers, his trust and vulnerability tugging at her belly. 'He's—'

'Heavy!' Marianne laughed.

'Beautiful, is what I was about to say.'

Juno appeared in the hallway, offering subdued greetings. She waited while Cassie heaved Georgie back into Marianne's arms to bestow her with one of her brittle hugs, and she allowed Luke a demure handshake.

'Good journey?' Juno asked.

'Not too bad,' Luke said. 'And thank you for inviting us, Mrs Greenaway, and putting on this pre-wedding gathering. What a wonderful idea. I was just saying to Cassie, how much I love this place. And now Cassie has left her job, at last, we can look forward to so much. Isn't that right, darling?' He put his arm around her and pulled her into his side.

'Absolutely,' she said.

Juno fixed Cassie with her knowing gaze and nodded silently.

They all went through the dining room and her aunt's parlour towards the large drawing room. Marianne, walking beside Cassie while expertly cradling Georgie, leant in to her.

'So, you are marrying Woodward, are you? You are going to be *rich*!' she whispered playfully. 'But more seriously, his mother is a delight. You're going to be so happy, Cassie. Isn't she, Georgie?'

'Yes... yes, I am,' Cassie said, chucking the baby under his chin, a strange uncertainty creeping over her. Anthea indeed would make a lovely mother-in-law, and Luke's wealth, in all honesty, barely crossed her mind. She had known him for so many years that it simply felt like part of him, like a coat he might wear. But happiness? She wanted to ask Marianne exactly how *she* had felt when she got engaged to Harry Brough.

The typical English summer's day wasn't quite warm enough to sit outside, so the French windows had been opened onto the terrace, and the chairs arranged to make the most of the view of the oak trees in the long sweep of the park. Harry got to his feet to greet them, and Lilibet ran giggling at her father, wanting to be hoisted up. Marianne set Georgie down on the hearth rug among a scattering of toy building blocks, while Luke sat in the armchair closest to Cassie's and shuffled it even nearer.

'Well, Cassandra and Luke, welcome,' Juno said. 'We have plenty of champagne for today and tomorrow when Rich and Miranda *finally* get here. Charles, will you fix everyone what they'd like?'

Charles gave a mock salute and headed for the drinks trolley.

'Splendid idea, thank you again,' said Luke. 'Seeing as we didn't have a chance to celebrate the engagement properly.'

Cassie could detect an edge in Luke's voice: a snag of frustration. Marianne looked over, giving him a puzzled glance.

Cassie thought that Luke had understood, and accepted, why she had wanted to stall, to continue with her work. It riled her that he still expressed his disappointment in front of her family, even now, with a month to go to their wedding. Hadn't he, moments ago in the car, been more than enthusiastic?

'So, the church in South Ken is still standing, is it?' Charles asked, handing Cassie a gin and tonic.

'I think it lost a few roof tiles to an incendiary three years ago,' Luke said. 'But relatively unscathed. The other church near Cheyne Row, however, took a direct hit.'

Cassie glanced at Luke, remembering that awful night, and

how he had come home ashen-faced after trying to help the people sheltering there. *You see*, she told herself, *he's a good, good man.*

'Although the V-bombs are getting nasty, aren't they?' Harry said. 'What else is Herr Hitler going to come up with?'

Luke agreed. 'It seems he hasn't wasted a moment. The Allies invade and he sends the rockets over. He must have had them primed and ready to go.'

'Argh, hush, please, not in front of little ears.' Marianne indicated Lilibet, who had begun to help Georgie stack his bricks. 'Cassie, how lovely for you to be married from home,' Marianne offered, her own face glowing with memories. 'It made it truly special for me.'

'It will be small and quiet,' Cassie said, not having considered much about it before. 'But a lot smaller than your wedding, Marianne. Exactly what we want.'

'Not that I have had much say in any of it,' Luke said.

Cassie tilted her head at him, expecting him to laugh at his own joke, but he seemed perfectly serious. He had written to her at Ferne House every other day, since last October, and she had seen him twice in London, at Christmas at Egerton Terrace and around Easter time when she had visited the house in Richmond. She had begun to imagine her life there – gentle, drifting and dreamlike, for it truly was a delightful spot. And she felt that Luke had very much had a say in many things.

Luke had taken her for dinner in the pretty high street at Richmond and later, over a night cap, offered hints about them sharing a bed, but she had demurred. And he had, ever the gentleman, respected her wishes. The spark, as she had admitted to Margaret at Ferne House, remained evasive, but Cassie felt sure that it would come once she had settled into the reality of married life. Because Luke was real, solid and dependable. And she needed Luke.

Cassie reached across the short gap between their armchairs and took his hand to console him. His disgruntled expression fell away, but with his glasses acting as a shield, she could not quite read his eyes.

'Come now,' she said, lifting his hand to her lips and kissing it. 'You know it's the bride's prerogative.'

Luke's face broke into a grin, widening with pleasure, and relief. He stood up and cleared his throat.

'Ladies and gentlemen, and children,' he said, gazing around the room. Conversations petered out. 'May I raise a toast, firstly to my beautiful bride-to-be, Cassie, who I have known and loved for many years and also... to my dearest and absent friend, Oliver. Who I also have... for even longer. Without him, and his enduring friendship, I would not be here, and on the brink of a happy, contented future.'

'Here, here,' said Harry.

'Bravo,' said Anthea.

Marianne nodded in agreement, but looked unnerved, and Cassie felt her pain. Oliver, and the danger he was in, somewhere in Normandy, in the battle for his life, brooded over Greenaways, following the family from room to room.

Juno's face tightened. 'Of course, dear Oliver,' she said quietly. 'We think about him every day. And raise a toast every night.'

'Have you heard from him recently?' Luke asked.

'No,' Juno said, 'I haven't, but...'

'It must be difficult,' Harry said. 'I hear that—'

'Enough!' Charles cried out. 'I've had enough!' He set his glass down on the table beside him with a clunk and pressed his fingertips over his eyes. In the shocked, thickening silence, he muttered, 'My boy, my lad. I can't bear it. My boy. He wasn't cut out for any of *this*.'

Juno hurried to her husband's chair, leant over him and rested both her hands on his shoulders. She spoke quietly, firmly to him, her face close to his. 'Now... now, hush, my dear...'

Her whispers did not quite reach Cassie's ears, but she had never heard Juno speak with such tenderness towards her husband before.

Charles groaned, his head drooping. Tears seeped down his cheeks. 'I just want him home.'

Cassie and Marianne locked eyes in shared distress, and Marianne left her seat to crouch by her children, distracting them with the toys. Anthea let out a mouse-like cry of shock and Luke and Harry looked the other way.

'We all do, Uncle Charles,' Cassie said, her mind clearing. *Even if her uncle is not Oliver's natural father*, she thought, *Oliver is still his boy.*

Charles sniffed hard, wiped his hand over his face and said with bravado, 'Goodness me, what a poor show. This will never do.'

'Why don't you go and have a nap, dear?' Juno said. 'When you come down later, you will feel more refreshed.'

He gathered himself together and stood up. 'Sorry about that outburst,' he said, straightening his shirt cuffs. 'Must be the drink. I ought to put a stop to it.'

'No need to apologise, sir...' Harry began.

'Mr Greenaway, I'm sorry...' Luke offered.

'Pa,' Marianne said, 'I will bring you up a cup of tea in a few minutes.'

Charles waved his hand to acknowledge them, uttering his apologies as he left the room.

Lilibet and Georgie carried on their chattering play.

'Well, now. Happy couple,' Juno said with false brightness. She sat back down, rearranging her skirt with a flourish, her mouth pursed, her curious seeking eyes glittering with unshed tears. 'Tell us more about your small "big day".'

* * *

After dinner, which Uncle Charles had felt suitably revived to join them for, Cassie went upstairs to fetch her jumper. On her way down, she spotted Juno waiting for her in the hallway and involuntarily slowed down over the last few stairs, alarmed by the look on her aunt's face.

'Come with me a moment,' Juno said with a hook of her finger, and walked along the kitchen corridor, and out through the back door.

Cassie followed her, a rash of nerves burning in her stomach; would this, then, be the confrontation that she had dreaded for so long? Would her aunt have it out with her, accuse her of telling tales, of spoiling her life, meddling in things – her affair with her father – that she couldn't hope to understand?

Walking a few paces into the rose garden, Juno fished a letter out of her cardigan pocket and handed it to Cassie.

'It arrived a week ago,' she said.

Puzzled and for a moment somewhat relieved, Cassie took the letter, its envelope, addressed to her, care of Greenaways, unopened, and squinted down at it in the gathering dusk. She recognised Oliver's handwriting, saw the postmark: 6 June 1944. She let out a small cry. Her blood churned with futile joy, and punishing dread. Her fingertips turned cold, and yet the letter she held felt like it was in flames.

Juno peered at Cassie, the skin on her usually sun-kissed

skin pale and almost transparent, the lines in it clearly drawn. Her cheekbones sharp, her eyes sad and unguarded.

'I know he loves you,' she said, with such raw sensitivity that Cassie expected her aunt to break apart.

'You do?' Cassie said, not knowing what or why she asked the question. She turned the envelope over in her hands, with its tatty corners, the censor's stamp like a mark of blood. 'He *does*? But why... he has written to me... why now?'

Juno folded her hand around Cassie's wrist and gently shook it.

'Go take a stroll, Cassandra. Read your letter. We are putting the blackout down in the drawing room and are going to play cards. Join us later if you like. If not, I will see you in the morning.'

She turned to go but stopped herself. 'And your uncle doesn't know about it. We haven't had a letter ourselves, you see...'

'Yes, I... oh, but Aunt Juno...'

'Aren't you a little old now to be calling me *aunt*, Cassandra?' Juno said and drifted back into the house.

Cassie stood still among the roses, not knowing what to do, where to take herself. But to walk, anywhere, must be the answer, to shake off such disabling, wavering confusion. Clutching the letter, she followed a path through the rose bushes, changed her mind, doubled back and decided on the long walk beside the drifts of lavender. The fading light intensified the colour of the dry, purple-blue fronds where half a dozen bees lingered, unable to find their way home. She came out near the pond, the water a deep olive-green, and found herself among the thickets at the bottom near the stream. Here, twilight deepened the spaces between the trees and the sound of the water rushing by created a little night music of its own.

'*Eine Kleine Nachtmusik*,' Cassie whispered as she made her way to their log, relishing the warmth of her memory of Oliver whistling with the blade of grass, the letter growing heavier in her hand the longer she waited to read it, feeling like much more than simple pieces of paper.

She sat down, shakily tore at the envelope and pulled out the letter, noticing immediately the sporadic black lines of the censor's pen. But, mercy, they had left her most of Oliver...

Dear Cass,

As you will have guessed by now, I still can't remember your address in South Ken (no rolling of your eyes, please), and I know that you are no longer at Cheyne Row, and damned if I am going to send this through the War Office PO Box. So, it's best, and safest, to write to you at Greenaways. One way or another, my letter will reach you.

You will know, Cass, where I am. We are penned into our camps near the south coast, hundreds of us. Earlier today, at dawn, we were primed and ready to go. Fixed bayonets, if you will. But there was a stand-down. The Brass changed their minds due to the weather forecast, and a lot of men were beside themselves with the dreadful trauma of it all. Everyone had steeled themselves, and there was nowhere for the adrenalin to go. The chaplain came round to talk to us, to bless those who wanted it. All of us, every man jack, asked to be blessed. Myself among them.

The Canadians are playing baseball – we'd call it rounders, Cass – now to pass the time. What strapping, well-fed lads they are. But the English boys, myself not included, are nonchalantly kicking a saggy old football about, or napping. Says it all, doesn't it!

I will have to be quick with this, because the chaplain is going to collect any last-minute letters and will post them tomorrow, I hope. And the King himself was here about two weeks ago to inspect the troops, and he gave a speech to rouse us. He's a slight man, although tall, quite fragile-looking, and he seemed as frightened as we are, his voice as light and as thin as he is. This somehow made me feel better. For I am not a brave soldier, Cass. I will come across as a fine captain to my men, but most of the time, I wish I was somewhere quiet, reading a book. I am a quiet man who studied Latin and loves art. I am a man who likes to draw. A man, Cass, who loves you.

This I have known forever. Who knows when it started, but it has always been that way. I know this will make you feel uncomfortable. It makes me uncomfortable, and ashamed, and a disgrace, and unworthy of much else but what is surely coming to me.

And I want to apologise for my behaviour at Marianne's wedding, and the day after. I should also apologise to Vee too. I can't really explain my recklessness and arrogance, but feel it was some sort of reaction to the turmoil I was feeling. And still am. It was disrespectful to everyone – but in truth, the only person's good opinion I crave is yours.

You fell asleep on the rug, Cass, and the day, the beautiful moorland all around you, was perfect, and you are perfect. We had talked, remember, earlier that morning and when we arrived at the moor, we talked about church bells and sheep, and I can confide in you. You read me. You know me. And I realised that the only person I ever wanted to be with was you. And when Vee's attentions towards me got the better of me, I am ashamed to say, on impulse, I did something to help erase you from my mind. To sabotage the very thought of you. However, it failed. Which is why I have not been in touch. I had to cut myself off, throw myself even further into this damn blasted war.

I know we cannot be together. I must be shocking and repulsive to you, Cass, and I am so deeply sorry, but this could be my last and only chance to tell you. If I come back from this, we will hopefully one day laugh at it – at my absurdity, and yes, my inappropriate, downright childish behaviour. But in a few hours, I might not be any more. We both know the life expectancy of an officer in these situations.

Remember, Cass: umbra sumus.

Be happy and go quietly on in your own sweet and determined way. And you will always be happy, because you are Cass, Cassie, Cassandra. And I wish I could say this to your dear, beautiful face.

I have left it to the last minute to congratulate you on your engagement. Forgive me, it should have been the first sentence I wrote. But I know that Luke will look after you. He stayed and watched over you while you slept on the rug on Dartmoor, remember. If he cares half as much as I do about you, you will be fine, and happy and safe. I trust him, as you should. He has always been a good friend to me.

The chaplain is nearly at my tent now, so I must go.

Cass, I am 100 per cent sure that this effort, that this operation, will be a success. Whatever happens to me, or anyone else here. It will work. I believe it.

As I have always believed in you.

Love always,

Oliver

* * *

Cassie sucked her breath in, as if she had woken suddenly, with a falling sensation, not entirely sure where she had landed. She heard a shattering in her head, the sound of glass breaking, and a disorientating lightness engulfed her, as if she had no flesh, or feeling, with nothing inside her.

She fumbled with the letter – he had written on both sides of two sheets of paper – and another page dropped from her hand, floating to settle on the ground. It landed face up. Dazed, Cassie stared down at it: in the gloom, she made out a delicate, detailed sketch of a wren.

She understood his intention with the drawing. To say something without words, to remind her. And at last, after all this time, Oliver had reached her, had spoken to her. But he left her with another secret to bear. Loving Oliver, and Oliver loving her, did not make Cassie whole or complete, or safe any longer; it frightened her, and she felt tired of being frightened. Cassie got down off the log and sat on the bed of the crisp leaves at its base, shed by the trees during the hottest days that summer.

'That poor little bird,' Cassie whispered into the dusk, gazing at the picture. 'I'm here with it, Oliver, in our beautiful place. And you are... where?'

She squeezed her eyes shut, fancying she would know, that she would hear him telling her. But the only sounds came from the stream, rushing blindly past her on its way, eventually, to the sea, and a gentle rustling in the tree canopy, black against the darkening sky above her.

Turning the pages over again, Cassie scanned Oliver's words, frightened that she would not remember what he had written, wanting to take note, to do as he asked. To go quietly on in her own sweet and determined way. And this meant marrying Luke – dear Luke, he did not deserve this. To do so would finally resolve the situation and save all three of them from themselves.

It was far too dark now to be able to read any more. Cassie carefully folded and slotted the letter and sketch back into the envelope, as if handling an injured creature, got to her feet and made her way out of the trees.

Night had fallen, but the summer sky held the last of its colour, a luminous, chalky, deep blue, and Greenaways itself, with its blacked-out windows, appeared flat and indistinct, as if blotted out of existence. Behind it hung the moon, having risen suddenly, encircled by a halo sending out a hazy, silver glow. Cassie stared, mesmerised, trying to remember what her uncle had once told her the halo meant: fair weather or foul, impending joy or disaster.

Approaching the house, she did not dare hazard a guess. She thought instead of Marianne's children asleep in the nursery up there, and her own childhood summers came back to her in snippets of joy and a little natural, unadulterated pain. She heard the rhythmic thud of the tennis balls, the squabbles and the laughter, the calling of her name and the song of the wren, and a shrill whistle blown on a blade of grass.

* * *

Earlier, Juno had shown Cassie and Luke to adjacent bedrooms, with an encouraging flourish, but Cassie had pretended not to notice, adamant to be proper about it and that nothing would happen between them until their wedding night. Now, exhausted, depleted, and feeling curiously empty, Cassie decided to go straight up to her room.

As she reached the half-landing, she heard gentle conversation easing through from the drawing room, and wondered if she should go back down, find Luke and sit by his side. Play a round of cards with them. Be with Luke, as much as he wanted to be with her.

She hesitated, hearing a cheerful boom from Charles, and Marianne's laughter. Juno's voice, underneath – chiding and delicate, and yet supremely strong – made Cassie want to weep. For now, she knew what it felt like to love the wrong person.

PART IV

24

At last, Cassie felt settled; at last, her life had been gathered into one place – childhood treasures and books from South Ken, some clothes left behind at Greenaways, and a few possessions that she had forgotten about at Cheyne Row. Luke, discovering this when moving out, had packed them into a small box for her, diligently labelling it.

Cassie had been grateful, of course, but felt she had no need for any of it; best, she thought, to let the past, its trials, and its mysteries go. And yet her present moments, as the new Mrs Dubois living in this truly delightful spot by the river in south-west London – or, as Luke from time to time corrected her, Surrey – held a dreamlike quality. But it proved to be a dream that she could neither control nor indeed remember much about. Life with Luke mirrored the years they spent together at Cheyne Row, the difference now being that they shared a marital bed. And time drifted, from day to day, through the most trifling of domestic moments.

'Sorry, Luke, I seemed to have burnt the toast,' Cassie said, presenting the charred slices in the dainty rack that had been a wedding present. From whom, she could not remember.

'Never mind, I shall scrape,' Luke said, dipping his crumby knife into the butter.

Cassie sipped her tea, averting her eyes from the mess and gazing through the French windows at the large garden, the prim flower beds, and the pristine lawn, across which Kipling trotted on his morning prowl. Here, she would *prefer* a little unruliness, for it all looked far too staid, far too suburban. Their garden needed, she admitted, the wild Juno touch.

'Perhaps when Marianne visits,' Cassie said, 'we shall have a trip to the nursery and pick out more plants. I feel the need to fill those borders to the brim, have them spilling over.'

'*More* plants?' Luke said, glancing up from his newspaper. He took a moment to register the look on Cassie's face. 'Whatever you like, darling. Are you still keen on setting up a greenhouse?'

'Absolutely. I shall ask at the nursery. They must know a man who can do the job.'

Luke turned back to the paper, gardening evidently holding no interest for him. Cassie continued to sip with creeping realisation that the joke about them being 'an old married couple' had truly come to pass.

She stared at the date on the newspaper's front page and gave an inward shudder. The sixth of June, as Margaret the Signals Officer had predicted, had become indelible on the nation's conscience. They had peace, certainly – Potsdam had been signed and Europe carved up between the Allied powers – but the scars lingered under the surface, the pain a constant reminder.

Within the week, it would have been three years since she left Ferne House, and her job with the War Office. Where had the time gone, Cassie wondered, as she stacked the breakfast plates, knowing immediately that it had gone around in a circle to come back, dragging her memories with it to haunt her.

Luke drained his cup, folded the newspaper. 'Back to the coal face,' he said, as he did every morning.

Cassie set down the plates and followed him out to the hallway, so wide, it always felt to her like another room. Sunlight glinted as a promise through the stained-glass panels in the front door, and the high windows above it. She did, she conceded, admire their house. Edwardian, detached, double-fronted and as square and as solid as Luke, it had been planned to contain space, elegance and practicality. Built some forty years before on this fine little avenue, lined with trees, the river but two streets away, surely with a couple like them in mind. And Cassie found it bleakly amusing how well she conformed as they wordlessly went through their morning ritual. She handed Luke his raincoat because, well, one never knew, gave him his briefcase propped on the hallstand and took his hat from the hook.

Luke planted it on his head, grinned at her and pecked her cheek.

'What time is Marianne arriving?' he asked as he opened the front door.

'Mid-afternoon, all being well. She is coming up from her friend's house in Guildford; she'll get a taxi from the station,' she said.

'Not Vee?' Luke asked.

'Ho, no, not Vee. She is still in Kent. Another friend.'

Luke flipped out his wallet. 'Here's five bob to pay for her taxi,' he said, handing her the note. 'I shall see you all later.'

He headed off down the path, with a cheery backward wave of his hand.

Cassie shut the front door and waited, listening, adjusting to the silence. Usually, after Luke left for work, the empty hours of the day lined up ahead of her like a series of grim obstacles. But today... Cassie smiled, hugging her joy and anticipation. Marianne, Lilibet and Georgie would be visiting and staying for the whole week. And she had much to do.

She went straight upstairs to make up the twin beds in the temporary nursery and then popped out to the garden to cut some flowers to put in the guest room for Marianne. With the birds singing blithely and the thin whirring of a lawnmower from somewhere along the avenue, the summer's day settled into its gentle sequence. Cassie, gathering a handful of scented pinks, sensed emptiness, along with a distinct lack of responsibility, and knew she should be satisfied. Her nerves were not stretched to breaking, nor her mind filtering great batches of information and figures; no longer translating at pace whatever disjointed phrases echoed in her ears. But not having much else to do did not come easily to her.

When a man got married, he could continue along in his life as if nothing had changed. But when a woman, when Cassie got married, everything stopped. Her purpose, her reason to be, had shifted. No, she corrected herself, it had been demolished.

'Morning, Mrs Dubois,' someone called, and Cassie spotted the woman who lived next door through a gap in the hedge.

'Morning. Lovely day,' she replied on reflex, conforming to be the person her neighbour on this quiet, cloistered street thought she was: young Mrs Dubois with her civil-servant husband, soon to celebrate their third anniversary, the years ahead already laid out for her. And yet, no one knew, not even Luke to any extent, the life she had left behind, the secrets that lay one on top of the other, the skeletons she must stack in the cupboard.

Returning inside and making her way upstairs, Cassie sensed her home's domestic peace, and certainly did not wish herself back, even though her work in the War Room and at Ferne House, alongside its catastrophes, had given her life meaning. She set down the little green jug of flowers by Marianne's bed and plumped the pillows, wondering if she had, in fact, been hiding. And now, free of it, and with time to be herself, to merely drift aimlessly around the house and garden, she must look herself in the eye and face her reality.

* * *

As soon as the taxi drew up, Cassie dashed down the front path to open the car door. Two immaculate children got out of the vehicle, wearing summer coats, white, knee-high socks and patent shoes. Lilibet's dark hair lay in two plaits over her shoulders, Georgie's cheeks ruddy from having only just woken up, and they stood side by side on the pavement with polite obedience, waiting to be told what to do next. With an excited cry, Marianne emerged from the other side, and scooted around, calling, 'Casseee... Casseee.'

They embraced, giggling and squeezing each other's shoulders, Marianne as fresh and elegant as ever, while the children watched patiently.

'Oh, my goodness, how well you look, Marianne,' Cassie said. 'And as for you two... my, how they have grown.'

'It *has* been over two years, Cassie,' Marianne said, chiding playfully.

'Do you remember, your Pa used to say that someone had stretched us, Marianne. And that's what I think has happened to you, Lilibet, and Georgie.' Cassie bent down to say hello to them properly. 'That's your grandpa. He used to say that to us.'

'Well, I am five,' Lilibet said, 'but Georgie is still only four. And my Daddy marks our heights on the wall.'

'He's using the same bit, by the scullery door,' Marianne said.

Cassie remembered those pencilled, dated lines at Greenaways; whenever she and Gerard were included once a year, they slotted in, with Cassie always at the bottom, and her brother right at the top, above everyone.

The driver carried the suitcase up to the front door, tipped his cap, and Cassie paid him.

'Oh no, Cassie, I was going to—'

'Please don't worry. It is on Luke.'

'Oh well, in that case. I know he's not short of a bob or two.'

They laughed together as they walked into the hallway. Cassie's guests took off their coats and hung them on the coat stand, and she showed them through to the downstairs room.

'What a lovely house you have, Cassie,' said Marianne, appreciating the large drawing room, with its panelled, folding doors halfway down open on to the space at the back with the dining table, and view of the garden. 'It suits you to be settled in a beautiful home. And all this lovely furniture...'

'A great deal of it came from Cheyne Row, some Dubois heirlooms,' Cassie said. 'All very nice, but a little old-fashioned, don't you think?'

'Oh, I wouldn't look a gift horse—'

'I know, I know,' Cassie said, 'I realised how that sounded, when Luke is so generous.'

She felt she shouldn't mention the cook who came in twice a week, the lovely laundry woman, the gifts of jewellery, and money for clothes. The help around the house certainly gave her freedom, but the other things merely left her with a lingering sense of guilt.

'You know how I am not the best cook in the world?' Cassie said. 'When we first married, Luke wanted to sign me up for a *Cordon Bleu* course and I told him I think we better start with basic home cooking.'

Marianne laughed, settling down into an armchair, and pulled Georgie against her knees.

'This one looks entirely worn out.'

'I thought you'd all be weary after your journey, so we shall have a sit down and some afternoon tea to refresh you,' Cassie said. 'How does that sound? I have spent the morning making sandwiches and fairy cakes – so the cookery course had its uses – and I have squash for you children.'

'I will have a cup of tea, please, Auntie Cassie,' Lilibet said, sitting on the edge of an armchair, folding her hands on her lap.

'I see, young lady, of course you may.'

'And no sugar, please,' Lilibet informed Cassie, her pale-green eyes unblinking in all seriousness, 'as it is still on the ration.'

Cassie laughed. 'Ah, she is so like you, Marianne. Has anyone ever said that before?'

'They certainly have. A good thing or bad, we are yet to discover,' Marianne said. 'Come on, children, let me take you to the lavatory and you can give your hands a thorough wash before Auntie Cassie gives us tea.'

As Cassie carried the laden tray in, Marianne was admiring Cassie and Luke's framed wedding picture on the mantelpiece.

'This was 1944, I realise, but has it really been two years since we last saw each other?'

'It must be...' Cassie mused, setting out cups on the little tea table between the armchairs. 'I haven't been to Greenaways for so long...' Her thoughts switched to when she'd read Oliver's letter in the gathering dusk, and she abruptly shut them down. 'The first Christmas after we got married,' she said, 'we were with my parents at Egerton Terrace. Of course, the war was still going on, and things difficult. But the next year, we spent the whole of Christmas and New Year in Edinburgh with Anthea. That was fun. But this year, we were here on our own.' And that, admitted Cassie to herself, had been rather gloomy.

Marianne said, 'We have been spending Christmases at Greenaways, of course.'

Cassie's question twitched on the tip of her tongue. '*All* of you, at Greenaways?'

'Harry's parents sometimes. Ah, but not Oliver. He has been rather a stranger to us. He threw himself into his teacher training, and now, obviously, his new job. Not even sure if Ma hears much from him. But I certainly haven't seen him. Have you heard from him, seen him?'

'Not since... no,' Cassie hesitated. 'We haven't seen him.'

'What? Even though he is renting that place in Chelsea from Luke? He hasn't been to visit *you*?' Marianne sounded astonished. 'But he is only up there in London, and you and Luke are his two favourite people. I am beginning to worry about him.'

'Who, Mummy? Worry about who?' Lilibet asked.

'Goodness, what big ears you have, Lilibet,' Marianne said. 'Why don't you both go and play in the garden, now that you have finished your tea. It's lovely and sunny.'

'I don't want to. I want to sit here and have more cake.'

'Can *I* go and play in the gar-din, Mummy?' Georgie asked.

'Yes, you may. Lilibet, will you do as I ask and go with your little brother?'

'Come on,' said Cassie. 'I will show you the way. It's a bit of a labyrinth back there.'

'I know you are only sending me off because you want to talk about grown-up lady things,' Lilibet said, reluctantly taking her little brother's hand and following Cassie out of the room.

'I'm afraid I haven't any toys for you to play with, children,' she said, opening the back door for them.

'It's all right, Auntie Cassie, we don't need toys.'

As Cassie watched Lilibet lead Georgie across the lawn, making him measure it with his little stubby strides, her mind drifted beyond the garden and down to the towpath along the Thames. She often walked there, watching the river flow downstream, knowing the water eventually made its way past Cadogan Pier, and Cheyne Row. And yet, unlike Marianne, she wasn't at all surprised Oliver had kept his distance. She had not replied to his letter, for she could not imagine how to begin, her silence the only way to communicate.

As she walked back into the drawing room, Marianne held her gaze, gently nodding.

'You're worried, too, about Oliver. I can tell.'

'I'm just glad he made it home.' Cassie sighed, stacking cups and plates ineffectually, the result no better than when she started. She gave up and sat down, the strain of hearing about Oliver, but trying not to ask, to wonder and to love, far too great.

'Of course, we all were,' Marianne said. 'Ma cried with relief. I cried. I think Pa might have, locked away in his study. Thank God it was all over, and Oliver was back, safe and sound. But Pa had wondered if he would stay in the army, to become a career soldier, like he had been. He had been ready for promotion.'

'Oliver would not have wanted that...'

'But as you know, he left as soon as appropriate and went straight into teacher training in London. Latin and art, naturally. And oh, we were all so grateful that Luke stepped in to offer him his old home when he got the job at that Grammar in Wimbledon. You have a good man there, Cassie.'

'Even though he once whacked a tennis ball at you.'

'I think we were all guilty of goading him. We were terrible, really,' Marianne said. 'We didn't know what he was going through. A good man, Cassie.'

'He is...' Her drifting gaze found her wedding photograph and she stared, puzzled, almost not recognising herself.

'Ha, I must say,' Marianne said, leaning over to pick up the piece of cake that Georgie hadn't eaten and pop it in her mouth. 'When Oliver did visit us, soon after he had been demobbed, so I'm talking nearly two years ago now, he left a book behind. Some tome on art history, and he had been using your old postcard as a bookmark! Saint-Tropez, wasn't it? I remember thinking, how lovely.'

Cassie sank back in her chair under a wave of sinking frustration, of pointless yearning. The thought of letting Oliver know how she felt hearing Marianne mention her postcard left cold, tightening prickles over her scalp. She had considered writing to him after he came home from the war, to thank him for his letter, the sketch of the wren; to tell him she understood. But how could she begin to shape it into words? Not as simple as an attraction, and something far greater than that, their bond incapacitated her then, and even more now it had been broken. And talking about it, confirming it, would do no one any good.

'Yes,' Cassie said weakly. 'I remember sending him that. My first holiday abroad...' She sighed. 'But Marianne, tell me, how is Harry's new job? Deputy head, no less?'

'Ah yes, he loves it, and what a turn up – the vacancy at Eastcombe School. Perfect, because there was a time when talk was of going back to Plymouth. And so, we shall remain at Greenaways, which, of course is... simply wonderful.' Marianne's face shone with joy. 'So, after this trip with the children, I shall be back home in time for school breaking up, and the summer holidays starting. The best time at Greenaways...'

Cassie's cousin trailed off, and the way she met Cassie's eye made her understand that she didn't mean to hark back to the past, with Gerard no longer being in the present.

But Cassie never needed reminding.

'Anyway, Lilibet will be starting at Eastcombe School in September,' Marianne said cheerfully. 'Georgie the year after.'

Cassie's cousin gazed through the windows at the far end of the room at her children, running in circles around each other in the centre of the lawn: a game, it seemed evident immediately, devised by Lilibet.

'Have you thought about children, Cassie?' she asked.

'Oh... oh, not really...' she replied, although she had. After all, surely, a baby would distract her, mend everything, and smooth over all her troubles.

'I'm sorry, that was pushy.'

'I don't mind. If anyone can ask, you can,' Cassie said. 'It... obviously hasn't happened. But I am not entirely sure that I want it to,' she added to soften the matter.

Marianne cocked her head in question.

'No, really. I have such space here, and so much freedom. Part of me doesn't want it to change,' Cassie said, realising how much like an excuse it sounded. 'I have been sketching; I am planning great things for the garden. I can walk, goodness me. There's the river, and enormous Richmond Park; we must go there tomorrow. The children can see if they can spot the deer. They are well camouflaged in the grass, but their ears and tails flick to give them away.'

'Do your parents visit?'

'Occasionally. I may spend a lot of time on my own, but sometimes, I prefer it that way.'

Marianne still did not look convinced. 'I must organise a family gathering. Invite everyone to Greenaways. The end of the summer, how does that sound...?'

'Wonderful,' Cassie said, the word crackling in her throat.

'That's settled then. Come on, I'll give you a hand with all this.' Marianne began to collect teacups. 'Let's go and see what the children are up to. Oh, and I meant to tell you. Vee has just given birth to her second, and is deliriously happy.'

'That's lovely news,' Cassie said, in all honesty. Some time ago, the mention of Vee would make her wince. 'I'm not surprised; from what she told me when I met up with her in Kent, she seemed over the moon with Reggie.'

'Good old Vee,' Marianne laughed.

Perhaps, Cassie thought as they went out into the sunshine, that would be the key. Happiness, and what Vee had hinted at whenever 'her Reggie' came home. 'Well!' Vee had said expansively, her eyes gleaming an even deeper brown across the pub table.

'At last, Mummy, you've come to play my game.' Lilibet ran over the lawn towards them, with Georgie trotting behind her. The little girl had clearly been making daisy chains and had put one around her brother's neck. Lilibet tugged at Cassie's hand. 'And you, Auntie. You must play too.'

Cassie tried to concentrate on the rules, to turn circles when Lilibet did, and laugh when she laughed, while her mind filled with Vee hinting at how going to bed with her husband was such a great pleasure. For Cassie, it had only ever felt like a puzzle, leaving her wondering how an awkward, sometimes boring, procedure could ever be described as sublime, never mind a joy.

* * *

Marianne put the children, worn out by their games in the garden, to bed reasonably early and not long after, Luke arrived home from work.

They retreated to deckchairs on the lawn, soaking up the sinking rays of suburban sunlight, sipping glasses of champagne. Cassie had prepared dinner earlier: salad with mackerel and horseradish sauce, buttery new potatoes and green beans.

'That sounds good, darling,' Luke said, 'but do give me lots of potatoes.'

'This time next year, I want to have grown all of the vegetables myself, Marianne,' Cassie said.

'Even the horseradish?' Luke asked, laughing. 'Cassie, we can get a gardener in to do that.'

'But I want to try,' Cassie said, wondering why he never took her seriously.

'Hurrah to that.' Marianne sighed with satisfaction, taking in her surroundings. 'It seems as though you have settled in well,' she said. 'Both of you.'

'Don't forget Kipling,' said Cassie, spotting the cat dozing in a little nest he'd created by squashing down a crop of wallflowers. 'I believe he is in clover with this space to roam, compared to his previous home, all those busy streets. Although his inscrutable expression never gives anything away. We never did find out where he went when he went missing.'

'It doesn't matter now,' Luke said, reaching over to pat her hand.

But for Cassie, it did. And she understood why an animal might take itself off and hide away during the most turbulent, unsettling times. As she had done. And now, the way Oliver was doing too.

'And this is delicious champagne, Luke,' said Marianne. 'I have heard good things about the Dubois cellar.'

'I brought most of it over from Cheyne Row when I moved here,' Luke said. 'And will probably have to start ordering some more, by the looks of it. I left Oliver a case or two, but he may well have got through that by now.'

'Speaking of which,' Marianne said, 'Luke, I was saying to Cassie earlier, that I'm surprised that Oliver hasn't visited you here...?'

'Ah, yes. I have invited him, certainly, many times.'

Cassie turned to look at him. 'You have?'

'Yes. Via a quick notecard through the post, here and there. But sadly, no reply.'

Cassie didn't blame Oliver. Gazing at the bubbles rising in her glass, she appreciated why he would decline.

'He isn't on the telephone,' Luke said. 'It got cut off at the end of the war, and I offered to reinstate the line, but he said he didn't want one. I often think of dropping in, perhaps on my way home one day, but then think better of it. He may not be in, and to be honest, it is a bit out of my way. And in any case, it seems a bit rude. Perhaps there is a lady friend on the scene.'

Cassie braced herself, expecting a repeat of the sickening jealously on seeing Oliver with Vee on Dartmoor. But this time, whatever she felt, perhaps curiosity, flickered quickly away. Too much time had passed, she decided. And perhaps Oliver himself thought better of it; regretted even, ever sending her the letter. After all, everything had been heightened then: love, life, death. They had all been poised one step away from unknowable disaster. Now, in more settled, more predictable days, what he had written, what he had confessed to her, the night before he left for Normandy, might now be considered excessive. They both had been, Cassie realised, so young and frightened.

'We haven't seen Oliver at Greenaways for a long time,' Marianne said, 'but Ma does get the occasional letter. No mention of a lady friend, though.'

'It sounds like he has thrown himself into his new teaching career,' Cassie said, enjoying her own speculation. 'Perhaps it is Oliver's way to forget the war, the desert, France... everything.'

'Well, I really must make more of an effort,' Luke said. 'We will make definite arrangements, Cassie. Drag him over here if we must.'

Cassie watched her husband ease the bottle out of the cooler and top up the glasses, bristling at his drive to take control, spelling out exactly what they will do, while also unable to imagine such an occasion.

'Now this is an odd thing,' Marianne said, sipping. 'And I meant to tell you earlier, Cassie. I have been having a tidy up of some paperwork at home; we are going to have Pa's study decorated, but that is by the by. I happened to find Ma and Pa's wedding certificate.' Marianne looked from Cassie to Luke and back again. 'And they were married a few months *after* Oliver was born. I had no idea.'

'Goodness me, are you sure?' Luke asked.

'Well, I know how old my brother is,' Marianne replied.

'Perhaps your parents were caught out. My mother always said how wild those times were,' Cassie said, trying to deflect the matter away from what she had discovered, overhearing her mother and aunt's conversation all those years ago.

'But it wasn't the Roaring Twenties, Cassie, dear,' Luke said. 'Oliver was born in 1919, soon after the war, the same year as me. We are practically twins.'

Cassie glanced at Luke, irritated by his patronising tone, and pondered what may well have happened: Alberte Rene fleeing from Paris to England as the Great War broke out, keeping Juno as his muse, as his lover. Abandoning her when she became pregnant. Dear Uncle Charles stepping in.

She turned back to Marianne. 'Have you mentioned finding the marriage certificate to your parents?'

'No, I put it back where I found it. I don't think Ma would mind but Pa would be mortified if he knew that I knew. We know what a stickler he is.'

'Obviously more to Mr Greenaway than meets the eye.' Luke chuckled, raising a toast. 'Here's to Charles.'

Cassie automatically lifted her glass, thinking how much Charles cared for Oliver, and tears stung her eyes.

Luke and Marianne settled back into a, thankfully, easier conversation, but Cassie remained quiet, struck by Luke's blunt manner. She must have got used to it or – more likely – given in to it over these past three years, but now an understanding flooded through her: a cold wave starting at her toes and sweeping steadily, inevitably, to engulf her. Luke, that troubled boy who had teased her and who she had secretly felt sorry for, now annoyed her even more. He controlled her with his kindness, his practicality, his directives. With his declaration of love.

What mind had Cassie been in when she had telephoned him from Paddington Station to ask him to marry her? Did she force herself to accept him? As a distraction, a punishment?

She heard Luke mention Oliver to Marianne again, and rightly so. He would be concerned about his friend. But if only Luke knew, she thought. If only any of them knew that Oliver's letter and the sketch of the dear little wren lay secure in a drawer where she kept – as her mother would put it – 'her feminine articles', for Luke would not dare look in there. Oliver's words, however, did not bring her pleasure; they never had done. They frightened and condemned her.

Cassie sipped her champagne, vaguely listening to the

conversation. She took in the garden and the house with one sweeping glance, appreciating her home's safety and its emptiness, and everything else here that would now be her lot.

* * *

Their 'old married couple' routine at night proved a little less predictable.

Luke wore his pyjamas, and Cassie her nightgown, and they both sat up in bed in the lamplight for at least half an hour: Luke doing the daily crossword, Cassie reading a novel. The soft, distant sound of the last trains through Richmond Station would filter into the room on warm nights when the window was open. And, depending on which way the wind blew, the odd hooting owl, or the ethereal cries of water birds on the river.

Some nights, Luke finished his crossword far too quickly, folded the newspaper away and shuffled himself down into bed. Cassie wanted to carry on reading, to lose herself in the story, to stay on the character's journey, whether hopeful or disastrous, she did not mind. For when she put the book down, she felt as if she had aged, had stalled, and her own world shrank back in on itself.

But switch the light off she must.

Cassie snuggled herself down in the darkness, her back to Luke. And in the silence, she heard the telltale shuffling as her husband took off his pyjama top and his hand found her, resting heavily on her hip. It became a wordless question, and one which she hated answering.

'Not tonight,' she whispered.

'Are you...?'

'Marianne and the children are here.'

'So...?'

'We have guests, Luke. They might hear...' She stumbled over her words, wanted to say *you*. 'They might hear us. And it would be awfully rude.'

* * *

All too quickly, a week later, Cassie stood on the pavement waving Marianne and the children off in their taxi to Richmond Station on the first leg of their journey home to Greenaways, leaving her to the quietness once again.

She started on her routine, stripping the beds and airing the rooms, and then ventured into the garden with a notebook. The day before, her plants had been delivered from the nursery – she, Marianne and the children had had fun choosing them – and she took her time now to examine each one, imagining it blooming in all its glory. She could always ask Juno for advice but had instead borrowed a huge book from the library to start her off. Perhaps gardening, then, would become her distraction, her life's work, Cassie thought wryly, as she assessed the scale of what she wanted to do.

Popping back inside to fetch the book, she heard the telephone in the hallway ringing. Wondering for how long had it been going – as the sound would not have reached as far as the garden – she hurried to pick it up.

'Hello, Richmond 5549,' she said, breathless.

'Cassie, it's Dad. Ah, Cassie, has Marianne left?'

'Yes, a couple of hours ago.'

'Is Luke there?'

'No, he's at work. It's a Friday.'

'You're on your own... oh.'

'What is it, Dad?'

'Cassie, sit down. Yes, better sit down. I have bad news...'

She did as he asked, perching on the stool next to the telephone table, her heart knocking in a hollow, brutal fashion.

Her father said, 'It's Uncle Charles, I'm afraid. He passed away.'

Cassie winced, uttered a silent, *Oh...*

'It happened yesterday but they have only just found him. Rather, an hour or so ago, I believe.'

'*Found* him?'

'He went on one of his walks yesterday afternoon. Didn't come home. Had been missing all night, Juno said. Mr Poulter and some others went up to Hound Tor this morning. We know how he likes— liked...'

'But Marianne!' Cassie gasped. 'Marianne is on her way home, with the children. She is...' Cassie squeezed her eyes shut, picturing her cousin's happy face, waving goodbye through the taxi window. Marianne would have five or six more hours of travelling, blissfully unaware of her father's death, and nothing could be done about it. 'And Mum!' Cassie cried. 'Is Mum with you?'

'Yes, yes... hold on. What's that, Miranda...?'

Cassie heard her mother's muffled voice in the background.

Her father came back on the line. 'Mum says that you are not to worry, that she is all right.' He whispered, but his voice sounded hard in Cassie's ear. 'But she isn't, Cassie. She is desperate to get down to Greenaways.' His tone straightened out. 'We are leaving now in the car. If only we had known sooner, we would have collected Marianne and the children on our way through. It's been sixes and sevens. A bit of a muddle.'

'And Juno... what about Juno?' Cassie asked, but in her mind, a small voice uttered, *What about Oliver...?*

'Juno telephoned us. She seemed... she seems to have titanic strength, that woman. But it's put on. We need to get to her. We both do. We need to be there for her. Look, your mother is impatient for the off. She says she will telephone you as soon as she can. Bye, Cassie, dear. Goodbye.'

Cassie continued to hold the receiver to her ear in a stupor, the long, droning, disconnected tone deafening her, dismay and shock ballooning through her mind.

'But what about Oliver?' she cried, as if her father might still hear her.

She slammed down the receiver and uttered again, with a groan of passion and despair, 'What about Oliver?' to the indifferent, empty house.

25

DEVON, JULY 1947

Wide awake at sunrise on the morning of the funeral, Cassie got out of bed, put on her dressing gown and went over to the window of the guest room at Greenaways. She had not slept well, felt numb and giddy as she slipped between the curtains and curled up on the window seat. She adjusted the drapes to create her own little sanctuary, while Luke continued to snore from the bed.

Dawn at Greenaways at the height of summer had always woven its own magic. Cassie gazed through the distorted old panes, listening to the birds tentatively breaking the silence. Had anyone else in the house, apart from Luke, managed to sleep, she wondered.

The light grew stronger, the birds louder and she heard the front door shut. Oliver appeared below, already dressed in smart mourning black, crunching across the gravel towards his car. On reflex, she withdrew further into the corner of the window seat. From that one glance, even though she saw his face for a second, she knew, she felt, his torment. Their last parting, a day or so after Marianne's wedding, remained a blur, and she had, over time, felt thankful for that. And yet Oliver appeared now, as if at the snap of a finger, and the six long years contracted into this one unbearable moment.

'Is that Oliver leaving...?' Luke asked sleepily from the bed, evidently woken by the sound of the car. 'He mentioned last night... ah yes, he arrived after you had gone to bed. He wants to go to the funeral directors in Dartmouth to make some final arrangements. Not this early, though, surely...'

'The funeral's at eleven. There must be lots to do,' Cassie said, pulling aside the curtain, feeling she had better come out of hiding. 'I suspect he wants to make sure everything is in order...'

'Come back to bed, darling.'

'Ah no, I can't sleep.'

Through the twilight in the room, she saw Luke reach out his hand, the colour in his eyes deepen.

'Not necessarily for sleep, darling...'

Cassie stood up in a flash of irritation. How could he be thinking about *that* on a day such as this?

'No, I am going downstairs to find Mrs Poulter and start helping her with the morning pots of tea.'

'She has help,' Luke countered drowsily. 'Isn't that daughter of hers around? I don't think you should be messing around with tea urns, Cassie. It must have been the eighteenth century when a Mrs Dubois last helped the servants.'

Cassie looked at him askance. 'Are you...? You're not joking, are you? I am going downstairs to help Mrs Poulter. It's the least I can do.'

* * *

Cassie stood before the full-length mirror and smoothed down her deep-black New Look-style skirt, with its full eight panels and nipped-in waist. The little jacket sat neatly on her shoulders, the sleeves midway between elbow and wrist, and the hat she had chosen from the milliners on Bond Street matched perfectly. She had wanted to make a supreme effort for today. For Uncle Charles. Although, the small voice inside her reminded her, she planned to appear to Oliver as an aloof, grown-up, married lady, and not the scruffy, adoring child who had traipsed with him along the banks of the stream. She wanted to distance herself, to crush the memories, place the barrier between them. And the outfit certainly did the job. In her reflection, she saw an elegant woman she barely recognised, her worried, harried face, her sharp and guarded eyes hiding far too much from everyone.

'My, my, that's quite an outfit,' Luke said, coming back in from the bathroom. 'Almost like a fashion plate. But don't you think it is a bit much for a country funeral, darling?'

Cassie glanced again at herself, wondering for a wild second if he knew, had seen through her. She fumbled with her handbag, looking for her black gloves.

Luke laughed. 'This time, I *am* joking. The dress is a sensation. It should be for what it cost me.' And this sounded to Cassie like a boast, not a complaint. 'Now, come on, help me fix my tie.'

Cassie went to him and quickly tweaked the knot. In the past, they would have laughed together through this little ritual. But that had been in the kitchen at Cheyne Row, when he had been her friend and not her husband who wanted to oversee everything and make ill-advised, rambling remarks. A friend, yes, she thought, her head pounding with frustration, but not someone she *knew*.

She messed up Luke's tie, had to start again. Tears filled her eyes. Her husband had unsettled her and dented her confidence, made her doubt herself. And this surely wasn't how things were supposed to be, especially on a morning like this.

Luke pulled out his handkerchief and gestured with it.

'Dry your eyes,' he said. 'Don't worry about getting make-up on it. I have plenty more. Look, Cassie, if this is too much for you, we can leave as soon as it's over. Or at least first thing tomorrow.'

'I can't do that,' Cassie said, aghast. She lowered her voice. As she knew full well, sound had the tendency to travel here at Greenaways. 'I want to be here to support my family.'

'Be that as it may.'

Luke sat down to put on his shoes, lacing and re-lacing them with infuriating precision.

'What on earth do you mean... *"be that as it may"*?'

Luke patted the bed beside him. 'Come and sit here; you are becoming overwrought.'

Cassie took a deep breath, an effort to control her temper, and did as he asked. She didn't want to sit by him on the bed, but she certainly didn't want an argument.

Luke gathered her hands in his and bounced them on his knee. He often did this in light-hearted moments, but now Cassie felt as if he wanted to pacify her, as if she were a child.

'Cassie, I see it all the time. You become upset when you are with your family. And I can understand why. You are not close to your parents any more, are you? Have been pretty much estranged from them for such a long while now. Since, if I remember rightly, you telephoned me – the first time – from that shop on the King's Road. So why now do you want to give so much of yourself to them?'

'Why not now? I want to make amends. To fix things...'

'Keep your voice down, Cassie. What things? You never explained to me why you wanted to hide away at Cheyne Row.'

She lowered her eyes, refusing to answer.

'You shut yourself off from me.' He pressed on regardless. 'When Marianne visited us recently, you seemed on edge the whole time. Not willing to give much... attention to me.'

'Luke, my cousin and her children were our guests. Of course they had most of my attention.' Cassie floundered, trying to form words through her astonishment. 'And I felt perfectly happy with Marianne. In fact, seeing her after so long gave me such a comfort. It reminded me of...' She hesitated, wanted to say *happier times* but realised what an insult to Luke that would be. 'It made me want to try to see everyone even more. And it is such a damn bloody shame that it comes to *this* for us to be together.'

Luke patted her shoulder, uttering soothing sounds.

'How about, then, after this is over with, we go away. Back up to Edinburgh if you like. August will be a good month, for I have saved my leave. You enjoyed it last time. Mother would love to have you. After all, you are part of our family now.'

Incredulous, Cassie felt her mouth fall open. Did her husband, with all his blustering and absurdity, pretend not to appreciate what she needed, or simply not understand her?

'But *this* is my family,' she said in a hard whisper. 'Here at Greenaways. This is where I have felt... so...' She squeezed her eyes shut, not daring to continue.

'You see, you can't explain it,' he said. 'Truth is, your family always seem to upset you.'

Cassie released her hands from his, went over to the dressing table to gather her handbag, check she had a clean handkerchief, straighten her hat.

'So now you are not talking to me, is that it?' he said.

Cassie turned to stare at him, a bolt of rage boiling through her.

'This is my uncle's funeral, Luke,' she said. The words flying out of her felt like a purge. 'And you are seriously questioning why I am upset?'

* * *

The weather that morning was exquisite. Birds, rising from the dewy heath, sent their song into the air, and friendly, white clouds moved quickly, as fleeting shadows over rock, heather and gorse. The beauty of the day seemed to be playing out one last time for Cassie's uncle: the scents and sounds, and the view he must have been taking in, before collapsing on the top drover's road. *Set fair*, Uncle Charles would have said, perfect for hiking. At the edge of the moor, Eastcombe Church perched like a gem in the ancient landscape, the lane leading to it, and the graveyard pathway, peppered with people in black, gathering like flocks of silent jackdaws.

Cassie, walking with Luke, her hand resting on his arm like any normal married couple, followed her parents into church.

'I'm sorry,' he had whispered as they'd walked downstairs. 'I'm sorry,' he had whispered as they got into the car. 'I just want us to be happy,' he said as they had arrived at the church.

'It's all right,' Cassie had assured him, her words and her smile a lie. 'It was a silly argument, that's all.'

The pews were almost full, much more so than for Marianne's wartime wedding; Charles Greenaway's reputation, honour, and influence undoubtedly spread far and wide. Parishioners and farmers, some of the schoolboys from Plymouth, now grown men. Townspeople from Dartmouth, moor folk and elderly army bods in Service Dress, medals gleaming and with black armbands, jammed in together, cheek by jowl.

Cassie sat down on the second-from-front pew with Luke and her parents. In front, Harry Brough sat waiting for Marianne and he and Luke struck up a hushed conversation.

Cassie's mother next to her, with watery eyes and a reddened nose – 'bearing up' as her father had assured Cassie – briefly grasped her hand and Cassie squeezed back, the gesture mutually comforting.

'You look beautiful, Cassie. I love your new dress. I meant to say earlier,' she said, gazing at her as if it hurt her to do so. 'I think I never said it enough over the years.'

'Thank you,' Cassie said, 'and I don't think I have ever said enough, either.'

Her mother seemed briefly puzzled before appearing consoled as fresh tears dripped from her eyes. And they waited together, while the musty book-scented air vibrated with a soft murmuring of sorrow and regret, the church and its very stones patiently containing the charged, expectant atmosphere.

The bell in the little tower began to toll, a primitive, clanging, singular note ringing as a summons, a declaration, a warning. The congregation shuffled to their feet. Cassie turned to see Oliver walking in with Juno and Marianne on either arm; and slowly, slowly, behind them, the coffin on the shoulders of mute pall-bearers.

Cold shock flashed through Cassie, tearing at her scalp. She had expected the years to have changed Oliver, but even so, she battled with disbelief. He held his shoulders with a mild stoop, his army training forgotten as he bore the weight and responsibility of his mother's and sister's grief. He kept his eyes down in supreme concentration.

And the bell tolled relentlessly.

Marianne looked radiant from weeping, her eyes, shining a deeper green, darting around, seeking familiar faces. Juno clung to Oliver's arm, her black net veil shrouding her face. Where yesterday, Cassie's aunt had appeared efficient, bossy and confident when she greeted them all, today, she seemed to have shrunk. She looked startlingly thin. Cassie had never seen her aunt wear black before and it certainly did not become her. As she passed by, Cassie noticed a ladder up the back of her stocking and supressed a gasp of compassion.

The pall-bearers worked in unison, tenderly setting the coffin down on the trestles by the altar. They bowed across the casket – the whole of Uncle Charles, his memory, his laughter, his energy, contained in a box smaller than Cassie expected – and departed.

The bell, finally, stopped.

Oliver guided Juno and Marianne into their pew, And Cassie, helpless in the face of his sorrow, fixed her attention on the pulpit.

Sunlight streamed through the stained-glass windows as the vicar began the eulogy. He relayed, with knowledge, respect and warmth, Charles's life growing up at Greenaways with his younger sister and brother, his army days and raft of medals, 'and when peace came, he met June,' he said. Charles's involvement with the parish, taking on the evacuees from Plymouth, and his enduring love of Dartmoor. The vicar's words conjured images of the past, and people dabbed with handkerchiefs.

From the corner of her eye, Cassie could see Oliver's profile as he stared at the coffin in disbelief. The last time they had been together, they had stood side by side, admiring the view that his father had loved so well. They had, as Oliver had reminded her in his letter, been talking about church bells and sheep, and the things that his father had taught her. And they had both longed for a time when they would hear the bells ring again. Neither of them had considered for a moment that it would be in this way.

A sudden, frail wailing rose from the pew in front and Juno slumped forward as if she had collapsed in pain, resting her forehead on the bookrest, her narrow shoulders shuddering. The sound of her grief pierced the air. Marianne, with Harry and Oliver, froze, almost recoiled with fear, but Cassie's mother and father stood up in unison and hurriedly squeezed into her pew. They sat either side of Juno, their arms around her, holding her between them.

As the vicar continued, reiterating how loved Charles had been, the mutual acceptance and admiration between Cassie's aunt and her parents struck her. Cassie felt years of horror and trauma release their hold on her, lift away and vaporise into the static, musty, ecclesiastical air. Could it be that love emerged in many forms; that it passed through barriers and knew no limitations?

'I know he loves you,' Juno had said when she had given Oliver's letter to Cassie. And at the time, Cassie had had no means, energy or ability to ask her how she knew.

* * *

Cassie walked unsteadily away from the open grave, brushing dirt from her hands. The committal had been humbling, intimate and visceral, but at least, Cassie consoled herself, Juno and her mother knew where Charles lay, close by and within sight of the moorland. Roland and Gerard would never be home. The funeral-goers began to disperse, shaking hands, embracing; Juno had wanted a very small gathering back at Greenaways: a simple tea for the close family.

Cassie hugged her mother and father, told them she would see them both back at the house and drifted off with Luke, towards the car parked on the lane. The intensity of the service and the finality of the burial continued to wash over her, and she needed to rest her hand on Luke's arm to steady herself. He chatted as usual, seemingly to have put their earlier argument behind him. Although for Cassie, it remained with her, burning a furrow through her mind. It, along with the funeral, left her depleted.

She heard footsteps behind them.

'Ah, here's Oliver,' Luke said, in a lowered voice. They turned to greet him. 'Hello, old chap.' Luke clapped him on the shoulder. 'Sorry I didn't get a chance to speak to you after the... just now. But I was just saying to Cassie, it went off all right, didn't it? Do you want a lift?'

But Oliver was looking at Cassie. This, the first time they had locked eyes for years, and he looked like he didn't recognise her. She tried to smile in sympathy, to form some sort of consoling sentence, but it proved hard to smile, when someone did not return it. But whatever she said would be of no help to Oliver, not in that moment. Her hand, still poised on Luke's arm, began to tremble.

'Ah no, not for me, Woodward,' Oliver said, turning to Luke. 'It's Mr Nesmith, the solicitor. Can you take him back to Greenaways? We don't have room in our car, and Ma is worrying. Pretty frantic, to be honest. It's not like her, but then this has hit her for six. Worrying Nesmith will be left behind. He is to read the will to us this afternoon, apparently.'

'Of course,' Luke said. 'Send him over. We're in the Bentley.'

Luke had once said to Cassie, in one of his flippant moods, that Oliver had come through the war unscathed. But standing this close to him, reading his eyes, she saw an entirely different story.

A year or more before, she would have wanted him to know that she had received – and read – his letter, but it seemed irrelevant, almost pointless, now. They had been children, even then, and it was all so long ago.

'Oliver, I am so sorry...' Cassie began, and she meant it: for the loss of Charles, for his sadness, for everything.

Oliver stepped forward and silenced her with a swift, polite embrace.

'I know, Cass,' he said, near her ear. 'Thank you for coming. See you back home.'

* * *

The small, low tea tables had been brought out onto the terrace, laid with linen cloths and set among the garden chairs, and everyone gathered with a sense of relief, voices low and gentle. Black suits, dresses and hats, gleaming in sunlight, felt at odds with the glory of the summer afternoon, but Lilibet and Georgie, having been released from their nanny's care, ran pell-mell across the grass to touch the nearest oak tree and back again, their joy and innocence a refreshing balm.

Mr Nesmith seemed to be the guest of honour, sitting close by Juno and taking with relish whatever sandwich or cake she offered him, while Luke held court with Cassie's father and Harry. Marianne and Oliver sat together exchanging earnest bonding conversation.

'Wasn't it a lovely service, Cassie?' her mother, next to her, said, as a tear leaked down her cheek. 'All those memories. Dear Charles. He *loved* this place. Our beautiful home. Of course, it will pass to Oliver now... I must thank the vicar.'

'Do you need another handkerchief, Mum?' Cassie asked. 'I have another in my handbag.'

'Oh, you are a good girl. Will you come and visit us soon? We miss you at home. *Dad*,' she emphasised, 'misses you.'

Cassie's father, sitting nearby, heard her. He looked over, caught Cassie's eye, and his expression softened, twisting sensitively into one of contrition.

Cassie, with a freeing sense of release, responded with a gentle, reassuring nod. Forgiveness, but not forgetting, seemed to bring her strength, to be the only way she could move forward.

Her mother looked past Cassie's shoulder at Luke. 'Both of you. Do come and visit us in town.'

'Certainly,' Luke said, 'although we are planning a *wee* trip to Edinburgh. Haven't seen my mother and Max for quite a good long while now.'

'Of course... of course. Perhaps we can book you in for Christmas?'

'Yes, yes,' Luke said, 'we'll have to discuss—'

Juno tapped the side of her teacup with a spoon to grab everyone's attention, and stood up, stalk-like in her black gown, wavering slightly as if in the breeze. The talking faded out.

'Sorry for the interruption, dear family and friends,' she said. 'But Mr Nesmith here is keen to get on with the reading of Charles's will. He must catch a train later at Dartmouth and time is pressing...'

'We dance to his tune, do we...?' Luke muttered to Cassie.

She frowned at him, shook her head. Why did he have to gripe so?

Mr Nesmith picked up his briefcase, got to his feet and cleared his throat. 'If the close family would care to join me in the study. That's Mrs Charles Greenaway, Mr Oliver Greenaway,

Mrs Harry Brough and Mrs Richard Marsh... if you would be so kind...'

Juno, Oliver, Marianne and Cassie's mother followed the solicitor though the French windows into the house.

* * *

In the ensuing silence, Cassie's father clapped his hands on his knees, announcing, 'I wonder if I should fetch that bottle of Charles's favourite whisky from the drawing room – let's raise a toast to him. I think we all may be needing a dram or two after this.'

'Good idea, Richard,' said Luke.

'I will collect some tumblers,' Harry said.

Leaving the three men gathered around their bottle, Cassie went to stretch her legs. She walked down the terrace steps to find the children, calling their names.

Lilibet ran across the grass towards her, with Georgie keeping up.

'Auntie Cassie, Auntie Cassie, have you come to join in?'

'You look like a princess in that dress,' Georgie said, in all seriousness.

'Haha, thank you, Georgie. I thought I'd see what you are both up to. All this lovely space for you to explore,' Cassie said, enjoying the sun on her face, a respite from the proceedings of the day. 'Have you been looking around the beautiful garden that Grandma created? My goodness, you could get lost in it. All those flowers. Which are your favourites?'

'The roses,' Lilibet said with conviction.

'Roses,' Georgie said.

'I think they may be mine too,' Cassie said. 'Let's go and have a look.'

But Lilibet tugged her hand. 'I want to go around to where the giant's leg grows out of the ground.'

'The giant's leg?' Cassie asked. 'Oh, the wisteria. You mean the wisteria stem. I used to be fascinated by it when I was your age. It is quite a mammoth specimen, isn't it?'

'Wish-teria,' said Georgie. 'Does it mean you can make a wish?'

'Ho, haha,' Cassie laughed. 'If you like, Georgie.'

Under the canopy of dripping, purple flowers at the front corner of the house, the children crouched down, giggling and elbowing each other as they settled. They each took their turns to rest their gentle, chubby palms on the twisting, gnarled root.

'Shush now, children,' Cassie said, kneeling next to them and placing her finger on her lips. 'The giant might hear you. He is nearly as old as the house is. Now close your eyes. And make a wish.'

Lilibet squeezed hers shut, but Georgie remained transfixed by the mysterious, huge, woody stem, springing from the foundations.

'And, remember,' Cassie whispered, 'don't tell anyone your wish or it will never come true.'

Someone shouted inside the house, and a door banged open.

The children flinched in fright, looked up at Cassie.

'What was that?'

She put her hand on Lilibet's shoulder. 'I don't know, I...'

Footsteps pounded, the alarming sound reaching Cassie through an open window.

Another indistinct voice, a woman's, possibly Juno's, pleading.

'But why didn't you tell me?' This time, Oliver. 'It's an absolute, utter lie!'

He walked swiftly out of the front door, across the gravel and straight to his car. He fumbled with the door handle, clearly distressed, and Juno raced out, almost catching up with him. But he slipped inside and shut the door. He revved the engine. Juno pressed her hands to the window, calling his name.

Cassie gathered the children towards her. Georgie looked like he wanted to cry.

Oliver wound down the car window.

'Ma, please. Move out of the way.' His intense, serrated voice carried across to Cassie crouching with the children beneath the wisteria. 'Please. Ma.'

Juno stood back, grinding her hands.

'Oliver, don't go, not like this...'

But Oliver sped off, leaving Juno alone, drooping in the middle of the drive, staring at the empty space between the rusted, old gates.

Lilibet whispered, 'Auntie Cassie, what is wrong with Grandma? What is wrong with Uncle Oliver?'

Cassie pulled the children closer to her as her aunt slowly made her way back into the house.

'Ah, I think Uncle Oliver is very upset about Grandpa. So, he has gone off for a little drive. He will be back at bedtime, you'll see. Come on, let's find your daddy.'

She took each of the children's hands to lead them back around to the terrace. Her father, Luke and Harry were sitting in a stunned silence, cradling their whisky glasses, having also heard the altercation echoing through the house.

'Cassie, did you hear...?' her father uttered.

Cassie gazed from his shocked face to the others, before bending down to say to Lilibet, 'Take your little brother to go and gather fallen rose petals in Grandma's garden.'

Always ready to supervise Georgie, the little girl nodded, and they set off.

Luke, his eyes widened with astonishment, said, 'Cassie, come and sit down. I'm not entirely sure what's going on...'

Cassie hesitated, an old, tingling fear creeping through her, the ground vibrating beneath her feet. Juno had looked devastated, and Oliver sickened. She sensed the rarified, heavenly world of Greenaways had been gouged open and knocked off its course, and not simply from her uncle's passing.

'I must find out if Marianne is all right...' said Harry, rising from his chair.

'Marianne's with Juno and the solicitor, Harry,' said Cassie's mother, coming through the French windows. She sat down heavily in a chair, white-faced and shaken, and wordlessly took the tumbler of whisky that her husband offered her.

'So, they both know now?' he asked her, below his voice.

Cassie's mother nodded.

'Know what, Richard?' Harry asked. 'What is it? Where is Marianne? Something seems terribly wrong. Are they still in the study...?'

'Best leave them for a while,' said Cassie's mother. 'It has been quite a blow.'

Her father plucked out his cigarette case from his jacket pocket, offered them around. Harry Brough snapped one up.

Cassie sat down, her throat thickening with panic, mistrust grating through her blood.

'I saw Oliver leave,' she said, her voice small, cracking. 'He did not look well. Not at all himself. What on earth has happened...?'

'It is not our place to say, Cassie,' her mother said gently. 'Better leave it to Juno to explain.'

'Here they are,' her father said, smoke billowing from his mouth.

Juno and Marianne came tentatively back out onto the terrace, with Marianne tearfully heading straight to Harry's side.

Juno sat down and held out her hand. 'Rich, give me one of those.'

'But you hate smoking, June.'

'Not today,' Juno said. She shuddered and her brisk efficiency of old resurged. 'Luke, would you be so kind as to run Mr Nesmith to Dartmouth? He has finished here for the day. I know it's a lot to ask, but Oliver had said he would, you see, and he...'

'Not until I know what is going on,' Luke said, putting his arm around Cassie's waist in a proprietorial manner, squeezing a form of reassurance. 'I don't want to leave Cassie here alone until I know.'

'Cassie is not alone.' Juno inhaled on her cigarette, winced and coughed, inhaled again.

'Be that as it may...' Luke said.

Cassie, sinking under the chaos, felt aware of herself edging away from her husband's grasp.

'This is certainly not the way I wanted to do this,' Juno said. 'But we are all family here. Oh, where are the children?'

Cassie, her mouth dry and tight, uttered, 'Over there, by the roses, I can see them...'

Stubbing out the half-finished cigarette, Juno took a shuddering breath, the sound of her words dry with smoke, an ominous betrayal. 'Charles is not Oliver's father.'

Cassie flinched, gave a shake of her head, staring at Juno as she absorbed the real and sorry truth. The truth, now admitted by her aunt – at last, spoken out loud – had been creeping up on Cassie for years: a truth that she could never bring herself to look squarely in the face. For thinking of her aunt's possible lovers, which included her father, forced her own private pain to funnel through her.

'Good God.' Luke exhaled.

Marianne began to chatter, wiping her eyes, '...but he is still my brother, always, it doesn't change anything, does it, and Pa loved him so much. So very much...'

'He did.' Juno's distraught expression softened with a faint smile. 'Charles loved him. Oliver *was* his son in so many... in *every* way. He adopted him, after we got married. Although Oliver was about three by the time... It took a while for the paperwork... some legal complication...'

'I'm only glad it is at last out in the open,' uttered Cassie's mother. 'Juno, I thought you and Charles were going to tell Oliver when he turned twenty-one.'

Cassie turned to look at her mother. 'So, you *did* know...?' she half-whispered, not entirely surprised. No one seemed to hear her.

'We weren't going to tell him while he was off fighting. We wouldn't put him through that. But now, I see, for it to come out this way... Such a shock.' Juno's hand fluttered over her face. 'Oh God, he is so desperately hurt.'

'I take it that it was written into the will?' Cassie's father asked.

'Yes, yes... but I didn't know that.'

'But Charles could have told him himself,' Luke said, outraged on Oliver's behalf. 'Why didn't he?'

Juno glared at Luke. 'It was never the right time. He always wanted the best for Oliver. And, Charles didn't know he was going to die, did he?'

An urgent, snapping noise filled Cassie's head. Oliver, her dear Oliver. Today, he had lost his father twice. Her pounding shock pinned her to her chair, battling with her instinctive desire to run and find him, to do all she could for him. But how could she help? What could anyone do?

'It makes sense now, doesn't it...' Marianne uttered to her husband. 'Ma,' she said, turning to Juno, 'I found your and Pa's marriage certificate a few weeks ago, and it baffled me, about the dates. But now I understand.'

'Yes, I was pregnant with Oliver when I met your pa...' Tears streamed either side of Juno's nose. 'I'm sorry, Marianne, that we have kept this from you, from you both.'

'But Oliver is my brother, no matter—'

'Look,' Luke said. 'We are all sitting here talking about him. Hadn't someone better go after him?'

'If you're taking Mr Nesmith in the car, I'll come with you,' said Harry. 'We might spot him on the road.'

'But you simply can't go haring off after him,' Cassie's father said. 'He could have gone anywhere.'

Cassie kept still and remained quiet, her bones singing with anguish for him. She had a fair idea of where Oliver might be, and she knew that he would not want to be found; he would need his peace and his isolation. Freedom to think. And he would find it at Hound Tor. She imagined him there, taking in the wild heath, with the ancient rock beneath him, hearing the sheep bleating, listening to the wind rustling the grass. On Dartmoor, as Cassie had done at Cheyne Row and again at Ferne House, Oliver could hibernate, place himself out of harm's way, keep everyone's voices at bay, while he tried to make sense of a world that had just been split open.

'You're right, Rich,' said Juno. 'And there's no point any of us going off, tearing around the countryside.' She looked directly at Cassie, her wet, pale-green gaze dissolving with utter empathy. 'The only person that Oliver would want to be found by is Cassie.'

Eyebrows raised, Marianne gasped. 'Of course, Oliver loves Cassie...' And one by one, people turned their heads to look at her. She sensed Luke's stare, right beside her, like the sun burning the side of her face.

Her father began to mutter about topping up drinks, wondering if any of the ladies would like a gin and tonic. Cassie's mother requested another whisky, but Cassie refused. She must stay calm and listen to the clear voice inside her head. She must think... think.

As Lilibet and Georgie came up the steps from the garden, everyone sank back into their chairs, the ill-feeling shifting and evaporating with the children's chatter.

The little girl was holding her skirt out, cradling her bounty of rose petals, while Georgie clutched his own haul in his stout, little hands. They went to their grandmother's side and began to fill her lap with petals: pale-pink and yellow, pristine white and deep burgundy, the colour of wine. Juno trailed her fingertips through them, weeping silently, fresh tears dripping from her chin.

Lilibet, her collection almost spent, came around to Cassie and delicately scattered the remaining petals over Cassie's mourning-black skirt.

26

LONDON, TWO WEEKS LATER

Morning sunlight beamed through the stained-glass windows in the wide, suburban hallway as Cassie handed Luke his sandwiches wrapped in a brown paper bag, and on reflex, reached for his umbrella on the stand.

'Now that is pessimistic, darling,' Luke said. 'Weather report on the wireless was dry and sunny all day. I'm not even going to put my jacket on, may even roll up my shirt sleeves.' He planted his hat on his head. 'And don't look so worried. We can go to see him together at the weekend. It will have to wait 'til then. I have taken far too much time off work as it is. And this way, it will give him time to calm down.'

'It's not about calming down, Luke,' Cassie said, suppressing irritation with a shaky laugh. 'Oliver has every right to feel the way he does. And it will take him longer than a few days to *calm down.*'

'In any case, until then, you have lots to occupy yourself with,' Luke said brightly, missing her point, as usual. 'You've much to do in the garden, Mrs Dubois.' He kissed her cheek. 'See you later.'

'I certainly have,' she said, forcing a smile. 'Much to do.'

She watched Luke head up the path, his suit jacket slung over his shoulder, waiting for him to turn at the gate to give her another wave, then shut the door and went upstairs. Opening her wardrobe door, she leafed through her clothes, wondering if she should wear her black again, although the day felt far too hot already for such formality. But she had plenty of time to decide, with no need to hurry. She would have to wait until after nine thirty to buy her cheap day return ticket into town.

Cassie pulled out one of her best floral, linen dresses and laid it on the bed, waking Kipling, who had been curled up like a stripy cushion on the eiderdown. He sat up, yawned and watched her, his yellow eyes narrowing in an entirely inscrutable yet disapproving manner, as she slowly, thoughtfully ran her brush through her hair.

'It's all your fault, Kipling,' she said, kindly, kissing the cat tenderly on the forehead. 'If only you hadn't gone missing that time... if only you hadn't come back home when you did...'

* * *

The mid-morning stopping service pulled into Waterloo with a great hiss of steam and screech of brakes, impatient passengers opening carriage doors, hopping down, and slamming them shut before it drew to a halt. Cassie didn't feel the urge to rush and waited until the train had come to a full stop before alighting. With unruffled confidence, and a peculiar light stillness inside her, she strolled along the platform to hand over her ticket. The station had a pleasant, echoey, excited holiday feel, with sunshine streaming through its glass roof, groups of chattering children gathering on the concourse, ready for their summer outings, and families with suitcases about to take a train to the coast.

Cassie thought about catching a bus but lingered in front of the Underground map on the wall, wondering how many changes she might have to make, before heading out to the taxi rank. It was such an ordinary-looking day; anyone noticing Cassie would see a young woman in her summer clothes, white gloves and perky hat, in town to visit, or shop or go to a gallery. But as the minutes and quarter hours of that ordinary day passed, it began to have an unnerving beat, a curious taste to it. Even then, as Cassie's taxi crossed from south to north over the river at Vauxhall, this strangeness had a pleasurable ring, a sense of necessity.

Cheyne Row appeared as pristine and elegant an enclave as ever; its fine terraced mansions in the dappled shade of plane trees, traces of the Blitz long swept away. Although, Cassie had noticed from the cab window a handful of bombsites nearby where buddleia grew stoically, the roots seemingly able to find sustenance in broken bricks and dust, their purple plumes attended by hosts of butterflies.

Standing on the kerb to pay the driver, Cassie spotted Oliver's car parked along the street and felt a tremor of anxiety. Of course, he would most probably be at home; after all, it was the summer school holidays. Cassie's fanciful excitement of making this journey switched abruptly to dry, uneasy reality and, as she tentatively climbed the steps up to the front door, cold fear laced through her body. Was she overstepping the mark? After the revelation at Uncle Charles's wake, Oliver may never want to see any of his family again.

Cassie paused on the step, rummaged instinctively for the latch key in her handbag, like she had done many times when she had returned to Luke's house at the end of the terrible days and nights in the bunker. The house on Cheyne Row had been her sanctuary, her place to hide, and she had never thought to give the key back to Luke.

He would know, Cassie thought, as she let herself into the house and wondered what would now constitute being Oliver's family. Luke would no doubt explain endlessly how Oliver and Cassie were related, now that everyone knew that Oliver was not Charles's natural son.

The hallway had a more battered and down-at-heel charm than Cassie remembered, as if the builders that Luke had engaged to fix the roof all that time ago had left scuffs on the walls, and had worn down the Turkish runner. A wireless played softly deep within the house, a ragtime tune, the sound, pleasant and upbeat, leaking from the walls. She pushed the door to the blue-panelled front sitting room open, but the shutters here were closed, the room unused. Backing out, she headed further along the hallway where the door to the salon stood ajar, the delicious music growing gradually louder as she approached.

Cassie stopped in the doorway, spellbound. She had only ever seen the salon in darkness, during the war years, blinds down, shut away, the furniture shrouded like crouching ghosts in the gloom. But now, the sun streamed into the long, elegant room through the huge panes of glass at the back of the house, capturing spiralling dust motes, as if the air itself glittered. Fine antique furniture gleamed, a sofa here, a pair of armchairs there, arranged ready for contemplation or conversation, and hundreds of books lined the shelves. And Oliver, standing by the window overlooking the small garden, book in hand, his attention caught by something outside or absorbed by the music on the radio, bathed in sunlight.

'Oliver?'

He didn't hear her; the music, as gentle as it was, must have taken his mind elsewhere.

She tapped on the door, as if to ask permission to disturb him, to break the spell, and tell him why she had come here.

He turned, his mouth opening in surprise. 'Cass...?'

Deep down, in the part of her that remained a child, Cassie had expected Oliver, no longer her uncle's son, to be different. But as he gazed at her, his expression flickering between amazement and relief, he remained, undeniably and simply, Oliver.

'Cass, what are you doing here...? How did you...?'

She walked towards him, opening her arms, feeling as if she was looking at herself in a mirror. For whatever she saw on Oliver's face blazed unwittingly inside her. He gathered her in his arms, and she held onto him, burying her face in his shoulder to withstand this entirely new sensation.

'I'm sorry, so dreadfully sorry,' she said, in utter, pure honesty, on the brink of euphoria, and she absorbed it and reflected it back at him, wanting him to feel it, like the heat from the sunlight through the windows.

'Oh, dear God, Cass,' Oliver whispered into her ear, and she heard, and knew, his pain. 'Thank God you are here.'

She felt his lips against her neck, finding her bare skin, a warm, brief pressure before he pulled instantly away. They simultaneously released their hold. Oliver went over to the wireless to switch it off, and they sat either end of the sofa facing each other.

'I feel I should offer you a drink,' he said, forcing gaiety. 'What sort of host am I? You've come all this way into town; you must be parched.'

'That can wait, Oliver,' she said, confused by his sudden high spirits. 'I had to come and see you. I wanted to make sure you were... well, I know you are not all right, how could you be...'

'You look lovely, Cass,' he said cheerfully. 'So bright and colourful. So beautiful in all this mess. Always have been.'

She ignored his compliment. 'You have had, and are still enduring, the most terrible shock, Oliver. But you haven't lost your family. We are still your family,' she said. 'You haven't lost me.'

Oliver's bravado fell and his face twitched with agony. The lines burnt in by the desert sun deeper still.

'It honestly felt like the end of me... Doubly so. I lose Pa... Charles, and then I lose him again. On the same day.'

Cassie wished she could damp down the agonised fire in his eyes. If only she could relay to him how much Charles had loved him.

'I might say that you survived the war, Oliver, you can survive this, but that sounds so trite,' she said, trying to rally him. 'But being here... at Cheyne Row.' She glanced around the room. 'It brings it back, doesn't it? We *did* survive. It was such an unsettling time, but how brave we were. Brimming with courage and laughing sometimes in the face of how ridiculous and random disaster can be.'

'We were young and, dare I say, stupid...' he began, 'but I see what you mean. You lost Gerard and yet you carried on, didn't you, Cass?'

'And you have fought in the desert, crossed France and Germany, and come back,' she said. 'And surviving grief... I threw myself into work. It is how I got through it. Endured that, and other... shocking things...' Her mind switched to her father and Juno, and she stopped.

'Cass, please don't upset yourself. Let me pour you a drink. It's so good you are here. I can't tell you...'

'Just water, please,' she said shakily.

He stood up. 'Then don't go anywhere. Please.'

Presently, Oliver came back in carrying a tray with a jug and two glasses. 'I can do better than plain old London tap water. I went to the grocer's this morning. I have a bottle of lemonade.'

'Will it be as good as your mother's, I wonder?' Cassie asked, hoping Oliver would smile.

He shook his head, failed to answer as grim memories found him.

'No wonder the army never suited me, Cass, like it did Charles.' He passed over her drink. 'He saw me having a career in it after the war, to follow in his footsteps. But he must have known what a hopeless choice that would have been.'

'But Oliver, you were made a captain, and you did him proud.' Cassie pictured her uncle weeping in the armchair at Greenaways, after D-Day, stricken with worry for Oliver. 'It's completely understandable that you would want to leave the military after the war and do the things you love. And you did. You are.'

'Perhaps Charles had an instinctive aversion to artistic people,' Oliver said, on the edge of bitterness. 'Perhaps he thought Ma was pining for my father, competing with a dead man.'

'Of course... your *father*...' Cassie muttered, not wanting to let on to Oliver that she had guessed a long while ago.

'No wonder, as son of Monsieur Rene, I am a fey art lover. And no wonder Charles did not really approve.' Oliver's voice broke. 'But I loved him.'

'Of course you did. And he loved *you* as his son, brought you up as his own,' she said. 'You *were* his son. Everyone still thinks that way. Did your mother get the chance to explain to you, much more about your adoption? She told us, after you'd left Greenaways—'

'— stormed off from Greenaways—'

'— that Charles had fought so hard to adopt you, after they married. How it took such a long time. All the bureaucracy. The fact that Monsieur Rene didn't abandon your mother but had died, soon after you were born, and their solicitor had to wrangle with his French lawyer. You were three years old before it was finalised, and they had already had Marianne by then. Ah, do you remember the old housekeeper at Egerton Terrace, Mrs Blake, saying that she remembered you?'

'Yes, yes, I do.'

'Your parents had come up to London to sign the final paper-work and had visited my parents at Egerton Terrace. Gerard would have probably remembered.'

'So, I had been to your house before. I don't remember, but then you don't from that age, do you?' Oliver fell quiet, sipped his lemonade. 'This isn't as good, is it?' he uttered, his thoughts trailing. 'I didn't give Ma a chance to explain any of it. I demanded to know who my father was, and she uttered Rene's name, and in that moment, I was spitting feathers. I wanted to hurt her that terrible day, after Charles's funeral. The fact that I had been brought up in a house with his paintings in every room, and there's me, oblivious. I felt like a fool and wanted to lash out. What an awful thing to do.'

'But you were in pain, Oliver, and everyone understood. We were all so worried. We didn't know where you had gone,' Cassie said. 'Although, I thought it might have been up to Hound Tor,'

Oliver turned to look at her, in admiration. 'You are incredible, Cass. You knew...'

'I did.' She unpinned her hat and set it on the low table, uttering to herself, 'I always seem to know.'

'Oh, Cass...' Oliver said sadly, watching her intensely.

'Have you spoken to your mother?' she asked.

Oliver brightened. 'I sent a telegram. Yesterday, in fact,' he said. 'To tell her how sorry I am. The succinct, stark words helped – it's all I could manage.'

'It's a start.' Cassie smiled. 'Something positive.'

'I knew you would make me feel a bit better.' Oliver reached for her across the sofa seat, and they held hands for some moments in silent, instinctive comfort. Outside, the sky began to cloud over in a typical English summer manner, while Cassie quietly sipped her lemonade. How wonderful it felt to be sitting here alone with Oliver. How perfect and natural, and yet she thought, as she spotted the chair that Kipling had ruined and evidently Anthea Dubois had decided to leave behind, it felt simply out of the question.

'Your letter, Oliver,' Cassie said, releasing her hand, her own frankness taking her unawares. 'And the beautiful drawing of the wren. I still have them, of course. But I have had to hide them away, you understand...'

'I am sorry to have done that to you,' Oliver said. 'It now seems completely unfair of me. I sounded like a rake. Such drama...'

'But we were all in utter crisis,' she said, acknowledging her own sense of relief that he chose to play down the contents of the letter.

'I did wonder at my life expectancy... I had been stationed at Inverary, in Argyll, for a long while before that,' Oliver said, 'in training for the Normandy landings, at Loch Fyne. We had to get it right – no second chances. We had to perfect the technique of getting men, tanks and guns ashore.'

Cassie winced inwardly, remembering this crucial turning point of the war, and the enormity of what Oliver and tens of thousands like him had gone through.

'I was at Ferne House,' she said, 'the communications post near Dover. And I had a fair idea where you would be at the beginning of June, camped on the south coast, ready to go. I worked all night, and I saw the sun come up, and knew that the inescapable was about to happen. This feeling of dread, and horrible momentum. And all I could do was fill my mind with you. Send you love and courage.'

'By God, I needed it,' said Oliver, and he looked straight at her, undaunted, unsmiling. 'I believe that I *felt* it.'

His knowing gaze softened, began to unwrap Cassie's protective layers, making her tremble with the need that she had for him. She wanted to reach for his hand and hold it again, for this had given her courage moments before. But it would be ridiculous, she told herself. As absurd as when she had been fourteen, hiding in Aunt Juno's wardrobe.

'I heard about your engagement, Cass, when I was in Inverary,' Oliver said, sadness escaping from him. 'Ma wrote to me that Christmas, 1943. Goodness me, Cass, I nearly went AWOL. I was going to jump on a train and come down to see you. Talk to you. I don't know, what would I have done? Luke is my best friend. I wanted you both to be happy. I went a little mad, having arguments with myself. I couldn't do what I wanted to do and be with you. I was in danger of making a complete fool of myself.'

Hearing his confession, his sincerity, Cassie felt shuddering desire creep through her, insistent, real and urgent, nothing she had ever recognised before, with Oliver at its centre.

'Of course,' Oliver said, lowering his voice, 'I didn't know then, what we know now...'

'You mean what you know about your... parentage?' she asked, understanding exactly what he meant, for it also lay behind why she had made her impulsive journey here.

He nodded. 'We share no blood, Cass.'

Cassie, terrified now, tried to reason with it, for them both.

'But, I don't understand what you are saying. This... is this worse, or better?'

'Worse,' said Oliver. 'Because when you have this feeling between two people, it is so rare. It must be, for I have never felt this with anyone else I have ever met, only you, Cass. It has lasted and lasted. I thought it might go away when we grew up. But it has never faded or failed. It has, in all honesty, become unbearable. Look how badly I treated Vee. And now we know this, about my father, it's even more difficult.' He drew a deep breath as if to bolster his nerve. 'Tell me, Cass, with Luke... you don't feel this, do you?'

Cassie pressed her lips together, shook her head, as if she would not allow herself to speak disloyally.

'I can tell,' Oliver said. 'The way you are with him. Even the way you sit next to him. At the funeral. You weren't together. Not like this...'

Oliver moved towards her, sitting close. He carefully placed his hands either side of her face, cradling her under her jaw. He pressed his forehead gently to hers; his mesmerising gaze locked her eyes.

'No, not like this,' Cassie whispered.

'You are the only one I want to be with,' he said softly.

Cassie saw the vulnerability in his eyes and watched as the long summers at Greenaways played out. Trailing along the riverbank, idling under trees, reading books. They had been children together, innocent, free and happy. But their maturity became complicated and had parted them. It had swaddled and suffocated Cassie, whispering tales of jealousy, lust and desire in her ear. And even now, floundering through her torturous craving, she must resign herself, her heart thumping, breaking. Oliver would always be a rare gift, given to her, but that was never going to be hers.

'Do you, Cass...?' he asked.

She felt no comfort or joy in his question. There was no happiness or romance. Instead, only deceit and transgression. And even if it proved not to be wrong, it felt impossible.

'Yes, I do. I love you, Oliver,' she said, gasping at the power of her own words. She drew away from him, 'but we cannot—'

'Cass, my love...'

He kissed her lips, and her surprise and her longing, her love for him, fused into an appalling truth. Was this, then, how it will be, she wondered. More secrets, lie upon lie. The day had started in such a humdrum way in suburbia, and now her life would never be the same. She began to weep.

'I know, I know,' Oliver whispered, wiping at her tears with his fingertips. 'We *cannot*. He is my friend. Poor Luke does not deserve this.'

Oliver sat back against the end of the sofa and gently pulled Cassie towards him. Clasping her, he wrapped his arms around her. She lay curled up against his body, clutching both of his hands to her chest, exhaling so hard that she felt as if she had been holding her breath for years. Curled up close to Oliver, she felt blessed, secure and loved absolutely, and wanted to shut her eyes to the sense of doom, their long and lonely lives spent apart, crawling towards them.

As the minutes and hours of that ordinary day ticked by, Oliver caressed her hair, took her hand to his mouth to kiss it, and Cassie wept, dried her eyes, then wept again. Outside, a Thames barge hooted out on the river, the sun went in, the room grew darker, and rain began to drum against the salon windows.

* * *

She woke gradually, emerging from her safe, warm cocoon, aware of Oliver's breathing as if it were her own, the ticking clock on the other side of the room, and the rattling of a key in a lock coming from much further away.

'Captain Greenaway, are you home? I have brought provisions.' Footsteps sounded in the hallway, the front door shutting. 'Hello? I've come to see how you are—'

'Oh, good God, Oliver,' Cassie uttered, sitting up in a daze, extracting herself from his embrace.

Oliver stirred. 'What's that?'

Cassie ran her hands over her hair in a desperate effort to smooth it down. Her arm felt numb from lying on it.

'Luke is here,' she whispered, poised to leap to her feet.

Oliver swore under his breath, grasped Cassie's hand, holding fast.

She stared at him, puzzled, tried to pull away, fresh tears prickling her eyes.

'No more lies in this family, Cass,' Oliver whispered, stroking her fingertips, urging her to sit back with him. 'No more.'

'But I can't... I can't do this to him...' Cassie uttered, panic thudding through her chest.

She went over to an armchair by the hearth, sat down, rearranging her crumpled skirt, holding Oliver's disappointed, broken gaze.

Oliver called out tentatively, 'In here, Luke.'

Cassie's husband strolled through the salon door, a man glad to be out early from his office, his tie loosened a little, his hat in his hand. 'I hope, Oliver Greenaway, you are in the mood for some Chateauneuf—'

He stopped dead, his benevolent smile frozen into a grimace, his baffled stare through his glasses flicking from Cassie by the hearth to Oliver on the sofa, as if he were solving a difficult mathematical problem.

'Hello, Luke...' Cassie began, her words failing as it dawned on her: her husband walking into his own house to find her with Oliver mirrored in some small way her stumbling in on her father and Juno.

'Good God, Cassie,' he breathed, and instead of greeting her as he usually might with a peck on the cheek, he slumped down on the armchair across the rug from her, tossed his hat next to hers on the low table, and placed a wine merchant's paper bag on the floor. He rested his arms on his knees, as if suddenly depleted.

'Luke,' Oliver said, getting up to shake Luke's hand. 'It's good to see you... Shall I fetch a corkscrew and glasses?'

Luke shook his hand, but did not answer him, his silence crackling through the room. Oliver returned to his spot on the sofa, his puzzled gaze finding Cassie.

'I couldn't wait for the weekend, Luke, you see,' Cassie said, tilting her chin as if this may cover her guilt, the betrayal in her eyes. 'I wanted to make sure Oliver was all right.'

'So I see.' Luke nodded, looking around the room, anywhere but at Cassie.

His gaze settled on the floor by the sofa. Sweat broke out over his forehead and his face blanched. He took his glasses off to wipe them on his cuff, and put them back on, exhaling through his teeth.

'I was at the office this afternoon, and I thought, damn this, I am going to leave early to visit my friend,' he said, responding to a question no one had asked. 'Because Oliver must need to see a friendly face. And I can lend a sympathetic ear, as always. Got the cabbie to stop off at my wine merchant in Pimlico, picked out quite a decent one, as you will discover. Headed straight here... I telephoned from the office, Cassie, to let you know I will be late home for dinner. But no answer... no answer...'

'Well, of course, Luke, because I came to see Oliver,' Cassie said with as much cheer as she could muster.

Luke would not look at her; he remained staring at the floor.

'Well, I won't ask you if you are coming home with me,' he said.

'What do you mean...' Cassie uttered, following his gaze to see what on earth held his attention. Beneath the sofa close to Oliver, her shoes lay untidily on the floor.

Luke picked up the paper bag and set it on the table, pulling out the bottle of wine.

'It's a fine vintage, this one, Oliver,' he said. 'So, I do hope you enjoy. And I do wish you well, my friend.'

'I was only just now saying to Cassie, I don't think the shock has sunk in yet, but at least I have made contact with my mother...' Oliver said, unnatural and hurried, as if the breaking apart of his world had been trifling. 'And I will see her soon, I hope...'

'Good... good. But as you will know, Oliver, dear man, that *in vino veritas*,' Luke said. 'And I certainly have experience of that wise and ancient idiom. Blurry eyed from this good stuff.' He tapped the side of the bottle. 'And I saw it. When was it, that first big raid? The afternoon the bombers got through. Imminent threat of invasion. The day, Oliver, you will remember, before you went off into the war. I saw it. And it all happened. Right here.'

'Luke,' Cassie said, 'Whatever do you mean...?'

He turned to her. 'Oliver loves you, Cassie. And I knew it, even on that night. That I wasn't good enough for you...'

'Oh, Luke, no, you are the most wonderful, kind generous man... You are...'

'Be that as it may. But not what *you* need, my darling,' Luke said, his face breaking into a wretched smile. 'I'm not a *stupid* man.'

'Luke, can we sort this out?' Oliver said. 'Because it is, honestly, has not been, and is certainly not, what it may appear to you now.'

'Luke, I came here to talk to Oliver...' Cassie's words stumbled, her truth not entirely whole. 'That's all.'

'That is worse, then. What, no illicit seedy affair? No meeting in hotels? Or snatching quick early-bird dinners in backstreet restaurants? Even I, not particularly a man of the world, knows about those.'

Cassie flinched, hearing her husband list the situations that her father and Oliver's mother had possibly shared.

Luke sighed, set his hat on his head and got to his feet. 'I'm not an army man, Oliver,' he said, 'but I know which battles to choose. And I won't win over love. *Real* love.' His gaze flicked in despair between Cassie and Oliver. 'I am so deeply sorry about Charles, Oliver. Another good man, gone. And, Cassie, I need to go home to give Kipling his tea, so I shall take my leave.'

'Luke, I really do care for you...'

'That is affection, Cassie, not love. Goodbye, my dear.'

At the door, he paused and turned to look at Cassie, and Oliver, his face softening with acquiescence as he took them in.

'You look so wonderful together, you two,' he said. 'You always did.'

27

DEVON, AUGUST 1948

The sleepy scented air, the stillness here at Eastcombe, seemed to Cassie to be full of noise: bees vibrating in the honeysuckle around the front door; the pinks and yellows of the towering hollyhocks singing outside her window; her patch of garden ripening and spilling over to its own merry tune.

'"Summer afternoon, summer afternoon",' Cassie whispered to her baby, who lay in his cot, batting his hand at his little, knitted duck. '"The two most beautiful words in the English language." Now who said that, I wonder? I think it was Henry James, but it has been a long time since English lessons at school. Daddy will know. Shall we listen together for his car?'

She lifted Laurie from his cot, carried him out of the cottage front door and sat down on the step with him to wait.

'Now don't you look lovely today,' Cassie said, enjoying her baby's soft, packed-in weight on her lap. 'A new little matinee jacket from Grandma, and nice little bootees sent by your *other* Grandma. You will see them both today, and they are going to have to work out between themselves what you must call them.'

Cassie hooked her little finger inside his pink, precious palm and waited, contentedly, admiring the unruliness of her cottage garden. She had only moved in at Easter, six weeks before giving birth to Laurie at a nursing home in Dartmouth. Juno had arranged everything: finding the cottage; at her side throughout her labour; and being with her when, on Cassie's arrival back home with her newborn, she had opened the envelope containing the Decree Absolute from Luke's solicitors.

'Good old Grandma Juno,' Cassie whispered to Laurie. 'I could rely on her to understand.'

She gently smoothed his gossamer hair behind his tiny, perfect ear, thinking how much had changed; how far she had come. Among the sweet sounds of the summer's day, the voice of her former husband rose and fell through her mind: *...my father is incandescent with rage... another Dubois divorce... but my mother is on my side... she has advised me... I refuse to engage the Dubois family solicitor and go down that bitter path... you, Cassie, are divorcing me... we will keep it as private as is humanly possible... I will pay to keep it out of the papers if I must... I saw it coming... you love him, go to him...*

'I love you both,' Luke had said, the last time she saw him at the house in Richmond, leaving Cassie with an overwhelming sense of guilt and gratitude that he had wanted to break the cycle of his own parents' acrimony. 'I am letting you go...'

And as much as her aunt had been wonderful through the distressing months that followed, her parents had been less than understanding. 'You are divorcing *and* having a baby!' her mother had cried, aghast, when she had broken the news at Christmas at Egerton Terrace. 'You are five months pregnant, and your husband is divorcing you? The *shame!*'

'*I* am divorcing *him*,' Cassie had muttered, but her mother seemed not to hear her, and Cassie could not bring herself to explain anything more of the delicate matter.

'You'd think a man would stand by his pregnant wife. I hope he is providing for you.'

'I don't want anything, Mum.'

'But they are stinking rich!'

'I don't want to be with Luke.'

'It's simply horrifying. It's the sort of thing you read in the newspapers. A wife abandoned!' Her mother had looked pale with anguish. 'You'll have to come home and have the baby here. We'll book you in to Queen Charlotte's. But, Rich, doesn't he have every right to take the child away?'

'Listen to what Cassie is saying, Miranda,' her father had said. 'I get the feeling he won't do that. Dubois is being noble, a gentleman. Even so, whoever is divorcing who, I still want to punch him on the nose.' He paused, thought it over, looked at Cassie with steady, calm eyes. 'Cassie, we only want you to be happy. That has always been the case.'

'I am happy,' she had said, without a trace of the misplaced, childish envy she used to feel for Marianne. 'And I will be happy.'

And because, she reminded herself of what Juno had said to her not so long ago: *Love finds us even if we try to hide from it.*

* * *

Only last week, at the beginning of August, Cassie had received a letter from her mother.

Thank you for sending the photograph of little Laurence. We trust you both are well and settled into your cottage. And we can't wait to see you, my darling, and meet our grandson for the first time. When I heard you had safely delivered, I cried, my darling. Thank goodness for Juno. I hope they were nice to you at the nursing home and had plenty of analgesics for you.

And thank goodness for Marianne and her bringing us together, arranging our family gathering at Greenaways. We do understand why you took yourself away to Devon, Cassie, when things have been so very difficult for you. A divorce in these appalling circumstances must have been unbearable. And tongues do wag in town. Our reunion at Greenaways has been long-awaited, and, thank God, will this time be in much happier circumstances.

We can't wait to see you, love as always, Mum and Dad.

P.S. I enclose a pair of bootees from a dear little shop on the King's Road.

'Here's the car, Laurie, can you hear, coming down the lane?' Cassie said. 'It's that funny old thing – all that Daddy can afford. But as soon as he starts his new teaching job in September, he might be able to choose a new one...'

Oliver pulled up outside the cottage and waved through the open window of his battered Ford.

'Is that you chattering away to Laurie again?' he called, laughing as he got out of the car.

'It certainly is. He is a such a good listener,' she said. 'Come and hold him for me while I fetch my bag and lock the door.'

'There's no need for that, Cass,' Oliver said, scooping Laurie into his arms and kissing Cassie's lips. 'No one locks their doors around here.'

Cassie laughed. 'I can't get used to it. It really is bliss...'

* * *

Cassie settled into the passenger seat, holding tightly to Laurie while Oliver drove along the twisting, dipping lanes, through tunnels of overarching trees, the hedgerows dripping with deep-summer green. On the horizon, the purple smudge of the moors.

'Have they arrived yet, Oliver? My parents?' she asked, the warm breeze through the window rippling her hair, and puffing at Laurie's fair little tufts.

'They have. Eagerly awaiting you and this little man.'

'And you are happy for us to...?'

'Absolutely. I couldn't be more so.'

He manoeuvred through the gates, passing the Greenaways sign, and Cassie's memories – nostalgic and brimming with laughter – spiralled and bloomed in her head. With a burst of joy, she kissed the top of Laurie's head.

'I must tell you,' she said, as Oliver cranked on the hand-brake. 'I had a letter from Luke this morning.'

'And how is Woodward?'

'Still in Richmond. Still working at Whitehall. Kipling is well. And Luke is due to take Esme out for dinner next week.'

'Oh,' said Oliver. 'Who is Esme?'

'I shared a flat with her for a few months during the war, and Luke met her then.'

'Esme, Esme... do I know that name?'

'She's another girl from the War Room.'

* * *

The front door to Greenaways had been propped open, and Cassie, carrying Laurie, walked with Oliver into the hallway and they strolled left into the dining room. The door to each room stood open and she could see right through Juno's parlour and into the drawing room at the end. To her right, the courtyard lay half in sun, half in shade, and the sash windows in each room had been raised an inch or two to let in the soft breeze.

She heard their voices blowing in from the terrace through the French windows: her father and her mother, Marianne and Harry, Juno, and the shout of a child, possibly Georgie or it could have been Lilibet.

'Ah, here they are,' Juno said, rising in all her bohemian elegance to greet them.

She rested a gentle hand on Cassie's shoulder, her bracelets chiming, and gave her one of her quiet, all-seeing gazes.

'You look happy,' she said, softly so that only Cassie could hear.

Cassie's mother looked around and gasped with pleasure, clambering out of her deckchair and darting over.

'My dear, my lovely Cassie.' Her eyes shone and her embrace felt firm and loving, 'and this little one, oh, look at him, Rich, oh my goodness.' Her gaze lingered on the baby. 'Can't believe I am a grannie. He is beautiful.'

'Ah yes, yes, he is indeed,' said Cassie's father, leaning in to peck Cassie's cheek. 'Wonderful to see you, my dear. And as for the boy. Little Laurence.'

'Laurie, really, Dad,' Cassie said.

Her father chuckled and turned to Oliver.

'Thank you for going over to Eastcombe to fetch Cassie, just now,' he said. 'I think my motor is past it; couldn't manage another mile today.'

'Yes,' Cassie's mother said. 'We were a bit ragged from our journey down here. But it is lovely that we are all here together.

At last. We will try not to leave it so long next time. Now we have our grandson.' She looked again at Laurie, her eyes widening in her radiant face.

Marianne bounded over. 'Cassie, the children have been desperate to see you and Laurie, jumping up and down with mad excitement, but they seem to have gone... Ah, no, there they are.'

Lilibet and Georgie came haring across the lawn, arms out, playing aeroplanes, making engine noises.

'Come and play, Auntie Cassie and Uncle Oliver,' Lilibet cried, pounding up the steps and across the terrace to stop short. She peered up at Laurie in Cassie's arms. 'So, he is the baby, is he?'

'He is. This is Laurie. Your and Georgie's second cousin, I believe,' Cassie said.

Her mother, standing with Cassie to stroke Laurie's plump little shoulder and smoothing his collar under his delicate chin, gazed hard into the baby's face.

She gasped.

'My goodness, Juno, have you noticed?'

'What's that, Miranda?' Juno came out of the French windows carrying a bottle of cold champagne, with Harry following with some glasses.

'Laurie...' Cassie's mother uttered, breathless, her eyes startled, fixed on her grandson. 'Laurie looks just like Oliver did as a baby.'

Juno caught Cassie's eye, raised an eyebrow, as if asking her permission, and Cassie gave her a succinct ghost of a nod.

Lilibet tugged at Cassie's skirt. 'Let's show the baby Grandma's roses.'

Oliver put his arm around Cassie. 'Come on then.'

They walked together down the steps to the lawn with the children running ahead and Laurie looking back over Cassie's shoulder at the others on the terrace.

They wandered among Juno's roses, immersed in the blooms, accidently brushing off loose petals that scattered to the ground, the fragrance following them, trapped along the narrow pathways. Voices from the terrace rose and fell, questions and answers flying back and forth, a cry of astonishment, and a single bark of surprise, all fading the further on Cassie and Oliver went.

'Do you think Laurie will be able to see the colours yet?' Oliver asked as they paused by a spectacular, luminous-red rose.

'I don't know enough about babies to answer that,' said Cassie, jiggling their son in her arms so that he could see the flowers.

'The baby will be able to see them soon,' said Lilibet, 'and if not, we will teach him, won't we, Georgie?'

Georgie looked like he agreed, but didn't say so.

Oliver glanced back at the house.

'We'll leave them to talk among themselves,' he said. 'Let it sink in a bit. And by the time we go back, it will be out in the open, and they will all have to get used to it. No more secrets in this family.'

Just one, Cassie thought, remembering the conversation that her father had had with Juno, standing right here among the roses that summer night so many years ago.

But for tonight, no more secrets.

Tonight, Cassie felt sure, she would dream again of Greenaways.

* * *

MORE FROM CATHERINE LAW

Another book from Catherine Law, *The Pilot's Girl*, is available to order now here:

https://mybook.to/PilotsGirlBackAd

ACKNOWLEDGEMENTS

The moment I walked down the steps into the Churchill War Rooms beneath Whitehall in London, I was on hallowed ground.

I explored those claustrophobic underground corridors with a sense of awe, taking in the low ceilings, the concrete walls lined with vents, pipes and girders, aware of how stifling and confined it felt. I peered into the infamous Cabinet Room, Map Room and the PM's Bedroom, and saw the cubbyhole where Mr Churchill spoke to President Roosevelt on the transatlantic telephone line. And, within this sobering and impressive wartime nerve centre, the personal stories shone through. The accounts of day-to-day life working in the bunker at the most crucial time of our nation's history stayed with me, along with details about the dreaded 'Dock', the pin holes in the maps, and the secretary who had typed out the message that her boyfriend's ship had been lost {reworked as Gerard's fictitious vessel *HMS Westray*}.

A year later, one glorious May Bank Holiday weekend, I travelled down to Devon to stay at a sublimely beautiful Elizabethan manor. Tucked away in the countryside, Cadhay House was an inspiring and enchanting place, complete with courtyard, Long Gallery, ancient wisteria and lily-pad pond. The walls seemed to whisper with the past and I was mesmerised. I said to myself, 'I will write about this place one day.'

As for most authors, these two contrasting events remained at the back of my imagination, quietly evolving, until I was ready to weave them into a novel. Three years later, they emerged as the story of Cassie, her family, the trials of working in the wartime bunker and the blissful peace of a Devon manor house that I have reinterpreted as Greenaways.

I also reimagined Abbot's Cliff Y (Wireless Interception) Station perched on top of the White Cliffs at Capel-le-Ferne, Kent, as the listening headquarters 'Ferne House'. The description of Mr Churchill being spotted strolling along the clifftop is based on the account of Patricia Owtram (b.1923) from when she worked at Abbot's Cliff as a special duties linguist with the WRENs during the Second World War. And, as usual, I have used my imagination to make it work for my story.

It is a pleasure and an honour to be able to create novels inspired by the ordinary people who lived through the war years. I recommend *Forgotten Voices of the Second World War* by Max Hastings, in association with the Imperial War Museum, as a wonderful and sometimes harrowing source of information on this fine generation's experiences.

Thank you to the fabulous Boldwood team, my editor Emily Yau for her support and encouragement, copy editor Emily Reader for the fine tuning, and Camilla Lloyd for her excellent proofreading. Not forgetting my wonderful agent Judith Murdoch, who has been championing me and my writing for twenty-five years.

ABOUT THE AUTHOR

Catherine Law is the author of several historical novels set in the first half of the 20th century, in and around the First and Second World Wars. Her stories are inspired by the tales our mothers, grandmothers and great-grandmothers tell us, and the secrets they keep. She lives ten minutes from the sea in Margate, Kent.

Sign up to Catherine Law's mailing list here for news, competitions and updates on future books.

Visit Catherine's website: www.catherinelaw.co.uk

Follow Catherine on social media:

facebook.com/catherinelawbooks
instagram.com/catherinelawauthor
goodreads.com/catherinelaw

ALSO BY CATHERINE LAW

Letters from
the past

Discover page-turning
historical novels from
your favourite authors
and be transported
back in time

*Join our book club
Facebook group*

https://bit.ly/SixpenceGroup

*Sign up to our
newsletter*

https://bit.ly/LettersFrom
PastNews

Boldwood

Boldwood Books is an award-winning fiction publishing company seeking out the best stories from around the world.

Find out more at www.boldwoodbooks.com

Join our reader community for brilliant books, competitions and offers!

Follow us
@BoldwoodBooks
@TheBoldBookClub

Sign up to our weekly deals newsletter

https://bit.ly/BoldwoodBNewsletter